BONFIRE

BONFIRE

BY

Dorothy Canfield

HARCOURT, BRACE AND COMPANY

NEW YORK

BONFIRE

PART ONE

1

THE PROUD skyline of The Wall was slowly drawn across the darkness, at first faintly in gray on gray, and then in transparent blue on gold. The planet that had been lording it in fire-color paled and died in the dazzle of white light which suddenly laid a high ceiling of brightness from The Wall to Hemlock Mountain. Down below this The Valley was still twilight-dim; but the wild life which, unsuspected of all save the Clifford dogs, nightly hunted and fed back and forth across the fields claimed by man, began an unhurried retreat. Along paths well known to them rabbits sauntered back to the brush and brambles of old clearings. Woodchucks ambled to the mouths of their holes. A deer floated like thistledown across a newly plowed field and up a wood-road.

Just before the first sun struck into the valley, two robins, wing-weary with the long journey from the south, dropped down over Lathrop's Pass, and, driven by imperious laws unknown to them, flew past hundreds of desirable nesting-places to alight with a chatter of triumph on the one foreordained corner under the roof of the one foreordained porch.

The first soul awake in Clifford was Sherwin Dewey's Don. He had started to his feet as that deer passed, half a mile away, and ever since had stood taut on the steps of his master's house, his nostrils and his vitals quivering. But he did not dream of racing off in pursuit. There was a great deal more to Don than the wild nerves which at that smell had broken into bloodthirsty clamoring. He might not be able to still their frantic lust for killing; but he

3

could resist it. He sat down slowly; with a mournful sigh he lay down, stretching his front paws out in a gesture of resignation, his beautiful eyes sorrowing over the burden of a dual nature laid on him by destiny. Then all his being concentrated on one hope, the only hope that was virtuous for him, "Perhaps He will take me with him on the mountain today."

Don's master had wakened but was lying still to listen to his brook. For seventy years its voice had been the first sound in his ears, and he knew its every intonation. From its timbre now he knew that the April sun was melting the snow around its springs high up on The Wall. He rolled himself out of bed, went to the window and looked out across the valley at Hemlock Mountain. It was time to start the breakfast fire but he paused to note that during the night the tide of spring had risen from the Crow Rocks, where it had been at dusk, up to the dark mouth of Dowling Hollow. Sherwin Dewey's eye, ranging along the mountain, transported him wherever it looked. He had been there—everywhere on it—so often that looking up at it from Clifford Street he could see and smell and feel any spot on it. Standing there by his bedroom window, tall and gaunt in his nightgown, he saw how green the valley gleamed through the white birches as you look down on it from Searles Shelf. He smelled the dark forest chill at the bottom of Dowling Hollow where the low branches of the old hemlocks still sheltered shrunken snowdrifts; Hawley Pond lay before his eyes, ice floating on its sinister black water; he climbed higher and looked over the universe as you see it from Perry's Point up on top and saw that the universe was made up as it should be of tumbled mountains, blue and bluer in the distance.

Having visited these favorites of his, he turned back refreshed, to wash his face and hands in the basin on his washstand and to pass a sketchy comb through his thick grizzled hair. Then he went down the back stairs to cook his and his wife's breakfast, thinking of his brother who had gone West and made money.

Not everyone in Clifford saw Hemlock Mountain when he woke, and looked out to see what had happened to the world since last

night. The Reverend Mr. Kirby—or rather Father Kirby—heavy-eyed after a white night saw that while he had been praying, a spider had woven a web from a branch of the pear tree to his window-sill. Every artfully braced thread was taut, the complex fabric accurately created during the darkness out of an old, confident skill. In the center of its linear beauty, adorned now with globes of dew, sat its hairy creator, devouring with relish the body of a white moth.

The Reverend Mr. Kirby—Father Kirby—shuddered, asked himself with passion how anyone could be expected to make sense out of such a world by his own unaided Protestant brains, and braced himself for another day of just such effort.

There was another spider-web in town that morning, across the corner of a kitchen window in the Kemp house when old Miss Bessie billowing in her calico wrapper went to open the door for her hired man bringing in the milk. That web too was beautiful and intricate, based on an astounding knowledge of stresses and strains and geometric laws, and as Miss Bessie glanced at it, its maker sprang out and clutched a fly whose frightened buzzing was like a scream in the morning quiet of the kitchen.

But the experienced old woman did not shudder. She reached for her broom and with one matter-of-fact gesture swept down to nothingness the beauty, the strength, the evil and the unanswerable question the spider had spent its night in creating.

What Isabel Foote saw, as she brushed her bright brown hair, was that the driveway had dried out from yesterday's rain. The Academy court would be dry enough for tennis! She scurried downstairs to telephone Cornelia and Olivia to bring their rackets to school, and was sent scurrying back by her mother's laughing, outraged, *"Isabel!* Go get dressed this minute! Will you ever learn you're too big a girl to go straminading around in your underwear where folks could see you!"

Mr. Lawrence Stewart did not look out of the window for some time after he rose. He went into his pale green bathroom, and

turned on the hot water—in his case it was his father who had gone away and made money—and stepped into the pale green bathtub. But there was no soap in the soap-rack. He bounded out, angry and dripping. "That woman has lost her mind! She forgets something new every day!" He snatched the soap from its niche over the lavabo, got back into the tub and began with care to clean his already clean skin. It was not till after he had shaved his clear-cut, early American statesman's face, that he remembered to look out at the world. A long black fissure in his lawn hid the shy radiance of the April morning from his eyes. Looking at it horrified, he chewed hard on life's bitter cud, and,—not for the first time,—called Heaven to witness that his help led him a martyr's life. "Of course Jo Danby *would* choose the time when the frost is coming out of the ground and the sod is as soft as butter, to steer his Ford off the side of the driveway!"

Downstairs on his front porch, Henrietta, the cat, watched Jo Danby taking down the winter entrance. She was outraged, having planned to have her this-year's kittens in a dark corner there. Unwinking green eyes fixed on Jo, she canvassed other possibilities. There were pleasant piles of soft things in the attic; but you never could be sure of finding the door to the attic stairs open. The kitchen was too public and too much mopped; and Henrietta always disliked Mr. Stewart's housekeepers as much as he did. The barn? No, she was no barn cat. She tucked her exquisitely white front paws more snugly under her snowy breast and gave it up for the time. There was no hurry. Still, spring was really here—the usual robins were back. She raised her head to watch them flying about, and permitted herself a ladylike lick of her chops. The robins knew the cat as well as she knew them. In fact they thought the house where they always built their nest belonged to Henrietta. So did Henrietta.

All these inhabitants of Clifford, looking at that day's world, saw different things. Yet, when the morning train whistled for the crossing, it suggested to most of them the same question:—Would Anna Craft really come back from France to take up her old work? And if she did, why?

They had but barely emerged, it seemed to them, from struggling with the question of why she had ever gone away. For two years they had asked themselves why ever Doctor Craft's daughter after ten years of district nursing should have taken up private nursing—and in Paris of all places! Everybody had had a different explanation.

Isabel Foote had thought, "Who wouldn't want to get away from here and go where something *happens.*"

Sherwin Dewey's fretful invalid wife had said it was just plain flightiness. Her husband protested, "Anna's had a nawful dose these ten years back, trying to make silk purses out of those measly Four Corners folks. Nobody with that down-hearted Knapp blood had ever ought to have got into such a forlorn way of making a living."

Mrs. Dewey's acid opinion was that "Anna's plenty old enough to have learned what we all got to learn, to eat what's set before us and make no fuss."

Her husband had thought but not said, "Oh, but Anna's awful young, some ways. There's lots she hasn't learned."

The Reverend Mr. Kirby had made no comment on Miss Craft's departure, although they were life-long friends. But not a night of the two years since then had passed without his praying, "O Lord, though she knows it not, it is Thee she is seeking. Help her to find Thee, O God!"

Old Miss Bessie Kemp had shouted to her deaf sister, "Well, when Anson landed that interne appointment I *hoped* Anna would bust loose. First chance since he started to college for her to lift her nose from the grindstone. But I was afraid she hadn't enough gimp left to do it. Ten years of doin' your duty is enough to addle anybody's brains."

Miss Gussie, hearing inaccurately as usual, said agreeingly, "Yes, indeed, there's never been a sister in this town who's done more for a brother and he only a half. She's sacrificed everything for Anson."

Miss Bessie could not let this pass and shouted, "So much the

worse for them both! Taking somebody's sacrifices is like taking counterfeit money. You're only the poorer."

"Oh, I don't know. I don't believe I'd want her to marry a *Frenchman*," said Miss Gussie in a reasonable tone.

Asked—two years ago—what he thought of Miss Craft's leaving her job and going to France, Mr. Stewart had silently congratulated himself for the thousandth time on being celibate, thinking, "She's running away from that tiresome Miss Ingraham! She's like a man who can't stand his devoted wife another minute!" Aloud he had reminded people that Miss Craft's war service had been in France and that she had probably been bewitched by Paris. . . . "But her idea that she can get enough nursing there to make a living is ridiculous! Mark my words, she'll be back in six months, strapped."

Clifford never did specially mark Mr. Stewart's words and at the end of two years had quite forgotten this prophecy. By that time the city-bred nurse who was Miss Craft's successor, shattered by her efforts to press Clifford granite into up-to-date molds, had resigned. Anna was written to and offered the place again. Would she accept? Everybody had a different guess. And when she did, their guesses as to her reasons were as various. Old Mr. Dewey's idea had been that nobody brought up in The Valley could be satisfied anywhere else. Isabel Foote, trying to keep her mind on a devotional book, thought, "To give up *Paris* to come back *here*—why, it's just like St. Francis giving himself to the lepers!" She did not venture to try the leper simile on her mother, but she went as far as, "Mother, don't you think M'Sanna is a saint? I mean a real Saint. Like in 'The Lives of the Saints.' "

Mrs. Foote took some pins out of her mouth to ask dubiously, "Hasn't she a good deal of the Craft quick temper for a saint?"

Isabel said spiritedly, "That's because she cares about poor people's troubles. She cares. She *cares*. Oh, Mother, *don't* make my skirt so long! It won't have a bit of style if it's way below the knee like that. Cornelia and Olivia have theirs *lots* shorter. I'll look like a girl off Searles Shelf if you keep it like that!"

Mr. Stewart, sitting down to his breakfast, was still of the opinion that Miss Craft's money must have given out. "Absurd to imagine

that a provincial American woman well past thirty could earn her living in Paris!" He struck the top from his egg, and sniffed. Suspicion darkened his eyes. He stooped his nose. But the cloud lifted from his face. The egg was all right. Now if only the coffee—he braced himself courageously for the fatal first taste of the coffee that would tell him whether it was one of the good days or not. A-a-h, the coffee was good, too. Mr. Stewart's serious face relaxed. His mind relaxed also, let serious matters like coffee lie, wandered at loose ends, "What could such a woman as Anna Craft make of Paris?"

Miss Ingraham had gone, of course, to meet Anna. Everybody had seen her square short-legged figure going down Depot Hill, had known she was going to meet the morning train and why. "She's probably all worked up over Anna's coming back," they surmised with the indifference that is felt for the emotions of unattractive women no longer young.

And there was Anna now—yes, you see she really did come back —climbing up Depot Hill, surrounded as usual by Miss Ingraham. She might have been no farther away than on one of her trips to Boston, to take some poor person to a clinic or a hospital there. People like Almira Boardman who were always rubbed the wrong way by Miss Craft went into their back rooms. People who liked her went out on their front porches to hail her. Isabel Foote indeed, as soon as she saw from afar the familiar red hair and pale face, raced down the marble sidewalk, her long legs flying, her arms widespread, "Oh, M'Sanna! M'Sanna! You're really here!" She flung herself on Miss Craft's bosom hugging and being hugged.

"Why, Isabel, how big you've grown. You're as tall as I," said the tall woman. A faint shadow fell on the girl's flower-like face. Miss Craft added hastily, "But you look only a big little girl, still, not a bit of a young lady."

"That's just what I think!" cried Isabel, her face brightening. "Mother keeps telling me I'm grown up. But I don't want to be. I want to have a good time first. How do you do, Miss Ingraham?

Is that a Paris hat, M'Sanna? Oh, I am *so* glad you've still got your freckles. How's your brother, M'Sanna?"

"All right. How are Cornelia and Olivia?" Miss Anna asked in her turn.

"Swell!" said Isabel. She ran back upon her porch calling over her shoulder, "It's simply corking to have you here."

Cora Ingraham said ardently, "Oh, Anna, how you put yourself into others' places!" Anna made a silent movement with her lower jaw which protested against Cora's tendency to make personal remarks, and said, "Isabel's grown to be quite a beauty, I see."

The two women walked on, passed the Randall, the Barney and the Gardner houses, exchanged greetings with their occupants, crossed Warm Brook, and in front of the small brick building that housed the Library, encountered a tall, thin, tired-looking man of no special age, a disfiguring blue birthmark covering all one temple, eye and cheek, a gold cross swinging over a clerical coat. He was walking heavily, his eyelids lowered, not looking where he was going.

"How do you do, Father Kirby," said Miss Ingraham. "And, "Good morning, Fred," said the returned traveler. He looked up, startled, snatched off his broad-brimmed, flat-crowned hat, and in a deep voice cried, "Anna!" as if he were surprised not that she was there, but that after Paris she was still herself. He shook her hand warmly and Miss Ingraham's dutifully. "How's Anson?" he asked, and after she had answered "All right," went on, looking intently at her, "Are you going to be able to stand our dull old backwater after being out in the . . ." He left his sentence hanging awkwardly in the air, as if he could not think what was the opposite of a backwater.

She waited a moment. Then, "It's not just *your* backwater," she answered. "It's mine, too." She added, "And God's."

The name gave out a mellow clang like a struck bell. They stood, letting the vibration die down into silence. When they nodded and separated, the clergyman walked on, smiling to himself, his fingers closed around the cross.

"You know *just* what to say to *every* . . ." began Miss Ingraham and stopped, halted by the movement of her friend's lower jaw.

They had quite a talk with Mr. Dewey—that is, Miss Craft did. Miss Ingraham listened.

As they crossed the culvert under which the Dewey brook ran, they could see him, the sleeves of his old flannel shirt rolled up over sinewy arms, his shaggy gray head bent over a grindstone which whirled, now rapidly with a high keen note, now slowly with a low growl as he bent his back to press down, or straightening up, let the stone skim around under the blade. Don sat beside him, sympathizing and admiring. Miss Craft called out, "Haven't you got that ax ground *yet*, Mr. Dewey?"

He took the ax from the stone and called back, "Ain't you got Clifford Four Corners cleaned up yet, Anna Craft?"

"A life sentence for us both," she agreed.

Mr. Dewey came out to the sidewalk, wiping his right hand on his threadbare pants, Don at his heels. "Well, we've had quite a rest from your bossing, Anna, but I guess we can make out to stand having you around again," he said, in a quick, high, twanging voice.

"How's everything?" she asked.

"Nothin' extra. That other nurse let everybody run right over her. Old man Burdick has been on the warpath most of the time. And they tell me there's a fourteenth or fifteenth Tobey baby on the way. Th' town won't have any money for roads and schools if many more Tobeys get born. Time you were back."

Don had been trying conscientiously to think what it was that people liked to have him to do. He remembered now and sitting down raised his right paw stiffly.

"Oh, he knows me," said Miss Craft, shaking it.

"Why not?" asked his master. "I did."

"How's Mrs. Dewey's rheumatism?" asked the nurse.

As he had for thirty years, her husband answered, "Worse," and shook his head. Then, "How's Anson? Somebody was tellin' me he's most ready to start practicin'. But I couldn't believe that."

The irony of his tone struck out a spark from Anson's sister,

"Anson Craft hasn't taken a day longer for this training than any other medical student. Not a day! Anybody that thinks he has just shows his ignorance. A person can't learn to practice medicine the way he'd learn to . . . cut down a tree."

"That's right. That's right," said Mr. Dewey, approving her sharpness. "If a person's folks don't stand up for him, who's gunto? You needn't worry, nobody that knows him ever thought but what Anson Craft has plenty of brains. Well now, Anna, did you find Paris any harder to boss than we be?"

"Couldn't be."

He laughed. "I bet Clifford Four Corners has Paris licked a mile for deviltry. Not to speak of Searles Shelf."

"Can you still see the Searles Shelf houses from here?" she asked, "or have the white birches grown up too thickly?" She turned to look up at the towering pile of misty blue. The morning sun fell slanting across it, modeling with transparent shadows the Hollows as they rayed out fanwise from Perry's Point at the top. When she looked back at the old man she saw that he too had lifted his face toward the mountain. She watched his brooding eyes for a moment before she said, "I tell you, Mr. Dewey, I didn't see anything sightlier than that, all the while I was away."

" 'Tain't bad," he conceded.

As the two women moved on, he called after them, "I sort o' hate to admit it, Anna, but I'm glad to have you back."

Miss Ingraham looked admiringly—but silently—at her friend.

They passed the Dean, the Merrill, the Nye, and the Jim Merrill houses, went by the Community House, turned the corner by the Town Hall, crossed another brook and approached the old Stewart house.

"There's not a handsomer, better-proportioned house in America," said Anna. "I'm glad the wind hasn't hurt those elms, yet. They're so old. . . ." She perceived Mr. Stewart in well-cut gray flannels, drooping his well-groomed gray head sadly over a muddy scar on his lawn. He saw her too, aroused himself to do what was to be done, took off his gray hat, shook hands, said, "I hope you're as well as you look. How's your brother?" did not wait for an answer,

inquired correctly, "Did you enjoy Paris?" and before she could open her mouth told her, "I hope you went often to look at Notre Dame from the back, from across the Seine. It's much less banal from there." He looked down again at his disfigured lawn and sighed.

Miss Craft said, "If you had that rolled right away while the ground is still soft that rut would be all smoothed out."

"*Would* it?" said Mr. Stewart eagerly. "Do you really think so? But I haven't any roller!"

"There must be one for the Academy courts," said Miss Craft. "They'd let you borrow it. Wouldn't they, Cora?" Miss Ingraham as teacher of Latin and mathematics could not answer for the Academy tennis players.

"I know they would," said Miss Craft. "Just ask them, Mr. Stewart."

"Well, I will." He turned quickly back towards the house, calling, "Jo! *Jo!*" The two women walked on, Miss Ingraham smiling broadly, Miss Craft permitting it.

On the front porch of the Kemp house the two sisters sat in their short-rockered, hickory-seated, eighteenth-century chairs. When Miss Craft and her companion came in sight on the other side of the Old Burying Ground, the old women rose, vast in their loose calico morning dresses, and went down the front walk to meet her. "Well, Anna!" said Miss Bessie. "Here you are!" said Miss Gussie.

"Why, Miss Bessie'n'Gussie!" the returned traveler cried. "How like yourselves you look!"

"How would you expect us to look?" said Miss Bessie.

Miss Gussie asked, "Had enough of Paris, Anna?"

"Plenty!" she answered, remembering to speak loudly. *"Plenty!"*

"Did the change do you good?" asked Miss Bessie.

"I didn't get any change," she said, going back with them as they returned to the porch and sat down.

Miss Ingraham remained standing, on the front walk. It would not be accurate to say that she was left behind. She stayed behind. After all, it was only seven years since she had come to the Academy to teach, and had fallen a victim to her passion for Anna

Craft. People "liked her all right" and had begun to get used to her but they felt her—she felt herself—an outsider. She was almost the only person in town who had no blood kin in Clifford.

Miss Craft leaned her forearms on the railing of the porch. "How many thousand talks have I had with you, hooked over this railing!" she called to Miss Gussie.

"Your mother and your grandmother liked to lean against it and visit, too," Miss Gussie remembered. She asked, "Well, Anna, did you really get any work in Paris? Lawrence Stewart would have it you'd starve to death."

"He was wrong, as usual," said Anna Craft. "I got all the work I could do at 'most any price I wanted to ask."

"That was your Nye blood comin' out," said Miss Bessie. "Set a Nye down in the middle of a swamp and he'd make a good living."

Miss Gussie demurred, "I always thought there was lots more Knapp and Craft than Nye in Anna." She went on, "Won't you find it pretty tedious back here? There's not much a-doin' in The Valley. No more now than ever."

"I won't complain of the monotony," said Anna Craft in an enigmatic tone that roused Miss Bessie's curiosity.

"See here, Anna, how d'ye mean you didn't get any change? You needn't try to tell me Paris is anything like Clifford."

They turned their heads to look up and down the street, the feathery-branched elms misty with spring, the clear windowpanes of the white houses glittering in the sun, the marble sidewalks snowy in the green lawns. Into the silence, as into all Clifford silences, came the murmur of running water.

"They don't *look* much alike," admitted Anna Craft. "But listen —you know what I get here in The Valley. The people I see, most of them, don't live here in The Street, they're Clifford Four Corners families. *You* know what *they're* like—the father drunk, the mother a moron with no morals, always running around with other men, too lazy to take decent care of the children. And my business to clean up the mess they make."

Miss Bessie recognized this picture. Miss Gussie had caught only

odd words, Anna's intention to speak loudly enough for deaf ears having lasted as long as such intentions usually do. She fixed her eyes intently on Anna's moving lips in the hope of reading something from them, and began as she always did, to read something else from her face.

"Well, I thought I'd had my share of that here, and I wanted a change. But in Paris—I might have known it—it turned out this way: the Americans who live all the time in Paris—if they're any good—know French, and when they're sick they have French nurses. There are plenty of nice Americans there temporarily who don't speak French. But they're professors or students. They haven't the money to pay a nurse. That leaves the dumb rich ones, don't you see? There are plenty of those, believe *me!* And they're the ones I've been working for. Well, except that their variety of deviltry costs them more money, they're just like the back-roads families here. The men drink and won't work, and the women run around with lovers, and neither the father nor the mother pays any attention to the children except to yell dirty words at them, and . . ." She was using for her satirical sketch a light dry tone, different from any she had employed on her progress up the street, and she kept it nonchalant to the end although here in the middle Miss Bessie caught the point and all her mountainous flesh began to shake. Miss Ingraham, seeing the old woman's face broaden into laughter, thought, "Anna always gives everyone what he needs."

"I've never seen any of our back-roads kids suffer more from the fool food their folks give them," the nurse went on, "than some of those I nursed in expensive hotels around the Etoile, children that were taken care of—if you want to call it 'care'—by servants who—well, by the kind of help that kind of folks have. The mothers don't know any more about what to feed their children or how to bring them up than any Searles Shelf Burdick. And they yearn to be taught how, just about as much as the Burdicks do. As for drinking—no Tobey man could get any drunker any oftener or knock his wife around any more than some of our fellow-countrymen abroad. Well, that's been the way of it. I've spent

my time trying to clean up those messes instead of the ones here; trying to get the men to sober up once in a while and to make the women act halfway decent and to keep the children from learning too much dirt from their parents' talk, not to speak of getting them into a bath once in a while and their teeth looked out for. I thought if that was all I was going to get, earning my living there, I might as well come home and get it here, where I'd have snow instead of rain for five months every year. Give me snowshoes instead of rubbers any day."

She took her arms from the railing and stood up with the manner of one who has just given a matter-of-fact explanation of a small matter of no consequence.

Miss Bessie wiped her laughing eyes with the hem of her voluminous wrapper. "It does seem good to have somebody back in this town who's got some fun in her," she said. "You make me think of your father. Is Anson growing to be like your father too? I haven't seen Anson, not more than to see him go by, as you *might* say, since he started in getting eddicated."

Miss Craft's eyes, which till then had been steadily directed outward upon her interlocutors, turned for an instant inward. And softened. "I don't know . . ." she murmured dreamily, "whether Anson . . ." Finding Miss Gussie's piercing eyes fixed on her face, she started a little, gave her head a shake and said, raising her voice to be heard by them both, "Why, I haven't seen much more of Anson than you have since he went to medical school. He did laboratory assistant work all through his vacations, you know, hardly came home at all." She hesitated, made a decision, and announced, "But you can soon pick out for yourself which of his ancestors he's like, Miss Bessie'n'Gussie. He writes that when he finishes his interne service in June, he's going to go into practice here in The Valley. As Doctor Cole's assistant up in Ashley. With office hours here two or three times a week."

The two old women exclaimed over this news and Miss Craft left them to exclaim, walking on arm in friendly arm with Cora Ingraham.

She was almost out of hearing when Miss Bessie called after

her, "Hey! Anna, wait . . . ! About you and Paris now—you just
remember one thing—no matter where we go there's plenty of
what we all want to fill our dippers with. But we can't fetch up
any more than our dippers will hold."

"Ah, that's just what makes me mad," answered the nurse over
her shoulder.

After she had quite gone Miss Gussie said, "I didn't catch all she
said—what was it you were laughing at so?—but I take it she gave
up Paris and came back because Anson is going to be here, and
she thought he might need her."

Miss Bessie looked at her sister, opened her lips to say something,
shut them, and leaning forward, shouted, "Yes, you got it right.
That is what she said."

2

ALL THROUGH the winter there had been plenty of snow, and
in March, to the disgust of the sugar-makers, it had rained
almost every day. But at least a wet spring soaked the world
so that by April it was safe—as safe as it ever is—for burning over
weedy upland pastures, and for lighting the great bonfires of brush
and tree tops left over from the winter's chopping. As Miss Craft's
Ford started out from The Street for her first round of visits after
her return, feathers of blue smoke stood up in the still morning
air all along the lower slopes of the mountains on both sides of
the valley. They added another beauty to a scene already lovely,
but the nurse's face, rather somber that morning, did not lighten
as she looked at them. Driving with one hand for a moment, she
reached back of her to make sure she had brought along her outfit
for burns. But the real danger was not to be coped with by carron
oil, bandages and heart stimulants. Her eye traveled down the valley from one smoke pillar to another to where a fire was licking its
way across the steepletop weeds of David Graudey's hill pasture.
"I never knew a year, let the woods be as wet as you will," she
thought forebodingly, "when anyhow one of those fires didn't get
out of hand. What possesses the men to set them going?" She

knew what possessed them:—"Every man of them thinks that the fire *he* lights will burn up just what he wants and no more."

She turned the Ford off the highway into the narrow Churchman's Road, and was soon in second gear, grinding slowly up through the spring mud. Knowing the road—knowing all Clifford roads—as other women know their pantry shelves, she swerved at just the right places to avoid certain jutting rocks at the sides. Not that she cared what happened to the hub-caps of her car. The maple woods on each side of the road here exhaled the exquisite and exciting odor of spring germination. Miss Craft breathed it in but did not note it. She had risen that morning to what she thought of as "one of my Knapp days," dreaded days when the inner springs of life were dusty, when she could take delight in nothing, nor sorrow either. The grim local cult of heredity which made it one with Fate, had from her childhood shut her in without hope to the misery of these recurring periods of apathy. Her mother's family were melancholy. Who can escape what comes to him from his forefathers? As one hard-worked year succeeded another, she had felt the cloud stoop lower, darken more of her days. This, cruelly, just when—at last—the goal of Anson's graduation drew near. She had thought, ". . . to be a burden on his spirit, just as he enters life . . . that would be past bearing!" and with a conscious effort of the will had prescribed for herself the traditional treatment of a change of scene.

But her foreknowledge of its futility had proved true. The two years back of her had but turned the key in the lock that shut her in, so plainly had they shown her—what she already knew—that zest cannot be, by direct intention, manufactured from any set of outer circumstances. She knew now once for all that when her inner eye was filmed with gray, gray was the life it looked at, whether in the Seine Valley or at the foot of Hemlock Mountain. This was one of the gray days. Struggling uphill in deep mud and likely at any moment to stick fast in it—what else was life for her?

The road grew less steep, less muddy, made a turn. Tragic blackened trees lined the road, stretched for acres on both sides. She stopped her car to gaze. That had been Ned Rollins's pine lot!

"Oh, they *didn't* pull through!" she thought, remembering the wild day of the fire and Ned's hysterical insistence that only the underbrush had been killed. "The bigger fellows'll pull through all right, give 'em another year. The bigger fellows'll pull through all right, Nellie! You'll see," he had said feverishly over and over— as if his saying so could make it so. But though he continually wiped it off, the sweat had continued to start out in big drops on his smoke-blackened face. And he had not once looked at his wife, standing silent in her gingham dress, gazing at the smoking ruins of their plans for the children's education.

That had been on the last day of Anna Craft's service, two years ago. To try to find more zest in life for herself she had left the man and his wife standing there in despair. And there she found them on her return, the woman facing the ruin of her hopes, the man the ruin of his marriage.

At first their anguish was like a troubled pulse in the air, around her, but outside her own inner numbness. And then it gave one faint but living throb within her. Her pale face grew paler. Here was the way out—a hard way, but the only escape she had ever found. But she knew from experience that to live through another human being meant sharing the bitterness of his pain as well as the vital warmth of his life. Facing, as so many times before, the choice between insensibility and suffering, she hesitated. Or tried to hesitate.

But something in her, not her mind or will, had already chosen. The dead pines had told their story. She saw them now not through her own but through the eyes of the man and woman whose lives, whose children's lives, had been laid in ashes by that fire. The hapless thoughts in the husband's mind—now she not only knew what they had been, she thought them too. Now her own heart burned in the wife's bitterness. She was the woman standing with locked lips thinking, "The only chance the children had— and he risked it to save himself trouble. We'd better never have had them than not to be able to do for them. Nothing ahead now, nothing to work for. We will be just like *his* family, back-road folks, raising ignorant young ones on a hill farm."

And she was the man who saw written in the smoke above his fatal blunder, "Nellie will never feel the same to me again, never, never. I've lived for her. But she's lived for the children. They were going to make it up to her for having married a Rollins, and living on Churchman's Road. We've had such a good time of it together and now it's all over. Nellie will never say anything to me about this. But she'll look at me the way she looks at Searles Shelf folks. She will never say a real word to me again!"

The nurse started her car and drove slowly through the charred unburied skeletons of the trees. Nothing had pulled through, she saw, nothing at all had pulled through but little lesser ephemeral growths, worthless alders and gray birches and popple and millions of tangled brambles, violently alive, thrusting up their thorny shoots to riot in the sunlight of which the murdered trees could no longer deprive them. She was sick with the despair and shame and anger she was sharing; yet she abandoned herself to pain—made no effort to turn her thoughts away, knowing that she must clutch this vicarious suffering to her till its clawing at her vitals aroused from sleep the creative fierceness of that Will beyond herself that was the master of circumstances.

But as she emerged on the level road leading to the Rollins house, a part of her brain that had not been stunned by that tigerish spring of sympathy stirred and cautioned her. Perhaps—that was two years ago—something else had turned up. Perhaps they had forgotten. She looked ahead of her keenly at the white house tiny under its massive maple tree.

Ned was in the side yard splitting wood. His aspect gave Miss Craft the first indication as to how things stood. Nothing is more expressive than the manner in which a man splits wood and Miss Craft knew the significance of every one of the many ways in which that task may be done—from the sulky awkwardness of the growing boy who wants to go fishing, through the glittering bravura of the young husband, master of his ax and glorying in having a hearthfire of his own to feed, down to the Voltairian neatness and enforced economy of effort of the old man with withered arm muscles but with brain cells stored with a lifetime's observation

of the ways of firewood. Opening the shutters of her eyes, the nurse exposed the sensitive plate within to the way Ned Rollins was handling his ax. It told her that the loss of his pine lot—his wife's feeling about it, that is—was a burden no lighter for the passage of two years.

Slogging away as he was, head bent over his wood, he did not hear the car. But his wife did. Miss Craft saw her shadow move slowly across the window of the ell; she came out on the porch, a small, thin, gingham-clad figure with bent shoulders, and called with dry severity, *"Edward!* Can't you see somebody's here!" The hardness of her tone added to the nurse's rage of sympathy for the man an unbearable pity for the woman shut up in the self-righteous misery of the blamer, always so much more angry and inflamed than the humble sorrow of the blamed.

And now at last she had suffered enough. The sleeping power within her awoke and shook itself. And as always when it woke, obstacles were not. Her way was clear.

The farmer and his wife recognized the red-haired, pale-faced woman now and called out, "Well, M'Sanna!" Their manner of saying her name welcomed her home.

They looked, she thought, much more than two years older. But as they came out to greet her their voices and accents were commonplace and natural. Mrs. Rollins did most of the talking. Ned stood back, tall and broad beside his wife's dry thinness, his head drooping. She said, "My! I bet you're glad to get home!" She asked, "How's your brother?" and then skimmed the cream from their own news all in one long sentence. Andrew's spelling was still terrible, it seemed, but he was two grades ahead of his age in arithmetic and geography; Gyp was dead and the new collie had no sense at all; old Mrs. Persons still taught Number 10 school ("just as cranky and hateful as ever") and was having an awful time with a lot of wild young ones down from Searles Shelf ("I have to look Andrew's and Mattie's heads over every day when they come home from school"), and with a big Burdick girl that was a holy terror; taxes were higher all the time; the season had been a bad one for making syrup. "Won't you come in, M'Sanna?"

"I don't know but I could . . . a minute," she said, getting out of the car, "if Ned'll put some water in my radiator."

In the kitchen, bright with sunlight and geraniums, fragrant with burning birch wood and baking cookies, she gave a look around expressing the praise which decency did not permit her to put into words. "It always looks nice in your kitchen," she said with the correct flatness of intonation. "I see you've still got your canary." She sat down, and said, "Go right on with your cookies."

She waited till the woman's face was bent again over the cookie dough before beginning to explain the idea she had. It was a plan for a Monday to Friday coöperative home in The Street for those Academy students who came from too far away to go home every night. As if she were explaining something quite new, she said to the silent woman, who went on cutting out cookies at higher and higher speed, but soon forgot to put them into the oven, "You know, Nellie, everybody wants his children to have an education, but lots of farmers just haven't the cash to pay board for them, and there aren't nearly enough houses in The Street where they can work for their keep."

Ned came in then, shut the door and leaned against it, his hands in his overalls pockets. Miss Craft turned to include him, "I was just telling Nellie that I don't believe but what I could get a house down in The Street and have it run as a home for out-of-the-village Academy students so it wouldn't cost but a little if any more than having them live at home and go to school." She went on with quickly improvised details, "The fuel would come from the farm woodlots; the young people would do the housework; the rent divided among several would be almost nothing for anyone." She spoke of furniture stored in attics and barns that could furnish the house, of its cellar stocked with preserves and vegetables from farm kitchens and gardens, of a cow loaned for a month at a time from one farm and another. As she talked the kitchen hushed its small sounds of crackling fire and restless bird and yawning dog, and held its breath to listen. "Of course there'd have to be a middle-aged woman with lots of good sense and nice ways, to look out for them. . . . But we could find somebody. And as for

tuition at the Academy, if we all stick together next Town Meeting I know we can get a vote passed to have the town pay the whole tuition instead of half." She pointed out to them what they had seen from her first words, "There'd be more to this plan than just saving money, too. The farm girls and boys living in such a house would be in their own home, as good as anybody, not hired help waiting on other folk's tables and washing other folk's dishes. They could have parties of their own, and invite their friends, and *be* somebody. All it needs to make a go of it is coöperation. What do you think?"

She stopped. Mrs. Rollins had long ago left her cookie dough and sat down. She had at first rolled her apron tightly around her hands. Then reaching forward she mechanically picked a dead leaf from a geranium. She rolled this to dust between her fingers, looking down at it as she listened to the nurse's matter-of-fact talk of ways and means. Once a tremor passed over her mouth and chin.

She said nothing now. Her husband took his hands out of his pockets and cleared his throat. "W-e-ell, I don't know but what mebbe that might work," he conceded.

Miss Craft stood up to go. Ned's wife sprang to her feet. "Oh, you must take some of my cookies home with you," she said quickly. "Couldn't you eat one now with a cup of coffee?" She flew to the stove to see if the kettle was boiling, and back to the shelf for the coffee pot. "I've got some slips from my begonia started in my upstairs window. Wouldn't you like a couple?" She ran light-footed up the stairs and down again with two little flower pots. She said wheedlingly to her husband, "Neddie, go get M'Sanna a bag of our popcorn, will you?" She told the nurse, "There's nobody in The Valley can grow popcorn as good as Ned's. Is your coffee right, M'Sanna?" She reached down to pat the collie's head. "He's nice with the children," she said, tacitly excusing him for his lack of success with cows.

But the fumes were already thinning from around Miss Craft. Through them she saw ahead of her the parched landscape of

realism which lies on the other side of intoxication. She began to count the price she would pay for this.

She had indeed one more golden moment. They went out to the car with her and stood by it talking as she got in. Mrs. Rollins was telling of her last summer's preserving and said in a cheerful voice, "We've got the best berry patch on the mountain now. You know—where the pines were burned off. The raspberries and blackberries have come in there as thick as they can stand. We got *some*thing out of the fire, anyhow. We'll never lack for filling to our pies." Her husband lifted his head and looked at her. The smile on his face was the last thing Miss Craft saw of them as she drove away.

For a time she tried to hold this between her and reality. But soon enough, "Good Lord, what have I let myself in for *now!*" she groaned. "Will I ever learn not to let myself go that way? Where'll I get the money to furnish the house? And pay the woman to manage it? And for light? And water? And repairs? And as to Town Meeting—never in this world will that vote pass!" Even if it did—she heard in advance the bickering and recriminations of mothers over the running of the house, the accusations of favoritism to this or that child, the quarrelsome claims as to the relative value of butter and firewood provided from the different farms. And as for managing a bunch of boys and girls at the crazy age! "Lord! Lord! the gossip-mill it'll make! Yes, 'all it needs is coöperation,'" she caricatured her own steady tone into goody-goody sentimentality. "'Nothing but coöperation!'" And ended savagely, "And I know who's got to furnish the coöperation."

She made her next two calls dry, cautious, impersonal, dressing the running sore on old Walt Henry's leg and bathing the unwanted new baby at the 'Gene Kemp house with a severity of manner which surprised no one. Everybody knew that M'Sanna had her ups and downs. They were laid sometimes to red hair, sometimes to her Knapp blood. The grumbling done about them was of the resigned sort evoked by the familiar cussedness of the weather. "There's nobody can be disagreeabler than M'Sanna Craft," people often said as they did of March and November, the

thought of the rest of the year diluting the acid of their resentment.

She was due that morning at Number 10 school for the spring inspection and having given far too much time to the Rollinses, where she had no business to stop at all, she was late. Noon recess had begun evidently, from the wild shrieks as of the tomahawked which rose from the playground of the distant schoolhouse as Miss Craft's Ford topped the rise at the end of Churchman's Road. By the time she drove in under the tamarack of the front yard, there was not a child in sight. Her old enemy, Mrs. Persons, more gnarled and craggy than ever, was sitting on the doorstep, eating lunch out of a pasteboard box. "They're playing coonhunt," she explained sourly as the nurse came to sit beside her. "And Elmer Highgate is the coon, so they'll probably run their legs off before they catch him." She had never concealed her dislike for Miss Craft and made no comment on her reappearance after two years.

Miss Craft resigned herself to waiting, to going without her lunch and to being silently reproached by Cora Ingraham for not taking care of her health.

Mrs. Persons relented enough to give her an eccentric sandwich of home-made graham bread, butter, and pickles which she ate as she began with the usual difficulty to drag from the old teacher some information about the tonsils, eyes, morals, adenoids, and skins in school that year. Just the usual run of Tobey eczema, Twombley fits, and Capen vermin, it seemed. Mrs. Persons professed to need no help from anyone, let alone a wholly superfluous district nurse except, "If you want to *do* something, get a job for that Burdick girl somewhere else. She's full old enough to work. I can't keep a decent school with her in it."

Miss Craft remembered now that Mrs. Rollins had spoken of a Burdick girl. "Which one is she?" she asked. "I thought those younger Burdick kids were boys. Aren't Jed's girls grown up and married off?"

"Yes, they are. This is Jed's niece. Didn't you ever hear about his older sister that was such a bad lot and ended up years ago by

running away with the York State lumberjack that came fishing in Hawley Pond, and died off somewhere—the sister did, I mean—and the Overseer of the Poor wherever 'twas, York State somewheres, found she had folks and sent her little girl back here? At least he claimed it was hers."

Yes, Miss Craft did remember some features of that typical Searles Shelf story and now making a long cast back into her memory fished up almost a blurred recollection of the child herself. "Wasn't she one of that bunch from here I took to the hospital five years ago to have their tonsils out?"

"I don't know but she was." Mrs. Persons implied by her accent her opinion of all that tonsil business.

"Who's the child's father?" asked Miss Craft.

Mrs. Persons laughed. She added, "She's just one of the Lord's mistakes whoever fathered her."

Her unfeeling voice made Miss Craft bristle in spite of her resolution not to let herself go again, not to put herself in anybody's else place. She thought, "I suppose the kid's got some life in her; isn't the wet dishcloth the old lady calls a 'good child.'" Aloud she said, challengingly, "What's the matter with her?"

Mrs. Persons answered acidly, "She's mean. As mean's they make 'em. When they're playing hide and seek and she's 'it,' she looks between her fingers. She always fixes it so somebody else gets blamed for what's her fault. And you never can catch her at it. At that or anything."

"If you can't ever catch her at it how do you know?" asked Miss Craft.

The corners of Mrs. Persons's grim mouth turned down. "You talk like everybody that don't know her ways. They all say that. She's the kind that visitors pick out to like. If they're men, anyhow. The children can't abide her."

Miss Craft thought, "There's something personal in this. The old lady has got some grudge of her own against the child."

The teacher brought out now the deadliest epithet in the vocabulary of The Valley, "She's *plausible!*" and added, "And she makes trouble."

In the language of the back roads as in other primitive tongues, to say of a female that she makes trouble means but one thing. Miss Craft reflected, "She can't be as young as I thought." Aloud she asked, "How old is she?"

"Who knows? She looked to be four or five when she was sent back and that's twelve years ago come Decoration Day. Maybe she's older."

"Do you mean the boys run after her?"

"No! They've been to school with her. But the men do. One married man . . ."

"Is she pretty?"

"She's cross-eyed!"

"Is she smart?"

"She can learn anything she *wants* to learn . . . !" said the old teacher as if this were another condemnation. "Let's quit talking about her. It makes me mad. You just get her a job somewhere else."

They went into the schoolhouse now, Miss Craft envying the simplicity of mind which solved problems by transferring them to other people's towns. Mrs. Persons got out the records of attendance and other reports and they set to work. Presently the children came straggling back to the playground, their stockings down, their shoes muddy, their eyes bright, and began to play "King *William* was King *James's* son," stamping around as though they were fresh from sitting still at their desks. Seeing them circling hand in hand, Miss Craft asked Mrs. Persons to point out the Burdick girl. The two went to the open door. Mrs. Persons stared, and called sharply, "Where's Lixlee?"

The children stopped singing and told her that on their run they had met Henry Twombley and he had taken Lixlee home to help his wife clean house. "She said she knew it would be all right with you, Teacher. She said you'd told her lots of time she was full old enough to work."

They began to circle again, chanting,

> "So *now* look east and *now* look west
> And *choose* the one that *you* love best."

Mrs. Persons turned her back on them. *"House-cleaning!"* she said with a snort.

"I didn't catch her name," said Miss Craft, "sounded to me like Lixlee!"

"That's what it is," said the teacher, "Calix Leota. They call her Lixlee for short. Regular Burdick idee. You know the heathen names they give their young-ones. You remember Fondelly Burdick, she that married a Twombley? Her name was Fonda Ellen. It's *her* husband, Henry, that . . ." She stopped herself and called the children in for the health inspection.

Since she was there and the mud so deep on the road up from the valley, Miss Craft decided to make a day of it in spite of no lunch. If she had had valley homes ahead of her, she could have counted on a glass of milk and a piece of cake. But she had passed the few poor but fiercely self-respecting farms that made up the Churchman's Road district. Before her now was first a long uninhabited road slanting south up across the mountain, and then the sharp turn back to the north that took you out along the overhanging rocky edge called Searles Shelf. It was safer to refuse than to eat the food prepared in the small, dirty, weather-blackened houses scattered along that stony lane.

And even if she had been willing to drink milk in a glass that had been washed by a Twombley or a Capen, not a cow was kept by the few families at this end of nowhere. They were not farmers although a few of them occasionally pulled the moss and steeple-top from a bit of land and planted (when they got around to it) potatoes and corn and a few pumpkins. And there were some marshy meadows from which in good years the grass was cut. But, though they bowed their backs very seldom to the drudgery of farming and had little milk and no butter they did not starve. In spring and autumn, they bought "store-goods" out of the wages some of the men made working on the road. In summer everybody, man, woman and child, picked ferns and sold berries. In winter there were occasional jobs to be had chopping in the woods. The women kept a few hens. A pig was killed Thanksgiving time.

But, in and out of the legitimate open season, hunting was the real occupation of the lean, powerful, care-free men. Their women folks might have sketchy notions about window-washing and clean beds, but they all knew how to make rabbit stews and could cook "deer meat."

Down in the well-painted white houses of The Street, the tidy housewives, staggering under the burden of their own standards of neatness, shuddered at the thought of the wild way people lived up on those back roads, could never learn the difference between Churchman's Road farmers and Searles Shelf hunters and Clifford Four Corners degenerates, and sometimes touched off Miss Craft's red-headed temper by admiring her for her courage in going among them. "There're all kinds of them—some good and some bad," she often said dryly, contemptuous of The Street's complacency, "just as there are down here . . . or anywhere."

She turned her car around the hairpin turn now and was on the Searles Shelf road. Patches of snow gleamed in the shadowed ravines of Hemlock Mountain, towering darkly on her left. Through a white birch grove to her right lay the valley far below, astonishingly greener than anything up here, two thousand feet higher. On her good days Miss Craft usually stopped the car at this corner, to look down the slope of the mountain to the fertile valley, across it, and up the darkly wooded slopes of Wall Mountain to its high skyline drawn against the east from south to north. Her eyes rested on this beauty today but she saw only the difficulties in which she had involved herself. "Why, that means organizing and supporting a dormitory, nothing more or less," she thought, in consternation. "Too much for the Academy to undertake these hundred years, and now I've pulled it over on me. I'm like a man with a weakness for whiskey. Put a bottle anywhere within reach, and I can't keep my hands off it."

At least she had the drunkard's embittered reaction of caution and as she went in and out of the unpainted ramshackle houses of the mountain settlement it was with a sour morning-after determination not to let herself get started again.

There was a good deal that might have started her. The city-

bred nurse who had replaced her had not liked any Clifford people very well, finding them all, as she often said, actively ungrateful for efforts made to help them and with a positive genius for being disagreeable. As for the back-roads families, she had simply given up, lumping them all together in the dictum, "I'd as soon try to work with Apaches." The result was that Miss Craft's first visit showed rather an accumulation of things that needed attention. She made many mental notes as she sat "visiting" in one and another of the weather-beaten shacks, listening to gossip, being shown new babies, learning of deaths, asking who this and that tall boy or girl was. For of course all the children were much bigger, and some of them were unrecognizable from having during her absence crossed the line on one side of which are the noisy game-playing, shoving, anonymous young human beings called children and on the other side the dangerous unexploded bombs called adolescents.

One of the first houses she entered was that of Henry Twombley. From what the old school teacher had intimated, she had gathered that she would find no house-cleaning going on, and was not surprised to find Mrs. Twombley sitting in a chair with one rocker gone, reading the almanac. In one arm she held a late baby, crusts of eczema on his head, a filthy sugar pacifier in his mouth. Around her the house lay quiescent in dirt and disorder. She was one of those who had enjoyed lapsing, under the absentee nurse, into unheeded shiftlessness and neglect of the children. To Miss Craft's question she answered stiffly, "Henery is up at the top of Dowling Hollow today choppin' for Mr. Dewey."

After this, Miss Craft, along with her other inquiries, dropped in each house a casual question about the Burdick girl. She gathered about the same impression from all the lean, overworked women—for Searles Shelf like other primitive human organizations gave men a good time and made women drudges. They were unwilling to say much. Lizzie Burdick, the aunt who had unwillingly brought her up, took a firm stand, "No, I ain't a goin' to talk about Lixlee at all, not to anybody, not so much as to say aye, yes or no. I don't want her bad will." Old man Burdick nodded

his head to this. "That's right. There's nothin' Lixlee wouldn't do to get back at somebody she thinks has done her dirt. She don't let on, but she bides her time."

In another house, a babbling young wife began to tell a story in which Lixlee, Mirella Capen's boy John, a quarrel, another boy, and poison ivy rubbed on a towel were mixed together so ramblingly that Miss Craft could make nothing of it. But as she broke in with a question, her young hostess' mother-in-law's gray head appeared around the corner of the door. "Nyanna, if you let your tongue get too long, it'll hang you!" she said severely. "Didn't your folks ever tell you the most becomin' wear for a fool is a shut mouth?" She came in, began to unbutton the young woman's dress, saying, "Now M'Sanna's got back, you show her that lump in your breast, and see what she thinks 'tis."

But though they edged off warily from talk of the Burdick girl they all seconded eagerly the school teacher's hope that M'Sanna would get her a job somewhere else. The only cheerful view of what would happen if she stayed on was taken by Mrs. Myron Capen, a faded aged woman of thirty-five. "Oh, I don't lose no sleep about Lixlee. Uncle Frank has got his eye on her. You knew he'd buried Emma last November?"

"But a young girl wouldn't marry that dreadful old man! Wasn't Emma his third?" said Miss Craft.

Mrs. Capen was amused at the spinster's simplicity. "Oh, he's quite an old beau, Uncle Frank is, when he goes courtin'. The more women a man's had the more he can get, you know. When Uncle Frank puts his mind to it the boys don't have no chance. He always gits his girl—knock down and drag out if he can't manage no other way. But he wunt hev to Lixlee. She knows he's about all she's likely to git—'less it might be some tough lumberjack from outside, like her mother. There was two of them Canucks came over last winter from beyond The Wall and hung around her some. None of our boys wunt hev nothin' to do with her—not in the marryin' way. They know her too well. And they're kind of scared of her. And water can dribble from married men's mouths all you want to hev it but it don't never git a girl nowhere. Yes,

I calc'late to hear most any day that Lixlee is married to old Frank.
And then she'll have a lot of kids and lose her hair and her teeth
and . . ." She gazed at a picture in her mind, lost the thread of
what she was saying, ended by noisily sucking the saliva back
from the corners of her mouth and wiping her lips with the side
of her hand.

Miss Craft shrank from the gloating malice of the woman's eyes,
thinking indignantly, "But the girl's only a child! And a motherless child! Isn't there one of them, not even her own blood-kin,
to realize a child's right to help and protection! They are like a
pack of dogs around a fawn that's lost its mother."

But that case was only one of many, all urgently needing her
attention. And her impulse to rush to the rescue had already that
day cost her a price. "Now, no more letting yourself go!" she
thought severely. "You've got yourself into enough trouble for
one while. Let well enough alone for once in your life!"

By the time she made her last call the sun had sunk behind the
high overhanging mass of Hemlock Mountain; but the valley to
the south and The Wall on the other side were flooded with long
golden rays streaming through Lathrop's Pass. Seeing none of this,
the nurse turned her car homeward. She was looking inward, trying to arrange in the order of their urgency the problems she had
collected. Among the younger children a new crop of tonsils and
adenoids cried aloud. Leonard Capen's wife's goiter was much
worse, probably should be operated on at once. Old Mrs. Moore's
oddities began to look alarmingly like paranoia of a dangerous
kind; it was criminal to leave her helpless little grandchildren alone
with her. There was that Burdick girl evidently on the point of
catastrophe. Those blotches on the Tobey children's cheeks were
not at all, as the old school teacher had thought, their usual non-
contagious eczema. It looked like impetigo that might run through
all the valley if it weren't headed off. In her mind a familiar
thought rebounded from its familiar answer. "I ought to get old
Doctor Cole up to look at that. No, no, I can give them calomel as
well as he."

And then startling her so that she stopped her car as though something had risen before her in the road, came the thought, "But there will be Anson. Anson will be here! Our long separation is over."

She had come home from very far because of that, but till this moment she had not really believed it, and now that she did, she found herself so affected—strange and terrible pleasure-pain to feel something for herself not through others—that she could not at once drive on. It was one of those moments, rare in anyone's life, almost unknown in hers, when the throb of the heart beats visibly in all the world, when nature no longer stands aloof and indifferent but bends tenderly close, suffused with sharing sympathy. For the second time that day she was altogether alive. She looked down along the mountain slope to the sweetness of the valley and across to where on the other side The Wall stretched its long bulk, clad as in velvet by the mauve bloom of early spring. She looked and saw—and felt her heart shattered into ecstasy by beauty and by love.

3

FOR THE first week after her return, Miss Craft thought it was only by chance that she saw Isabel Foote so often. By the end of the second week it was plain that Isabel, not chance, was responsible. She ran in early while Miss Craft and Miss Ingraham still sat at breakfast, "to bring over a bunch of hepaticas from the Academy woods": the instant Miss Craft stepped into the Post Office for her mail, Isabel was at her side to help carry the packages home; at noon she rushed down the hill from the Academy to spend most of her lunch hour hanging around the cubby-hole in the Town Hall that was called "M'Sanna's office," perhaps taking care of an obstreperous baby while M'Sanna looked out for its mother, perhaps sorting over or mending the old garments, bedding and shoes donated to M'Sanna's work and kept in the dark back room. And in the afternoon, as soon as her classes were over, she looked up Miss Ingraham, found where Miss Craft's visits had

taken her that day and walked off in that direction. Sometimes her long wood-nymph's legs had carried her for miles along a back road before she heard the rattle of the nurse's Ford. Miss Craft came to expect, as she turned almost any corner at that time of day, to see the tall comely girl, sturdy in her warm sweater and short woolen skirt, her bright brown hair gleaming, standing knee-deep in the steepletop and bracken beside the road signaling for a lift, sure of her welcome with the smiling confidence of a cherished child who has always been welcome everywhere.

She talked a great deal during these rides. Mostly it was young magpie chatter about Academy dances and tennis, a new dress, one of her many boy-admirers, a little sister's prank. But sometimes, almost without transition, she would break into talk so earnest that it made her cry—about life and herself and the strange, strange feelings she had, and her passionate longing to live so that her life would not be the mere vegetating it was to "every single woman I know except you, M'Sanna! Oh, you can't imagine what it means to me to have *some*body I can talk to! None of the other girls seem to feel this way. Cornelia's always wrapped up in Charlie Dean— as much as she ever could be about anything, you know how frightfully *placid* Cornelia is! And Olivia is such a kid. All she really cares about is tennis. What *would* I have done if you hadn't come back!" As her confidence in the nurse grew, she even confessed some of the immature notions she had had when she was still an inexperienced child:—"I wanted to go and live on that Hawaii island and take care of the lepers. But of course, now I can see that was just a crazy kid's notion. And then I thought for a while I wanted to take vows and join an Order—I fairly pestered Father Kirby to get him to make Mother say I could. But he just laughed. And now I see he was right. *Now I know* what I was born to do!" The present plan was, it seemed, to enter a nurses' training school as soon as she graduated from the Academy next year (she would be nineteen, nearly twenty then) and follow in Miss Craft's footsteps, working as a district nurse in the country. "I'd feel there was some *meaning* to life then," she said, with a fierce frightened scorn of its present meaninglessness.

But no matter how freely she had poured out her heart in one of these long uninterrupted talks in Miss Craft's Ford, Isabel usually invented an errand that would give her one more glimpse of her present idol before going to bed. She always found Miss Ingraham correcting Latin and algebra papers, and M'Sanna across the book-lined living-room, reading a serious social-welfare magazine, or seated at the desk that had been her father's, vainly trying to cope with the reports and letters to be written to and about the many people dependent on her for sympathy and help—orphaned children in foster families, physically and mentally sick men and women she had helped to place in hospitals and prisons and reform schools and insane asylums and homes.

"Good evening, M'Sanna. Good evening, Miss Ingraham."

"Well, Isabel, what can I do for you?"

"I can't find our copy of 'The House of the Seven Gables,' and I have to write a theme about it. Can I borrow yours?" Or, "Mother made such a swell ice-box cake for supper, I brought over what was left to you two."

But when she went away it was, "Oh, M'Sanna, come out a minute to look at the stars!" Or, "Don't you simply *adore* a rainy night? Step out here on the porch and listen."

Once she had the nurse to herself in the dark, her good night was a long, ardent embrace. Miss Craft understood very well that this belonged not to her but to some young man in the near future. As she sat down again at her desk to her dusty impersonal work, the remembered pressure of those violent young arms and the petal smoothness of the young cheek made her feel rather dustier than usual by contrast.

Clifford pople noted what they spoke of as Isabel's latest crush and commented on it each in his own language. Miss Ingraham called up the unjealous tolerance she had fought so hard to learn and remarked, smiling, "It could be said of you, Anna, that 'to have had a crush on her is a liberal education.'" Isabel's father stopped Anna on the street one day to say stiffly, shyly, "I want you should know I appreciate your being good to Isabel at a time when she's at a . . . It all seems very serious to *her,* of course."

He repudiated this cant phrase as a betrayal, flushed and corrected himself, "It *is* very serious . . . she'll never feel anything any more deeply. I remember from my own youth (you do too probably) how overwhelming it all looks at that age. I'm . . . I'm *very* glad you don't laugh at her!"

"Oh, Doctor Foote, who could do that!"

"A great many people," he said sadly and went his way.

Sure enough it was with an easy laugh that Isabel's mother (she who had been Hilda Nye) said to Miss Craft, "I hope the child doesn't bother you, Anna, tagging you round so. She's got to the excitable age, when children have to tag somebody—somebody outside the family, of course. But it won't last long, probably. She'll soon be off on something else"—this with her usual comfortable matter-of-factness. She had already successfully brought up two children older than Isabel who were now happily all through with this soulful business, and she had two younger ones, rapidly coming up into stamp collecting, cave digging, the cowboy fever and other phases recently left behind by Isabel. Miss Craft, revolted by her belittling common sense, thought, "Isn't Hilda a Nye through and through! No wonder Isabel doesn't confide in her. They haven't a thing in common, not a thing. Isabel is her father all over."

Old Sherwin Dewey, as sure of his equilibrium as of Hemlock Mountain's, said tenderly to Miss Craft, "Isabel makes me feel the way some April mornings do. Nice girls that age, when they're all ready for their first beau but he hasn't come along yet . . . gosh! I'm like butter in the sun when I look at them. I wonder where all the cussed women come from anyhow? All the girls are so nice."

Mr. Lawrence Stewart, although he thought of himself in these middle years as entirely absorbed in the maintenance of an esthetic and dignified pattern of life, had been once or twice disagreeably startled by the violence of the impression made on him by a young girl, the younger the worse. Of Isabel he said severely, uneasily, "All those adolescent fits! I wish she'd get them over with."

Father Kirby said, "God is calling the child, Anna, and she is trying to answer. Even to try to answer is more than most of us do."

This last text received a footnote from Miss Bessie Kemp:—
"We're all glad you got back, Anna. Everybody would enough
sight rather have *you* be her lightning rod than a minister." At
Miss Craft's inquiring look, "Oh, hadn't anybody told you? Hadn't
Fred Kirby? I thought he told you everything. She's been em-
broidering an altar-cloth and considering going to be a Deaconess
for the last six months. When she wasn't playing with her dolls. I
didn't know how much longer Fred, even though he is a Reverend
Father, could hold out. When a good-looking full-blooded girl of
eighteen gets lighted up with religion, she's about as easy to handle
as a forest fire. And I'd hate to have Isabel marry a Reverend. I
don't think *really* religious men ought to marry anyhow. They
have too many children if they do, you must have noticed *that*."

Subtracting from these comments the varying personal notes, from
Mrs. Foote's Nye literalness to the Rabelaisian touch dear to
Miss Bessie, Miss Craft perceived back of them all (except, of
course, poor Mr. Stewart's) a warm friendly concern for the girl's
welfare and happiness. Like an invisible shield this stood between
her and danger, as she ran forward into life, glorying in the tragedy
of her isolation in a dull and insensitive world.

To perceive this did not—quite the contrary—help Miss Craft
throw off the weight on her conscience she had brought down from
Searles Shelf. That Burdick girl with the preposterous name—
what had it been?—was probably about Isabel's age, and was probably, like her, a vessel almost shattered by the ferment of youth.
Miss Craft often took pains to tell the Gardners, Footes, Barneys,
and other substantial respectabilities of The Street that experience
had taught her that the only difference between ignorant and dirty
people in small weather-blackened shacks, and comfortable well-
washed people in large white houses with clean window-panes, is
a difference of opportunity. The tingling contacts with Isabel, heavily charged with the high-powered current of youth as the girl
was, repeatedly shocked her into remorse over the difference in
opportunity between the two adolescents. Both girls were at the
age which most needs the protection of the older generation, but
the defenseless youth of the Searles Shelf girl was surrounded not

by affection and solicitude as was Isabel's, but by lust and envy and ill-will. She too, thought Miss Craft, had probably just now broken through the shell of childhood, and half in and half out, startled to see the stars high over her head, was reaching her arms up towards them. She, too, probably was flinging herself here and there in life wildly, idiotically, generously. But the only eyes that followed the struggles of the penniless orphaned girl were those eager to put the basest interpretation on all she did. The picture had been plainly drawn for the nurse up there on her first visit. She could not look away from it . . . the friendless, motherless, unwanted girl-child now in the dangerous flower of her age, an unwilling enemy to the peace of other women, not one of whom would lift a finger to save her from the hairy hands of the old satyr spying on her from ambush. ". . . and then she'll have a lot of kids, and lose her hair and teeth and . . ." While down here, Isabel, no more in need, not half so much in need, was walled around from danger by indulgent, watchful, understanding protectors and well-wishers.

Finally, one windy darkly clouded May afternoon, she gave in to that inner pressure. "If I'm not here to do what families should do, for folks that haven't got families, what *am* I here for?" she asked herself, and considerably sooner than she had planned, set out again for Searles Shelf. As she turned from the highway into Churchman's Road, she was thinking that people wrought very oddly on each other's lives. Isabel, quite unaware of the Burdick girl's existence, was responsible for this second trip up the mountain. It was Isabel, warm in the safety of a cherished child's life, who had not allowed her to forget the darkness and cold around the unfriended girl.

She ground up the first steep slope of the road. She passed the burnt-over lot without seeing it, she went by the Rollins farm with only a vague recollection of the formidable price her sympathy for the Rollinses had cost her. All her thoughts were now concentrated on the probable difficulties of the case before her. Wherever could she find work for a Burdick girl off Searles Shelf—assuming that the girl wanted work and was fit for it. She and Cora Ingraham

needed no houseworker but their competent neighbor, Mrs. Randall, who for years had come in for work from after breakfast to before supper. Of course someone should be in the Dewey house to help the devoted old man take care of his crippled wife. But as her husband said, if the Angel Gabriel should offer to wash dishes and cook for Mrs. Dewey she'd be afraid a feather from his wings might drop into the soup. It wasn't likely that she would ever let a Searles Shelf girl into her kitchen. Nor any more likely that her husband would, after all these years, put his foot down and refuse to go on being martyrized. Mr. Stewart's housekeeper it was true, was looking for a second girl, Mr. Stewart having disliked the voice of the last one. But . . .

Well, she would better wait before trying to plan. Perhaps the girl might be too dumb to learn the varied tasks of a houseworker. The Burdicks *were* dumb, pure-blooded, Anglo-Saxon peasant stock that they were. It might be better to try to find a small job for her in the brush-back factory, where she would be required only to repeat one simple operation.

She steered her car around the hairpin turn and came out on the stretch of level road that looked down through white birches to the valley. There among the slim immaculate stems of the trees stood a girl—not Isabel—knee deep in bracken. She was shading her eyes with her hand and looking expectantly at the turn of the road as if she had heard the car approaching. As Miss Craft automatically slipped her clutch and put on the brake, her practiced eye as automatically passed the girl in review. She was not ruddy and sturdy in a thick wool sweater. She wore a draggled sleazy green rayon dress with very little under it. Her dark matted hair did not gleam with health and vigorous brushing; it had been, Miss Craft accurately guessed, clumsily curled with a hot iron, scarcely combed for fear of "spoiling the wave," and ever since tied up in a cloth at night. She was either very pale or had a very white skin; there was something queer about one of her dark eyes. And she looked half frozen.

By this time the Ford had stopped. "Did you want a lift?" called Miss Craft, although the other had made no sign.

As soon as Miss Craft spoke she began to push forward through the tall new ferns and stiff resisting stems of the steepletop. She moved slowly, not looking down to pick her way, her unsmiling gaze searching the nurse's face. By the time she had come out into the road and up beside the car, Miss Craft had added an item or two to her appraisal. Muddy high-heeled shoes run over at one side; pink cotton stockings; rather a flat undeveloped body for a girl of that age, with that unchildlike expression on her face; probably underfed during adolescence; something unusual about the way she walked.

The girl came up close and put one thin grimy hand on the door of the car. Though she moved quietly, almost with a wild-animal wariness, there was desperation in the air about her.

Between them flowed a silence full of blind swirling cross-currents. The nurse asked again, "Were you wanting a lift?"

"Yes, I be wanting a lift," said the girl in a deep husky voice, and then wildly pointing back towards Searles Shelf, "But not that way, M'Sanna! Not back that way!"

As if her words had been thunder breaking a before-storm oppression, she burst into tears, bowed herself forward over the door, her face hidden in her arms. From where Miss Craft sat, nothing could be seen of her but the top of an ill-cared-for head and a bony young back, both very touching to the nurse's professional eye. She was trying to choke back her sobs so that she could speak, but she could never get beyond, "Oh, M'Sanna, don't. . . . I've *got* to get away. . . . They're so *mean* to me. . . . M'Sanna, can't you . . ."

After the first moment of surprise, Miss Craft stepped hastily out of the car and putting her arm around the thin young body drew her down on the running board. She said nothing at first, trusting to the healing gift of physical nearness. Presently the dark tousled head was on her shoulder and she felt herself shaken by the girl's sobs.

She was thinking with austere self-blame, "I should have come before. Sitting down there in a well-padded chair, making out fool reports in duplicate! Probably now I am too late."

She drew the shivering girl to her, trying to use her own tweed-clad body as a shield against the gusts of cold wind, which, damp with the impending rain, roared in the tree tops on the overhanging mountain and swooped down on them at intervals, whipping the white birches into a momentary frenzy.

But when the girl had cried herself out and they had a talk, sitting side by side on the running board of the car, it appeared that she was not too late. In answer to a cautious inquiry about Uncle Frank, Lixlee said passionately that she'd kill that damned old goat if he ever tried to touch her. Miss Craft remembered the ax-man's sinewy gorilla arms and looked doubtfully at the flaccid white flesh that hung on the girl's slim bones. She also noted the language and mentally checked off most of the respectable valley houses where she might have placed the girl.

That was, it seemed, Lixlee's hope—to get work somewhere else. Anywhere else. Any kind of work. Her ignorance of everything except Searles Shelf was so complete that she could ask for nothing more definite than to be taken away from it. She dared not try to run away since the day at Ashley, last year, County Fair Day, when, conquering by a terrific effort of the will her mountaineer fear of strangers, she had stolen away from the Searles Shelf people down at the Fair for their annual day of rowdy fun, and had gone from house to house in the town asking for work. "They looked at me so!" she told the nurse, the tears bursting out again at the memory. "The women shut their doors. The only place I was even asked in was where an old bachelor lived by himself, and the minute he had me in there, he began to . . . I had to . . ." Shuddering she hid her head again on Miss Craft's shoulder, finishing the rest of her story so brokenly that not a word could be heard.

Miss Craft did not need to hear. From the moment the girl began to speak she had known what there was to hear. Indeed, now it seemed to her that she had known it from the first of the old school teacher's harsh unfeeling words. Once more she let time pass for the quieting of the girl's nerves, employing the pause by thinking profoundly. Or rather, in abandoning herself to a certain stir and movement in her mind which, when she needed it most, came from

below the plane of thought. When she was trying to steer a course through a complicated situation this subterranean current was, she had found, rather more to be trusted than her reason. She now let it carry her where it would, and was genuinely surprised to have it take her straight to the unexpected conclusion, "Well, not in Lawrence Stewart's employ, anyhow." She chided herself, "Pshaw! I'm getting like any other old maid. As bad as Almira Boardman."

As yet she had seen the girl's face only long enough to note that she bore no resemblance to the flaxen-haired blunt-featured Burdicks. Feeling the second storm of sobs subside, she thought, "I must have her talk and look straight at me, so I can get a line on her."

But when Lixlee lifted her head and, fixing her eyes on the nurse's, began to tell the story of her troubles, Miss Craft found her own gaze caught by what seemed a very slight cast in one or the other of the girl's dark eyes. Was it the left or the right one that had just a hint of . . . ? No, no, it was not a cast, perhaps the way the light fell. She leaned closer to see more clearly, decided it was nothing at all, caught again a faint hint of something oblique, leaned closer yet, till her own gaze drowned in the swimming darkness of the girl's velvet eyes. . . .

She did not know how long a time had passed before she came to herself with a start. How long since Lixlee had stopped talking? There was no sound now but the wind blowing loudly. How long had the silence lasted? How long had she been gazing into that liquid pansy-black iris, set, she noted it now for the first time, not in a clear blue-white eyeball, but in one of a faintly creamy tone.

Nettled to feel herself confused, she said in a dry businesslike voice, "Well, I'll see what I can do. . . . It's not always easy to find a job for an untrained person!" To herself she thought with annoyance, "And after all my staring, I still don't know what there is about that eye."

But still slightly shaken as she was by that momentary stopping of her sense of the passage of time she was unwilling to risk too long a look at it. A sensible and practical explanation of her long in-

voluntary gaze occurred to her, "It's the sort of dizziness you have when you try to fix your eyes on two moving points," she thought, and shot a hasty glance at the girl, her curiosity still unsatisfied.

Her glance showed the girl's eyelids now dropped over her eyes. Seen so, the rather long, pale and oddly modeled face looked quite different from what Miss Craft had thought it. "I hadn't noticed her eyebrows were so black and fine, and her cheek bones so high . . . why, I haven't really looked at her *yet!*" thought the nurse, feeling the currents in the below-thought layer of her mind swirling uncertainly here and there in the dark.

Under her gaze the girl's eyelids, thick and very white, slowly lifted. She raised her dark eyes imploringly. Their impact on Miss Craft's was startling, sending her subterranean current suddenly down a steep straight channel to a well-formulated conclusion, "Why, the girl's a man-eater. One of the natural-born sirens. She all but got *me* going!"

Glancing now at her wrist watch, standing up to go, the nurse began the maneuver of retreat. She was astonished to find that nearly an hour had passed. As she asked herself uneasily where all that time could have gone, the trees on the mountain above them bent suddenly under a huge invisible wave of wind that broke over the crest and poured itself in rough noisy eddies down the slope to the road. It whipped the skirts of the two women around them, and enveloped them for a moment in a blinding scurry of last year's dead leaves, flung up from the forest floor. A few first heavy drops of rain came with it, spattering ominously here and there. Miss Craft backed off still further, "Well, I'll see what I can do," she repeated noncommittally.

"I'll wait right here for you, M'Sanna," said the girl, her husky voice broken by tears. She took Miss Craft's hand in both of hers. Nothing could have made a more moving appeal to the nurse's professional instinct than those pathetically thin young fingers, the dry uncared-for skin only just covering the delicate bones. It was with an effort she kept her own hand cautiously limp.

The girl held it close as she went on, "Ever since I heard you were back I've come down here to the turn of the road to watch

for you every minute *she'd* let me go." Throughout the long story she had told of her life "she" had been her uncle's second wife who had brought her up.

"No, no. Don't wait here. It's rather a lonely place for a girl by herself." As Miss Craft spoke, she noticed that although they were out of sight of the nearest house—the decent one where the decent branch of the Capens lived—they were quite near enough for a call to carry. She shifted her ground, "That would be a great waste of time. I can't tell at all when I'll be able to come up again. I know the way to your Uncle Jed's house. I'll drive right there. If I succeed in finding work for you, that is," she added hastily, determined to promise nothing till she had had time to reflect.

"But I want to! I want to wait for you! I ain't got another friend in the world but you, M'Sanna!" cried the girl desperately, fixing tragic dark eyes on the nurse's. Miss Craft looked the other way and climbed into her car. As she backed herself around in the narrow road she called once more, "Well, I'll let you know if I find anything," and drove away rather fast.

As she made the sharp turn she glanced up and saw that, in spite of the rain which now began decisively to fall, the girl stood motionless, gazing after the car. She looked anything but dangerous— thin, strengthless, uncouth—and pitiably alone. The next glance showed her walking stumblingly in the cold rain toward the turn of the road, as if she were trying by a few poor steps to lessen the distance the nurse was putting between them. Miss Craft's heart melted in a shamed revulsion of feeling. What nonsense had she been thinking about the unfriended hapless child!

"Well . . . !" she said to herself straightening around in her seat, and taking a firmer hold of the wheel as the Ford began to buck viciously over the waterbars of the steep road. "Well . . ." Knowing a long stretch of uninhabited road to be before her, she settled down to a leisurely mental examination of the data she had brought away with her.

But one more item was to be added. She had gone no further than to think, "If that is a cast in one eye it could be corrected by glasses. And tonsilectomy might clear up that queer huskiness of her

voice," when she heard a new rattle among the many well-known old ones of her car. She stopped on the next waterbar, got out, saw that the rough road had jolted her radiator hood loose, and snapped the fastening down. When she turned back towards the door of the car, she was aware of something distant moving across the outer edge of her retina . . . something on the road back of her, leading up between its thick green walls of trees and brush. She lifted her head and saw a man's back near the top. In spite of the ladder steepness of the road, he was racing up in long rapid strides. He must have been in the bushes as she went by and have stepped out after she had passed. A Searles Shelf poaching pot-hunter? She looked to see if a rifle were over his shoulder. But he was too far away to be sure of this or anything else about him except that he was tall and in rough old clothes.

As she looked, he stopped short, as if he had only just then noted the cessation of the noise from her car. And flashed around to look back. He had no rifle.

Seeing her, standing there in the rain by the car, looking up intently at him from below, he made a startled plunge towards the shelter of the bushes at the side of the road. It was the lithe, supple movement of a powerful man in his prime.

But after that one involuntary reflex movement, he stopped again, his back to the nurse, and stood for an instant, considering. Then coming to a decision he strode on up the road.

4

As they sat down to supper that night, Cora Ingraham looked across the table to see if the long-expected letter from Anson had come. The listless way in which Miss Craft was spreading butter on her biscuit showed her that it had not. "I could kill him!" thought Cora, pouring out her tea. She helped herself to the honey and looking unusually plain, tried resolutely to think of the weather which was making itself very audible, the wind-blown rain dashing against the closed shutters, the water overflowing in streams

from the eaves-troughs. The meal was almost finished before she ventured to knock at the door of her friend's life and ask to be let in. . . . "Well, Anna, how did your day go?"

"About as usual."

"Did you see that girl on Searles Shelf you were thinking of finding work for?"

"Yes."

"Well . . . ?"

"Oh . . . I don't know. . . ."

Miss Ingraham took a resigned swallow of her tea and said no more. Miss Craft felt the unspoken pull of the other's longing to share life with her and this time yielded to it not unwillingly. Cora was no fool. To talk that perplexing matter over with her might cast some light on it.

"Well, Cora, now that I've seen the girl . . . I understand more how it is she sets everybody up there by the ears."

"Quarrelsome?"

"No. Oh, no, not that way. Not that kind. The kind that makes you keep looking at her to see what there is about her . . . especially men, I should think."

Miss Ingraham was astonished at such a report of a resident of Searles Shelf. "Not good-looking?" she queried, incredulously.

"No. Worse."

Miss Ingraham thought she recognized this as a piece of Anna's dry Vermontism, laughed, and asked, "What kind of work could she do?"

"She *looks* as untrained and unbrought up as a barn cat. I don't suppose she could hold a needle, or cook so much as a boiled egg. She certainly doesn't know how to wash her face and hands."

Miss Ingraham rose in revolt. "She sounds impossible. Oh, Anna, why do you have to take on all the impossibles! Why are *you* responsible for her? The girl's not sick, is she? You're a nurse, you're not God! Suppose you hadn't come home from France. Suppose you didn't know about her."

"But I do," said Miss Craft in rather a somber voice. She got up and led the way into their sitting-room, its old red curtains drawn,

its two reading lights bright on desk and table, chunks of apple-wood burning on the hearth. She sat down in front of the fire, "I imagine that what keeps God on the job—if He is—is just that, His knowing about everything. As soon as you know about something you're responsible for it, aren't you?"

"I suppose it makes *you* responsible," admitted Miss Ingraham, unable as usual to resist Anna.

There was a silence in which the ordered self-centered comfort of the living-room silently wove against the wind and rain and blackness outside, the cushiony spell of walled-in pleasantness with which fire-lighted homes protect their owners from the greatness and confusion of life. It was the spell with which Cora Ingraham wished she might always surround and protect her friend. She let it fall sweeter and warmer around them for a time before she asked, persuasively, "But, Anna, why are you so sure God would take that girl away from the background she's used to and try to make her over into something else? Why need you always assume that God wants the course of action that will give you the most trouble?"

Miss Craft thought, "I like Cora's irony. I wish she had more of it," and answered, "Yes, I suppose we do love any formula that'll protect us from really thinking!"

"Well, then, this time really think!" Miss Ingraham pressed her advantage. "What *could* you do with such a girl?"

"I'd have to find first of all somebody willing to take her in and civilize her, housebreak her. But who?"

"Not Cora Ingraham!"

"No, not anybody who couldn't be on the job twenty-four hours a day. See here, Cora, let me tell you the whole thing as far as I know."

In a colorless narrative, she laid before her housemate all the facts she had gathered.

At the end, Cora Ingraham conjectured, "I suppose the man on the road was the old gorilla widower stalking her. A good thing she was near enough a house to call for help."

"No, it was no old man. His leap was like a tiger's."

"Oh!" Miss Ingraham thought an instant. "Was it the husband

who wanted her to help with the house-cleaning, do you suppose? Yes, yes, of course, it must have been. And *he* was the person she had gone to the turn of the road to meet, not you at all. He'd just waited in the bushes till you went away."

"Well, of course," admitted Miss Craft, "that came into my mind. But I couldn't believe it. Nor I can't now, when I remember the girl herself, and the way she cried, and her poor, starved, bony young body. . . ."

"Her being thin hasn't anything to do with it."

"You didn't see her! I know what it sounds like. But I tell you she simply couldn't have been putting all that on. Nobody could. She's desperate. Like an animal caught in a trap."

"Maybe it's just as well that kind of a girl is safely in a trap."

"Now look here, Cora, *you* don't know what kind of a girl she is! Nor I don't! Nor she doesn't! We don't *know* that man had a thing to do with her. With peace and good food and decent training, she might grow into something just the opposite of what she seems now. Remember Alta Capen and Marden Twombley." (She was referring to two forlorn, unpromising Searles Shelf infant orphans whom she had placed long ago with farm families on The Other Side and who had grown up to be sober, hard-working, useful young people.)

"It's too late for that in this case. Could you get any decent family to take in this girl . . . at her age, with what they'd hear about her when they asked Searles Shelf people?"

"I don't suppose I could."

"Anyhow," continued Miss Ingraham, "why in the world pick her out of all the others as somebody you've got to get out of there. You don't feel under any obligations to move down all the Searles Shelf young ones into respectable families in The Valley. Quite the contrary. You're always taking the wind out of our sails by telling us that in lots of ways they're better off and happier being lazy and shiftless than Valley people working their heads off to keep ahead of dirt. Why should it be a trap she's caught in, more than any other Searles Shelf girl? Answer me that."

Miss Craft was sure there had been an answer to that question

somewhere in her impression of Lixlee, but pacified and relaxed
as she was by the domesticity around her, she could not bring it to
mind; nor indeed, now, bring the girl very clearly to mind. She
sat silent before the hearth, looking at the drowsing fire, tamed
and housebroken blood-brother to the unvanquished wind shouting across the top of the chimney and wrestling with the tall
maples around the house. Presently she said, "It's this way . . .
I'm not worrying about her having to work hard and live hard.
That does nobody any harm. But—I don't say I'm sure of this—
just suppose for argument's sake that there is some special quality
in her that wouldn't have a chance to live at all up there with those
narrow, hard-headed people who have had her faults under a mag-
nifying glass all her life. I don't mean an artistic gift or anything
like that—but a special kind of personality—a quality that would
give her prestige anywhere else—you know what I mean—what
you and I haven't got an atom of."

"Sounds like sex-appeal."

"No, not exactly. . . . Not so simple." She looked around the
book-lined room and up at the steel engraving of the Forum her
grandfather had brought home from his European tour. "Now
that I try to get it into words it seems silly. She was such a draggle-
tailed stray cat! I don't know what made me think there was
something about her . . ."

"Well . . ." Miss Ingraham squared herself for some logic.
"Isn't it one of two things? Either she's an ordinary Searles Shelf
girl headed for a Searles Shelf life that, on the whole, is the suitable
one for her, or . . . if there is anything in this funny business of
her having some personal glamor only she can't work it on the folks
up there because they know her so well they see right through it to
what she really is . . . why not, for heaven's sake, leave well
enough alone and let her live with the one group in the world
she can't fool? Isn't that sense?"

"It certainly sounds like sense," admitted Miss Craft with relief.
By this time she could scarcely remember Lixlee at all, except as a
slatternly girl who needed a bath and a shampoo. She stared dreamily into the fire. How good it was to be loosened and vague. It

was very rarely that she felt so. She had been right to talk it over with Cora. Presently turning her head she said, "You're a comfort to me, Cora. I'd be very lonely without you."

The room was filled as by a bright fountain, with the astonished gratitude of the other woman. "Oh, *Anna!*" she said.

Miss Craft got up and went to her desk. In a moment their two pens were scratching on, making a dry old-maidish noise, quite audible in the hushed room against the roar of the wind and rain outside.

Later on Isabel came in, rain drops sparkling on her bright wind-roughened hair, her eyes wide from the darkness, shining like stars. "Good evening, M'Sanna. Good evening, Miss Ingraham."

"What can I do for you, Isabel?"

"Mother thought you'd let me borrow one of the hoop-skirt dresses in your cedar chest. I'm the grandmother in our class play."

"Yes, of course." Miss Craft pushed away from her desk to go in search of the costume but paused, her eyes on Isabel's face, rosy and fine-textured as an arbutus flower. "The grandmother!" she said, breaking into one of her rare laughs. "You'll make a fine grandmother, Isabel!"

She went to bed in this appeased state of mind and at first slept soundly. But towards morning she woke up to a sky still black except for a faint hovering of gray above the line of The Wall. It had stopped raining. The wind had died down. Her room was dense with the before-Judgment-Day hush which precedes dawn. The doomed and terrified girl under the white birches stood beside the bed and looked piteously at her. She thought, "There's a great deal more to that business than Cora and I touched. It's deep! It goes to the roots of things. Cora got me side-tracked. It's never safe to stop being alone. Letting somebody else in who loves you always lets you down. No matter what they say, all they're thinking about is how to keep things little and tidy and comfortable for you. This is no question for prudence and good sense to decide. It's a question of Life against . . . Is it against Death? No, it's the *whole* of Life against . . ."

But she was very tired, and fell almost at once again to sleep.

When her alarm clock rang at half-past six, she stood up from bed into an amiable spring morning of sun and wandering breezes and well-intentioned little white clouds. Of her moment of wakefulness at dawn there was nothing left but an uneasiness she could not label. "Can it be time already for Mrs. Dean's confinement?" she wondered and ran downstairs to look at her calendar. No, Mrs. Dean's baby was not due for a fortnight. Could it be another "Knapp day"? Her heart sank.

After a rather grim silent breakfast, she walked across her back yard to get out her Ford for the morning round. Across the valley, Hemlock Mountain was all vaporous blue and gracious down-dropping lines. Along its flank, a line delicately cross-hatched in white, stretched the birches that marked the Searles Shelf road.

After a time Cora Ingraham, familiar by now with the seasonal preoccupations of her adopted town, called out from her bedroom window, "Anna, whatever are you staring up at? Do you see a fire on the mountain?"

"I can't seem to make out from the look of it *what* it is," Miss Craft called back and went on to her car, trying to dismiss the Burdick girl from her mind. At least she knew now that the shadow over the day did not come from her Knapp inheritance.

But the Searles Shelf question was as hard to dismiss as to find an answer for. All that day, and the next, and the next, she felt herself taut in the involuntary muscular expectancy of a person who has noticed a rock about to fall, or a bird poised for flight. Even when her back was squarely turned to Hemlock Mountain and she was facing the unsubdued growth of never-inhabited forest on The Wall, she felt the high-hung road on the mountain behind her leaning more and more ominously over the comfortable little town. Several times, wheeling quickly to look up at it, she was surprised to find it still in its old place, far across the valley, a mere hint of a line no stranger would have noticed.

Her usual routine went on, monotonous in its variety. Tuesday morning was her regular time to visit Clifford Four Corners. This group of shacks and shanties at the foot of The Wall where the road

ended, had nothing of the mellow, dignified, slightly smug self-satisfaction of The Street in having subdued to cleanliness and decency
its corner of the epic mountain magnificence of Windward County.
Nor did it breathe free in the wild, bold, backwoods lawlessness of
Searles Shelf. Clifford Four Corners had only epilepsy and hopelessness and dirt and incest and imbecility. More than once that
morning the nurse thought, "Here and thus—if I do nothing—is
what that friendless girl will be."

On Wednesday she had calls to make on The Other Side. This
was the name of the upper highway leading north over the foothills
of The Wall from The Street to Ashley. Only a few old people like
Miss Bessie'n'Gussie Kemp remembered the satiric origin of the
name. It had been given to the road in the eighteenth century by a
sharp-tongued rector of St. Andrew's, exasperated by the un-Samari-
tan aloofness from other people's troubles of the well-to-do church-
going families who lived along it. The same rector it was who had
given to the back road from which nobody ever came to his services, the ironic nickname of Churchman's Road. As in his time,
The Other Side was still the road of prosperous dairy farms and
apple orchards, of clean red-cheeked boys and girls, and well-read,
hard-handed, hard-headed men and women. They considered themselves the only real Vermonters in the region, and were very scornful (a little envious, too) both of the shiftless ease of Searles Shelf
and of the parasitic way in which the villagers in The Street—
storekeepers, professional families, a few with small unearned inherited incomes—contrived with uncalloused hands to live off their
neighbors with horny ones. These successful folks had mixed feelings about Anna Craft. She was connected with them by the ramifi-
cations of kinship, hence her existence, unlike that of an outsider,
was not open to question. She belonged in The Valley. Moreover,
worshiping competence above all other human qualities, they could
not but respect M'Sanna's professional skill. But as heartily as their
ancestors they detested demands on them to take care of "the lame
and the lazy" as their traditional phrase ran (they meant the poor);
and years ago they had been the very last voters to stand out at
Town Meeting against the modern foolishness of paying sacred

tax money to a nurse to help folks who ought to be made to help themselves. When they were finally out-voted, and the nurse was actually among them, of course they made as much use as possible of her services, though suspiciously on their guard against her annoying habit of never letting well enough alone. She always had plenty of calls for nursing from The Other Side.

It ran parallel to the main road below it, and also to the much higher Searles Shelf road across the valley. On that Wednesday as the district nurse dressed the bed sores of a bloodless old invalid ending his life in a clean white bedroom, or the navel of a red new baby beginning life in another, she could not but see across the valley the line of white birches. When this made her too uncomfortable she defended herself by asking, "You don't happen to know of anybody who's looking for help, do you? There's a girl from Searles Shelf who wants to . . ."

As she expected she never was allowed even to finish that sentence. She was always cut short by an emphatic Other Side formula, like, "Not on *this* farm!" or, "I never let one of 'them' inside the house."

"Even if it were quite clear that was the thing to do I *couldn't* get her a job," she told herself, disingenuously.

On Thursday old Miss Gussie Kemp sprained her ankle. Miss Bessie sent over to the Town Hall for Anna Craft. On her way to the Kemp house she stopped to get the old ladies' mail and handed them a letter which Miss Bessie read out shoutingly to Miss Gussie while her ankle was being bandaged. "You know who this is from, Anna, he's a relative of yours too," she said as she began, "Emory Harliss's no-good boy. They live out West in Ohio. I bet he wants money. He got himself into some kind of a mess awhile ago. Anyhow no Harliss ever wrote anything but a 'gimme' letter."

The letter proved to be what she expected. Miss Craft, kneeling to wind adhesive tape around the swollen ankle, thought it touching. For a misdemeanor apparently trifling, the boy was in prison for a short term and was soon to be released. He wrote humbly that he dreaded returning to the town and the circle of acquaint-

ances which had proved his undoing, and asked his old kinswomen for a little loan to help him make a fresh start elsewhere.

At the end Miss Bessie snorted. "An awful lot of 'I'm sorry' but mighty little 'I won't do it again' in that letter. He had his nerve to ask us! If he was any good, somebody where he's always lived would be ready to help him out. He and his father are just two of a kind. You couldn't connect 'em with a decent job of work—not with a log chain!" She paused, drew a deep breath and summed them up scornfully, "They're *plausible!*"

Miss Craft stopped her bandaging and sat back on her heels. "Plausible?" she repeated. After a look at the old woman's granite face, she leaned again over the hurt ankle. "You're not going to help this boy?"

"Why, Anna, I've just told you what he's like. If he ever gets around to do anything in this world, it'll be harm. Why should anybody help him get at it?"

"Don't you . . ." Miss Craft hesitated, "don't you ever feel any doubt about whether . . . ?"

"What under the sun, moon and stars would make me feel doubtful?"

"Well, isn't it rather a responsibility to refuse to save a human being from drowning? No matter who?"

Miss Bessie's massive face broke from grimness to laughter, "Just give me the chance to *push* a few people in this town into the water, and the responsibility wouldn't set heavy on my mind, not for a *ninstant!* Why, Anna, where's your good sense? Who'd put fertilizer around the weeds in a garden? You hoe 'em up."

"How about giving sinners a chance to repent?"

"Now, Anna! *You* haven't any birthmark! Don't be pious! Who said anything about sinners? I said the boy was worthless. I sort of like a good energetic sinner, myself. Life would be pretty monotonous without any sinners around. But a worthless person . . ."

"What will you write this boy?"

"Write him nothing! Light the fire with his letter!"

"And sleep soundly tonight?"

"Why, Anna, how young you talk! Well, of course you *are* young.

You're so sensible, mostly, I forget that. I suppose it is only when a person's seen ever and ever so many two's and two's added together that she'll believe that nobody can ever make them add up to more than four."

"How do you know they're two's before you've given them a chance to see what they'll add up to?"

"By using the sense you were born with!" cried Miss Bessie, out of patience.

"Let me see that letter," said Miss Gussie, now, putting out her hand. "I didn't half hear it. You mumble so."

"I hate to let her see it," grumbled Miss Bessie, giving it up. "She'll be sending him something behind my back."

When Miss Craft emerged on the Kemp front porch, her ear caught the regular beat of footsteps on the marble flagstones of the sidewalk and her eyes noted vaguely that someone was walking towards her along the empty street beyond the Old Burying Ground. From that distance he looked like anybody and before she glanced up at the clock in the tower of St. Andrew's, she had had no more definite impression of him than that he was a countryman and not from The Street. But as she focused her gaze on the clock tower, thinking only of the time of day, her attention was caught by a change in the rhythm of his footsteps. They skipped a beat, slowed down and stopped, suggesting that he had met someone coming from the other direction and had stepped to the grass on one side to make room to pass. But there had been no one else on the street. Miss Craft brought her eyes down from the clock tower and turned her head. The pedestrian had turned off at right angles from the sidewalk, and was now walking with considerable speed across the Old Burying Ground, the long grass muffling to silence the sound of his footsteps.

As Miss Craft knitted her brows in an intent look at him, she heard Miss Bessie calling, "Wait a minute, Anna, there was something I forgot to . . ." Arriving at the door, she stared and exclaimed, "Why, what's that man doin' in the Buryin' Ground?"

He had now reached the stone wall on the far side. Laying a

hand on this, he vaulted over it with a pantherlike leap. The back lane on the other side being lower than the cemetery, he vanished instantly.

Anna stirred and stepped down off the porch.

"Wherever could he be goin' to?" asked Miss Bessie blankly. "There's nothin' but my night pasture on th' other side th' lane. Did you see who he was, Anna? He had a Searles Shelf look to me. The way he moved."

"I've rather lost track of the folks up there since I've been away," said Miss Craft, moving down the walk.

Miss Bessie dismissed the matter as insoluble and of no consequence anyhow and repeated, "Wait a minute. I forgot to ask you something. Gussie got this sprained ankle goin' down the cellar stairs with a pan of milk, you know. Now we're too old, both of us, to keep on doin' all our own work. Fat as we are, and old as we are, we oughtn't to be goin' up and down cellar stairs. But we haven't an extra cent to pay help. I don't suppose there's left in the whole world what there used to be plenty of in my young days, an old widow-woman, or a girl so hard-up, they'd work for their board and lodging. I wouldn't care who 'twas. There'd have to be something the matter with her of course, or she'd want wages. The one my mother had when I was a girl, had fits. But so long as what she had wasn't catchin' and she had two arms and two legs to run errands with, she'd do. I'll supply the brains."

As if considering, Miss Craft turned her head and looked off into the distance at the line of cross-hatched white on Hemlock Mountain.

"I thought," added Miss Bessie, "that going around among poor folks the way you do, you might hear of somebody."

"Well, I'll bear it in mind," said Miss Craft, walking on.

She passed Lawrence Stewart's fine old house with her usual look of admiration. Henrietta, the cat, was basking in the sun on the front doorstep. Miss Craft's glance showed her that Henrietta's time had nearly come. It was not only her broadened body that showed this, but an emanation of tranquilly heightened intensity of life. Henrietta was not dozing. Her wide-open eyes were fixed

on nothing in an insolent tranced enjoyment of being doubly alive. The nurse stood a moment to look at her with envy. A consciousness of being observed came into the cat's impassive face, but she did not stir nor turn her eyes.

This was on a Thursday. On Friday the Reverend Mr. Kirby came into Miss Craft's office. Isabel was there as usual—it was the noon hour—sitting cross-legged on the floor, matching pairs out of a bushel basket of rubbers and shoes sent down from The Other Side. The nurse was changing the dressings on a scalp wound for an old workman in the brush-back factory who had had his head cut open by a snapping saw-belt. With the unceremoniousness of one old playmate to another, she made a sidewise motion of her head to suggest to the clergyman that he sit down and wait. He did so, hanging his hat on a nail, nodding to Isabel, and with an automatic movement which Miss Craft remembered from their childhood, turned the unsightly scarred side of his face toward the wall.

Over the unkempt white head she was bandaging, Miss Craft observed them both. Isabel did not change her position by a hair, still bent her sleek pretty head intently over her work. But every line of her body, every movement of her hands and arms changed; the very expression of the round white nape of her neck was different, was the expression of a girl who knows that a man—any man, even a disfigured man—had come into the room. After all, if it were not for his birthmark, and if he weren't so skeleton thin, Fred would be a distinguished-looking person.

"No, she's not a child any more," thought Miss Anna, "that commonplace mother of hers is wise in not letting her act like a little girl any longer, no matter how honestly she thinks she still is one."

The thought reminded her, as of a debt that would not let itself be forgotten, of the girl who was Isabel's age and had no mother to be wise for her. For an instant she looked again into desperately imploring dark eyes, that seemed to be wholly—but were not—focused on hers. She looked away from them with impatience, buried that debt once more under the common sense which proved

it not to exist, and to keep her mind from it, glanced across the room at Fred Kirby. One look showed that, conscious though Isabel might be of his masculinity, he had forgotten that she was there, had—apparently—forgotten where he was, looking dreamily out of the window, his deep eyes fixed on a something very much more remote than the mountains flowing like blue waves along the other side of the valley. "What a coarse old heathen Miss Bessie Kemp is!" thought the nurse, with an inward laugh.

"There, Phil, that'll do," she said to the workman, "and mind you get your accident insurance for that. I'll go into court for you any day. I'd like nothing better." He thanked her and went away.

The Academy bell rang. Isabel fluttered off. Father Kirby came back to life, drew his chair nearer her desk, and put the question he had come to ask. It was about a camp for younger boys which was a regular part of the nurse's summer undertakings. He had a candidate whose name he presently brought out. Miss Craft started. To herself she thought, "I wouldn't let that dirty-minded boy within a mile of camp." To the clergyman she said, "Oh . . . Paul Marbadie . . ." and fell into silence as if considering the matter. She was, rather, considering the man before her, his hand closed around his cross. With an effort familiar to her, and an interest which was, she sometimes thought, the only genuine one in her life, she began to project herself out of her own personality into his. When she had arrived there at his point of view and was looking out of his eyes at the hapless boy and at herself stonily determined to give the little degenerate no quarter, she was able to say, quite naturally, "I suppose Paul is the one our Saviour would care more for than all the others."

From his quick melted look, this was what he had been trying to say. "Oh, what a liar I am!" she thought, ashamed. She sank back into her own mind; found there the rather indignant thought, "Haven't the other boys *any* rights even if they are decent?" and threw out a hesitating, "Well . . . ?" She saw then that Father Kirby had gone beyond her reach. He simply sat there, silent, his eyes dropped to his fingers fumbling with his cross.

"Praying, probably," thought Miss Craft, attempting mentally to stand between her camp and that prayer.

But what he said was, as he stood up to go, his gray eyes on hers, "Well, Anna, you are the one to decide." His deep voice was almost tender.

"Praying for *me,* he was," thought the nurse, taken aback.

For an instant she saw herself as he saw her, a soul wandering in darkness outside the Kingdom of Heaven, as much an object of compassion, as much a subject for prayer, as the little boy with the twist in his character that would some day land him in a penitentiary.

At the door he stopped, turning his shabby, broad-brimmed, black hat nervously around in his hands. "Did you ever happen to think, Anna . . . it's been in my mind a good deal lately, but you know what a failure I am at expressing my thoughts . . . how, well, how *commercially* we take that noble 'Judge not that ye be not judged.' You'd think it was offered to us as a way to bribe God to look the other way from our faults. But isn't it really a sort of warning to . . . at least that is what I've had a glimpse of lately, only I can't find any words for it . . . isn't it a warning to us not to presume to measure with our poor inch-long human yardsticks what is so . . . don't you see, what *we* think is evil may be only a deeper part of . . . God's plan is so vast and we . . ." He gave it up, shook his head, stood defeated.

Miss Craft said respectfully, "I *almost* understand what you mean, Fred." She was thinking, "I never do understand a word that mystics say, and yet . . ."

He tried again, this time bringing the words out hastily as though catching at them as they fled through his mind, ". . . as if we should try to make swimming safer by drawing off part of the ocean, when everybody knows that it's not the shallows but the deeps that bear the swimmer up." He repudiated this attempt as a grotesque misstatement like the others, "No, no . . . not . . ." and stood silent again, looking down at his hat, wrestling with his thought. Finally very earnestly he said, "The *wholeness* of life . . ." put on his hat and went away.

He left the room murmuring like a sea-shell in the echo of his deep voice—filled with the mood he had evoked. Miss Craft put out her hand to pick up the crumpled pus-stained bandages on her desk. But she let it fall and sat, gazing dreamily at the soiled gauze, seeing not that but the top of an ill-cared-for dark head and a thin young back shaken by sobs. Something dim and powerful within her stirred and bade her rise and set about doing what she had known all along she must do. Fred's effort to take her with him into the far reaches had been fumbling and inarticulate as always, but as always, he had made her lift her eyes from the immediate and look beyond. What mean cautiousness could have made her hesitate to open the door to that imprisoned and endangered young life? What else was she in the world to do? What had she been afraid of? She could hardly remember. How could there be any risk in placing the poor child in that safe old home, with those two life-seasoned old women to train and civilize her? Anna stood up and reached for her hat.

But the door opened and let in a troupe of little children, unwashed and unkempt, with quick squirrel-bright eyes and ill-shod little feet that protested with scuffles against the shovings of the faded woman back of them. "Oh, how do you do, Mrs. Capen?" said Miss Craft, hanging her hat up on its hook again. "Down to see about shoes? A new lot came in only yesterday. How's the baby? Has that tooth come through yet?"

They tried on shoes and shoes and shoes, talking of the weather and the prospects for fern picking that summer, and how little Maliza would be of school age come next September. Mrs. Capen remarked that she hated worse'n poison to have Maliza under that cussed old teacher.

"That reminds me," said Miss Craft, "I've been wanting to ask some of you what it is Mrs. Persons really has against that Burdick girl?"

Mrs. Capen was glad to tell the story. "Well, Lixlee kind of put it over on the old lady for a while. Jed's folks had quit tryin' to do anythin' with her—I guess they never tried very hard—and she was growin' up like a wildcat or a reg'lar Indian, and old Mis'

Persons got it into her head *she* could give the kid some bringin'
up, if her uncle'n'aunt couldn't. So for a while there she used
to take her home after school and wash her up and read aloud to
her and sew for her, and I don't know what-all. Lixlee took hold
real good. She ain't overly bright, they say, for book-learnin', but
any other kind she can pick up as fast as a sheep's tail picks up
burrs. If she *wants* to, that is! Mis' Persons talked big about what a
good learner she was and how *she* was goin' to make somethin'
out'n her. None of us never said anythin'. Let her try. 'Twan't any
of our business."

"What happened?"

"Oh, she found out Lixlee was makin' a fool of her. Right under
her nose. She all but had a stroke she was so mad."

"How do you mean—made a fool of her?"

Mrs. Capen looked at the children drinking in what was being
said, coughed expressively, lifted her eyebrows and shook her head.

"Oh . . ." said Miss Craft, and changed the subject.

After her visitors had gone away she tried to remember what she
had been about to do when they had come in. When it came to her,
she recoiled, astonished that Fred Kirby could have led anyone of
her experience into such visionary ideas even for an instant. "Fred's
a dear, but he hasn't as much common sense as you could put on the
point of a pin!" she told herself. "I've always known that. I don't
know how many dimensions there may be to the world *he* lives in,
but there are only three in mine . . . when I'm awake, anyhow.
He puts things over on a person with that voice of his. Cora is right.
The place for that girl is right where she is. That's where she belongs." Once more she dismissed the whole matter from her mind.

The next morning, Saturday, five days after her return from
Searles Shelf, Miss Craft arriving at the Post Office a few minutes
before the mail was sorted, stood on the broad marble doorstep to
wait. Her mind was full of Anson and the letter from him that
might now be inside in a mail bag.

She waited outside as did several other early people—rather

than inside—because it was the spring of the year. The Clifford Post Office did not at all hold itself aloof from the ebb and flow of the seasons. It shared heartily in the life of The Valley. Blindfolded and set down in it, the smell would have told any Clifford person the time of the year. In winter there was a faint spiciness of spruce and hemlock mingled with the dry heat from the big pot-bellied wood stove; in autumn one caught mellow whiffs of ripe apples and sharp vinegar reminders of pickle-making; in summer it was a mixture of curing hay and dust. But in the spring when manure was being hauled from out the barnyards and pigsties, and phosphate applied to the land, people usually waited on the doorstep till the mail was ready to distribute.

A dog came limping around the corner, one ear torn and bloody, long scratches on his nose. "Why, Don, what's the matter?" called the nurse, and whistled him to her.

Don's master appeared in his turn. He was in his outing clothes, shapeless black coat and pants greenish with age, and a black felt hat with a hole in the crown. His rusty shoes were smeared with wet leaf-mold. One hand held a blood-stained handkerchief around the other. By the peacefulness of his eyes he was just returning from one of his long brooding communions with his mountain. He looked at the little group on the doorstep and smiled. Miss Craft thought it was as if he had held up his hand to bless them. "The grand old man!" she thought. "He's the biggest person this town ever had. As big as Nature."

Someone asked, "You and Don been mixin' up with a hedgehog, Mr. Dewey?"

"No, 'twas a wildcat," he answered mildly.

"I didn't know our little Vermont wildcats ever attacked anybody," said Miss Craft, surprised, "I thought they always ran away."

"This one couldn't. He was in a trap."

Elmer Merrill said sharply, indignantly, "A trap? *Where?* The season's closed long ago."

"Up Dowling Hollow way," explained Mr. Dewey. "Hadn't you ever noticed those Searles Shelf hunters are what you might call 'careless' about leavin' traps around after the season's over? Both

forefeet in this one, the critter had. Caught but not broken. He surely was one mad cat, wa'n't he, Don?"

"Couldn't you shoot him without getting in reach of his claws?" asked Miss Craft, "or didn't you have a gun with you?"

"I didn't shoot him. I opened the trap and let him go," said Mr. Dewey steadily.

Miss Craft started and looked at him attentively.

"Why in the . . . ?" began Elmer Merrill, outraged.

"I couldn't shoot him. You couldn't've, either, Elmer, if you'd seen how he was r'arin' around. So much more life in him, after Lord knows how long in that trap, than in *me*—! If there was any shootin' goin' to be done, he was the one that had ought to have held the gun."

"But see here, Mr. Dewey, they do a great deal of harm—chicken-yards and . . ."

"Oh, harm—!" said Mr. Dewey, looking meditatively down at his bandaged hand. A trickle of bright blood oozed from under the stained handkerchief. He shook it off and said easily, "What harm could he do that would be half as bad as my not lettin' him go?"

PART TWO

1

ON NEW YEAR'S DAY every calendar, large and small, has the same number of dates. But we soon learn that the years are of very different lengths. Nobody knows beforehand which ones will swing along at the steady pace of seasoned soldiers, which ones will caper past like children at play, and which will crawl by, dressed in black, headed for an open grave and bearing something precious that was once alive.

Sometimes the Clifford years slid forward as evenly as a clock ticking, from the brilliance of January axes flashing in snowy woods, through sap-boiling time with steam clouds veiling leafless maples, into summer thunderstorms, and around again before you knew it through September school bells to Thanksgiving strawrides and then to trips to the woods for spruce and hemlock greens to decorate the church at Christmas. And nothing had happened, nothing whatever, except that all the children were an inch taller and the requisite number of pounds heavier (or M'Sanna Craft would have a thing or two to say to their parents) and all the old people had stepped one rung lower on the ladder that leads down into the burying ground. Yes, there were years like that, when nothing happened to anybody. And then there were others. . . .

It is by looking at a calendar that modern city dwellers know when one season gives place to another. Only one of the old felt folk dates has survived industrialism. Even city people know that summer ends and autumn begins when school opens, when nine

o'clock in the morning once more resumes its dread eminence over
the other twenty-three hours of the day.

Clifford still counted all its seasons by folk dates. Summer there,
for instance, did not begin on a certain printed date in May or
June but on the day when the "summer schedule" went into effect
on the railroad. This meant that the two through trains north and
south (mistakenly called "The Cannon Ball") began to stop at
the Depot every afternoon without being flagged. And when this
happened, summer people began to arrive.

Clifford people had watched for so long the marvelous timing of
the birds' autumnal flight from cold, and the alarm-clock mechanism in tulips and snowdrops, that they had grown to take for
granted all the other accurate miracles of life's adaptations to en-
vironment; and hence gave no thought to the equally mysterious
and accurate instinct which year after year so timed the annual
arrival and departure of summer people as to avoid any contact
with the communal life of the region. Neither the travelers who
stepped from the Cannon Ball to the platform of Clifford Depot,
nor the natives who impassively watched their arrival, thought of
the significance of their folkname. "Summer people," they were
called, summer people they were.

And being such, they never arrived until after the last of the
year's social activities, when everybody had finished sucking the
human marrow out of the fact-bones of the Academy Commencement, when the Academy building was locked and shuttered, when
nothing was going on at the Community House, and few young
faces were to be seen on the street. Why wouldn't they assume that
static quiescence was the usual color of the town life? They did.
How could they know that a period of quiescence was imperative
after what went on in the winter—weekly meetings of the Bridge
Club and St. Andrew's Guild and the Fish and Game Club and
the Sacred Name Society and the Masons and the Women's Club
and the Catholic Daughters of America and the Order of the
Eastern Star and the local chapter of the Red Cross and the Young
People's Club, church suppers and bazaars, community sings, lec-
tures by professors up from the University; not to speak of the

dances and hikes and plays and skating parties and entertainments given by the different classes at the Academy and by the Parent-Teachers' Association, nor of birthday parties for young and old and showers given for the season's brides. Not having any idea what the summer people thought about anything, residents of Clifford had no idea that they were supposed to be thin-blooded decadent descendants of gloomy Puritans, incurably morose, unsociable and pleasure-hating. But if they had known it they would have made little effort to correct that impression. What the cottagers thought seemed no concern of theirs. They wrapped themselves relishingly in the mantle of invisibility cast around them by city people's ignorance of them, and, unseen, unguessed-at, front-row spectators, followed appreciatively the annual comedies, tragedies and farces enacted for them by the summer colony. What audience ever thinks of reaching across the footlights for a handshake with the troupe? To explain Clifford people and their lives to those summer actors would, it is true, have been a proof of what effusive people call the common humanity of us all. But why prove the obvious? Especially when such proof would spoil the show. A good show, too.

And then, if the truth must be poured out to the last drop, many of the summer people were not exactly to Clifford taste. Professional families who did some of their own housework, wore old clothes to go berrying in, hated cordial back-slapping as much as you did, and knew how to recognize a dry joke, soon melted indistinguishably into The Valley. And so did the few city-bred families—even when they had plenty of money—who stayed all the year around and got quite country and plain. But those butter-smooth, middle-aged summer ladies with white gloves and liveried chauffeurs! The more ingratiatingly they smiled on you, the glummer you felt. They were like good coffee spoiled by too much cream and sugar. They took you up at a word in such a hurry, did to your feelings with their wordy cordiality what with their excellent manners they never dreamed of doing physically—stood too close to you, breathed too warmly in your face. Invisibility was really the only way to cope with them.

Mr. Lawrence Stewart did not agree with his Clifford neighbors about this. There could never be too many butter-smooth, middle-aged summer ladies in white gloves for his taste. Invisibility to summer people was the last thing he wanted. Yet he insisted to them on his status as a native.

"Yes, indeed, I'm related to everybody in town," he told callers brought by summer-colony dowagers to drink tea out of his fine blue willow ware. They learned before the first swallow that it had not been acquired in an antique shop. He was amusing about people who bought their family antiques. "This cup is a native, too, was put on our pantry shelves in 1824, the year my great-grandfather brought his bride here to live. Not a piece of it has ever been out of the house since," he often said, turning an old cup around in his hands, white, well kept, with an incongruous growth of thick, reddish and quite ungrayed hair on the backs. Now was the time for the dowager who was showing off Mr. Stewart to diagram the joke about his being a "native." "He's lived as much of his life in Rome and Copenhagen and Paris as in America," she would explain with gusto, "and speaks nobody knows how many languages."

To which Mr. Stewart always cried out, smiling, showing his fine teeth, "No, no, dear lady, I'm none of your rootless Europeanized Americans. My dear father did bring me up at one or another European court, it is true, but nothing could ever make me anything but a Windward County, Clifford Street Stewart like my forebears! If the James family had had a *home,* Henry could not have deserted the American scene. Why, I could no more deny the claims of my own town and my own townspeople on me than I could deny my mother's claim."

This was a theme which admitted and received at his hands many variations. But he had plenty of other themes, too, from Colonial doorways to life at the Danish Court in his boyhood; almost as many themes as he had callers and that was saying a good deal, for it was part of the regular routine of the summer season to go to drink tea with Mr. Stewart in that perfect early-American house of his. If you were a summer person you took your every guest to see his century-old maple furniture made here

in town, and his Currier and Ives prints that had never been off the walls since his grandmother bought them, and to hear his excellent talk about the responsibility of leisure-class Americans to create stability in our restless country.

No matter how incautiously you had led your visitors on to expect a good deal, he never let you down. He was always glad to see callers, always had plenty of time for you, always looked just as he should, with none of that slicked-up Park-Avenuish new expensiveness, rather with the crumpled well-worn English look that is just as expensive, always served you perfect tea in marvelous old china, and according to the lead you gave him, turned on one or another kind of good talk. Leaning back in his great-grandfather's writing-arm Windsor, he would take the front wall off from any house in town and show you the skeletons hanging in its every closet. Had a guest asked you, "Who are those extraordinary fat old women in gingham Mother Hubbard wrappers who live next to the old cemetery?" you answered, "Wait till we take tea with Mr. Stewart and ask *him*." Even when you knew beforehand what he would say it was amusing.

"They are Miss Bessie'n'Gussie Kemp. The Kemps were one of our good families, who built that house in 1769—or was it '70? Miss Bessie is seventy-eight now, remembers her great-grandmother, who was born in 1775, and remembered Ethan Allen. A sharp tongue, a great conversationalist. The local saying is that she would rather talk than eat. Nobody dares go by without passing the time of day."

"And the other one?" your guest might ask.

"Nothing to tell about Miss Gussie except that she is very deaf. She provides comic relief in that way. One whole chapter of our local joke book is devoted to Miss Gussie and her deafness. It starts with her saying years ago to the minister condoling with her about her mother's death, 'Well, yes, the heat *has* been very trying!'" He paused a moment for the laugh. "And goes on to a Rabelaisian one about an entertainment given in the Town Hall one winter years ago by some wandering vaudeville actors. One of their acts was a very raw song. As the words—considerably more than suggestive—

came rolling out, all the decent people in town froze into horrified silence, except Miss Gussie. She saw the laughter of some hard-boiled lumberjacks who'd drifted in and the grins of the Searles Shelf men, and when they applauded at the end, she clapped her respectable hands together, too, all smiling appreciation. But, of course, to get the flavor of that story one must, as one describes Miss Gussie's innocent applause, repeat the words of that song,— which are, I assure you, quite, quite unrepeatable. But of course carefully passed on from generation to generation of boys."

"I should have thought her sister would stop her," the visitor sometimes commented.

"Miss Bessie? It was a joke after her own heart. Nobody laughed louder than she."

House guests of the summer colony found it "too priceless" to be able to ask about anyone whose appearance had stirred their curiosity and have the leaves of his personality thus turned and read aloud to them. "The tall lean old man in rusty black, with jutting eyebrows, who is he? With a shaggy dog always at his heels."

"Sherwin Dewey. Mr. Dewey plays the rôle in our town—traditional in all farces—of the man-afraid-of-his-wife's-tongue. It is said that when he married her his wife was like a rosy peach. But she turned out a very sour apple. She nagged herself into invalidism thirty years ago. Ever since, he's done the housework and waited on her hand and foot, absolutely cowed by her incessant scolding. That's all there is to his life except that as a refuge from her, he has taken up local history very hard. His house is full of old papers."

"But *how,*" a city lady would perhaps inquire, "does such a man make a *living?* How does anybody here get a living?"

"Well, take Miss Bessie'n'Gussie Kemp. They have a small dairy farm, on the edge of town. Miss Bessie runs it by bossing an elderly hired man, and supplies us all with milk and cream. We don't dare not buy it of her. The milk money pays the hired man and their taxes. The farm supplies most of their food and all of their fuel. They probably have inherited several small savings bank accounts that come perhaps to five thousand dollars. The income from

that buys their clothes and groceries. They do their own house-work, of course—or no, I've heard that since Miss Gussie broke her arm or something last May they have a poor person in to work for her keep—some back-roads woman our district nurse found for them."

"Two hundred and fifty dollars a year!" one lady would exclaim to another. "Why, Mr. Stewart, it's a perfect revelation! Tell us, what does the hen-pecked husband do for his living?"

"Mr. Dewey is our wood merchant. From one side of his family he inherited any amount of mountain land—he owns most of Hem-lock Mountain—and from the other side, a saw mill. By cutting around here and there, year after year, he keeps going. His income is the difference between what he pays his sawyer and his choppers and what he gets for his boards and firewood. Perhaps some savings bank interest too. Nearly all of us have some. He probably lives and takes care of his invalid wife on five hundred dollars a year. His brother is a millionaire out in Seattle."

"Forty dollars a month! Imagine it!" The city ladies would make little gestures with their hands to express their astonishment. "In that beautiful old house!"

"Is your district nurse a local character too? Or did she come from outside?"

"Oh, Clifford to the marrow of her bones! Daughter and grand-daughter of our local doctors. Her grandfather born in 1830 is still 'Doctor Craft' in our talk. Her father, although he practiced medi-cine here for thirty-three years, never was called anything but 'young Doctor Craft.' There's no name left for her half-brother, our present doctor, but 'Doctor Anson.' I suppose his son will be 'young Doctor Anson.' A combination of many bloods the Crafts are—like all of us humans, of course, only with the Crafts they never seemed to mix. I remember older people used to say of her father, 'young Doctor Craft,' 'Well, here comes Anson. What'll be on top today? Will he be a rough-and-ready, high-stepping Gardner, get-out-of-the-way-or-I'll-kick-you-out? Or a meek and lowly Merrill, dry-washing his hands and butter not melting in his mouth? Or a plain, practical Nye, come, come, no caterwauling about your feelings,

stick to your knitting and it'll all come out in the wash? Or a pious godly Barney, dearly beloved brethren, we are ga-a-athered together in the sight of the Lo-o-rd . . . !' "

Animatedly suiting action to phrase, Mr. Stewart always had his audience laughing by this time. But although there were many more lively family characterizations to that story, he never gave more than four, knowing that summer people are tragically subject to ennui and are only saved from it by constant change of subject and tone. When the laughter died down, "But Anna's mother was a Knapp," he would say gravely, "and for us, Knapp blood means just one thing . . . melancholia."

"Oh," said the ladies, softly, sympathetic and hushed. And after a pause, "Is that why she never married? She is not unattractive. A good figure. And really fine hair."

Mr. Stewart, pushing in one stop, pulling out another and pedaling briskly, would reply, "No, that reason is too picturesque. The real reason is probably the quick temper that goes with that hair. But perhaps not. Perhaps because she has had to do so much for her half-brother. She is the soured and sacrificed Mary Wilkins New England nun of our town. Mayn't I put another cushion back of you, Mrs. Lodge? That chair was made for a big-boned Green Mountain great-grandfather of mine, not for a Dresden China shepherdess like you. Yes, Anna's mother died when she was a little girl. Her father's second wife was rather an invalid and Anna spent most of her girlhood bringing up her half-brother. She did get carried away out of her rut once, by the war, did do some military nursing in France. But her stepmother chose that time to die and she had to give that up and come back to make a home for her father and brother. Just try one of those sugar cookies, Mrs. Vanderburg. They're made by an old family recipe. And then the doctor died, leaving his children nothing but bad debts. Nobody ever thinks of paying a country doctor, you know. Everybody in town owed young Doctor Craft. So they salved their consciences and saved their cash by making his daughter district nurse. She already did something in that line, in a volunteer way. Every town, you know, has some female with no sex-appeal who is in a fever to

make the world a better place to live in, ha! ha! That's Anna
Craft. Never lets well enough alone. I hear she has a new bee in
her bonnet now. Special help for students from back-roads farms—
she wants them to be paid out of our taxes for condescending to
come and be educated at the Academy, I understand—or some such
camouflaged Socialism. If it shows signs of going too far I shall
just mention the word 'Socialism' and stop it right there. Vermonters can always be counted on to react in the sane and sound
way to *that* word! Where was I? Oh, yes—well, out of the pay of
district nurse she has put Anson through the rest of his Academy course and college, *and* medical school. Ten years of it. And
now Anson is back, a full-fledged sawbones, and what does he turn
out to be? One of your sulky superior young men, called nowadays,
I believe, 'sophisticates.' Our grandfathers called them 'sulky dogs.'
Bored to death with us country boobs, and his old maid half-sister
he is,—you know the kind, Menckenized to the core; probably
furious because he couldn't land a job that would keep him in the
city. Have another of those maple hearts, Mrs. Peabody, do. My
housekeeper makes them very well, being to the manner born. I
make it a point to have only Vermonters around me. No Japanese
or Filipino need apply at the old Stewart home!

"Our New England nun? Why, I can't think of anything else
to tell you about her. Except that she has a very dull wife. Yes,
wife. Haven't you ever observed that women who take a man's
place in the world can't escape clinging vines any more than men?
Anna's is a Miss Ingraham, the Latin teacher at the Academy. A
New Jersey woman. Or was it Ohio? Impossible anyhow. One of
those incredibly charmless women who should be chloroformed at
birth. Buck teeth and no chin. Almost as soon as she came here—
six or seven years ago—she annexed herself to Anna. You've seen
such ménages. Must you go? Well, do at least take time for a
turn around the garden. Not one of *your* grand professional affairs,
you see. Just the same old perennials where my ancestresses planted
them. This border of pinks is much older than I. And these are
eighteenth-century roses. Very much more distinguished with their
few simple petals, I think, than the later varieties with their ruffled

Victorian petticoats. Ah, good afternoon, Isabel, you still in town?
I thought you were going to spend the summer with Helen. Oh,
you go tomorrow? Well, good-by. Have a good time!

"Yes, she *is* rather a pleasant-looking girl. Oh, no story in *her*
life, dear lady, she's a blank page in a book that will never have
anything written in it but very small beer. What's known as a nice
girl. One of the typical, hiking Girl Scout, worthy, disinfected
American girls who disconcert European men so amusingly by
not being women at all in the European sense. I rather like the
way the iris grows off towards the birches over there, don't you?
Who is her father? Ah . . . Doctor Foote. The trouble with those
late tulips is that they take so long to ripen. . . . No, not M.D.
He is . . . ah . . . our . . . ah . . . local dentist. Well, Henrietta,
how are your kittens today? Allow me to present Henrietta, who
has, in a manner of speaking, lived continuously in this house and
slept every night on the foot of the owner's bed since 1790, when
her great-great-ancestor was brought here by my great-grandfather's
mother. Henrietta, do you hear what our witty visitor says, that
you are an authentic antique, too! Ha! Ha! Ha! Very good! Good
day, Mr. . . . Father Kirby, how are *you* today? Our minister . . .
or priest as he would have it. Oh, no, no, not Roman . . . Anglican
Catholic. Did you never hear the story of the settlement of The
Valley in 1764? How settlers coming over the mountain from Connecticut were stopped at Ashley and asked which church they belonged to? If they were Congregationalists they were sent to the
best land, that fertile upland stretch along The Other Side. If they
said Methodist, they were directed around the mountain to Haton-
ville, if Church of England they were told to settle here in Clifford
village, and if they said they didn't believe in 'no damn God, nohow'
they were sent up to Searles Shelf. Full of savor, aren't they, those
old local stories? And lasting. To this day, The Street is solidly
Anglican, and Searles Shelf is still godless. Well, for that matter
St. Andrew's down here isn't exactly what anyone would call God-
intoxicated. You know the old saying that Episcopalians think it
underbred and low class to love God too loudly. Most of our rec-
tors—we've had only ten in a century and a half—have been in-

terested chiefly in their vegetable gardens. But we have now—you saw that hideous blue birthmark—a rector who's rather an eyesore, and consequently the religious thermometer of our parish marks a higher temperature. How so? Now don't tell me, dear Mrs. Peabody, that you have never noticed how a disfiguring physical infirmity turns a person's thoughts to religion? Yes, we might have known years ago when poor little Fred Kirby with that blue scar on his face was playing around our street that he would end by wearing a straight collar around his neck and a cross on his watch chain. Oh, must you go? Let me give you what we call a 'bokay' of my old-fashioned flowers. How beautifully that larkspur repeats the blue of your eyes, Mrs. Lodge. *Do* get Mrs. Peabody to bring you again. I'll show you the costumes and bonnets in the attic the next time. Any time. I'm always here. Henrietta and I are always at home, aren't we, Henrietta?"

It was a picture, they said to each other, leaning out of the windows of their car for one last smile, as the chauffeur put his heart into the operation of starting the engine smoothly and succeeded so completely that nobody noticed it at all—it was a perfect picture, that distinguished man, there before his dignified old house, in his garden that had been tended by all those generations of his family, with his cat who had always been there too. The way he spoke of his cat—how quaintly humorous—so Vermont! It was wonderful to see *one* American with roots. What devotion to these simple mountain people he understands so well. Something magnetic about him, too, my dear . . . oh, very! . . . that makes you feel that if he wanted to he could still make love beautifully, in spite of his gray hair! You can tell from his manners that there were plenty of conquests in that European youth of his. What was his father . . . consul? No, I've heard it was Ambassador.

"I tell you . . . Mr. Stewart makes me realize what Henry James *would* have been if he had felt the local responsibility that English country gentry feel. He never once intimated to us, you notice, that it is the aristocrat's duty to enrich his country by living in it, as he does. He is far too much of a reticent Anglo-Saxon gentleman to

say such a thing. But 'noblesse oblige' certainly ought to be carved up over his door, or somewhere," they said to each other, his recent visitors, settling themselves on the velvet upholstery of their car and waving a last white-gloved hand at him.

At least this was what Mr. Stewart, still standing in his garden with his cat making love to his legs, hoped they were saying.

2

"Upon his breast he wears a *star*
That *points* the way to London Bar,"

sang the children, circling hand in hand under the dreamy September sun.

"So *now* look east and *now* look west
And *choose* the one that *you* love best,
If she's not here to take her part,
Go *choose* another with all your heart,"

they wisely advised the little boy in the middle of the ring looking from one little girl's summer-tanned face to another.

Another summer season was safely over with nothing happening to anybody in it—except, of course, what annually happened to Henrietta's kittens. Mr. Stewart's white-gloved audience had gone, leaving him rather tired—he was not as young as he had been— but happy and fulfilled, quite ready to begin another arduous behind-scenes period of preparation for the next presentation of his little piece. Isabel Foote had been far away in foreign parts visiting a married sister in Rhode Island. Miss Gussie Kemp had watered her vegetable garden with her sweat in hot mornings and walked alone with God in it in cool evenings, and Miss Bessie had taught the Searles Shelf waif how to can everything, from dandelion greens through wild strawberries to raspberries and currants, down to Golden Bantam corn and lima beans. Father Kirby's congrega-

tion had swelled with the addition of elderly summer people, trained in their youth to go to church once a week, and shrunk again to the usual Clifford faithfuls.

For now another autumn had begun, although the swamp maples were the only trees that knew it, had begun with the trampling of young feet on Windward County school yards and the gathering together of the various adults charged with the impossible tasks of doing the right thing for children's health and education. The district nurse and the doctor stood on the steps of the school in The Street, waiting to go on with the health examinations started the day before.

Anson had been back more than three months and yet Anna, her eyes on the unchanging child life flowing at the base of the unchanging mountains, yielded to an impulse which those months had taught her always led her into making the wrong remark. "Don't you think it's nice, Anson," she asked, "their playing those old games we all played, here on this very playground? Doesn't seem more than yesterday that you were the little boy in the middle. And I suppose to Father it didn't seem more than yesterday that *he* was."

"What is there particularly interesting about that?" inquired Anson, his tone stripping the interest from the idea as one strips the tender green leaves from a plant.

Anna, left with the bare stalk, knew that what he meant was what he generally meant, "Oh, don't be an effusive bore." But the forward impulse of her heart towards him betrayed her into answering the question as if it had been a question. "Why, isn't today deeper when you can feel all the yesterdays in it? I don't mean just our personal Craft yesterdays. That song-game, from the words, must have been sung in England in the seventeenth century."

Anson thought, "What of it," so distinctly that Anna heard him, though his lips had not moved from around the pipe clenched in one corner of his mouth. She told herself gloomily, "I'm rubbing him the wrong way again." But on a last chance that the trouble was that she had not made her idea clear, she went on, though

timidly now, "Well—when you hear back of our own Clifford kids singing today, a couple of centuries of children's voices—singing on the trail from Connecticut to Vermont, and before that, all the way from London Bar across the Atlantic Ocean . . ."

"I doubt if they sang much on shipboard," remarked Anson, bleakly.

Zerah Colburn, the young first-grade teacher, came out and pulled the bell rope heartily. The bell responded with a bronze clangor. The children playing "King William" dropped each other's hands and scampered towards the door. Other children, older and younger, burst up out of the grounds and followed into the forming lines. Clifford housekeepers set their kitchen clocks at two minutes of nine. Anna Craft standing near the head of the line looked down it, and, mixed with Lamarches and O'Keefes and Pulaskis, saw faces familiar to her even when she did not recognize them individually—Gardner and Nye and Craft and Merrill faces, come along with their song-games down the centuries and across the Atlantic—lines of children reaching back into the past, streaming forward into the future—children, children, every September bringing in more of them to stand in line, helpless in the fumbling hands of the older generation, soon to become the older generation, conscious of its impotence and unwisdom, standing shamefaced before lines of helpless little boys and girls. Doctor Craft knocked out his pipe on the heel of his shoe with a dry rap. His sister started and looked at him apologetically. Through the open schoolhouse door, skipping and hopping, wonderfully young for their age, came the notes of the "Joyous Farmer." The lines of children began to sway and to move forward with a rhythmical shuffle.

Inside the schoolhouse the hall vibrated to the *left,* right, *left,* right of the march. It grew fainter as one after another classroom door swallowed up its share of the procession. There was nobody left but the first graders, trotting into their room, their eyes turned with adoration up to the clear young face of Zerah Colburn. She did not look at the tall personable young doctor behind them. She looked down on her children with a welcoming smile. The door shut gently after the last little trotter. The clock struck nine. Around

them the hall, the classroom, the building were silent. As a seashell is silent.

Forgetting once more that Anson found that kind of remark flat and sugary, Anna Craft said, impulsively, "Zerah makes a grand teacher, doesn't she? How she loves it! When I think how hard she had to work to earn her way through Normal School . . ."

Doctor Craft shut his eyes, drew a long breath and asked, "Tonsils and adenoids in the third grade, wasn't it?"

"What *is* the matter? Where have we got off the right track? What have I done or not done, and when?" thought Anna Craft, holding a child's head so that the doctor could have the right light for the nose inspection. "It was his own idea, to be a doctor. I never urged him towards it. I never dreamed of asking him to come back here to practice. I've begged him not to think of paying back what I've spent for his education. It was his own plan, from the beginning," she told herself, trying with the little plumb-line of reasonableness to fathom the dark ocean of human personality.

"Don't wriggle so, Paul," she said severely to the child standing between her knees.

The elderly principal came in to greet the doctor and nurse, both of whom had gone to school under him. Anson looked up. Instantly, by a strange alchemy there was in the young doctor's look, the worst in Mr. Wright rose to the surface from the depths where it was usually hidden, and turned into even worse than it was. His deprecating mildness became mean cowardice that would knife a righteous but unpopular cause in the back—not that the opportunity to do this would ever occur in Mr. Wright's life—his good nature became weakness, his skill in running his school without periodical explosive quarrels, appeared only as an abject ability for compromise.

Mr. Wright, not knowing what had happened to him, said cheerfully, "Hello, Anson—I suppose we've got to learn to call you Doctor now—how goes it? I hear you're settling in Clifford?"

"No, in Ashley," Doctor Craft corrected him, still attentively

studying his face. "I'm to have office hours here, three times a week, in Father's old office, but the rest of the time next door to Doctor Cole."

"Ah-ha? Wants you handy, does he?" The words were jaunty but the tone uneasy. Mr. Wright had begun to feel Anson's eyes.

"Yes, for night calls and confinement cases on back roads. And drives at two in the morning to where one lumberjack has taken an ax to another. For the dirty work that doesn't get paid for."

Mr. Wright gathered that this was intended for humor and gave a propitiating laugh. He flinched away from something formidable smoldering under the young doctor's cold words, began to rub his hands and to sidle away, "Well, if everything's going smoothly with you medical people here, I'll just go on—furnace—water-pipes— janitor—broken window." Doctor Craft looked after him with an expression of contempt so open that a breath would have turned it into words. He opened his lips to speak, his eyes still on the door which had shut after the rabbit-man's retreat.

"Sh! Anson! Sh!" said his sister sharply, reminding him by a glance at the little boy standing between her knees. With no change of expression Anson transferred his gaze to her face. After a pause, in a level tone, "I was going to ask you to hand me that swab," he said. The nurse gave him the swab in silence. The examination went on.

"I must keep my head," thought the nurse. "There's always a way out if you don't lose your head." But her heart was physically quivering from the hurt of his look and tone. She could not think for the pain. "What *is* it I do that hurts him so that he must hurt me back? I would better say nothing—nothing at all."

The child under examination was dismissed. The doctor and nurse waited in silence for the next one. The ticking of the clock, most potent of all the comforters of mankind, slid minute after minute between Anna and that pain till it was muffled to an endurable dullness. She began again to indulge herself in small reasonable thoughts and plans and hopes. "It probably means only that he is worn out with the murderous length of a medical education. For ten years he and I have thought of nothing else, have tried for

nothing else. Of course, now we get it, it doesn't seem like much. There's bound to be a reaction. He's gone without everything young men like and need. He's twenty-six and I suppose he hasn't had a carefree moment of fun since Father died. What he needs is more enjoyment—let me see, how can I get it for him? What do other young men here enjoy? Hunting? We could easily arrange a hunting party for deer week in November. He ought to join the Fish and Game Club. The Friday evening dances at the Academy will soon begin. Perhaps he'd like to play some bridge. I must see that he gets off to Boston for the theater once in a while. I'll subscribe to the Mercantile Library. That will give him all the books he wants."

The stricture on her heart loosened its clamp. With patience and ingenuity on her part . . . ! She had as yet encountered nothing in life to shake her faith in what she could accomplish by patience and ingenuity.

The next child to be examined appeared in the doorway—a little girl helped into the world eight years before by Miss Craft, alone with the case on a zero night because old Doctor Cole's car could not get through the impassable snowdrifts over which her snowshoes had carried her.

"How d'do, M'Sanna," said Lettice, running up to the nurse, unafraid of the doctor because M'Sanna was there.

"Only eight years!" thought the nurse, putting her arm around the solid little body. "How's your rabbit, Lettice?" she asked.

"*Oh!* She's turned out to be a *mamma* rabbit!" cried the child. "Hadn't you *heard?* Five cunning baby bunnies she had, *five!*" She showed with her roughened little country hands how small they were, with the mother-look on her face, how sweet they were.

Anna thought, "Anson can't help enjoying her. A little, anyhow—if I don't say anything sugary, don't look as though I expected him to." She kept her eyes fixed on the glowing child-face.

"Come, come, Anna," the doctor rapped out, "we'll never get through at this rate!"

The nurse turned the child's sunny head towards the light. "Open your mouth, Lettice, wide. Wider."

Presently the little girl, turning and twisting incessantly out of position, was too much for her ruffled nerves. *"Will* you keep still!" she said savagely, giving the child a shake.

"Anna! You ought to be ashamed of yourself!" said the doctor, shocked, his professional standards outraged by a show of temper in a nurse on duty. Little Lettice shrank away from him, clinging hard to M'Sanna.

"I am," said Miss Craft. The examination went on.

At a quarter past eleven they were walking back to the Craft house where they had both left their cars. Anna was trying out another plan. To say nothing at all was impossible, of course. She would wait passively till he had spoken and then chime in with whatever tone he used.

But now, as often happened when there had been friction, open or hidden, between them, Anson made a great—and a very apparent—effort to be innocuous. Grotesquely innocuous, Anna thought, smarting under the implications of his manner. "Does he think I'm an idiot fit for no talk but about whether we'll have rain today?" But she could think of no way she could speak of her resentment that would not invite the retort, "Well, what *do* you want?"

Then they approached the Stewart place and in the garden saw Lawrence Stewart in tweeds arduously superintending an overalled Jo Danby muddied to the eyes by the usual September work of separating and re-setting perennials. Henrietta, exquisite in white and yellow, lay on the sun-warmed wall, superintending them both. Mr. Stewart, naturally, had taken no vow to wait till Anson had spoken and then follow his mood. He came out towards them, sociably. Behind him Jo Danby stopped digging and leaned on his spade to listen, Clifford fashion, to any bits of news. Henrietta yawned. It was not exactly news that Jo picked up from the dialogue between the young doctor and his employer, which ran, "Ah, how're you, Miss Craft? Well, Doctor, how many legs sawed off this week?"

"Not as many as I could wish," this smilelessly from Doctor Craft, his cold blue eyes successfully bringing the worst in Mr. Stewart to the surface.

"Ah-ha! Ha! Ha! Very good! I sometimes wish one of mine *were* off, so I could have a chance to sit still a moment. I'm driven to death. I never have a chance to call my soul my own in the summer season. I *wish* summer people would leave me alone! What they want to bother me for, I can't understand! All my work gets behind. Those iris should have been separated weeks ago. And the peonies—*I* don't know what to do about the peonies!"

"Well, when you break down under it, let me know and I'll prescribe something for you," said the young doctor in a smoothly savage tone that made Jo Danby turn around quickly and bow himself over his spade. Henrietta, half way through another yawn, remembered that she had been interrupted in her toilet that morning and had left a spot half way down her left hind leg. After she had attended to it, put her leg down, and looked around, the visitors had gone, and one of her servants was superintending the other one again.

Anson Craft, not very far from the Stewart garden, was beginning a remark in a not very low voice. "Of all the fetid . . ."

"Sh! Anson! Sh!" said his sister hastily.

Anson burst into a wild laugh. "The motto of this town!" he cried. "Its motto and pass word! '*Sh!*' That's really all that anybody says to anybody else! '*Sh!*' That's what they send their children to learn of that old cotton-tail back there in the school. '*Sh!*' Open their hearts and you shall see, graven inside them, '*Sh!*'"

His voice fell like vinegar and salt on Anna's raw heart. He broke off, shocked by the pain in her face, and said with an impatient groan, "Oh, I've hurt your feelings again! I *didn't* mean to! Honestly, Anna. But I never know what's going to! I always forget you're such a sensitive flower."

At this last, indignant tears sprang to Anna's eyes. He said hastily, with an accent of sincere repentance, "Oh, Lord! I just put my foot in it worse all the time. I *am* sorry! I will try to do better. I wish I were more what you want."

They walked on in silence, Anna bewildered at her shaken nerves, wondering helplessly, for the thousandth time, why, ready

as she was to give or do anything, she could not lay hold of this
situation and straighten it out as she had all the other situations
she had encountered. Time blowing on the heat of the friction between them cooled it off. Presently Anson asked, "What was it
Lawrence Stewart's father made his money at? A patent coffin?"

"Why, no!" said Anna, taken in by the seriousness of his tone.
"He was a dentist! One of the first American dentists to take American methods to Europe. He was a great success, filled lots of Royal
teeth. A very smart man he must have been, but a frightful old
rip. A household tyrant too. The older people always say his wife
died to escape from him. And you know Lawrence had an older
sister who hated their father so she ran away from home. Not with
a lover. That was the original thing about it. By herself. Like a
bold angry young man, not a girl. She was very different from her
poor brother."

Anson drew a long breath of boredom at having inadvertently
brought down on himself another old-time Clifford legend. "All I
could remember was that his son doesn't like to have him mentioned," he broke in. "I'll have to go in some day when he's enter-
taining summer people and talk bridgework and amalgam fillings
to him. Anna! Don't be so solemn! I'm trying to make a joke!"

Anna thought, "But why must *all* the jokes turn on despising
somebody?" and turning her head from side to side because of
an ache in the back of it, perceived to her surprise that the day
was still sunny warm and quiet—like a June day, but filled with
autumnal peace, purified of the restless pain of June's imperious
lust for life.

They approached the Kemp house. On its front porch sat the
two old sisters, twin mountains of checked gingham. Their faces
were turned towards the front door where, at that moment, the
Searles Shelf girl appeared as though to ask a question. She had
a broom in one hand, a clean white cloth bound around her head,
and looked very neat in a blue percale work dress. Anna thought
gratefully, "You'd never know it was the same person! The old
ladies are pretty expert civilizers." To Anson she said in a low
apologetic tone, "I hope you won't mind taking just a moment

here to pass the time of day. Miss Bessie'n'Gussie do like to have people stop for a chat."

"You do it," said Anson. "I haven't been back in Clifford long enough to learn the art of talking when I have nothing to say."

So they did not stop. Anna waved a hand as they passed; Anson took off his hat without turning his head. Behind them they heard Miss Bessie yell to Miss Gussie, "Anson has got the Merrill hair, hasn't he? But the shape of his head is like the Crafts'."

Anna was amused by this and smiled.

"Good *God!*" exploded Anson, "talk about Mohammedans being fatalists! They're light-minded triflers compared to these heredity hounds! As if there weren't enough bars in the New England prison without that!"

Anna stopped smiling. She thought, "That's so. It really isn't funny at all. Anson is very acute. We all do that too much. And it's dangerous. He has a *good* brain."

They passed the Community House being cleaned and opened up for indoor activity after the summer's concentration on outdoors. Mrs. Peter Merrill came to the door to shake a rug. "Oh, M'Sanna," she called, "the Bridge Club meets this evening. Can we borrow your cups again?" She meant, "We are going to borrow your cups," and so without waiting for an answer turned to Anna's brother, "Doctor Anson, now you're back to stay," she said, persuasively, "*you* ought to join the Bridge Club. We have lots of fun."

"I never play cards," said Doctor Craft, his gaze turning Mrs. Merrill's comfortable enjoyment of life into sodden acquiescence in the ignoble, and her own plump comely person into a cipher, "except poker—when I can afford to bet enough to make it interesting."

"Oh," said Mrs. Peter Merrill, "I see." She took her still unshaken rug back with her into the house.

Mr. Dewey, Don sitting beside him, was driving into his side yard with a wagon load of cord wood. Seeing them, he drew rein. "Does nobody in this town ever go about his business without shooting off his mouth?" murmured Anson. But all that Mr. Dewey wanted to tell them was, "What say! The fringed gentians are up

in the Rollinses' back pasture this year. Funny! I never saw 'em there before. Those darn little fellows just grow where they darn *want* to, don't they?" He clucked to his horses and drove on.

The reminder of something that did what it darn wanted to softened Anson's face so much that as they approached the Craft house, Anna asked, "Can't you stay for lunch with me, Anson? It wouldn't delay you."

"Would Miss Ingraham be there?"

"Not till later," said Anna, hastily. "We'd be through by the time she came. It's all ready. Boston brown bread and one of those fish chowders Father liked. And a rice pudding with spices. You know how we make them. Or baked apples if you'd rather. You wouldn't have to talk to Mrs. Randall either. She always leaves the table set for lunch and the tea-kettle on the stove, and goes home to get her husband's lunch. I'd just have to make coffee."

"That menu sounds better than anything I'm likely to get in my Ashley boarding house," admitted Anson. "God! This native New England cookery is toxic!"

But though he ate a great deal of the fish chowder and brown bread, had two helpings of rice pudding and drank three cups of coffee, he said nothing about their non-toxic qualities. "I wonder why?" thought Anna, asking from everything help in understanding Anson. "It looks as though it came from expecting that everything is going to be right, and naturally only noticing and mentioning the things that are wrong. But expecting everything to be right is optimism, isn't it?" She hurriedly put this idea out of her mind in a panic at the thought of Anson's indignation if he should catch her fancying that he was an optimist.

Lunch had gone too well to risk spoiling. Anson had evidently again made a resolution not to be rough, and this time made better work of it, keeping the conversation on their work—the only thing in the world, Anna began to think, that he respected. They had passed from a variation in the use of insulin to the rôle of calcium in para-thyroid trouble and thence to late theories about the disuse of plaster casts in bone fractures. The half hour had been peaceable. But Anna, all one longing to give Anson what he wanted, was no

nearer knowing what that was. Strange, as other people came towards her on the street, it was as if they wore around their necks a placard telling her what they lacked. She could always escape from one of her forlorn "Knapp days" by giving them what they wanted, could warm her cold hands at the reflected glow of their pleasure and relief. That is—she remembered the Rollinses—she could kindle that light if she were willing to pay the price. For Anson she would be willing to pay any price, but, fumble as she might, she could not find the clew to what he wanted.

"Where do you keep your matches, Nansie?" asked Anson. She sprang up to fetch them, thrilling over his use of the nickname, and ventured to suggest, "What do you say we sit out by the rock instead of inside here? It's so sunny and warm today."

The luck of having Cora Ingraham so late might be rounded out to perfection if she could manage so that he would need to no more than nod to her from a distance.

"Okay," said Anson. "Where's the afghan?"

She snatched the ragged old ruin out from the hall closet as they went by, thankful that she had resisted her impulse at house cleaning time to burn up this relic of the past which had in it so many hours spent with the little Anson sprawled on its knitted reds and blues beside their rock.

He could not sprawl his long mountaineer's body on it now, apparently took it along only as an old comrade, for as soon as they were out by the rock, he handed it to her and lay down at full length on the carpet of pine needles under the big tree he had so often climbed. Anna sat by him, her back against the rock thinking, "Oh, isn't this too good to be true. I have somehow done the right thing," and trying to push away the question, "But what was it? How shall I know the next time?"

Through the silence came first the murmur of the brook back of the rock, and next from a distance, the clock in the tower of St. Andrew's striking a quarter hour. Cora Ingraham was due. Anna was pierced by the dreadful possibility that Cora might think it necessary for politeness to come out to the rock and greet Anson. "It would," she thought despairingly, "be just like Cora!" She

looked at Anson. His eyelids had fallen shut. She looked up anxiously. Yes, there was Cora turning the corner from Academy Street, hurrying a little because she was late, rather more graceless than usual because she was hurrying. If Anson were asleep it might be safe to get up and run to meet Cora and tell her—what could she tell her? That her brother disliked her so much she hoped she would not . . . But Anson was not asleep. He turned over on his side now, pillowing his head on one arm, looked up at his sister and smiled.

With startled tears in her eyes Anna put that loving smile in the safest corner of her memory. Even if Cora came up now, this instant, and spoiled everything, she would forever have that smile. In no matter what pain, she could comfort herself with the memory of this moment when Anson had let her know he loved her and knew that she loved him.

But Cora did not come out to spoil everything. As she approached, her heavy footsteps loud on the marble sidewalk, her eye caught Anna off under the big pine, leaning against the rock. Her gait slackened as she looked. And then she saw who was stretched on the pine needles. For an instant, as though her feet were left without orders from the brain above them, her steps fell irregularly. But at once that brain resumed its usual command. Miss Ingraham walked briskly on, waved a silent greeting to her friend, sent her a cheerful nod and smile as she passed, walked steadily ahead, past the house where her lunch awaited her, purposefully past the next one and disappeared down the street, the sound of her steps coming back more and more faintly till they quite died away.

Anna Craft thought, remorsefully, "How intolerable—all that capacity for selfless love—ignored because she has bad teeth and a thick waist. Where *will* she get any lunch, poor Cora? A sandwich at the drugstore, perhaps."

Anson sat up, yawned comfortably, and said, "Let's move around where we see old Hemlock."

Anna threw Cora overboard. "Oh, let's!"

They settled themselves on the afghan, their backs to the rock looking off across the valley to Hemlock Mountain.

"Any game left up there?" asked Anson.

"Oh, yes. All kinds. Deer, lots of deer. Rabbits, partridges, pheasants, a bear once in a while, wildcats. Why don't you join the Fish and Game Club?"

Anson yawned again. "Not on your life! It's just all I can do to stand my fellows citizens one at a time, as patients, when I'm paid to. A lot of them at once coagulated into a lump . . ."

Anna threw the Fish and Game Club after Cora. She did not feel so unshaken a confidence in patience and ingenuity as solutions to all problems. Anson drew out his watch. "I've got five minutes more." He looked back at the mountain, the hollows rich with purple shadows, the ridges green-gold in the sun. It was one of the noble days, done in the grand style.

"I haven't been called up on Searles Shelf yet," he remarked, following the white birches with his eye. "Do you go up often?"

"It depends. Sometimes. I had a case last spring that took me back and forth a good deal."

"Maternity?"

"Oh, no, not nursing at all. A girl up there they all wanted to get rid of. I found a job for her here in The Street."

"You're pretty smart if you found a job in The Street for a girl that Searles Shelf wanted to get rid of," commented Anson. "What was it?" He slid down till he was again on his back, his arms under his head.

"Oh, I don't mean she was . . . She wasn't . . . It was rather an interesting case. Unusual. I thought perhaps changing her background . . ." Anna was thinking, "Why, he is interested. He did ask me. This is—at last—just what I looked forward to! Sharing my work with Anson, talking over my problems with him." Her watchful care not to bore him relaxed. She went ahead impulsively, "My first impression of that girl didn't make me any too enthusiastic about placing her down here. But when Miss Bessie'n'Gussie needed somebody to work for her board and lodging, it seemed worth trying. They've done wonders with her. Miss Bessie says she's the

best learner she ever saw. Doesn't that seem to you a perfect labora-tory proof of what a better background will do for any young per-son, even the most unpromising? It's made me surer than ever that we *must* make it possible for the brighter boys and girls from the poorer farms to go through the Academy. If the town would only vote full tuition and give a little help to start a coöperative home where they could . . ."

Something in the air gave her a warning. She was seeming senti-mental, flat, tiresome, priggish, prolix—whatever it was in her that Anson so frantically couldn't endure. She shrank together and was silent. Anson did not stir. After a pause she looked down at him, dreading what she would see on his face. But what she saw was not exasperation or scorn. He had dropped his eyelids again. His face, undefended by his fierce blue eyes, lay open to her gaze. She was horrified by its sadness.

He put his crooked arm over his eyes now as if to shut out the light and from under it said in a quiet, almost gentle tone of de-spair, "Oh, Anna, Anna—all this patching up of dreary human beings that had better never have been born—so they can go on living their dreary lives out. Don't you suffocate . . . not to have any goal but that? I do."

She would gladly have given her life to know how to make the right answer to the hopelessness tolling in his voice. But the right answer was not for sale in exchange for a life any more than it ever is.

This was the first time he had said anything to her that he really meant. She knew the moment was a crisis. But she could not rise to it. She lost her head, began brokenly to speak of her own escape-device from those moments when the skull of life shows grinning through its smile, remembered that she had always thought her melancholy came from her Knapp mother and that Anson did not share that inheritance, caught herself back, exclaimed, and stopped short, pressing her hands together, trying to collect herself, trying to separate what she had thought from what she had said.

The spell was broken. Whatever she had said had been wrong. Anson opened his eyes, fierce hard eyes, and said, "Ha! Ha! Ha!"

in a sardonic voice. He sat up, leaned forward to brush some pine needles from his trousers, remarking, "Yes, it *must* upset you, Anna, to have your heredity formula work out the wrong way! Not a drop of Knapp in me, and yet not so damn sure the snail on the thorn proves where God is. Can't make it add up, can you?"

He saw her face whiten in pain, and said between exasperation and compunction, "Oh, gosh, Anna! Use your sense. It doesn't take Knapp blood to account for a person's occasionally wanting to lie down and die at the spectacle of Windward County life. Ordinary red blood is enough."

He defended himself with some heat against her trembling lips. "I don't mean to hurt your feelings all the time, Anna. But darned if I can tell beforehand what's going to. I've heard you put down more than one smug Valley person by telling him those red Indians up on Searles Shelf are the only people in Clifford who know how to enjoy life. Why should you take it as a personal insult when I say the same sort of thing? You know as well as I do that all these damn mean 'nice' people are so scared they don't dare make one single honest-to-God grab at life from their birth to their death. They haven't even got the guts to do as they like when nothing's to hinder them—wound up like cocoons in 'What'll people say?'"

His words went by her ear unheeded. What his voice told her was that he was still trying to talk to her about something that mattered to him. He had heard her knocking at his door, and in his way was trying to open it. Now or never. She rushed blindly at the cold steel of her habit of reticence, trying to tear its bars down, to tell him that in all he said she heard but one thing—that he was not happy—and wanted but one thing, to know what to do to make him so. But even as she fought her way forward with confused badly chosen words, she brought herself to a shamed halt. For she felt the door closing.

"Oh, I'm all right, Nansie," he said, trying to mask his evasion of her by the nickname. "You worry too much." He got to his feet and took out his watch. "Maybe I'm bilious. Isn't there bilious blood in the Crafts or the Gardners or the Perrys or some of our ancestors?"

She remembered sickly that to stand up, glance at her watch and say something casual was her own device for evading Cora Ingraham's unasked devotion.

Still looking at his watch, Anson remarked tentatively, almost timidly, "Your first idea about anything always is, isn't it, Anna, what *you* can 'do'?"

"Why not?" She felt as if he had tacitly criticized the law of gravity.

He slid his watch into his pocket, said ruefully, "Well . . . sometimes . . ." gave her an uneasy baffled look and did not go on. Then stiffly, awkwardly, "I certainly do wish, Anna, that I made a better return for all that you . . ."

With a shocked desolate gesture she cut short his unendurable dutifulness.

It was no use. Words were not tools for them but clumsy weapons. Falling back on the older surer language, he took her hand in his and pressed it. She showed by a nod that she knew his intention was to be kind, and said, "I mustn't make you late. Didn't you say you were to telephone the hospital?" The overtones of her matter-of-fact voice said, "I understand now that you don't want to let me in where you really live. I'll try not to knock again."

"So I did. I'll call them up now," he answered, his voice brightening. He walked briskly away into the house, his back expressing relief.

Anna followed him slowly.

Someone skimmed down the walk and over the grass towards her—a girl in scarlet and white, Isabel Foote, back from her summer with her sister. Tanned, tall, deep bosomed, a young woman, her bright brown hair grown-up in a knot at her nape. But her long arms still gave a little girl hug.

"Well, Isabel!"

"Oh, M'Sanna!"

She glinted like a brook running in sunshine. She was as fragrant with youth as a lilac bush in May. She was full of herself to the brim and intoxicated with that headiest of all draughts. Her first report of her visit was broken by little laughs overflowing plash-

ingly from her high spirits. She had played in a tennis tournament and done well. Had gone to dances with men—not boys. Helen's baby girls were too wonderful. She had taken care of them all by herself once, for two days. She had had orchids sent her, orchids! By a silly old man, to be sure. But still—orchids! M'Sanna wasn't by any chance going to drive to Ashley, was she? Father'd left the car in an Ashley garage for repairs and . . .

The door in the house behind them opened. A tall dark young man, gauntly built, with a roughly modeled bony face and a beautiful mouth stood on the porch looking at them out of warm blue eyes.

"Oh, it's Doctor Anson," said Isabel. She had seen him several times before going away for her visit. Every particle of her flesh and even her hair took on the expression of a girl at whom a young man is looking, but now it was the self-confident, irresistible glow of a girl to whom orchids have been sent.

"How're you, Isabel?" said the doctor, walking out towards them. He spoke nonchalantly enough. But he looked a little dazzled, as well he might.

The thought-threads tangled into a hard knot in Anna's mind loosened and lay open to her eye. Why, of course, she knew now which one to pull, saw that if that were straightened, the knot would be undone. How childish of her to have thought that little patient ingenuities on her part could accomplish anything. It was the moment for the entry of one of the vital forces of life. Anson needed to love like a man, not to be loved like a child. She had asked herself longingly what he wanted, so that she could give it to him. Now she knew.

"My brother is just starting to Ashley," she told Isabel. "He'll take you along to the garage."

3

ALTHOUGH Father Kirby always looked more or less like a skeleton he was never ill, never had any occasion to consult a doctor. His attacks of indigestion came from a cause medicine could not remedy: the occasional lapses from bad to frightful of the cooking done by the incompetent elderly cripple who was his "help." But how else could old Hiram Rudd earn his board and lodging? Who else in Clifford would put up with his laziness and bad temper? Father Kirby's only recourse was to use the periods of superlatively barbarous food as seasons for fasting. People who fast a good deal seldom need medical care. It was not illness but an accident that sent him to Anson Craft's office one rainy afternoon in late November.

Driving back rather fast—he drove fast as a general thing—from a visit to a bed-ridden parishioner on The Other Side, he forgot the outdropping of clay at the turn beyond the Foster house and did not slow down as he went around it. His Ford skidded, slewed itself into the ditch, slowly toppled over against the bank. By the time he had struggled out through the window Bud Foster had arrived with the farm truck to pull him out. Bud's mother had noticed the Rectory Ford flashing by at its usual speed and knew what would happen on that rain-greased clay.

After the overturned car was back in the road and the mudguards hammered approximately into place, Father Kirby climbed in, stepped on the starter, put his head out of the broken window, called in his deep voice, "She'll run. Much obliged, Bud!" and was off.

But though the engine seemed to have taken no harm, its owner soon found that something was wrong with his own mechanism. Every time he drew in a breath, a small knife slid its point into his lungs and once, coughing incautiously, he was transfixed by an anguish on the left side which he recognized. He had had broken ribs before now. So instead of driving to the Rectory, he went at once to Doctor Anson's office.

As he slid carefully out of his Ford, favoring his left side, he saw that a prodigally long limousine with a liveried chauffeur waited before the door. A grove of palm trees would have been no more surprising a part of November in Clifford. Even before he knew why, Father Kirby sickened in a familiar misery and drew back. Then his mind caught up with his instincts. That car meant a stranger, a stranger meant a startled horrified glare at the first sight of his disfigured face. "I'll just wait till Anson is alone," he thought and turned towards his own car. But he stopped, stood still a moment, his head bent. Then, his gray eyes quiet, he walked up the side path into the little waiting-room.

No one else was there. A laying-down-the-law voice sounded from the office. Looking through the half-open door Mr. Kirby saw that the speaker fitted the voice. A bulky, domineering, gray-haired man was leaning across the table towards Anson, driving home something he had said with an authoritative gesture. He looked heated, like a person outraged at opposition. Anson's attitude was one which Father Kirby recognized from his little boyhood as a storm signal, backbone steel-straight, hands in his pockets, head held high and stiff.

"I'm really justified in not staying," thought the clergyman, and retreated hastily, calling out, "Never mind! Nothing of any consequence. I'll come in later."

But Anson, for once, was glad to see him, springing up with evident relief to say, "No, no, come in. No need to wait. Doctor Colchester, Mr. Kirby."

In the six steps he took to cross Anson's office, Mr. Kirby went involuntarily through a familiar and bitter mental sequence— "Now he'll turn his head indifferently towards me—now his eyes will widen and fasten like leeches on the birthmark; now with a start they'll flash up to mine and bore greedily in to see how much I've been warped by carrying around a hideous blemish; now when he has seen all there is to see, he'll remember that well-bred people do not stare, self-righteously lower his eyes and very well satisfied with his own good manners murmur some greeting."

"Ah, how d'you do," muttered Doctor Colchester awkwardly,

snatching his startled gaze away from the newcomer's disfigured face and looking down at his hands.

While Anson was explaining, "Mr. Kirby is Rector of the church here," and asking, "Well, Fred, what have you been doing to yourself?" Mr. Kirby was forcing himself to go through another familiar mental sequence— "No, don't go putting yourself up on the pedestal of a special grievance. Your birthmark's like anything in anybody's life—just what you make of it. He didn't mean to stare. As soon as he could, he stopped." He answered Anson matter-of-factly, "Nothing serious. Skidded off the Foster turn and tipped myself over. Only a window and a rib cracked, I think."

Anson welcomed his news. "Oh, I'll strap you up in a jiffy!"

Mr. Kirby began with difficulty to take off his coat, wincing at the stab of pain and thinking, ". . . the dark angel at the ford . . . Jacob wrestled with him through the night . . . and *'at the breaking of the day he blessed him there.'*"

Anson now said to the visitor, "You'll excuse my not going on with our talk, Doctor Colchester."

The older man's sardonic smile indicated that he saw through Anson's attempt to dismiss him. Claiming a professional privilege, he curtly set it at naught. "Oh, go ahead, Craft, and strap up the Reverend's rib. I'll be your assistant and hand you the scissors. We can go on with our discussion afterwards."

Anson sent him a resentful look and began to help Mr. Kirby take off his shirt.

Silence filled the room bleakly. The clergyman tried to relieve the situation by some casual remarks, picking his way cautiously since he had no indication which wires were the live ones. Not cautiously enough. With a vague idea of showing that he was on Anson's side, he said something about the old friend's interest he had always felt in Anson's medical career, having watched it since Anson's boyhood.

Doctor Colchester pounced on this, "An old friend's interest, hey? Well, now's the time for any friend of his to head him off from the biggest mistake any young medical man can make—the one they all try to make—grabbing at the first chance to make money

with their new M.D. instead of using a little gray matter to plan their lives intelligently. Here's the situation:—I don't suppose anybody here knows it, but Doctor Craft showed in his student days really exceptional ability in research work. There is not, heaven knows, any too much of that around. When he graduated we wanted him in our laboratory—we want him now, to work on some absolutely first rate research on poliomyelitis. He could get something done there that any scientist would be proud to do. But like so many other young fools, he insists on cashing in at once, on his father's being known here, and ruining his chances for something better by . . ."

Anson flung his roll of adhesive tape down on the table. "Doctor Colchester, I prefer not to have that matter mentioned, certainly not discussed with people whom it doesn't concern." His face had run up the threatening "No Trespassing" sign that always frightened Anna.

But the older man was not Anna. He matched Anson's look with one as black and said overbearingly, "You prefer! You prefer, hey? What makes you think that settles it? By what right should you have what you prefer in this world? Any more than other people! There's nothing secret about this proposition. I could put it in the newspapers if I wanted to. See here, Mr.— What'd you say your name was? Kirby? Judge for yourself. . . ."

Anson made his lips stony. He took up the roll of tape and went on working. His blue eyes froze to harder and harder ice, as the older doctor laid the case before the very uncomfortable clergyman but he said not a word in his own defense; not even at the end when the orator launched into a vitriolic description of what was before him if he persisted in remaining in general practice in the country. . . . "Bridge champion of the village, that's what *you'll* be, Craft— or maybe end-man in amateur minstrel shows." He ended goadingly, "Of course the laboratory position barely pays living expenses. I understand that. But for God's sake did you go into the practice of medicine to make *money?*"

Anson had now finished strapping up the broken rib. He handed

Mr. Kirby his shirt and coat. A look of mulish obstinacy was on his face. He was evidently determined not to open his mouth.

But he was not prepared for what was now in all innocence said by the clergyman.

Offering what seemed to him a natural defense of Anson's position, Mr. Kirby remarked, "Don't you think, Doctor Colchester, that a young man might very well consider general country practice more humanly useful than work in a laboratory, even in the most interesting research? Could there be a truer form of missionary devotion than just what Doctor Craft is—"

He had hoped this was what Anson wanted him to say. It was not.

Anson let him go no further. Leaning across the desk to the older man, he flared out, "I hope you're satisfied, Doctor Colchester! I hope you like what you get when you call in someone who doesn't know what you are talking about." He visibly withdrew from his heat of anger into a zone of icy distaste. Emerging a few inches from this, he continued, "Since we're going into the facts, let's go into them. I hate general practice as much as you do. I'm crazy about that polio work, have been from the first time I stepped into your laboratory. The reason I don't take up your offer is because I can't. No *missionary* ideas about it. Just ordinary commercial honesty. My half-sister has given ten of the best years of her life to helping me get my medical education. I can't do anything else till I have paid back the money—at least *the money*—I owe her. General practice here, where my father practiced, where everybody knows me and I won't have to wait for patients, is the quickest way I can make money." He shut his handsome mouth. And opened it a very little to add, "Now I've told you. Don't you try to tell me you wouldn't do the same thing in my place. You know you would. Anybody would."

"Oh!" said Doctor Colchester, taken back. "I didn't know . . ."

Mr. Kirby felt himself very much in the way, and drifted towards the door. Anson called out apprehensively, "Wait a minute, there. Wait a minute," followed him out into the waiting-room and shut the office door behind him. November rain hung a dismal gray

curtain at the one window, but it was light enough for the clergy-man to see that the angry young doctor had changed into an agitated boy. "See here, Fred," he said nervously, "Anna must never know about this. You know what she'd do!"

"She'd move heaven and earth to make it possible for you to take that laboratory work," predicted the clergyman with certainty.

"Yes! I couldn't do a thing with her. You know I couldn't. Don't tell her," Anson begged him.

"But she'd rather do that than anything else in the world, Anson. Why not let her?"

Anson cried out in a panic, "I knew you couldn't understand! I knew you'd say that! That's what she'd say!"

"I didn't say it. I asked it," corrected Mr. Kirby. "I still ask it."

"Why, because! Because! Because she's done too much as it is! I can't . . . ! It puts me in a . . . ! Oh, you can't argue about such things, Fred. It's just *so!* I couldn't argue with her. It's not just the money. That only stands for something else. To pay it back is something I *can* do. I don't mean you can pay back a . . . It's not just because it's an obligation, you understand. . . . A man must, he *must* . . . Oh, hell! It's everything!" He flung out his arms in a despairing attempt to indicate by a gesture the vastness of what he could find no words for and ended somberly, "But of course you can't see it."

The clergyman's reply was unexpected. "Yes, I can."

Anson took hope incredulously. "You *do* see how impossible . . . ?"

Mr. Kirby nodded and said, "Yes, of course the point is . . . Even when . . . At least she should . . ." He flung down all his beginnings as hopeless. "What you feel, and quite right, is that . . . You have . . ."

Anson, all his life, had heard Fred Kirby struggling like this, vainly trying to fit words to ideas he found too big for words. Until now the young man of science had thought with a silent conde-scension, "Most likely not too big, just too vague and religious and formless." But for the moment he was humbled by his own en-counter with a passionately felt conviction, perfectly clear to him

but mountainously too bulky for any words he knew. He listened almost with sympathy to the other's stammered beginnings. Finally Mr. Kirby stopped, stood silent for a moment, took a long breath and brought out intensely, "Disproportion!" as if Anson would recognize it as the keyword to what they had both been trying to say.

"Yes, perhaps that's it," agreed Anson. "That's always the devil. But anyhow the important thing, right now, is that Anna shouldn't know of this. I couldn't make her listen to me."

"No, she wouldn't listen to you."

"And you see how it wouldn't *do* to have her go on and on . . ."

"Yes. I see that."

Anson's face expressed enormous relief. "Well then, all *right,*" he exclaimed. "Just let it go at that!" The distracted boy turned back into a dignified young doctor. "I'm glad you see it as I do," he said, one professional man speaking to another. "Just let me know if the rib gives you any trouble." He hesitated and added clumsily, "I suppose I owe you an apology for the tone I used about missionary work. I regret it."

"Oh, never mind about the missionaries. Never mind!" Father Kirby made light of it.

"I rather lost my head anyhow. Just the possibility that Anna might come to know about this is enough to . . ."

"Yes, yes, Anson, I quite understand. I'm afraid of her too," said Mr. Kirby, smiling.

The smile caught Anson still shaken, still a step or two outside the walled prison of his reticence. He said quickly, "See here, Fred, I don't want you to think . . . I want you to know that I . . . I really *appreciate* Anna."

"Ah . . ." breathed the other. He turned away to the door and stood a moment in thought. Then he remarked over his shoulder, "Well, Anson, so do I."

4

PEOPLE sometimes—when they thought of it—said it made them feel bad to see poor old Miss Gussie Kemp so shut up in her deafness. It must be terrible, they told each other, to be so out of everything. Look at the way she sat in the vestibule of the church, come time for Christmas greens, winding away on the wreaths and ropes, just having the hard work of it, poor old soul, with none of the fun.

Sometimes, when the door opened to let in a crowd of the young people bringing in a fresh supply of greens from the woods, stamping their feet to get off the snow, laughing, pushing each other, carrying on like wild things, you'd feel so sorry for poor Miss Gussie looking her eyes out at them and not hearing, that you'd lean over and pass their news on to her in a yell, "They say the snow up in the Rollinses' sugar bush is two feet deep a'ready," or "Both the Foote twins went through into Cold Brook. Isabel had to take them home to change their clothes." But of course, such rags and bobtailed tags of talk didn't amount to enough to make it worth the bother of shouting them. You soon got tired and left her alone again. It was too bad. But what could anybody do about it? Sometimes looking at her, you wondered what in the world she could find to think about, to fill up all those hours-without-end she sat by herself.

A good deal of the time Miss Gussie was thinking about the expressions on people's faces. She had a great collection of them in her memory, and was always adding new ones to it. She never forgot an expression that had struck her. Sometimes when she had seen a person her sister had missed—an itinerant umbrella mender or an automobilist stopped to ask his way—Bessie asked her, "What kind of a looking man was he?" and when Gussie could not say whether he was tall or short, well-dressed or shabby, went off into one of her great laughs over her sister's wool-gathering wits. Gussie knew better than to report what she had seen of him, that his eyes

were those of a man who has lost his way in life, or that his mouth
looked as though he should have wielded an ax in a slaughter house,
turning life into death.

When Bessie described their father, she told people he had been
a fine tall man with a thick beard and brown eyes, like the Gardners,
his mother's family. What Gussie remembered of him were the
expressions of his face—his guilty look when his wife scolded him
for endorsing a note for a shiftless neighbor; the astonished relief
as from some gnawing inner doubt when he heard he had been
elected Town Representative; the tenderness with which he looked
at his deaf daughter; and—grandest of all Miss Gussie's thousands
of remembered expressions—the fearless quiet of his eyes as he lay
dying.

(Lizzie Randall leaned to shout in her ear, "They say eggs are up
to fifty-five cents!")

The deaf woman sometimes wondered if the clatter of sound in
normal ears did not distract the eyes from seeing. The loud snoring
dreadfulness of their dying father's breathing had so horrified poor
Bessie that his death-bed had given her nothing but a terror from
which she had never recovered. That or something. Miss Gussie
was by this time inured to life and to the expressions it caused on
the faces of its victims, but there were still two she could not bear:—
the look in poor Almira Boardman's eyes at a wedding, and the
dreadful cringe of fear in Bessie's face when a hearse went by the
house, when the bell of St. Andrew's tolled a death, when she read
in the Ashley *Courier* the obituary notice of one of her contempo-
raries, above all when she had one of her heart attacks. Watching
expressions as the deaf woman often did on their front porch or
now in this group of women chattering as they wound Christmas
greens, she sometimes saw her sister's animated laughing old face
like a mask worn through, no longer—to her eyes—hiding the
anxious glare of fear that lay below it. (Lavinia Gardner told her
loudly, "They're tellin' about a Searles Shelf girl at the Fair, spoon-
ing the froth off'n an ice cream soda and tryin' to eat it—first she'd
ever seen.") If she had been younger, she would have worn herself
out trying to think of some way to comfort Bessie, to reassure her.

But she knew now—she was nearly seventy—that nobody can help anybody else.

The door burst open, a delicious coldness perfumed with pine and hemlock eddied into the vestibule. Miss Gussie, not hearing what the young voices were saying, looked at what the young faces said. Most of them, those of boys and girls alike, shouted, "I'm alive! I'm alive!" and nothing more. The Foote twins (Isabel had evidently dried them off quickly enough to let them join the crowd again) wore another expression which for a moment Miss Gussie could not identify. Then she saw the twelve-year-old girls lay their armfuls of ground-pine down in a pile by itself, away from the rest, and call the attention of the nearest woman to it. Miss Gussie at once dropped their expression into a pigeon-hole (a full one) which she had mentally labeled, "Keep your wits about you or somebody else will get credit that belongs to you." She knew what their school life was, she knew what kind of marriages they would make, she knew how they would bring up their children. She knew that when they had climbed to the top of the long grade of childhood and adolescence and from Grownup Hill caught their first glimpse of life spread out before them, they would waste no time crying out like their sister Isabel, "Oh, wonderful!" or like Anson Craft, "Is *this* all?" Quick, quick, they would stoop and pick up here and there little advantages lying close to their feet, little profits, little credits.

Smiling to herself, Miss Gussie stooped over a pile of ground-pine. She was thinking, "The Foote twins will make out very well in this world."

When she sat back in her chair again, the whole group, heavily seated women and fluttering young people, had stopped what they were doing to laugh over some joke. Miss Gussie saw the mirth—inaudible to her but not invisible as to other people—as bright waves, eddying around and around the room, dashing up their rainbow sprays against the gray cliffs of people's faces, usually so stony and dry, now glistening and streaming with gayety.

Kind Sadie Warner stopped laughing long enough to tell the deaf old lady in a piercing voice, "Barney Randall says Mr. Kirby

stopped that little Ellen Nye and asked her what she learned in Sunday School last Sunday and Ellen told him, s'honest as you please, she'd learned that 'God-the-Father-Almighty will get *you-u-u* if you don't watch out!'" Miss Gussie laughed then herself, and enjoyed the joke. But not more than the sight of those human beings ransomed from themselves for an instant by laughter.

The young people finished distributing the freshly brought greens among the workers and streamed out again for another trip to the woods, letting in as they went a burst of radiant cold. The big oaken door closed slowly with padded ecclesiastical dignity, shutting out the sunshine, and dulling to a murmur the clatter of the cranking of the old Ford truck and the frolicsome shrieking of the girls being hoisted into it by the boys. The church vestibule was left to the many-colored light from the stained glass window at the side, the women were left to their gossip, Miss Gussie to her thoughts.

For now on the faces bent over the spicy twigs and ground-pine sprays there were no expressions worth looking at. Everybody looked like herself, the least interesting expression, Miss Gussie often thought, of all those possible to human beings. Being a Clifford woman, she called it "the Nye look;" and made her excuses to the Nyes by reminding herself of what everyone knew, that they were the nicest kind of folks, steady, kind, sensible, good to sick neighbors and to poor people. Of course, you had to be either sick or poor before they saw you needed help. Miss Gussie glanced over now to Mrs. Foote, she that had been Hilda Nye, and saw from her expression that she was as usual looking at the world from well back inside herself. How safe she was, like a turtle inside his shell, thought Miss Gussie, compared to people like her daughter Isabel who—you could see Isabel doing it—was always flying out through her eyes to be a part of what she looked at.

Mr. Kirby—they who had known him as a little boy, left it to the girls to call him Father Kirby—came in now from the church, pale in his cassock, one hand about his gold cross, the blue scar on his face like a stain of colored light from the window. The other women looked up to listen to what he said. Miss Gussie looked,

too, to see whether his expression was worth collecting. She liked some of Father Kirby's expressions. And others that she found rather painful, interested her because they were different. What was to be seen on most Clifford faces was by this time as familiar to the old specialist in expressions, as clover and daisies to the accomplished botanist. Like other experienced collectors she was always on the lookout for rare and unfamiliar specimens. The girl from Searles Shelf whom Anna Craft had persuaded Bessie to take in and train had brought into the Kemp house several expressions unknown to Miss Gussie. They had baffled her for a while. Then she had thought she had fitted them together into an understanding design. And now, all of a sudden again, there was this new one she could make nothing of. But she was losing her chance to look at Fred Kirby, the only other person in town whose face could still present expressions that were hard for her to read.

She dismissed the Searles Shelf girl from her mind for the time and followed the clergyman around with her eyes as he went from one to another of his parishioners, talking and listening to them talk. Miss Gussie could see from their gestures that he was helping them decide whether they had enough green crosses, and whether eighty feet of evergreen rope was enough for the chancel. Not hearing his cheerful words, she saw that there was a shadow in his eyes. They were always veiled by his preoccupation with something far on the other side of the trivial things that make a disorderly confusion out of everyday life. But this was no transparent veil; it was darkness. "Why, he's got something on his mind!" thought old Miss Gussie, almost shocked. She had thought him as above personal cares as she was.

She wondered if the hearing women had any clew from his words, and after he had gone on, out of the front door, she asked Sadie Warner, "What'd he say?" But Sadie thought she had done her duty by deafness and only shouted, "Nothing much!" She added, with compunction for her shortness, "He was real pleased with the greens."

"Oh, well," thought Miss Gussie, reasonably, "maybe it is indigestion. They say what Hiram Rudd cooks for him would kill

a horse." She had not lived to be nearly seventy without learning the need for caution in identifying troubled expressions. Experience had taught her that indigestion accounts for a great many of them.

Her thoughts went back to the other hard-to-read face of which Fred Kirby had reminded her. Her practiced fingers binding the green twine round and round the spruce twig stems on the wreath someone had given her to finish, she sent her thoughts back to the beginning, went over again those first days of the girl's stay with them, smiled to remember how Bessie, then as now, had seen in the girl's expression nothing but a docile willingness to learn. Well, it did look a good deal like that. Miss Gussie could understand how a person whose eyes were muffled by the ability to hear could mistake it for docility. Certainly Lixlee's actions had been docile enough. She had really tried to profit as much by Miss Gussie's lessons in history and geography and spelling as by Miss Bessie's in cooking and preserving and sweeping and dressmaking and brushing her hair. But either she had no head for book learning, or Miss Gussie had too little of the impulse to make people over and make them different. The attempt at a daily study hour had soon ended by being just a talk, disguised as a lesson in English by Lixlee's writing out her side of the conversation with the deaf woman to whom her deep husky voice was entirely inaudible. Miss Gussie kept those scraps of paper covered with unformed scrawls and sometimes looked them over. Little by little, from them and from her day after day watching the girl's face, she had formed an opinion of her which ran, "She ain't really what I'd call an extra *bright* young one, for all that Bessie says about her being quick to pick up manners and clothes and neat ways. And I imagine she'd be kind of a wildcat if you crossed her. But I kinda like her. There's something there."

As these daily, half-written, half-oral conversations went on, Lixlee's answers to her questions gave her repeated glimpses of what the girl's childhood had been. What she learned caused her a shocked pity. She kept this to herself as she kept most things, knowing that people with ears rarely felt as she did about anything. And accustomed to be non-existent, especially for young folks, it

did not occur to her that her interest and sympathy would mean anything to Lixlee. She would pore gravely over the ill-formed handwriting and only say flatly in her deaf voice, "Dumb has a b to it, Lixlee. You ought to have known that. You had it yesterday." Or, pointing, "Don't use that word. It's not respectable to." But what was in her mind was, "There ain't a dog or a cat or a pig in The Valley that wa'n't better looked out for when it was little."

After more weeks of these "English lessons," the old teacher thought to herself, "Well, she didn't take it lying down, anyhow. She's one to give as good as she gets. I never see a better hater. And who'd blame her?" Later, some indications too slight for any but Miss Gussie to notice, made her hazard a farther guess. "She couldn't be so hot to hate, could she, without she's the kind that would jump in the river for anybody she set store by?" And finally just before the attempt to give the girl any book learning was given up as a waste of her time, "But a person'd have to be ready to do the same by her, I guess, or there might be trouble."

Anna Craft had brought Lixlee to them in May. By Thanksgiving time Miss Gussie thought she had learned the language of her face. She had a habit of receiving in a momentary silence any remarks, questions or instructions addressed to her. Miss Bessie simple-heartedly took for granted that this pause was a docile one made in order to be sure she understood what was wanted of her. Miss Gussie often amused herself by reading in the silent down-dropped look, unexpressed sentiments that would have outraged the masterful Bessie had she guessed them. "That young one is a master-hand at not lettin' on," thought the deaf woman, "and why shouldn't she be? A good-looking girl without any money or any education or any folks of her own to look out for her, how's she goin' to keep the breath of life in her if she don't learn how to say what folks want to hear instead of what's so?"

Modestly pleased with the sharpness of her self-trained eyes, the old woman had settled back to watch this new phase of the comedy of life. But just the other day . . . Her fingers busy with the spruce twigs, slowed down and stopped, while she passed that little scene

once more before the eyes of her memory. There was nothing to it.
Perhaps she had been mistaken. She had been watering the flowers
in the bow-window, Bessie sat reading the Ashley *Courier*, Lixlee
came in from the kitchen and asked Bessie a short question. Bessie
had nodded a "yes, all right," and returned to her newspaper. Lixlee
had gone away. Miss Gussie had not caught a single one of the soft-
spoken words, but the moment the door had shut behind the girl,
she had asked Bessie, startled, "What ever was the matter?" Bessie
had replied from behind her paper, "Nothing's the matter. Somebody at the back door asking for the job of splitting our firewood.
What made you think anything was the matter?" She had expected
no answer to this question, and Miss Gussie gave her none. But she
had lain awake nights since then, recalling the shut expression on
the girl's quiet face, and trying in vain, as she did now, sitting
tranced in thought in the midst of chatter, to put a label on it.

The front door opened and Mr. Stewart appeared. Miss Gussie
was delighted to see him, as always, and gave him her whole attention at once. What a place Clifford was for interesting things to
look at! Miss Gussie was sometimes fairly tired out, there were so
many of them, one right after another. But she never was too tired
to look intently at Lawrence Stewart. Not because he was the only
son of sweet Emma Merrill, who had been her most loved girlhood
friend. There was nothing of his mother in Lawrence except what
Miss Gussie liked least to remember of Emma, her weakness. Nor
was it as other Clifford people liked to look at him, enviously at
his camel's hair overcoat, curiously at the fuzzy felt of his expensive imported hat, mockingly at the tan spats neatly fitting over
the mellow brown of his English-cut shoes. Miss Gussie saw nothing but the expression on his face. To see it there was for her like
eating when she was hungry. For under the various moods thinly
overlaying it, what she always saw was incredulous joy. She shared
it now joyfully as she had shared it the happy day she first saw it—
the day, thirty years ago, when the blessed news of his father's death
had reached him. Hearing people had not seen it then as she had,
because their ears had been full of all there was to hear—items nobody bothered to relay on to the deaf woman till later—details of

the accident, conflicting surmises as to why Doctor Stewart had ever happened to be down on the railroad tracks on foot at that hour, arrangements with the undertaker, futile efforts to locate the runaway daughter to notify her of the funeral. Only Miss Gussie's eyes, freed by her shut ears, saw the expression that all day long came rushing to cry out from young Lawrence's eyes, "Can it be true? Can a man in one moment pass from shame and helplessness to life, livable life? *Can it be true?*"

Miss Gussie knew people thought it one of the oddest of all her inexplicable doings, her crying her eyes out at that old reprobate's funeral. She never told them they were the tears of thanksgiving Doctor Stewart's young son dared not shed. She watched Doctor Stewart's middle-aged, gray-haired son now, thirty years later, talking with his professional sociability, making a show of being interested in the greens, opening his mouth very wide as he talked in that foolish foreign way he had, and she thrilled over the happy ending of that story as though it had happened yesterday. He put his hand in his pocket and took out his bill-fold. Miss Gussie gave a happy bounce in her chair to see in his eyes the never-dulled surprise that he was free to put his hand in his pocket as he chose. He left a ten dollar bill with Hilda Nye Foote. It was no more than they had looked for, but of course they went through the motions of being astonished and pleased, though Miss Gussie knew they all thought him rather a silly old fellow. He nodded, smiled and went out, leaving Miss Gussie radiant, as a sight of him always did. She wished Sherwin Dewey had been there to share the fine flavor of the moment.

Just for the pleasure of it, to brighten by contrast her enjoyment of his present safety, she called up for an instant the expression the young Lawrence's face had worn during those few terrible years of his early manhood, after his mother's death and his rebellious sister's flight had left him helpless and alone in his father's clutches.

("Is this light too dim for your eyes, Miss Gussie? Why don't you stop working?")

"No, no, I'm all right."

"I noticed you put your hand up to'em as though they hurt you."

"It was nothing.")

No, *no,* it was a mistake ever to remember the boy he had been who could neither die as his mother had nor fight back and run away like his sister. To remember the shamed and servile look in those young eyes had made Miss Gussie sick. She took her hand down, thinking, "Let him live to be a hundred and play the fool with summer folks all he wants to . . . 'twouldn't begin to make up for what he went through when he was young." She sent a grateful thought to the house, the china, the old furniture he acted so silly about. They gave him, as nothing else could, what his father had stamped and burned and clubbed out of him—the feeling that he *was* somebody.

Hilda Nye Foote held up the bill and shouted to the deaf woman, "He left this for greenhouse flowers for the altar, Christmas Day."

"Very nice," said Miss Gussie. She added seriously, "In memory of his father, I suppose." It was safe to make the little joke. Doctor Stewart had died so long ago nobody but the oldest people remembered about him.

"I suppose so," agreed Mrs. Foote innocently.

Miss Gussie was amused to see her sister dart a sharp look at her. Bessie was sure she was the humorist of the family! She wore her jokes out telling them to everybody. Nothing entertained Miss Gussie more than to let Bessie catch an occasional whiff of the rare aroma of one of her jokes, the kind that were too good to tell, that one sipped by oneself.

There was a stir among the wreath makers. Enough had been done. They were going into the church to wait till the men and boys came in to put up the greens. Someone pushed the swinging doors open and held them so till they passed through.

It was about half-past three, almost December sunset time in The Valley. Light from the sinking sun poured through the two stained glass windows in the west-facing chancel, filling the church with long level scarlet and blue and green and golden rays. The

air was still and warm, a little close, with a faint odor of burnt wicking from the now cold candles on the altar. The women scattered in twos and threes, to consider how the decorations were to be placed, although everyone knew that in the end each wreath and cross and length of green rope would be where it always had been. Where else?

For the moment there was—for those women always busy about many things—no work to be done, no thought to be taken, no decisions to be made. An exquisite emptiness began to make itself felt in the church, in the minds of the waiting Marthas. Miss Gussie saw them sink down here and there, in the pews, on the chancel steps, saw one after another energetic face soften and become gently vacant. She sat down in a corner pew, her eyes on the chancel window that was a memorial to her Gardner grandfather. She knew, they all knew, exactly how the high ridge of Hemlock Mountain swept from left to right behind the red and blue robes and golden halo of St. Andrew. But though she tried, she could not imagine it there on the other side of the glass, so filled were her eyes by the throbbing glory of color. Not a ray of the stimulating cold whiteness of the winter sun could penetrate the luminous barrier of the windows. Not a glimpse of the shouldering bulk of the mountain wall, of the daunting vastness of the outside world did they permit to reach the eyes or the imaginations of the dreaming women. Nor a breath of the winter wind's harsh challenge. So proudly did their colors take on the vibrations of life, they ended by seeming not merely to transmit the light but to create it. With but one thickness of brittle tinted glass, they eliminated from existence whatever lay outside the church walls. Life was what was inside, lighted in a fixed and harmonious pattern, windless, warm, circumscribed, smelling a very little of candlewick.

Miss Gussie, pulsing with the glowing rays, thought dreamily, "Well, it *would* be sort of nice."

But old Hemlock though hidden by the ecclesiastical mosaic of glass was none the less there. And as the globe turned over, the mountain began inexorably to hide the sun. Slowly the window faded from living flames to glimmering coals, from glimmering

coals to dim bits of glass. The church sank from mellow twilight to duskiness.

Someone—Isabel Foote's mother, probably—knew where the switch was and turned on the lights. At once the windows became quite black. People blinked in the raw glare of electricity, stirred, turned to each other and began to ask what could be keeping the young folks. Then Miss Gussie saw them hearing something, and guessed that it was the party from the woods noisily arriving. But she did not move from her corner pew. There would be plenty of hands now to do the work. She had been far and could not at once find her way back. If she moved now, if she returned to life too hastily, she risked doing one of the queer things that startled people. She would just sit quietly, she thought, in the empty church till all those intimations that had quivered into wakefulness had sunk again into their usual safe half sleep.

But the church was not empty. Even after the other women went out into the vestibule she was not alone. She could not at once smooth down and close those opened inner eyes. She looked around her. There in the pew before her sat May Barney at her husband's funeral, she who sixty years ago had taught a little deaf girl how sorrow looks. And beyond her, John and Nellie Cole gazing down again on the baby who had almost died, gave to the deaf woman behind them a picture of joy as strong as sorrow. In the mourning pew at the front, young Lawrence Stewart sat alone, looking guardedly down at his black-gloved hands while the rector read out the horrifying words, "I am the resurrection and the life." Down the aisle walked young Merrill Foote, his face pale with the bridegroom's exaltation, and beside him walked Hilda Nye in her white bride's dress, rosy, satisfied, composed, sure that there was nothing in married life any more than anywhere else, that couldn't be kept in order by Nye hands. Miss Gussie looked back sadly through the years at the well-remembered shining on the young bridegroom's face. That white passion of consecration—it had been ground into flour and made into bread to feed little dry souls. It had looked like

something immortal come down to earth. But earth would have none of it. What had become of it? Where was it now?

The door to the vestibule opened and fell shut again. A young man and a girl had come in. The girl did not see the old woman sitting motionless in a corner, nor her parents' bridal procession coming down the aisle towards her. The blind brilliance of her eyes seemed to see nothing at all although in answer to gestures from her companion she turned her head here and there. She moved a few steps up the aisle and stood now by her shadowy young father, his ardent eyes on his bride. She looked back at the young man. Miss Gussie could not help seeing her face. And having seen it, the old woman shrank together and tried to look away. The young man nodded and stepped back through the door into the vestibule.

The girl, left alone, bent her head and fixed her eyes on the ground. The church hushed itself to a deeper silence around her. Presently Miss Gussie, not looking and yet seeing, saw the young body shaken by a long tremor, loosened and softened, saw the girl slowly lift her head towards the vaulted ceiling as if to open her heart to an invisible consecration pouring down from on high. The light fell full on her pale face.

Miss Gussie put her hands over her face and fell on her knees. But she was not praying. After a time, she felt someone shaking her shoulder. She looked up. The vestibule door was propped open and a line of spruce trees coming through it, their bearers hidden in their thick green branches. Anson Craft was at the top of a step-ladder, hanging a wreath. Her old sister Bessie stood over her, half amused, half scandalized to see somebody being devout out of church time. Nobody else was paying any attention to her. Miss Gussie was always doing queer things.

Miss Bessie was moved as she sometimes was, by pity for poor Gussie, so out of things, never knowing what was going on till it was all over. She sat down and tearing out the fly leaf from a hymn book—she never cared what she did, Miss Bessie, so long as it was what she wanted—wrote on it, "Anson Craft went with them on that last trip to get the spruces. Anna had asked him to. They say

she's managing so he sees a good deal of Isabel, and that it's beginning to take."

Miss Gussie read this piece of news and nodded to show she appreciated her sister's thought of her. Miss Bessie took the fly leaf back and scribbled, "A very good idea of Anna's, too. It's just what Anson needs. And he needs it bad."

Miss Gussie's lifted eyebrows showed she did not follow.

Miss Bessie turned the fly leaf over and explained, "Don't you remember Grandmother used to tell us that nobody was quite so half-baked as them that had lots of education and no experience?"

Miss Gussie wrote back, "You talk as if marriage was an oven."

Miss Bessie laughed at this and looked pleased at having something to laugh at.

5

ALTHOUGH she knew it to be a very useful tool for getting done the kind of social welfare things she wished done, Anna Craft had never had much patience for the Nye temperament. But that winter she admitted to herself that the cool Nye way of taking life had its good points. Isabel scared her. She felt like Ned Rollins helplessly gaping at the devouring flame-genii sprung up from what he meant to be a serviceable little fire to clear his pasture of weeds. To begin with, there had been but harmless-looking little spurts and crackles, as after that first drive, "Why, M'Sanna, he's perfectly marvelous, your brother is! I've heard people talk about magnetic personalities. Well, now I know!" And soon after that, when Anna had invited her to stay to supper one evening when Anson was there, "It doesn't seem possible that anybody so . . . so . . . Well, think of anybody like that in *Clifford!*" In November, Doctor Foote—never one of the lucky ones—fell off a stepladder and had to spend a fortnight in the hospital with the resultant torn ligaments. Anna occasionally took Isabel up to Ashley and left her to visit with her father, with the understanding that Anson would bring her back when he came down to Clifford to see a patient. After this had happened several times, Isabel told her,

"We have the most wonderful times on those drives! Last night the stars were out before we got here and he told me the names of some of them. All my life long I'll never be able to look at the stars without . . . Never." The hushed tremor of her voice gave Miss Craft a little warning of what was to come. A little. But nothing prepared her for the speed with which those harmless little spurts of feeling leaped into devouring flame.

She could not escape the sight of them for she was now more than ever—as Anson's sister—the one person Isabel trusted to understand her. "I'd go crazy with it, M'Sanna, if I had to keep it to myself. And who else could I say a word to? Mother would think I was crazy already. Olivia, too. And Cornelia—you'd think Cornelia would understand *some*thing about it—you know she and Charlie Dean have always been sort of engaged and now he's got the promise of a job after he graduates they really are. But all she talks about is what kind of vacuum cleaner she's going to have. It'd scare Cornelia to death if I talked to her about how it really feels, to . . . It scares *me* to death, M'Sanna. It . . . scares . . . me . . . to . . . *death*." But as she spoke life blazed in her so hotly that Anna shrank back from the reflection of it.

She slowed down at once on making occasions for Isabel to see Anson, telling herself (a little late) that it was better to let such things take their natural course without steering them from the outside. In fact only once more was she responsible for their being together. Anson had made a wry comment on the joylessness of Clifford life, and she had pointed out that he absented himself from all the traditional occasions for folk fun. "Don't you remember what lively good times everybody had decorating the church for Christmas? Well, they still do. Tomorrow's the day. You just try going out with the young people to the woods for greens." Remembering that Isabel would be among them she added seriously, "I wish you *would*, Anson. To please me."

It had happened—or had it only just happened?—that in the pairing off of that expedition Isabel and Anson had been together, had plunged through the snow side by side, had driven to and from the church in the same car, had walked around in the church de-

ciding where to stand the spruces, and then that Anson had invited her to go back to Ashley for supper at the hotel and to go to a concert given by the Middlebury Glee Club afterwards.

"I bet you had a good time," Olivia told her enviously the next day.

"Yes, I had a good time," Isabel answered.

But to Anna she said, "I don't know what's the matter with me, M'Sanna! I feel myself beginning to imagine . . . I try *hard* not to, but it's no use . . . how . . . how," an agonized pause and then in a rush, "how it would be to have him . . . put his arms around me. But when I do imagine it . . . it almost kills me. My arms and legs go all limp as if I were going to faint away . . . as if I were going to die. Yes, truly, M'Sanna, it feels like dying. All my joints so loosened . . . ! I couldn't close my hand on anything and hold it, then . . . not if my life depended on it. M'Sanna, what *is* it? What can it be? What ought I to do?"

The startled nurse who would have known exactly what to do had the symptoms been of typhoid fever or appendicitis, could only say, "Keep busy, Isabel, work hard at your studies, fill your mind with other things and it'll be all right."

"Yes, M'Sanna, I will try. I do try," Isabel would say, humbly accepting absurdity for good advice because she knew no better.

One of the Academy traditions was that no one could graduate who had not in his Senior year gone up to Perry's Point on snowshoes. The expedition was taken that year as always. Anna happened to pass the crowd of young people as they came back rocking lightly over the drifts on their webbed shoes, singing the Academy song. Isabel was as red-cheeked and bright-eyed as the others.

But three days later, the girl told her, "M'Sanna, every night now I dream that we are climbing the mountain together, and all the way up I know what he is going to do, and just thinking of it makes me float along as if I were flying. Then when we get up to Perry's Point . . . M'Sanna, it's so real I can *see* The Valley down below us blue in the shadow, and The Wall lilac-colored in the sunset! Then he leans towards me, and the mountains begin to shake and flow like waves and he says, 'Now I'm going to kiss you,

Isabel, for the first time!' *His very voice! It is his voice. I hear it!* And all the next day no matter what anybody says to me, what I hear is, 'Now I'm going to kiss you, Isabel, for the first time.'"

"Take plenty of exercise in the open air, Isabel, and sleep with your windows wide open no matter how cold it is. Don't let yourself sit still and dream. As soon as you begin to, get right up and take a long walk, even if there's a snowstorm. It won't hurt you to get very tired."

"Yes, M'Sanna, I will. I see what you mean. I *do* try."

"Good heavens!" thought Miss Craft sometimes as she let Isabel out of her car. "Good heavens!" Sometimes after such a talk her own hands were shaking, her own pulse drumming fast.

But, of course, in this case it might—probably would—turn out all right. Might even, for all she knew, be just the usual thing, startling to her only because—although she had listened to many wives who hated their husbands, to many distracted mothers, even to some husbands wrought to frenzy by the misconduct of their wives—she had never before been the confidante of a young girl in love. Perhaps they all felt like this. Perhaps this was the preliminary madness without which no one would take the mad step of getting married.

Nothing astonished her more than Isabel's skill—where could she have learned it?—in concealing most of what she felt when she was with Anson. She always, it was true, said yes to Anson's occasional offhand invitations to drive up to Ashley with him on one of his rare free evenings, to go to the movies or hear a concert. But with a self-respecting art that left Miss Craft speechless, her yes was casual, not eager. Sometimes she even said, "Well, I'm not sure, Doctor Anson. Suppose I telephone you tomorrow morning. I'll know then whether I can." Unless he were observing her very much more attentively than he seemed to be, Anson must, his sister thought, have gathered the impression that she sometimes said no.

The girl had a sixth sense which told her when he was staying on with his sister for supper after his office hours in The Street, for she often ran in on an errand at such times, and sometimes sat down for a neighborly chat. Anson always seemed glad to see her,

joked her about her low marks in Latin and about the English teacher who was one of her many admirers, told her solemn nonsense about a two-headed baby born up in Clifford Four Corners, evidently enjoyed looking at her, as who would not. And Isabel—except for a certain shortness of breath and a melting softness of eye—took all this with a natural manner as if he had been anybody. Watching, Miss Craft would tell herself, "Oh, I must be mistaken." But afterwards alone with the nurse in the car, "M'Sanna, sometimes I think I'm losing my mind. I've *got* to talk about it to you! You're the only one who knows a thing about it! I'd die before I'd let Mother or Father know. It's getting so I don't know what's really so and what I imagine. When I'm sitting in the room with him I want so much to go over and touch him that sometimes *I think I have!* Honestly I don't know whether I'm there by him, leaning over him . . . or still sitting in my own chair. I'm afraid I'll *do* something some time that people'll notice. Do I show it? You don't think *he* notices? Oh, M'Sanna, *do* you think he likes me? Sometimes I think he does."

"Why, yes, Isabel, he wouldn't ask you to do things with him if he didn't."

"Oh, just those . . . ! They're nothing! Anybody would ask anybody as much as that . . . to the movies once in a while."

"But you're the only girl he *does* ask. And he went with you young people to get the Christmas greens, and took you to the concert and all."

"Yes," whispered Isabel, going off into a trance. "Yes . . . Yes . . . that day . . ."

Presently she remembered to breathe, and asked tremulously, "Doesn't he . . . doesn't he ever *say* anything?"

"He doesn't talk much to me at all, Isabel, since he came back."

Isabel, ferociously deaf to the sadness in the other's voice, insisted, "I didn't mean . . . I thought perhaps he . . ."

"Here's where I have to turn off, Isabel. You'd better get out here, or you'll be late home. I've got to go up Searles Shelf way."

"All right, M'Sanna."

Looking after her, swinging off down the snowy road, robust

in her tweed skirt and leather jacket, her head coiffed in its blue béret, Anna Craft thought anxiously of the things Anson occasionally said about her, "Yes, she's a nice kid." "Beefsteak and rice pudding." "Sure, *I* like her all right."

But perhaps, reflected Anson's sister, letting her clutch in thoughtfully, perhaps Anson, like Isabel, did not say what he felt. At the thought, her hope breathed freshly, her heart filled with daydreams of Anson married to this sweet ardent girl, Anson with little children, his love for them the solvent of whatever the dark questions were that tormented him now. No young man in his senses, she thought, could resist Isabel's loveliness, her youth, the softness in her eyes as she looked at him.

She did not realize she was driving by the Rollinses' house till Ned and his wife came out to stop her to talk over the campaign for Town Meeting. How many votes did M'Sanna think she had in line? They had made sure of everybody on Churchman's Road. M'Sanna told them The Street was about half and half. She was on her way to Searles Shelf. Taxes being little or nothing to those propertyless people they never cared *how* they voted except they'd rather than not vote so's to spite the people in The Street. "Speaking of Searles Shelf, how's the Burdick girl getting along down to The Street? You don't say! Well, you never can tell, can you? I guess we must ha' been all off about her. Miss Bessie Kemp is a smart old woman, all right, maybe most as smart as she thinks she is." Of course, she told them, every house on The Other Side was solid against any plan that would cost tax-money. Not a vote to be had there. They received this in a stubborn silence, broken to say, "Well, we mustn't keep you. The days are getting longer now but even so, it gets dark early this west side of the valley, old Hemlock cutting the sun off so. Are your chains all right, M'Sanna? The snow's drifted terrible on that level stretch through the white birches up there. Sure your chains haven't got any broken links? By the way, they tell me Henry Twombley is working real good this winter . . . yes, sawing and splitting wood, around. A good thing, too. His wife says he never worked so steady since they were married. He better! She's expecting again, I hear. Well, good-by! Good luck!"

She left them without getting up her courage to tell them that, figure as closely as she might, she couldn't make the budget for the students' house balance without help from town money, in addition to covering the full tuition. They would know as well as she how little chance there was of ever getting enough yes votes for that.

That evening when, very late to supper, she drove her car into her side yard, light still streamed out over the snow from the south wing. Anson had been delayed, it seemed. A man brought in from the woods with a broken arm. Shrugging on his heavy coat, he looked at his sister with solicitude. "What *have* you been doing, Anna? You look as though you'd been dragged through a knot-hole."

"Up on Searles Shelf, trying to get votes. It's less than two months to Town Meeting."

He had forgotten about that project of hers, stared, remembered it and said, "What on earth makes you!"

She was too tired to abide by her knowledge that this was but an exclamation of disapproval, and answered as though he had really asked what it was that made her, "Because people on the poorer farms . . . like the Rollinses, they can't . . ." He did not say a word, but to drown out what she saw in his eyes she raised her voice, pleadingly, "Their children are *every*thing to them, Anson! All they have to live for!" She sank down on the bottom step of the stairs more exhausted by his expression than by her long tussle with snowdrifts and frozen ruts.

"Of all the innumerable ways of passing the buck," said Anson, turning up his coat collar and drawing on his heavy driving gloves, "that 'living for the children' one seems to me the most low-down. A fat chance for drawing the breath of life it leaves to the children! What's the matter with enjoying your *own* life! Anybody'd think there was a law against it in this State!" He opened the door, lowered his head against a crack of the whip from the zero wind outside, cried, "God! What a climate!" and slammed it behind him so hard that the steel engraving of Seward wavered on the wall.

His sister's first reaction was a flare of resentment that warmed her like fire or alcohol, so that she sprang up, all her fatigue gone, and began to snatch off her wraps, crying to herself, "If he worked half as hard at doctoring as in thinking up cutting remarks to make about everything I . . ." She heard Cora Ingraham start down the stairs, and hastily composed her face.

Her resentment went on blazing under the "No, not so bad as I've seen that road," "Well enough," and "Oh, all right" with which she answered Cora's attempts at conversation; till in the middle of the evening meal her anger and with it most of her vital warmth was blown out to blackness by the cold thought, "Was that a personal reference? Did he mean me to understand that he has been feeling suffocated because he is everything to me, all I have to live for?" She answered Cora, "No, no, I didn't get chilled. You know I never have any color in my face." And thought bitterly, "If he has any idea that his staying on here gives *me* any pleasure . . ." But even this side glimpse at the possibility of his going out of her life wrenched at fibers deep in her heart. "Perhaps that *is* a tyranny," she thought with an infinite sadness, saying to Cora, "Yes, yes, I like it all right. It's very nice. I just don't feel hungry," and thinking with an impatience that seemed to her natural and justifiable, "Oh, I wish Cora would leave me alone!"

She woke up in the night to remember ruefully the pleasure she had had in thinking of Anson as a father, accepting children as the answer to life's enigma.

But when other people criticized his manners she always defended Anson with a flare of temper. For, of course, Clifford resented his brusqueness and his cutting criticisms of their way of life. Not as much as brusqueness would have been resented elsewhere, where urbanity is prized more than pungency. While by no means as gratuitously hateful as some of the summer people thought them, Clifford people had sharp tongues and were connoisseurs in razor-edged retorts. Jo Danby had a great success retailing the dialogue between Lawrence Stewart and young Doctor Craft. "'Well, when you break down under it come to me and I'll give you a prescrip-

tion,' says he as natural as you please." And not only could Anson Craft plant a barb neatly without waving his arms or raising his voice, he was a darned good doctor. This fact was another that counted for more than it would elsewhere. Clifford people had never learned or tried to learn the modern method—necessary when most human contacts are casual and transient—of estimating people by what they say and seem. Their own human relationships, mostly very lasting, showed during long periods of time what people really do; and their estimates were largely based on such data. This habit, a quite unconscious one, explained the local esteem felt for some dour-spoken persons, the local distrust shown for certain smiling agreeable ones, judgments which summer people thought could come only from a native dislike for pleasant manners. It explained their enduring from Anson Craft talk that would have boycotted a city boarder.

Capable as they were of seeing what people do under the smoke-screen of what they say, Anson's fellow townsmen could not but be aware that, in spite of his spoken attacks on conventional ideas and conventional morality, the young doctor himself led an ascetic, useful, laborious life; that his rough manner was not infrequently a cover to kind actions and that he could be counted on for absolute devotion in all medical matters. He took hold of bad accidents and difficult cases of sickness with a vigor and resourcefulness they were not used to, and were very thankful for. His professional conscience extended to smaller ailments. It was a comfort to have somebody who took a sincere interest in your varicose veins, or morning sickness or sinus headache—a nice change and none too soon, from old Doctor Cole's grumbling exasperation with you for bothering him by being ill. And he had prestige. There was no denying that. The girls fluttered over his blue eyes and masterful ways and the boys tried to copy his clothes. Many responsible citizens resented his prestige with the young as dangerous, and resented even more his unconcealed disapproval of every Clifford institution and habit; his caustic refusal to join any of the innumerable social organizations, his scorn of the local passion for bridge playing; his often-repeated comment that The Street cared much

more about the success of the Academy football and basket ball teams than about the danger of another World War; his ridicule of their fanatic accuracy in the details of local history. Perhaps as much as anything else they resented his envenomed objections to hearing a story more than once, even one of the good old local stories that had—they felt—more bouquet and aroma the more often it was repeated. That hurt their feelings more even than the crazy opinions he expressed (when he condescended to talk at all except to give medical advice), his claim for instance that Soviet Russians were ever so much smarter than Vermonters; his hooting jeers at the local chapter of the D.A.R.—such *nice* old ladies every one of them!—his whole doctrine of life, which seemed to be as near as they could figure out that the world would be better off if everybody did what he damn wanted to no matter what ministers and old women said. Especially puzzling and vexing was his glorification of the drunks and wastrels and failures of town as the real successes. "I'm all for rebels," he often said. What did he *mean?* A coarse saying went around among the men, the end of which ran, ". . . get your fingernails full of manure and drink till you puke, if you want Doctor Anson to think you know how to enjoy life." Some people said loudly they wouldn't have stood his talk a minute if he hadn't been a Clifford boy and related to all of them.

The very old, it is true, those who had lived long enough to learn that the few acts of life's little-varied drama always repeat themselves, refused to look up from their knitting and whittling to join in the shocked relishing talk about Doctor Anson's wild ideas, " 'Twun't last," they said. "Never does with that kind." The middle-aged and respectable were not so philosophic. They said to each other that the sore head Anson Craft had got out of his education was as big as a wash tub; they asked, "For the Lord's sake, what does the cub *want?*" They cried out, "Does he call that setting a good example to young folks?" They smacked their lips over experience as the inexorable teacher of wisdom, "Just wait! He'll soon find out that's no way to get on in the world." They wagged their heads, "Let him get married to some nice girl. That'll put ordinary sense into him." But none of them, young or middle-

aged—with the exception of Miss Bessie Kemp, who said whatever she felt like saying to anybody—voiced their criticisms of Doctor Craft directly to his sister. Sometimes, aggrieved or indignant, they went so far as to report sharp speeches of his, tacitly asking how she could explain his flying out so on everything that other folks thought was nice. Her retort sometimes took one form and sometimes another, but it was never more in substance than the red-headed person's reflex of "Mind your own business!"

She understood no more than they what it was that so exasperated him in herself, in the familiar life they all took for granted. Miss Bessie Kemp, walking back from the Post Office with her one day, said, "Anson acts like a man with the toothache. You know how they'll snap your head off if you say it's a fine day, or that the morning train was on time. Why should he think his teeth are the only ones that ache? Everybody's do. What's the use of hollering about it?"

Anson's sister answered warmly, "My brother is a very intellectual man, who's been living in one of the great cities. It's not surprising that he can't always be patient with our stagnant backwater."

"There's plenty everywhere of what we all dip our dippers into," said Miss Bessie, "but we can't fetch up any more than what our dippers will . . ."

Anna turned and left her abruptly.

February came in with a great storm that added a foot of snow to the twenty inches that were already making Miss Craft's pre-Town Meeting campaigning difficult. The month wore along without a thaw to lessen the great drifts heaped across the side roads. Miss Craft tied a snow shovel on the back of her Ford, and put a pulley and a length of rope under the seat, to warp herself out from a near-by tree when stuck too deep to get out by shoveling. The month was about like every Clifford February. The Masons gave their annual ball. The Academy gymnasium shook with the swift feet of basket ball players and rang with the yellings of spectators. The Woman's Club discussed a play by Galsworthy and read

a book on Japan. The Men's Club had a pool tournament. The Senior Class in the Academy gave "She Stoops to Conquer," Isabel Foote acting Kate Hardcastle, trembling with hope that Doctor Anson would come, in a panic when he remarked casually perhaps he would, sunk in heartbroken disappointment when he did not. About the middle of the month there was a scare about measles— the Foote twins spent a week-end with their married brother in Boston and brought measles back with them. A hasty arrangement of the family during the quarantine was necessary to allow Isabel, who had had her measles years ago, to keep on attending the Academy, and her father to keep on earning their living. Doctor Foote went to sleep in an extra bedroom in the Sherwin Dewey house and to get his meals where the Academy teachers boarded. And Isabel . . . Isabel had looked at Miss Craft, just looked at her, and the nurse with no volition of her own had said, "Isabel can come over and stay with Cora and me." Quarantine had been prompt enough, thanks to the excellent Mrs. Foote's vigilant eye, so that no other cases developed. Two lumberjacks were hurt in a logging accident up on The Wall, and another one poisoned himself with wood alcohol. Yes, it was just like any February—a falling tree grazed Mr. Dewey's leg and all but broke it. Something happened to him in the woods every winter, now that he was no longer as spry as he had been. He was laid up for a while, M'Sanna going in to change the dressings on his leg. Miss Bessie Kemp got her usual midwinter bronchitis. It was no worse than usual but she always worried about herself when she was sick and insisted on having the doctor to see her every time he was in town. A doctor, a stranger, called on young Doctor Craft . . . "no, not that high-and-mighty one with the bay-window and the Packard car that was here in November, he was from New York anyhow. Or Boston. This one was from over Burlington way, one of the professors in the Medical College, somebody said, the one that knew about hearts. A big bony old fellow, talked kinda like a Caledonia County man." A bear was shot up beyond Searles Shelf, and the pelt bought for ten dollars by Lawrence Stewart to use as a rug in his library.

("Yes, we Vermonters have not lost touch with Nature up here. There's a saving bit of the primitive left in our lives.")

The people on the farms along The Other Side were more and more out of patience with M'Sanna's notion of paying out town money for poor folk's tuition at the Academy. ("We pay our own way, and our children's way. Let other folks do the same.") Miss Craft remembered the four or five voters back in Emery Hollow, who never appeared in Clifford at all except on Town Meeting Day, and made her way up there on snowshoes. ("Naw! We pay too much for schoolin' as 'tis. Readin'n'writin' rots the brains, I allus tell'em.")

Miss Bessie's bronchitis was worse or she thought it was. Miss Craft asked her brother, who now went to the Kemp house nearly every day, to tell Miss Gussie to be sure to call on her if she was needed; but Anson said the girl who worked there did what was necessary.

Isabel's presence in the Craft home meant that the usual shorthand talk between Miss Craft and Miss Ingraham had to be explained if Isabel were to follow it—or at least Miss Ingraham felt that decent manners demanded this. That night, for instance, Miss Craft said, "When I remember, Cora, how I boggled and hung fire about giving that Searles Shelf girl a chance down here . . ."

("The one who works for her board with Miss Bessie'n'Gussie," explained Miss Ingraham in a rapid footnote to Isabel.)

"Anson says she takes all the care of Miss Bessie. Have you seen her lately, Cora? I saw her out sweeping the snow off the front porch today. She's not exactly pretty—her face is too long for that. But now she has some muscles on her bones, she's quite graceful. And she has very nice black hair now it's kept washed and brushed and those burnt, curling-iron scriggles have grown out. She must be up and down all night to wait on Miss Bessie. When I remember how I'd been ready to let her stay up on Searles Shelf and fall into . . ."

Miss Ingraham raised her eyebrows, looked at Isabel and said

hastily, "She was a very poor orphan, Isabel, who was . . . well . . . there was a very horrid old man who wanted to marry her."

"You just bore Isabel, Cora, with your York State politeness. I don't believe she hears a word either of us say."

Isabel aroused herself from her dreams to say, "Oh, yes, M'Sanna, I *do*. I'm *very* much interested."

Miss Craft gave this statement the credit it deserved and said grimly to Miss Ingraham, "Well, it's encouraging to have something a person does turn out well. I need encouragement."

"Votes?" asked Miss Ingraham.

"Lack of'em. Not a fighting chance for that proposition. Property owners in town would like to kill me. From the looks of things now I could lose my job over it."

"Why don't you give it up?" This pleadingly from Miss Ingraham.

A forked flicker of indignation darted across the table. "What do you mean, Cora? *Give it up!*"

It was as usual Miss Ingraham who gave it up. She thought a moment and asked, "Have you thought of the Altar Guild?"

"No! That's a fact. I haven't. That's a good idea, Cora. You do have good ideas."

"M'Sanna is working hard on a proposition, Isabel," explained Miss Ingraham, unable to abandon the manners of civilization, "that will make it possible for the boys and girls of high school age on the poorer farms, those who have up to now always had to work for their board, to have much better living conditions and a better chance than . . ."

"Yes, yes, I know," said Isabel absently, "one of them worked for her board at our house a couple of years ago. But Mother said she was more bother than it was worth. I'll speak to her about it if you want me to, but I don't believe she'd try it again."

The next day, acting on Miss Ingraham's suggestion, M'Sanna extracted the promise of seventeen more votes from the ladies of the Altar Guild. Not that they cared. "Just to please *you*, M'Sanna," they told her. But there was still a stonewall majority against her.

She had known from the first there would be. Lawrence Stewart did not even bother to dust off "Socialist" and wave it. She could judge by that, if by nothing else, how impossible the proposition was.

The thermometer, before letting up once for all, dropped very low so that everybody asked hoping for a new record, "What was it at *your* house this morning?" There was more snow. The coasting down Depot Hill was the best in years. The young people bobsledded there till all hours every evening. As usual Mr. Kirby kept Lent as hard as though he thought he could make up for everybody else keeping it so easy. Sherwin Dewey's leg healed up, or almost. He would after all be able to go to Town Meeting. It was very important to him, to everybody, to have him at Town Meeting, as he had been Moderator for thirty-two years. Miss Bessie Kemp's bronchitis hung on. Every time young Doctor Craft was in town he went to see her, even if it were late at night.

Once, in that last cold spell, M'Sanna's telephone bell rang wildly, long past midnight. It was Luella Gardner, she who always gloated over Miss Craft's occasional mistakes of judgment and saw that they were well advertised. M'Sanna shivering in her nightgown judged from the agitation of her voice that Luella had lost her head again and argued with her vigorously; but, "Oh, yes, it *is* croup, M'Sanna, this time it is! The poor baby is fighting for his life with every breath. Do come quick! But I *have* tried. I've tried both doctors. Doctor Cole is at the hospital with an accident case and nobody knows where Doctor Anson is. Oh, M'Sanna, come *quick*."

So Miss Craft drowsily put on the layer after layer of clothing needed for that sub-zero night and plodded on foot through the snow to the Gardner house, under a black sky, studded with malevolently blazing stars. A tree snapped loudly once in a while. The snow creaked like chalk under her overshoes. The white houses were cubes of snow. The only light visible was the one waiting for her at the Gardners'.

The croup turned out as she expected, to be a cold in the head with snuffles. M'Sanna warmed herself by giving a piece of her

mind to Luella and started back, going around this time by Church Street to avoid an icy stretch on the sidewalk where on the way over she had slipped and almost fallen.

Across the street from St. Andrew's, something dim and black loomed up. A car standing by the curb. But nobody left cars out at night in this weather. It was in front of the Kemp house. When she came up to it, straining her eyes in the starlight, she recognized Anson's car. Miss Bessie must be worse. The nurse looked up at the house wondering that she saw no light till she remembered that Miss Bessie's bedroom was at the back. Ought she to go in and offer to help? She hesitated. She was very tired. It couldn't be anything serious. She knew Miss Bessie's bronchitis. Probably the old lady, like Luella, had lost her head. If there had been nobody as nurse but deaf old Miss Gussie—but they had that new girl, young, active, and now so well-trained and competent to wait on them. The clock in St. Andrew's tower struck three. She went on.

Two or three houses beyond she was as surprised to see that another living person was out at that hour as she had been to see a car. A dark figure was coming towards her, not walking on the sidewalk like a person going from one house to another, but slogging down the middle of the street with a heavy stride, in the rhythm of someone who has come a long way. A poor man, or he would not have been on foot. Many poor men came tramping so through the darkness to Miss Craft's door with news of a wife whose time had come, or of a dying child. Knowing that she was unrecognizable in her winter wrappings, she called out to him, "Were you looking for the nurse? I am Miss Craft."

He started, stopped short and jerked his head around towards her. Apparently he had been so absorbed with his thoughts or his anxiety, whatever it was, that he had not noticed that someone else was abroad. He stood motionless now, a tall figure whose silhouette, blurred by the dim light, suggested the fur cap, sheepskin-lined canvas coat and high laced boots worn in winter by the countrymen of The Valley. He made no answer. She said again, "I thought perhaps there had been an accident or somebody sick and you were looking for the nurse. I am Miss Craft." She had another

thought and told him, "Or if it's for the doctor, Doctor Craft happens to be in town just now, for a sick old lady at the Kemp house. That's his car, down there."

There was something eerie about calling thus to this unknown human being through the arctic coldness of the deserted street. In the thin air her words rang louder than she had meant. He made no answer to them. But she could see that he turned his head to look towards where the car stood, black against the glimmering snow.

And now he moved forward toward it, the snow creaking under his boots. Had he, with the curt silent gesture of the taciturn men of The Valley, nodded, to show that he understood? Miss Craft was not sure. She waited a moment longer to see, and, watching the shadowy figure, made out that he had stopped by the parked car and was looking up at the Kemp house. Then, that the gray blur was moving towards the house. Yes, she had made him understand.

The vigilant cold, always watching its chance to strike down any living organism incautious enough to be still for an instant, had been making its stealthy way through her thick clothing and now reached her at the core of them, gripping her hard. She felt herself shudder and started on at a quick step, stamping her feet and thrashing her arms against her body. It must be thirty below that moment, she thought, planning to make the rounds of the fires in the house before she went back to bed.

The next afternoon, seeing Anson about to step into his office, she went into the hall to ask him, "How's Miss Bessie?"

"Oh, about the same. More scared than hurt."

"I never knew it to last so with her," remarked the nurse. "She usually gets over those attacks in less than a fortnight. This one has lasted more than . . ."

Doctor Craft flashed around, his head flung up. He always looked very handsome when he lifted his chin indignantly. "Do you mean to insinuate . . ." he began in a stormy tone, but was halted by the extreme astonishment in his sister's face. His own face subsided

from startled resentment, became neutral. "Nothing," he said awkwardly. "No matter." He went into his office and shut the door.

"What is it *now?*" Miss Craft asked herself. She took her mind for a moment from what lay before her at Town Meeting to consider what she had said, and perceived that to a supersensitive young doctor the turn of her phrase might suggest that he was nursing along a case for the sake of the fees. She sighed. How could Anson?

She had meant to ask him also if the countryman on foot had found him last night. But now was no time to ask him anything else.

And then the 27th arrived. February was over. Another of the dull Clifford months had gone by with nothing happening to anybody.

6

Town meeting always comes on the first Tuesday in March— thence its other name of March Meeting. That year the first Tuesday fell late. Those who were working for the coöperative students' home still had seven days for their last campaign. York State people would not have recognized what they did as campaigning, or have identified as political arguments and offers of bribes the casual rambling talks about the roads in winter, the questions about the children's health, the offers to swap a day's work. Every respect must be paid, of course, to each free-born citizen's right to vote as he pleased. An outsider would scarcely have realized that the annual exercise of self-government was at hand, but everybody in Clifford, for and against M'Sanna's proposition, knew that this year's Town Meeting was one not to be missed for anything short of a broken leg.

"Calc'late on goin' to March Meeting this year?"

"Wa-al, ye-es. I sort of thought I would."

Another skirmish in the battle was on, the old battle, the endless battle between the well-to-do, determined as usual not to ruin themselves for the lame and the lazy, and the poor, longing to

help their children get more out of life than they. The never-dying spark of that longing was once more fanned into flame by hope, unsteady and flickering, for the odds were heavy, but burning up bravely whenever M'Sanna's red hair and pale face appeared.

She attended with a fierce thoroughness to every detail of her work, knowing that the enemies of her plan would be quick to accuse her of neglecting what she was paid to do. But she was now so identified with the cause that when she went into a house to give a hypodermic, or to look over the preparations for a confinement case, everybody was reminded of the question that was to be voted on. She was gloomily aware that reminders of that question did her cause little good. They only made the majority resolve once more not to be stampeded into voting more taxes, no, not for anybody. It was the principle of the thing, they often told her, either in belligerent words or in their stubbornly resisting thoughts, a stand had to be taken *some*where about taxes going up all the time. This was one of the stonewall objections to the proposition. Others, spoken or unspoken, ran, "Our fathers and grandfathers got along all right without, etc., etc.," "No woman, especially no red-headed woman, is a-goin' to tell me how to vote," and, "Where are we going to get our hired men and factory hands if everybody learns about chemistry and Latin?"

"Are we going to get more snow? I heard the Forge roarin' last night."

"No—no, most likely rain. Mebbe a sugar snow. March Meeting mud."

Even talk of the weather slid into some mention of what was before them.

Of course there were those in town who paid no more attention to this Town Meeting than to any other. In the Stewart house, for instance, neither Henrietta nor Lawrence bothered their heads about it; Lawrence because of his thrilling discovery of eighteenth-century French landscape wall-paper on the walls of a slant-ceilinged room in his third story. He himself—nobody else could be trusted—was soaking off the many layers of sprigged and striped

and figured papers which every ten years or so had been put on to freshen up the room. It was absorbing and responsible work. Hard on the nerves too, as any false move might make a jag in the holy original paper. He could scarcely be expected to think of Town Meeting. For Henrietta, too, this was not an ordinary spring. Not only was it the regular time to think of where to have her kittens, but her nerves had not recovered their equilibrium after the excitement of her affair with their father. For the Footes' large, yellow, bob-tailed tom was not as usual the father of Henrietta's kittens. He was, as a matter of fact, not even alive any more, having been killed by a fierce brindled cat from the woods who had taken his place with Henrietta, a masterful, coarse-haired, savage male raging down on Clifford backyards from off in the forest wilds of The Wall. No human, of course, knew anything of this—the Footes thought that an automobile must have run over their Tom—but it had been a terrifying, thrilling episode in Henrietta's life and was often in her mind as she sat in the best chair in her study, looking wide-eyed into the fire glowing on her hearth. She always liked a little wood fire kept going, Henrietta did, even though her house was quite sufficiently warmed by her furnace.

Doctor Foote, the dentist, was another one who gave no thought to the approaching Town Meeting. There was no room in his heart for anything but aching love for his dear daughter. He did not see her as often as usual these days, scattered by the quarantine as the Footes were. But he thought about her constantly, his head bent over someone's wide-open mouth. His eyes might be fixed on the cavity in a tooth; what he really saw was the expression on Isabel's face when she was telephoning to Doctor Craft. It took him back. Yes, it took him back to his own youth. He sighed heavily. Isabel was the only one of the children at all like him. He was sorry for her. "It'll have to come out. There's no saving it," he would say sadly to the anxious patient in the chair, asking himself, "What kind of fellow *is* Anson Craft? Is all this talk of his just talk? Or . . . ?"

And you certainly know more than to imagine that Isabel's

mother, gloriously wrestling with two cases of measles, wasted any time thinking about Town Meeting. She was in her element, Hilda Foote née Nye was—nursing, cooking, cleaning, washing, scrubbing and reading aloud. Calm, masterful, breasting the seas of work with strong arms, she knew the deep satisfaction of fulfilling a natural destiny. As for Isabel and her crush on young Doctor Craft, Mrs. Foote knew that either Doctor Anson would—as seemed rather likely since he had begun a little to ask Isabel out—marry her, which would give Isabel a nice home, though, of course, a doctor's meals are very irregular; or else he wouldn't, and then the child would get over this crush as she had her others, and when she grew up, marry somebody else. Mrs. Foote had little patience for people who worried over their children's love affairs. Her life motto was, "Don't make a fuss!"

Isabel thought as little as her mother about Town Meeting, worked almost as hard. But it was not mere satisfaction she felt, it was bliss. Her heart had almost broken with joy when the measles quarantine sent her to live in the house where Doctor Anson came and went. It was as if God Himself in His infinite love for her had arranged things for her happiness. The quarantine would last for another fortnight, perhaps more—an eternity of happiness.

For she was now actually helping him. Almost at once she had asked M'Sanna if she might offer to help out in the office as she helped Miss Craft sometimes. M'Sanna had not forbidden her, and the doctor had said why, yes, if she wanted to. And this had led to more. As Town Meeting drew nearer, M'Sanna was hardly at the house at all. Isabel was often the only person to answer the doctor's phone calls, and to note down who wanted him and for what. Sometimes she copied this little report three or four times before it was fit to show him. She arranged and re-arranged the magazines on the table in his waiting-room, she grow bolder and set his office in order, asked M'Sanna to show her how to run the sterilizer. This last was almost a mistake for it made M'Sanna notice her for a moment and say, "Look here, Isabel, you mustn't neglect your

studies. Your mother wouldn't like that. You're a Senior this year."

"M'Sanna, let me! *Let* me! I love to do it!"

M'Sanna had been too busy to go on noticing, so after a day or two of attention to school books it was safe to go back to the office and palpitating with ecstasy to carry out a wastebasket filled with soiled and blood-stained bandages. "It's almost," she thought reverently, as she set the match to them in the wire basket in the backyard, "it's almost as though I were his—as though I were a doctor's wife." Holy and sacred work in life—to be a doctor's wife! How could she ever have thought of any other.

He noticed her, too! He noticed more and more how she helped, how interested she was in his work, how little she shrank from things—blood, groans, pus—that would have frightened or shocked other girls, how naturally she was fitted for . . . He let her do more and more, depended on her more and more. By the end of February he was leaving her medicine and directions for patients who were to come in later, he was asking her to keep track by telephone of varying temperatures. It made occasions for their talking together, for her to stand close to him, to have a reason to watch his beautiful, cleanly drawn lips as they spoke to her.

On the last day of February something extraordinary happened. He was busy with an old lady come for a regular sinus treatment when a big lumberjack came lurching in with a broken shoulder. Forgetting apparently that Isabel was not his office nurse—or his wife—Doctor Anson called to her to cut off the man's sleeve and get the instruments and bandages and hot water ready. And when he cast his keen blue eyes over what she had done, he said, "Very good. Very good, indeed. You certainly have a knack for this sort of thing." By the next day Isabel distinctly remembered what he said as, "You'd make a good doctor's wife." It was almost as if he had said, "I wish you were my wife." All day long and the next day and the next, she could hear him saying in the voice whose every accent shook her heart, "You'd make a good doctor's wife." And the mountains rocked as in her dream. But this was no dream, this was real.

Nor was it a dream that every day he spent more time in Clifford. Those six days in March before Town Meeting were full of his comings and goings. On nearly every one of them he stayed to supper after his office hours. That was too wonderful. To Isabel he was, of course, always there. She never stopped thinking of him as long as she was awake. But to have him materially there, to pass a plate to him, to take a teacup from his hand, to lose herself in watching his eyes . . . ! Nobody else had such eyes, so blue, so living, so *his!* Although she did her best to brace herself for the shock of their occasionally meeting hers it took her a long time to get her breath every time that miracle happened. In the interval when he was talking medicine with M'Sanna, she could just look at what she knew so well—his hands, his long-fingered strong hands with the adorably masculine hair on the backs. And his neck; once before she could stop herself she thought how that firm man's neck would look without the collar . . . and felt herself blushing wildly. She knew his voice from hearing it all day long in her memory—and all night too—yet to hear him actually talking always added something new to her treasure-store of remembered intonations and accents. At night she lay in her bed trying them over in her mind. "No, no, only one lump," or, "I begin to think there's something *to* old Doctor Neale's idea about the value of accumulated observations on angina." She did not hear the words, they served only to carry to her ear the dear voice she was learning by heart.

Miss Ingraham had no love for the voice to shut out the words. Yet she did not make much sense out of them. She had never understood Anna's brother, but she had never before thought him fitful and changeable. He certainly was in these days. Sometimes he seemed almost—incredible as that was—to find something he liked in Clifford life. This was mostly when he and Anna were talking about a suggestion made to him by that old doctor, grouchy old Caledonian, who had recently visited him. Miss Ingraham could not follow their technical talk, but she gathered that Doctor Neale had asked Anson to collect data from those of his patients who had bad hearts. She could not imagine why this should at times make

Anson better natured than he had been since he came back to Clifford to live. Nor why at other times he was preoccupied and touchy as the devil. Nor why he was occasionally swept by a mood of heightened vitality so that he stepped around light and quick on his feet like a man who is getting the best of a fight. Nor why he flared up over nothing at all. One evening, for instance, she chanced to mention that she was trying to teach a few manners to her Latin class as well as how to read Cæsar. "Manners!" cried Doctor Anson indignantly. "Manners! Trained dog tricks!" He illustrated what he meant by grotesque caricaturing gestures. "Taking hold of your napkin, so. Instead of so! Using a fork for this kind of food and a spoon for that kind and your fingers for something else! It's a crime to judge human beings by such nonsense! To think less of somebody with forty times more capacity for living than those who have been taught to balance the food on their noses and wait till somebody has said, 'One, two, three,' before they gulp it down . . . It's infamous! We ought to be ashamed of ourselves for having such standards. *Manners!* Vitality, beauty, courage, love, all nothing if you don't or do crook your little finger as you lift your cup."

Miss Ingraham's attempts had been directed towards preventing her class from trampling each other down at the doorway as they came in and restricting their sprawling legs enough so that she could walk down the aisle to the blackboard. But she did not explain this. Nobody knew, nobody ever would know or care, but the fact was that Miss Ingraham disliked Anson Craft as much as he did her, as much as she helplessly loved and admired Anson Craft's dear sister.

Anna too noticed that Anson seemed in a period of heightened awareness, but in those few days before Town Meeting she was for once too much absorbed by other things to focus her attention on Anson. It was not only the energetic—though now hopeless—campaigning for votes. Other things worried her. Isabel. She knew she had been wrong in yielding to Isabel's silent peremptory demand to be where she could see Anson often. The child should have gone

to her aunt's during the quarantine. She frightened Anna, sitting at the table as she did, smiling dreamily down at her plate or up at the ceiling, breaking her silence only to say, "Doctor Anson told me to telephone the Bacons about ten o'clock," or to ask, "Did you hear Doctor Anson say that a George Arliss film is coming to Ashley?" or, "M'Sanna, does Doctor Anson like blue or red better?" And one day, Miss Craft, called to the telephone, picked up a writing pad she had thought hers, to write down a message. When she turned back the cover she saw the first page all covered with "Anson, Anson, Anson" in Isabel's handwriting. Still . . . why not? Anson was paying more attention to her every day, and he acted almost as strung up and nervous as she. Wasn't that a good sign? Wasn't that the way young men act when they are falling in love? Miss Craft often succeeded in quieting herself with the thought, "It's probably just coming to a head between them." But an hour later she would avert her eyes, shocked by Isabel's tenseness of hope and fear as she waited to see whether Anson would sit down beside her on the sofa to finish his pipe, or choose the armchair at the other end of the room.

And this was not all. Something entirely different sprang up from another direction to disturb her. Two days before Town Meeting she went in to talk to Mr. Dewey about the best way to present her project. Not that she expected him to swerve a hair's breadth from the even-handedness as presiding officer that was part of his personal religion. But she knew the childless old man to have a deep concern for young people and thought he might suggest the right person to stand sponsor for her hopeless scheme. She put the matter before him as she changed the bandages on his injured leg, Don's anxious eyes following her every move. Mr. Dewey laid down a yellowed old map to listen. He had been employing his shut-in days by minute researches into the location of the first roads laid out in town. When she finished he asked, "How would Merrill Foote do? There's as few in town that have it in for him as for anybody, I should say. And Hilda's bein' in quarantine with the twins, he'll be let to do as he wants."

Yes, Miss Craft agreed, Doctor Foote would be the person.

The old man added in a kindly warning, "I hope you ain't lottin on that plan's gettin' many votes, Anna. A lot of people in this town—well, murder'd be no load on their minds compared to taxes."

"No, oh no," she told him, resignedly, standing up from the finished bandages, "but since I'd got started on it . . . It seemed like letting those back-roads families down, if I gave it up without at least trying."

He nodded and reached for his map. She turned towards the door to go. But, "Hold on, Anna," he called after her. "There's somethin' I've been wantin' to ask you. Do you know who Henry Twombley is?"

The name knocked at one and another door in Anna's memory, found the right one. "Oh, Henry Twombley!" she said, and sat down again. "What about him?"

"D'you ever happen to run into him up on Searles Shelf?"

She said cautiously, "He hasn't been at home when I was there. But I know his wife and children very well. I'm always having to look out for them. He's not a good provider."

"He's earned enough workin' for me winters in the woods to take good care of 'em if he'd a-wanted to. But he's regular Searles Shelf—half-hound, half-hunter, all Injun. Well, this winter he's been workin' some for Bessie'n'Gussie Kemp, splittin' their wood."

"I didn't know that."

"No harm in it s'long as he stuck to outside work. But since I been shut up here I hear their Noah has got the lumbago again, and this Twombley is doin' th' house chores, too. Well now, Bessie'n'Gussie probably don't know it—and I don't know whether you do—but Henry's reppitation for honesty—or anything else—ain't any too good, even up on Searles Shelf. He's all right in the woods, a nawful smart man with an ax or a rifle. But I wouldn't want him inside *my* house. And if he was, you bet I'd count the spoons night and mornin'. Kind of a rough customer, too. A mean temper. Now I don't believe in bein' prejudiced, I always tell folks I'd trust a good York Stater as quick as a white man, any day.

And I don't hold with talkin' behind people's backs. But Henry Twombley ain't reely the man a person'd want workin' for old ladies, one of'em sick and one of'em deef. I thought maybe it might be so that you could drop'em a word."

Miss Craft said, "It's hard to drop any words in Miss Gussie's poor ears. And Miss Bessie's still too sick to be bothered. But I'll go around there and see."

She found Miss Bessie still in bed, feeble, fretful, anxious—it was impossible to believe that Miss Bessie sick and Miss Bessie well were the same person. Lixlee was with her, noiselessly tidying up the sickroom. Miss Craft looked at the girl more intently than she had since the time, almost a year ago, when she had sat beside her on the running-board of the Ford and watched the birch trees helplessly shaken by the invisible onslaughts of the wind.

"How are you these days, Lixlee?" she asked, to have something to say and to make the girl look at her.

After a brief pause, "I'm very well, thanks, M'Sanna," said Lixlee, keeping her eyes on the oiled mop she was pushing back and forth, her slim body moving slowly and rhythmically in time with it.

"She's not so skinny as she was, is she?" said Miss Bessie. "You weigh a hundred and twenty now, don't you, Lixlee?"

As if wishing to be sure of her accuracy, the girl took a moment to think before answering, "A hundred and twenty-one, Miss Bessie."

"She made that dress she's got on herself," said Miss Bessie, with a teacher's pride in an apt pupil. "I was going to cut it out and let her do the puttin' together. But when I took sick she did it all. 'Tain't so bad. She don't look what you'd call ridiculous in it."

Lixlee smiled at this praise, enduring with composure the gaze of the two women on the plainly cut, well-made and very becoming green jersey.

Everything about her was different, was transformed, thought Miss Craft, the hoarseness of her voice cleared, her speech correct, her hair glossy as a black panther's pelt, her body filled out.

"Ain't you goin' to take my pulse, Anna?" asked Miss Bessie querulously. Miss Craft laid her fingers on the wrinkled wrist and restrained the start that Miss Bessie's strange pulse always gave her. She sat noting it, wondering how much longer the laboring old muscle could last, not paying much attention to the stream of complaints poured out by the patient—about Anson's failure to relieve her, although he came to see her so often, about Gussie's queer half-cracked notions, about the smoky chimney, about Lixlee's naughty refusal to use the glasses they had bought for her. "Doctor Bancroft said he could get that crossed eye of hers straightened out in a year's time if she'd wear his glasses faithful. But you know girls, there never was one of'em that wouldn't trade her soul's salvation for her looks. There! She ain't got'em on this minute. Lixlee, go get your glasses and let Miss Anna see'em."

The girl went out, silent in her felt-soled slippers. She had a very slow, graceful way of walking, thought the nurse. When she came in again, large horn-rimmed spectacles framed her eyes. Through them she looked steadily at the nurse. Yes, it was true. There was not the slightest obliquity in the dark gaze now.

"Yes, I see," said Miss Craft. She looked more intently, struck by the transformation of the girl's face, and exclaimed, "Isn't it strange how glasses can change a person! You look like somebody else in them, Lixlee. I don't mean they're unbecoming. They look very nice. Only they make you look different."

"She looks good in'em, *I* think," said Miss Bessie, "and they cost us eleven dollars. She'd ought to wear'em. But she leaves'em off half the time. And Gussie backs her up in it. Says whose eyes are they? There's times when Gussie acts real tiresome. She's got all of Aunt Mett's contrariness and some of her own to boot."

While she ran on from Gussie to other grievances, the nurse sat watching the girl's leisurely movements as she stooped to get her mop under the highboy, straightened up, reached for a duster, lifted a hand to her head to put back a lock of hair. She had a beautiful figure, soft, firm, supple and harmonious. Extraordinarily fine shoulders, a flexible round waist, the flowing lines from the waist to the knee unbroken and cleanly drawn. Strange, thought

the nurse, who knew the human body so well, knew how little one varies from another—strange the life-and-death difference made by a little more or less depth of chest, length of tibia, angle of neck. Items that meant nothing, nothing to health or strength, gave poor Cora a body that was a clumsy barrier between her and life, gave this girl one that held the eye like a work of art.

As if feeling the gaze on her, Lixlee looked up at her through the round rim of the glasses, a straight, quiet, school-girl's glance, that made Miss Craft think, "Why, the thing to do is simply to ask Lixlee herself if this man is the same one—and if she is troubled by his being here."

Miss Bessie, rolling over like a restless behemoth, caught sight of her face in the mirror across the room. "Mercy on us!" she said, anxiously, "I must have a fever again. My face is as red as a spanked bottom. Lixlee, go get me a glass of water and those blue pills the doctor left."

The girl walked from the room.

"You really like Lixlee, don't you, Miss Bessie?" asked the nurse.

"Well . . . yes," said the old woman. She explained her grudging accent. "She's awful still!"

"I shouldn't think you'd mind that," said Miss Craft. "You wouldn't like it if she were noisy."

"Well, I like folks to holler and fly off the handle once in a while. That's nater. When they don't, how is anybody a-goin' to know what they're thinkin' about?" said Miss Bessie, fretfully. There was no pleasing her when she was sick.

Lixlee came back with the water and bent over the invalid, presenting her profile to Miss Craft. She had taken off her glasses. Something in the closed expression of the quiet young face made Miss Craft decide on an impulse, "No, I don't believe I'll say anything to her—yet. Not till I know something more about it."

She went downstairs, thinking, "Of course there is still Miss Gussie." But how could the gulf of deafness be crossed by the light, casual tone that would be the only prudent one in which to ask, "You haven't noticed anything special about this man who has been splitting your wood—and your hired girl, have you?"

And even if she could have reached Miss Gussie, the deaf woman would have been the last person to have guessed at anything under the surface, she who never knew what was happening in plain sight till somebody had shouted it in her ear.

She let herself out of the side door and was halted by the display of well-split and well-piled firewood, filling the semi-circular opening of the woodshed. She looked at it hard, and away from it up at Hemlock Mountain. She had half a mind to drive to Searles Shelf this minute, and have a talk with Mrs. Twombley. After all, having placed the girl here, she was in a way responsible for her welfare and safety. But the snow was still formidably deep on the mountain roads and Mrs. Twombley, she remembered, was not only a fool, but one of those hostile to the nursing service and to her. In half an hour she was due at the office of old Mr. Warren, owner of the Warren textile mills, an important person and large taxpayer, for whose vote and influence she meant to make a try.

"I'll just wait till after the seventh," she thought, moving on, "and then really look into this."

This was the fifth. In a mere couple of days what harm could come to anyone in a place like Clifford, where even the smallest event took so long to happen?

And now it was the day before Town Meeting, the 6th of March, and a marvelous great thaw, such as often comes about this time. All at once the rigors of winter dissolved. The sun shone. There was not a breath of wind. Where for months icicles had hung glittering, drops of water now fell gladly, splashing up from pools of melted snow. The Street was awash. Every passing car threw up plumes of jeweled spray. After the first appraising morning look out of the window, people kicked overshoes into corners and rummaged in under-stairs closets for rubber boots. Over the party telephone lines reports came in that as usual Crazy Brook was rising out of bounds. The Necronsett was already brimming

over the lower meadows. If any one of the summer people had come up from the city that day (but of course none of them ever did) The Street and The Valley would have startled him—fresh from walking dry-shod on dusty pavements—by its grimly enduring wintriness. But Clifford people basked in a summery relaxation more authentic than anything felt in Italy or California. Looking up at Hemlock Mountain from his bedroom window, Mr. Dewey thought, "Well, nobody need to try to tell me the Lord didn't make a go of it."

Of course life went on, even though men stopped, their rubber-booted feet in ice water, and took off their fur caps to feel the sun on their bare heads; even though women, out to sweep their porches, only leaned on their brooms and gazed into vacancy. Life went on and everybody continued to act in obedience to the laws of his nature. Mrs. Foote was happy in facing an adversary after her own heart, concrete and actual, who could be measured with mercury in a glass tube and fought with ten strong fingers. Lawrence Stewart had a slight rise of temperature from joy when he found on the margin of the border of the sacred paper, the name and address of the manufacturer in France. Henrietta's kittens were imminent and she knew it with the calm sense of power she had at such times. She knew that if she wished and so decided, she would, in spite of anybody, have them in the middle of the silk spread on her spare-room bed—which indeed, that year, she did. Miss Bessie Kemp kept her deaf, stiff old sister and her supple young attendant running up and down stairs on errands she invented to keep away the thoughts that stood coldly by her bed when the room was quiet. Sherwin Dewey tried out his bad leg by walking for the first time to the Post Office and joining in the conversation there as people waited for the mail. Lawrence Stewart was talking big about foreign parts he'd lived in. The mail was late. He had time to say a good deal. Finally, in his quick, high voice, Mr. Dewey remarked, "Yes, Switzerland's all right I guess. Kind of an imitation of Vermont, I take it, from what I hear," and turned away to smile mischievously at the executors' notice tacked on the wall.

But that was on the surface. His thoughts were really all on the duties and responsibilities of the next day. When facing the hundreds of standing men, roughly and well clad, poor and prosperous, old and young, he stood up on the platform of the Town Hall assembly room and called the meeting to order, he was vowed as solemnly to fair play as any priest to his God. To deserve the confidence in his impartiality felt by every one of those serious citizens looking up at him gravely as with the knock of his gavel they all addressed themselves to the work of self-government—that was a goal that gave life a meaning to Sherwin Dewey. For him, on the day before March Meeting, life ran deep and still.

The three women living in the Craft house got through the day on their three different formulæ; Isabel's, "He will be here at five and if I pray to God very hard, he will perhaps stay to supper." Miss Ingraham's, "Only one more day and it will be over—poor Anna!" Miss Craft's, "I was a fool to start it. I am always being a fool. It will be worse for the Rollinses and all of them, than if they had never had it to hope for. This time tomorrow I'll be ashamed to look any of those poor people in the face. And maybe I'll have given a black eye to the whole system of district nursing."

Father Kirby was, though nobody noticed it, in St. Andrew's a good deal that day, praying. Late in the afternoon, he came out and walked resolutely around to the Town Hall to Miss Craft's office. She looked up at him rather blindly from the card catalogue of voters she had arranged in three boxes, "for," "against," and "unknown." The "for" box, its cards leaning wanly against each other, had a hang-dog look compared to the "against" box, so well filled that the cards held each other up, straight, firm and sure of themselves, like all majorities.

"Oh, Fred," she said, very glad to see him, and forgetting the careful "Father Kirby" with which she occasionally remembered to indulge his ideas. "I haven't canvassed you yet. Can I count on you tomorrow?" Remembering his notorious absence of mind, she thought it prudent to add, "You know, Town Meeting and my . . ."

"Yes, Anna," he broke in, taking off his flat-brimmed black hat and sitting down, "you can count on me."

She shifted a card from one box to another, and looked back at him to see what he wanted. Apparently he did not know very well what it was himself.

After a moment, "Was there something special?" she asked.

"Yes," he said, "there was." But he did not get on to it.

She waited, looking at him, at the unsightly scarred face so familiar to her, at the sensitive, thin lips, at the gray eyes set far back under the strong arched bone of the sockets. She remembered from her childhood the shadowed look of his eyes.

After a time he shook his head in a helpless gesture and reached for his hat. "It's no good," he said in a low voice, "I never can say anything."

Anna took it from this that what he had wanted to say was something mystical. Everybody knew that he could speak with ordinary fluency about ordinary matters but fell into stammering incoherence whenever he tried to bring into words something of what (people supposed when they thought about it) filled the long hours he spent on his knees. "Let the Reverend Kirby get started talking about God," the local saying ran, "and there's no actor living that can give you a better imitation of a man that's had too much booze." Anna Craft's every thought had been for weeks centered on the hopeless charge she was to lead the next day at Town Meeting. And for years she had braced herself with a mixture of sorrow and exasperation against the inexplicable religious fervor of her old friend which, ever since they had grown up, had set a gulf between them. She was too tired to make the effort with which she usually met such moments, of transferring herself into another's personality; and in the case of Fred Kirby, his sincerity made her uneasily aware of an element of duplicity in that technique. She sat silent, pale, rather forbidding, looking down at her voter cards.

"It's about Anson," said the clergyman.

Anna's face softened. Her eyes made their never-failing response to her brother's name. She pushed back the card catalogue and turned her chair to face the other who was looking at her wistfully.

He dropped his shadowed eyes from hers at once, opened and closed a thin hand, opened it again and began to speak.

It was no better than ever. He plunged forward, halted, gave that sentence up and went back to the beginning, and was no more clear at the end of the second or third attempt. But he had something to say about Anson. Anson's sister patiently gave him her whole attention.

Presently from among his false starts and impatiently abandoned beginnings a phrase pierced home, ". . . you keep thinking that it is something in *you* that Anson hates and fights against, but . . ."

She shrank back, wincing. Used as she was to Fred's intermittent shafts of divination, it astonished and shocked her that his eyes had pierced to what she had thought her most secret and hidden pain.

He probed again to the quick. "Why always bring yourself into it, Anna! If you could stop that, you might guess that perhaps it isn't all hatefulness in Anson, that perhaps it is despair . . ."

"Despair!" she exclaimed, astonished at the book-word stalking with its tragic mien into ordinary talk.

"Yes, despair. Remember, this is the first sight Anson has had of what living is. He's been a—he's been in the ante-room till now— a student, though a grown man. Yes, yes, Anna, Clifford, our poor Clifford, represents human life for him. And of course he's right. That's what it is. But he sees only one side . . . the outside. What shows to the eye. He thinks that's all there is. And he can't stand it. He can't stand it, do you understand!" Seeing from her bewildered look that she did not understand, he burst out, his deep voice trembling as if in reproach, "Oh, Anna, he's right. Anybody who thinks that's all and *can* stand it, is rotting on his feet, dead to . . ."

Anna knew that he checked himself before saying, ". . . dead to God!"

There was a silence while he struggled for breath. Waiting for him to go on, she drew her eyebrows together, trying to collect herself to see if there might be something she could recognize as true—for her—under the religious phraseology that always made her sure beforehand there wasn't.

The clergyman began, more quietly, "Can't you see, Anna, he must protest against anything you say, anybody says, that seems to show satisfaction, that isn't an echo of his own horrified discovery of the wrongness and stupidity and cowardice everywhere? You're always putting yourself in other people's places . . . can't you put yourself in his for an instant? You'll see that every time you call his attention to something he might like, you look to him as if you were pretending that everything is all right, when he knows that it is not. See here, Anna, if he thinks that of us, you wouldn't *want* him not to be loud and angry with us, would you?"

Her eyes fixed on his, Anna was making as great an effort to follow as he to speak. She felt now, dimly, that there was an idea for her behind his words. It was not in the language in which her own ideas came and went through the doors of her mind. But it was there, halting and fumbling with locks it had no keys for. If only she could let it in. . . . No one but Fred ever came so near as that to entering her inner life. She forgot to resist the organ tones of his voice, to suspect that they wrapped a richness around his words beyond their meaning. For an instant she forgot the gulf between them.

He said now urgently, imperatively, "And you are just mistaken in thinking that you can cope with all that happens to human beings by practicing the ant qualities of patience and ingenuity. There come times, Anna, when nothing but the great spiritual forces . . ."

She took him to mean membership in his Church. The gulf between them yawned wide. She turned cold. He was always failing her like that.

He felt her withdrawing, and stopped. Drops of sweat stood on his forehead. He fumbled in his pockets for a handkerchief and found none. Anna silently took out a clean one from a drawer in her desk. He passed it over his face, haggard now with his struggle to find the right words.

The ones he now found were by no means the right ones for his listener. "But that horror with what the eye sees in material life is what we must all go through with, if we . . . It *takes* anguish,

Anna, it takes despair with the dreadful surface of things, to turn a man away from it to the depths, to the inner life where the only splendor is to be found . . . to turn a man to . . ."

This time Anna mechanically completed the sentence, ". . . to God."

But he was not taken in. *"Stop that!"* he cried, in angry rebuke, and gave it all up, rising and making for the door.

She asked of his back, "But, Fred, you say everybody goes through such doubt. You never did, certainly? I thought your faith had always been . . ."

He turned around, presenting his defaced blue-scarred cheek and eyelid full to the light. He did not hesitate or stammer as he answered her. It was no lofty new conception he was bringing into words, only an old sadness as familiar to him as his hand. "Why, Anna, when was there ever a moment from the day of my birth," he asked her steadily, "when the surface of life could tempt *me,* when it could bring me anything but horror? You know what people say of me—that a man so mutilated is good for nothing but religion. . . ." (So he knew they said that!) "They think that shows up what religion is. Of course it only shows up their own poor ideas. The truth is that every infirmity is the savage benediction of the dark angel at the ford. Why isn't it a blessing to be forced to turn to God's love by being cut off from human . . ." But he had overestimated his strength. From one word to the next his voice failed him. ". . . from human . . . affection . . ." He stopped, catching his upper lip in his teeth, his mouth compressed into a line of helpless pain. Before Anna could stir, he had gone.

She was swept out of her own suffering, filled with horrified sympathy for his. But in the upper layer of her brain, colored with the condescension the irreligious person feels for the believer, was the thought, "Yes, yes, of course, such people could not live without religion."

He came rapidly back up the corridor, and stood in the door. "Anna, I know what you're thinking. It's what you always think. It's what you use to shut me out with, whenever I try to say anything to you. You think I'm talking about . . . you think I can't

talk about anything but the Church, dogma, the Holy Trinity, the sacraments—what you insist on thinking is all there is to religion for me. No! No! No! What I'm trying to talk about is the search for life. For Life! And whether you know it or not, that's what Anson's searching for!" He spoke with passion. With authority. His deep voice filled the room. With three long steps he was towering over her desk. "Anna, you think religion is what's inside a little building filled with pretty lights from stained glass windows! But it's not." He flung up his arm. "It's wings! *Wings!*"

This time he did not come back. Anna sat staring at the open door, her nerves still shaken by the echoes of his voice.

She sat thus a long time. She had the sensation of thinking deeply but she could not have told of what. If anyone had asked her suddenly where she was, she could not for an instant have answered. Presently her hand, wandering aimlessly among the papers on her desk, fell on her card catalogue of voters. She pulled it mechanically to her. But when she saw what it was, she gave an exclamation of astonishment to see how different it looked, how shrunken from the daunting pile that half an hour ago had hid the rest of the world from her. "It's always so. I never have the least idea what Fred is talking about. Yet . . ."

Her eyes fell on the clock, and she sprang up. It was long after five. Wasn't there some special reason for seeing Anson before he went back to Ashley? What had it been? Oh, yes, the warning Mr. Dewey had given her. Anson, coming and going professionally in the Kemp house, was, of course (till she could really go into the matter herself), the right person to whom to pass that along.

She found him still in his office, but could not then repeat what Mr. Dewey had said because Isabel was there, competently clearing away the litter left from making a plaster cast for a broken arm. Young as she was, she really would, thought Miss Craft, make a fine helpmate for a country doctor. And it began to look as though a country doctor would marry her. "Propinquity does it" runs the proverb. Since the quarantine at the Foote house, there had been no lack of propinquity between Anson and Isabel. She looked at the two young people now, standing close to each other, looking

into each other's eyes as they talked. The last three weeks had taken them far along the road of intimacy.

Anson turned, took up his medicine case, stopped by the door and said earnestly to Isabel, "If that Pulaski child's temperature doesn't go down, you'd better telephone me." He added, "I know I can depend on you to remember."

"They sound," thought the nurse with the naïveté of the celibate, "almost as though they were already married."

She followed her brother out to his car. Although Hemlock Mountain had hid the sun from The Street for more than an hour, the thermometer was still above freezing—miraculous to have that dripping mildness continue even after sunset! The swimming softness of the air did nothing to rouse Anna from the mood in which Fred Kirby had left her. She continued to float in the vague remoteness from what she thought of as "real life" which often followed one of his futile attempts to take her with him into what was for him real life. It had shrunk her array of hostile voters from being bulkier than Old Hemlock, back to being only a card catalogue. Enough of it still hung in the air so that Anson too looked different to her.

He reached into his car to turn on the headlights. One of them was blank. With a murmured word of impatience he lifted the hood and began to tinker with the wires. Anna thought it safer to wait till he had finished before speaking to him, and sat down on the marble mounting block, left over from the horse age. From under the piles of snow shrinking all around her, trickled the liquid song of winter melting gladly into spring. As it flowed over her loosened nerves, she mused, "I sort of see what Fred means about Anson."

The reflections of the sunset, hanging in the eastern sky over The Wall, faded from misty pink to the misty blue of twilight that came drifting down off the mountain towards the valley. Dreamily the nurse thought, "How could I have taken it for nothing but nervous irritability? Or for just disapproval of *me*."

Dusk, floating down the street like a blue veil, fell about her, blurring the visible world to dimness. She told herself, "Fred is

right. I've been awfully personal about Anson. But I shall know how to do better now. I shall understand. Somehow, Fred's got the clew over to me."

The headlights, both of them, flared up yellowly. Anson shut down the hood and got into the car. His sister called, "Wait a minute. There was something I wanted to ask." But she had been so far away that for an instant she could not remember. Coming up close to the side of the car she could make out that Anson was leaning forward, one hand ready to turn on the switch. He waited, looking expectantly towards her.

"What *was* it?" she asked herself aloud, and then, "Oh, yes, I remember! Nothing important. I just wish you'd notice when you go in to see Miss Bessie, whether the man that's working for them is around inside the house very much. And whether there seems to be any special—well, familiarity, or understanding between him and—"

"Old Noah Haskins?" asked Anson, surprised.

"No. No, of course not. Since he's been sick they have somebody else, I hear, a man from Searles Shelf."

"I didn't know that," said Doctor Craft. He dropped his hand from the switch.

Twilight had deepened so that he was only a blur to his sister's eyes, but something about his attitude made her uneasy. Was he restraining his impatience at being bothered with trivial details that were not part of his work? She told him hastily and baldly what Mr. Dewey had said to her, adding, "But Mr. Dewey doesn't know the real point. That girl who is working for the old ladies, well, she and this Henry Twombley certainly knew each other very well and perhaps more than that, while she was still living up on Searles Shelf. It was one of the things they all had against her, her turning a married man's head so. Mr. Dewey's news gave me rather a turn. And I thought to myself it wasn't the Kemp spoons he was after. I don't suppose there's anything to worry about. But of course I really don't know much about that girl. And Miss Bessie'n'Gussie are too old to have anything unpleasant happen in their house. And I'm responsible for the girl's being with them.

If Miss Bessie were well, I'd tell her and she'd send the man packing. But Miss Gussie always gets everything mixed up. You haven't happened to hear Miss Bessie or the girl—or any of them—say anything about him, have you?"

"No," said Doctor Craft, sitting still in the dusk.

"Well, don't take any special trouble about it, but the next time you go there just have it in mind, will you?" said Anna, stepping back from the car to the sidewalk.

"Yes," answered her brother, leaning forward to turn on the switch.

Through the noise of the starter the nurse called, "See you tomorrow at Town Meeting."

But the car leaped forward suddenly, and to this last Doctor Craft made no answer.

8

B EFORE Town Meeting is called to order, the Town Hall is like a beehive. From whichever direction you approach it you can hear the loud hum the minute you turn into The Street especially if, as happened that year, there has been in the night a fall of soft late "sugar snow" to deaden the sound of cars and horses' hoofs. And though from afar it is nothing but a toneless buzzing, almost like something inside your head, you know from past years as if you heard the separate voices and words, what is being said. Still out in The Street trying to find a place to park or hitch, throwing a blanket over your horse or the radiator of your car, you know that the simple and earnest many are discussing conscientiously the pros and cons of the items in this year's Warning for Town Meeting; you know that the slick few are silently moving from group to group, listening to the serious people giving themselves away, making up their minds whose interests to play off against whose, so they can get what they want.

Town Meeting being the one great gathering of the year, there was always, of course, some ordinary news-talk mixed in with arguments. But not much. Gossip and personal news was left mostly

to the few women who since woman suffrage attended Town Meeting. Women did not yet seem to appreciate the stark fact that the votes that day decided what the town taxes would be for the year to come. Mostly the deep-voiced men's talk that murmured in your ear from the end of The Street, hummed loudly from every window of the Town Hall as you started up the front steps, and roared like the river in flood time when you pushed open the swinging doors and went in, was of a lofty impersonality. Bridges, roads, schools, the care of the poor, of the insane, all the heavy burdens of collective life were faced that day. The talk was always grave with responsibility, and often anxious with care. For, though this particular Meeting took place at the climax of a period of hysterical prosperity elsewhere in the Union, times are (relatively speaking) always hard in Clifford, cash is always scarce, the margin of existence always narrow, taxes always too high for incomes, living up to one's civic responsibilities always painful. There is some laughing and joking at Town Meeting, it is true, but strictly confined to the irresponsible poor, those whose empty pockets allow them to sing as they cross the dark plains of life, those who, because they have no possessions, have no taxes to pay except the annual two dollar poll tax. This is their day, the one day when they are at an advantage over the thrifty. A vote from a Clifford Four Corners man counts just as much as the vote of the owner of the woolen mills. This is the day when prosperous people seek poor men out, talk to them—man to man, appeal to their well-known intelligence to vote against the folly of spending any more tax money to mend the road up Dowling Hollow, or to put more windows in the East District schoolhouse. Serious arguments presented reasonably, democratically, by the well-to-do voter trying not to see the satiric glint in the poor man's eye. Yes, the few guffaws and high-spirited back slappings on Town Meeting Day come from poll-tax payers alone.

Knowing the battle that was before them at Town Meeting that year, everybody had expected to hear the distant buzzing of talk even louder than usual. And so it was. Farmers from The Other Side, in good-looking overcoats, steering their well-washed automobiles around places where last night's fall of snow had been

churned into muddy pools, heard the hum of voices above the accurate burr of their well-oiled engines, and braced themselves to defend their bank accounts with courage. The proletariat, French Canadians and Polish, from the textile mills and wood-working shops, splashing on foot up Depot Hill through the slush, heard it and with the defeated fatalism of wage-earners brought up in a tradition of poverty and oppression, thought, "It's no use. We might as well turn around now and go home." Poor farmers in worn sheepskin-lined coats, driving aged Fords or slow farm wagons drawn by winter-shaggy work horses, heard it, tightened their already tight lips and looked disagreeably down jutting Yankee noses, coldly determined not to give up till long after they had been beaten. The irresponsible sub-normals trickling in from Clifford Four Corners and the slum part of town near the Depot called "Mississippi" heard it and their dull eyes brightened a little with the prospect of something interesting that they could understand, namely a fight. Desperately for, firmly against and dully indifferent to M'Sanna's project, the voters of Clifford moved towards the Town Hall.

From the corner by Depot Hill it looked just as usual on March Meeting Day. Up and down The Street the cars and farm wagons stood thickly parked, and the sidewalks were filled with people moving in one direction. As you came closer, you could see that, as always happened before the Moderator called the Meeting to order, people had overflowed from the tightly packed assembly room upstairs, and had come down to stand around in groups on the steps outside, on the walk, and on the trodden-down new snow that covered the piles of left-over winter, shoveled from the side-walks in February.

But they didn't, as you came quite close, and could see their faces, they didn't look at all as they usually did. Everybody seemed to be talking at once, loudly, excitedly, and yet asking questions of his neighbors too. Arms were being waved, fingers pointed down the street, heads craned after them. Something had happened. You hurried your steps to join them, but before you could open your mouth to ask, "What is it? Whatever in the world is the matter?"

there was a rush towards you, and everybody was asking you, "Have you heard . . . ?" "Do you know . . . ?" "Ain't nobody told you . . . ?" And before you had even begun to take in the sense of the incredible words they flung at you, "Shot!" "Doctor Craft!" "Last night!" they had turned from you in a rush to the next newcomer, and were shouting at him, "Have you heard . . . ?" "Do you know . . . ?" "Ain't the folks down your way heard . . . ?"

Most of the people arriving from the country had heard not a word, and the few who had, had caught but incredible distorted bits relayed over party telephone lines. To the hail of questions most of them returned a startled, "No! What?" "What tell?" the foot up-raised to mount the steps halted in mid-air.

They got it then in excited exclamations, "What? Hadn't ye heard Doctor Craft was shot last night?" "Two o'clock in the morning." "And a Searles Shelf girl too." "Both dying." "In Miss Bessie'n'Gussie's house." "Both dead." "In her room." "No, not dead yet." "Their hired girl." "Not so bad, broken her shoulder and his arm." "No, it went through his lung and into her shoulder near the collar bone. . . ." "The jug'lar vein. . . ." "No, not that vein, at all, 'twas . . ."

The newcomer was usually too stunned to do more than gape, his jaw dropped, his eyes unable to believe that the excited faces before him were real, his ears unable to take in the inexplicable words they seemed to hear. He had breath for no more than to repeat inanely a phrase or two of what had been hurled at him. "In Miss Bessie'n'Gussie's house?" "Shot?" "Last night?" Two or three added, almost coherently, the question that had no answer, "But why should anybody want to shoot Doctor Craft?" One, in the first staggered innocence of his astonishment, asked, "But whatever was he doing in her room at two o'clock in the morning?" Several said, their minds foolishly catching on the unimportant item, "But I didn't know Miss Bessie'n'Gussie *had* a hired girl from . . ." And two or three, before they had time to remember that the hunting season had been over for weeks, brought out mechanically,

"Spent ball?" In deer week this was the first thought of Clifford people about stray bullets.

A fresh hail of exclamation bore down this question, "No! No! No, *sir!* No spent ball! Fired from close. A hole in the window drilled as clean as you could ha' cut it." "Must ha' been fired from the woodshed roof, you can see into that room from there." "No, no tracks—nothing—no sign, anywhere—this snow must ha' been falling then and covered everything. No hide or hair of a track left."

They drank in greedily the dazed stupefaction of each newcomer's face for in it they lived over again the raw intensity of their own first shock. It was again new to them, as it had been an hour before, incredible, high-powered, prodigious. Drama. To the faltering questions put by the newcomers, "But who . . . what happened . . . did somebody . . . ?" everybody answered, all talking at once, "*He* was knocked out—never knew a thing after the shot— *she* tried to bring him to, without telling anybody. But the old ladies—Miss Bessie—heard the shot and ran up to . . ."

"Miss Bessie was sick! She couldn't get up out of bed to . . ."

"Not now she ain't sick! You just try to get near the house. She's out of bed now all right. Not sick enough to make it safe for anybody to . . ."

"They called M'Sanna on the phone. . . . The ambulance . . . The hospital . . ."

But usually by this time, some new person was approaching, tramping unconsciously through the soggy snow, and with the recent newcomers with them they all turned to fell him with "Ain't ye heard? Hasn't anybody told you?" They were between hopes that he had heard nothing so that through him they could once more live through that first frantic exquisitely staggering excitement, and hopes that somehow he might have heard, might have noticed, might have guessed the missing parts of the story, without which the part they knew made no sense. A good many of those who came latest had heard, but only grotesque incredible fragments, not to be believed till contact with a crowd brought into play collective credulity that can believe anything.

Finally just before the bell from St. Andrew's tower struck ten,

sending them indoors for business, a new light was cast over it all. Pete Danby, Jo's brother, the garage mechanic, drove up in the good car the garage used for taxi service. But when he got out, he was in his oil-stained work clothes, as if he had been hurriedly summoned to be driver. His face was full of shocked, pleasurable importance. They crowded towards him as he approached, holding their breaths to hear what he had learned. He said in a rich, dark, secret voice, as if at a funeral, "I took the Reverend Kirby an hour ago up to the hospital—hurry call."

"Dying?" asked one of the tall big-boned men crowding around him, craning their necks to catch his words.

"Married," he said. And added, "Maybe dying, too. I didn't hear. I guess likely."

Ten o'clock began to sound from St. Andrew's tower. Another car drove up. The district nurse's Ford. She and Mr. Kirby got out and came up the walk towards the front door. The crowd fell back silently and let them pass, their eyes on Miss Craft's pale stern face. Mr. Kirby went on up the stairs to the assembly room. Miss Craft let herself into her office and closed the door. The men waited a moment, drew long breaths and without another word trooped heavy-booted up the stairs.

Inside her office, Miss Craft stood motionless in front of her closed door, her white face expressionless. Her eyes were dry and widely open. With a mechanical gesture she lifted one arm to her head and took off her hat, showing her red hair ruffled and disordered. Her arm dropped to her side, the hat dropped from her hand to the floor. She continued to look straight ahead of her at a point on the blank wall opposite her as if she expected something to appear there.

But it was from the direction of the back room that there came now a faint sound. She stepped stiffly to that door and pushed it open. There on a pile of old blankets crouched Isabel Foote. Their eyes met. From Isabel's expression it was plain that Miss Craft was the person she had expected to see when the door opened. From

Miss Craft's astounded look, it was plain that she had forgotten that such a person as Isabel existed.

The girl stood up and said in a whisper, "I had to come in here, M'Sanna. It's the only place where I could be by myself—if you'll just let me stay for a while, till I . . . M'Sanna, I *had* to come! I'm —I'm all right, M'Sanna, except that I'm cold! I can't get warm. But I don't feel anything at all, really, M'Sanna, not anything. If I could only get warm, I . . . I . . . would be all right." She tried to smile, and at that smile Miss Craft sank, sank where she stood and laying her head on her knees broke into dreadful tears.

The girl came quickly to stand by her, to kneel beside her, putting her arm timidly around her, saying in a trembling voice, "Yes, I know it's terrible for you! Harder for you than for . . . for anybody else. You mustn't think of me, M'Sanna. I'm . . . I'll be all right. Don't cry so, M'Sanna! I don't feel anything. Not anything at all. Except that I can't seem to . . . seem . . . to . . . get warm. Don't feel badly for me, M'Sanna. I'm so sorry about it for you. M'Sanna, you mustn't cry like that. M'Sanna, it will kill you to cry so."

But Miss Craft could not stop crying, could not get her breath. She was strangled, suffocated with weeping. The frightened girl ran for a glass of water, knelt beside her again, called to her, shook her gently, shook her harder, tried to take her in her arms. Miss Craft did not resist her. It was as if she did not know that another person was there. Isabel stood up, started towards the door, stopped, stood still and wrung her hands. The desperate choking sobs from Miss Craft went on. She ran out into the deserted vestibule and up the stairs to the assembly room, and stood there before the swinging doors, trembling, her teeth chattering. A vote was being taken. She heard the Moderator say crisply, "All in favor of this motion signify it in the usual way by saying 'Aye.'" A few scattering "Ayes" followed. "All opposed . . ." A deep roll of "No" shook the door on which she had just put her hand to push it open. Her hand dropped from the door as though it had been struck down.

In a panic she tiptoed away, ran wildly down the stairs and to the front door to look up and down The Street for help. No one

was in sight. Steps behind her. Father Kirby was coming down the
stairs. She flew to him, catching at his hand with icy fingers. He
listened unsurprised to what she told him in broken whispers, his
shadowed eyes dark. She tried to pull him towards Miss Craft's
office but he shook her off and stood for an instant, his gaze turned
deeply inward. Then making the sign of the cross widely from
forehead to breast, he turned back up the stairs and vanished inside
the swinging doors. When he came out, he ran down past Isabel
to Miss Craft's office, went in and bent over her where she had
sunk, where she lay, undone with weeping.

He said clearly, "Anna, Doctor Foote is just presenting your
plan to the Meeting," and waited a moment. Her sobs stopped.
She sat motionless, her head on her knees. He put his hand out as
if to lay it on her shoulder, drew it back, and said, "I don't suppose
you feel you can go up to speak for it . . . now."

She lifted her head. She got to her feet in one movement. She
said angrily, "What do you mean! Of course I can." Without a
look at him, without so much as raising her hand to wipe off the
tears glazing her cheeks, she walked rapidly past him, past Isabel
as if she did not see her, up the stairs and through the swinging
doors.

The standing men were crowded closely together, their eyes fixed
on Doctor Foote who was just finishing speaking. The ones nearest
the door felt her hand pushing them aside. They turned their heads,
gave one look at her face and started back, making a lane for her
to pass. Mr. Dewey on the platform saw her and held up his hand
for quiet.

In an intense silence she walked rapidly forward till she stood
before the platform, asked the Moderator with her eyes for permis-
sion to speak, turned and faced the crowd. She spoke to them in her
usual voice, just as she had spoken many times to every one of them.
They saw her, pale, her red hair disordered, unconscious of herself,
just as many times they had all seen her in their own homes, exhausted after a night's battle with death for one of their children,
one of their old people. But now they saw her as none of them had

ever seen her before, not once, deeply marked by suffering and pain that was not theirs but hers.

Reeling before their eyes in what they knew to be the ruin of her own life, she summoned all her authority to speak for the poorer children of town. She did not plead their cause. She would have scorned to plead a cause so righteous. Disfigured with weeping, her eyes red and swollen with tears, she but stated their cause, with a deeply moved sense of its dignity. She described her plan in full, and stated dryly and unflinchingly the amount of money that would be needed to cover the budget as she had it made out. She went on to what was evidently to be her statement of the principle involved, "You'll hear people say because the Academy is more than a High School, gives some higher teaching that is like a college, that it's too much to provide for poor folks' children. But it is exactly because their parents haven't the money to . . ."

The telephone on the platform rang sharply. It might be, and they all knew it, the announcement of her brother's death. She was silent, turning her white face towards the man who tiptoed across the platform to answer. As she waited, all those eyes hypnotically fixed on her perceived that her lips and chin were trembling uncontrollably. In the silence, they understood for the first time what had happened. It moved from the plane of abstract drama into reality, away from their startled nerves into their hearts. This was not something that had happened in a movie, in a book. It was M'Sanna's brother who lay at the point of death, the brother for whom she had always lived.

The man at the telephone turned away, hanging up the receiver, motioning to them, "No. Nothing. A mistake. Not for here."

Immediately the ardent, urgent, so-familiar voice went on. . . . "That is, of course, the very reason why they need a better preparation for life than we've provided for them up to now. That's why they need the best we can give them." She gathered herself together, her eyes burning. *"Don't dare think of this as charity!* Or let anyone else call it charity. Its name is decency. This would not be a *gift* to the young people it would benefit. It would be an opportunity they have deserved by being born Americans. Every American,

every Vermonter, every Clifford man, should feel ashamed that any man's children have less of a chance—a *chance,* that's all this is—than his own."

She leaned against the platform, spent, and nodded to the Moderator that she had done.

Mr. Dewey looked over the dense crowd of men, standing now so motionless, their serious lean faces turned towards his. He asked gravely, "Is there any discussion of this motion?"

There was not a sound. Not a move. His eye went from one to another, received the same message from all. "If there is no discussion," said the Moderator, "I shall put the question."

He paused. Those hundreds of living breathing human beings stood rock-still, granite-silent.

"All those in favor of this motion signify it in the usual way by saying 'Aye.'"

The windowpanes shook and rattled in the rolling thunder that followed.

"Those opposed—?"

Silence filled the room till there was scarcely air to breathe.

Mr. Dewey said quietly, "The 'Ayes' have it."

PART THREE

1

THE FIRST reaction of Clifford people to Doctor Anson's marriage and all that went with it was a reflex group response such as follows an earthquake or flood—something that happens to all as much as to one. No matter what their individual temperaments, they all cried out the same things when they talked, held their tongues by instinct on the same occasions. For, of course, even the children knew enough to shut their mouths during the few days when detectives, newspaper reporters and other prying outsiders were around, vainly looking for clews. And naturally when M'Sanna was in earshot their sympathy for her showed itself in a decent silence. In a language more expressive than that of their threadbare words, Clifford had told M'Sanna that it knew what she was, honored her for it, and stood staunchly back of her in her trouble. Every man of them in the Town Hall had poured out and held to her lips a full draught of brotherly sympathy knowing that it would cost a price, willing to pay. When they spoke of her brother to her now it was only to ask, "How's Doctor Anson gittin' along?" To which according to the news from the hospital Miss Craft answered, "The doctors say he has a chance now." "Not so well to-day." "Very bad, another hemorrhage." "Very low again from loss of blood." "No worse," and then after weeks of ups and downs, "Better." "Better." "Really gaining."

This silence in her presence about what in her absence was the subject of everybody's talk was decreed by an old local tradition. Summer people ignorant of this as of all other local traditions often shocked Clifford by being so full of the wish to express themselves

and to make their presence felt that instead of showing their reverence for sorrow by silent, self-sacrificing action, they blundered ahead into speech, pouring upon surfaces too raw for the lightest touch, the wordy sympathy that cost them nothing.

On the other hand, with an instinctive delicacy that would have astonished the summer people used to thinking of Clifford natives as anything but delicate in human relations, people went out of their way to make natural-sounding comments to Isabel Foote. "Whatever *do* you suppose possessed the doctor?" "The sheriff says he can't come across the least thing to show who did it." "Well, they say *she's* out of danger now. Whether that's good news or not remains to be seen." "Tom Merrill says he thinks it *must* have been a spent ball. Some fool boy tinkerin' with his father's rifle. Who would ha' wanted to shoot Doctor Anson?" To have preserved with her the same conscious silence as with M'Sanna would have been to recognize publicly that she, like the doctor's sister, had a special reason for sorrow. The accurate kind rightness of this treatment of Isabel came not from any unusual affection for her—she was just a nice girl that everybody liked—but from the fact that she was one of theirs, hence wholly human. The keen eyes that followed with a relishing satiric curiosity the emotional adventures of the daughters of summer people turned away in pity from the sight of suffering they recognized. Everyone understood why not to notice (in Isabel's presence) that she was pale, with dark rings under her eyes, that she listened to you apathetically, answered you from a distance.

This ritual pretense that she was what self-respect demanded that she seem, was like one of those frameworks used by surgeons in war-hospitals to keep the intolerable weight of the sheet from a shell-shattered body. Isabel, deeply one with her own people, knew that she could count absolutely on it to protect her from the intolerable weight of spoken sympathy. The only person who could not control himself to stand aloof was her poor father, always less iron-strong than those around him. Once or twice, at the first, overpowered by his dreadful divination of her pain, he offered her a caress, a look, an intonation that bore witness to the pity bleeding

in his heart. Isabel, sensitive daughter of a sensitive father, was too kind even in her misery to shrink away openly at this profanation of her secret, but her father felt her wince at his touch. Shamed and humiliated, he drew back then, like the others. She knew that she hurt him, but she could not—not now—think of that. Perhaps years later, as an old woman, long after her father had died, she might remember with vain remorse. Now, like a person being operated on without an anesthetic, her whole being was centered in the attempt not to cry out. Her mother, newly released from quarantine, was the one to whom she clung; she said to M'Sanna once, "Mother is such a comfort. She doesn't understand *any*thing!"

But she was wrong. What her mother understood was the need to survive. Dryly she recalled Isabel's attention from her present excitement and pain to the inexorable years before her. She did not allow her the poisonous pleasure of living over the past, of pressing the knife slowly home. She would not let her lie down and die. Without the exchange of a word between them she told her daughter as people of peremptory good sense like hers tell newly made cripples by the implications of their voices, "Oh, just because you are mutilated there's no need for being a burden to other people. There are plenty of useful things you can still do."

"What do you say we get this business of Isabel's training settled?" she said to her husband in Isabel's presence the evening of Town Meeting Day. "We can plan better if something definite is decided on. I don't even know what kind of clothes to make for the child's summer now. When does Easter vacation begin, Isabel? Monday? Well, papa, you haven't been to visit Eph and his family— not since their baby came. Why don't you and Isabel take the Cannon Ball Friday afternoon? You could stay with Eph's folks and go around to the different hospitals to talk things over. I'll write Eph's wife today to expect you."

So, although Isabel's interest in nursing and medicine had blown out of her mind like a dry leaf in a hurricane, down to Boston went the silent humbled father and the pale daughter walking as though in her sleep. They bore letters of introduction from Miss Craft, and took along for the married son and his family some new-laid eggs

from Mrs. Foote's Rhode Island Reds and a gallon of this year's syrup from the Rollinses' sugar-bush.

The presentation of these presents to the family and of the letters to hospital superintendents, the taking and dodging of horrible trolley cars and suffocating subway trains, the insensate noise of the rush to and fro on the streets of those unwanted, meaningless strangers—four days passed for Isabel as though she had been literally drugged by an opiate.

At the end of the week she and her father returned, paler and more silent even than when they went away, having between them, with no will of theirs, decided Isabel's future. Under her mother's direction, she had listlessly put a tip of her finger between two cogs of the hospital training-school organization and as her mother had foreseen, that powerful, well-oiled machine had pulled her in bodily. She was to enter training a week after Commencement. Her Clifford life was over. Her childhood, sadly shaking its little bells, walked away from her to nothingness.

But no other silence about Doctor Craft's marriage was kept in Clifford other than the little oasis of it about his sister. And, except when Isabel was present, communal curiosity raged like a lion. It was felt that self-control need go no further. In fact talk and plenty of it was called for. To exclaim and to condemn was right and proper. It was harvest weather for professional slanderers like Almira Boardman. The facts silenced even those tiresome people who spoil the delicious acidity of gossip with their sugary, "But remember, we haven't heard the other side yet." From Mr. Dewey himself came many a repetition of the old axiom, "Expeer-eye-ence is a hard school but fools will learn in no other."

As is the nature of our two-faced race they exploited with all their might the possibilities for malice afforded by a tradition they themselves had created in the interests of kindness. That they never mentioned Anson to those who cared for him enabled them to criticize him as savagely as they pleased, with no one to defend him. No one even who cared to point out self-evident contradictions in the harsh judgments passed on him. They could thus—a luxury generally for-

bidden by logic—have it both ways, eat their cake and have it too, say loudly that Anson, far from being so smart as the young folks had thought him, was just a dumb-head who didn't know enough to keep out of the clutches of an ignorant vicious girl that was somebody's hired help; and in the same breath could point out triumphantly, "Now you see! All that new-fangled hollering of his about how 'twould be better if folks were let to do what they damn want to—all he meant was that *he* wanted to be let to do what *he* wanted to, and that was to get around a poor orphan girl that two nice old ladies were trying to bring up right." The "nice old ladies" motif ran unabashedly side by side with reports of luscious sayings of old Miss Bessie restored to vigor by wrath. Her comments ran from a repeatable, "I call a spade a spade and Anson Craft a fool," to "Married, are they? Well, they're two that'll have to go to bed backward to get anything new out of that!"

There was, of course, a great raking back and forth of the facts known about the Searles Shelf girl but these were exasperatingly few. Surprisingly enough Miss Bessie had little to tell. When questioned she merely blew up in one explosion after another, claiming—what seemed improbable not to say impossible—that she knew nothing about her after having had her in the house nearly a year. "She made a fool of me . . . of *me!*" cried the old woman, her face congested. "At my age I've been made a monkey of by a somebody off of Searles Shelf! She's as secret as a well! And what's new to me, she don't let on she is. There I was—old simpleton!—thinking I was making such a good job of training her! Why, you've heard me say that! 'She's a good learner,' says I, forty times if I said it once. 'And I do like a good learner!' says I. And all the time she never giving me a real word, nor so much as a real look. You can't look straight at her the way you do anybody else—she puts it over on you with some kind of a squint in one eye. And smooth . . . ! All that 'Yes, Miss Bessie,' and 'No, Miss Bessie,' . . . it had no more to do with what she was cooking up than a silver spoon has with a manure pile."

Nobody took this very seriously as a report of fact. Miss Bessie like other people with lively tongues was regarded as a source not

so much of information as of entertainment. But it was always fun to get her going, and at first callers baited her purposely. But twice in one day, she frightened visitors by going off into a terrible heart attack, in the midst of a tirade. After that people no longer brought up that topic and when she did, raising her voice and beginning to turn purple, they excused themselves hastily and went away. There was never of course anything to be had in the way of news out of Miss Gussie, shut away from the real world as she was. And too, she seemed to be in one of her contrary moods. If she was present when Miss Bessie began to get up steam about the capacity of the Searles Shelf girl for deceit, she would put in, "Don't talk so like a fool, Bessie. If you'd thought from the first minute you drew breath that there wasn't a person in the world that you could count on, wouldn't you keep your mouth shut about your own affairs? You'd be the first to!" Or, "Good land, who blames a deer for learning how to leg it faster'n the dogs? How else is he a-goin' to keep the breath of life in him?" It was plain the poor old thing, deaf and an old maid to boot, hadn't really taken in what had happened. She never got anything quite straight.

Nobody else in town seemed to have seen the unknown girl enough to have anything to report about her. At least nobody who was willing to admit it. All the women suspected all the men of knowing more than they let on, and most of the men were sincerely regretful that they had been so unobservant. Opinions differed even as to her looks, some people remembering her as plain and cross-eyed, and others as "having had something or other about her." Curiosity ran so high that trips of inquiry were made to the hospital. But of course professional etiquette easily repelled these inexpert attacks. Questioners came back to Clifford with no more to report than that a nurse or attendant had said, "I never heard how they did manage to get a marriage license so quickly." Or, "Oh, he was perfectly conscious at the time—he was the one who insisted on it—it was the only thing to quiet him." Or, "I wasn't in the room." Or, "I haven't heard anybody say."

Some people even went up to Searles Shelf, for local surmises turned around and around the theory that the melodrama might

be connected in some way with something that had begun in the girl's life up there. But for all that could be found out along The Shelf, nothing at all had ever happened to her or to anyone connected with her. The hospital was not the only place equipped with a technique for repelling questioners. That of Searles Shelf had, moreover, been stiffened by the encounter with the baffled sheriff of the county. He had repeatedly tried to cross-question Searles Shelf people, coming away, as he knew beforehand he would, with nothing but evasive answers and perfect alibis. Much experience had taught him that all hunters stand solidly together against anybody connected with the law, the law having for them no purpose but to enforce the closed season for game and thus prevent their making an honest living. Having shut their mouths to legitimate official inquiries, it was not likely that Searles Shelf would satisfy the idle curiosity of The Street. In fact, behind their blank poker faces they were delighted at a chance to take down people who washed their necks and worked regularly and had money in the savings bank. The weather-beaten, loose-jointed men, lounging before their rickety shacks and keeping questioners away from the squaws inside, rolled something better than tobacco under their tongues as with vacant faces they brought out one "no" after another.

"No, never noticed nothing particular about her." "No, none of *our* boys." "Her mother's dead. Died off somewhere in York State, years ago." "None of us never knew *who* her father was." "No, she ain't never been back here since M'Sanna took her away. None of us ain't ever laid eyes on her since then."

Miss Craft went to Searles Shelf, too. Mrs. Henry Twombley's time was now so near that she ought to have the new layette at hand. But the little weather-blackened house stood empty. She looked up a Twombley house of the older generation and asked a question. Henry had found him a steady job somewhere off in York State across the Lake, she was told. Or was it down in Massachusetts near Pittsfield? She looked at them hard and remarked that his own sisters and aunts must know where he had gone. "Oh, sure

they know where. It's over in . . . what *did* he say? Em, where was it Henry was a-goin'? Was it Haltonville?" Oh, no, Em was sure it wasn't Haltonville. "Sounded more like . . . I can't seem to bring it to mind. Seems as though he left it written down on the almanac. Look over there, M'Sanna, on the cover of the almanac hanging by the stove. My hands are in the dough." But his new address was not there. By this time though they assured her that if it wa'n't there, it must ha' been on Aunt Lu's almanac he wrote it, M'Sanna knew that she would never find out where he had gone. And this suited her just as well. What difference did it make?

She left the layette with an "expecting" Capen wife—the world would never lack for Capens—and drove back through the white birch grove at which she pointedly did not look. She meant to pass the Rollins farm without stopping, but they were full of the Town Meeting victory and when they saw her car, ran out, shouting and waving exultant arms. And then were so obviously stricken by shame at having forgotten her trouble that she could do no less than stop and give them a chance to excuse themselves. She answered the usual questions as they came: "The doctor's not so encouraging today. His last hemorrhage was very bad. I'm on my way to the hospital now. . . . Right through the lung. . . . Yes, oh, yes, he knows me. He's conscious most of the time. But the doctor won't let him try to talk." The Rollinses having known Lixlee ventured to ask directly about her and were told, "She's not in so much danger. A flesh wound in the neck and shoulder . . . a bad one, but no bones struck. It's healing normally." They nodded, respecting her quiet voice; stepped back and let her drive on down towards the main road, passing through what had been a noble company of tall young trees promising magnificence in their maturity . . . what was now a mournful assemblage of dead bodies overgrown by blatantly vital brambles, very useful for filling preserve jars and pies.

2

B ut it is in the nature of every fashion—fashions being by definition communal movements—to rise higher and higher in favor till the weaker souls, currying favor with the majority by overdoing their obedience to its commands, go to an extreme that drives the majority back into a reaction. Those fashions pass from favor most quickly, of course, which have been most unanimously followed, because they use up soonest the very small capacity of human beings for continuity in anything—material or emotional. If Doctor Craft had been able to return at once to Clifford, the encounters of every day would have fed the fire of disapproval with the new fuel which it now lacked. As it was, that fire burning freely and unchecked all during his long illness, presently began to burn itself out. The stronger souls, their own personalities emerging a little from collective mob feeling, began out of sheer boredom with hearing the same facts combed over and over, occasionally to turn the conversation to something else. Of course the weaker ones did not perceive this gradual change. Led by Almira Boardman they went on as such people do, fatuously exaggerating a fashion beginning to pass, talking big about their intention never to leave Doctor Craft step inside their house, no, not if their mother had a broken leg and he the only doctor in Windward County; demanding that the School Directors have the common decency not to let such a man go on conducting tonsil and adenoid examinations; proposing to boycott him if he ever dared return to town. But while they babbled their way from one absurdity to another, time was dissolving into individual human beings the mob on whose brute unanimity they counted. People went back to their own naturally different ways of looking at life and began to perceive that some of the stones being thrown came from houses with a good many glass windows.

Time was not the only force that pushed the seven days' wonder off the center of the Clifford stage; the late northern spring came rushing on with its imperious summons to crowd into a fortnight

work that in other climates would last for months. Every vigorous organism was caught up by the onward rush taking place outdoors. Man and woman, filled to overflowing by the new life brought by the new sun, burned up in passionate house-cleaning and plowing the same springtime excess of vitality which the trees were spending in their annual explosion into foliage. They couldn't go on talking forever about what Doctor Anson had done long ago in March.

And as for that, what *had* he done? The sun shone provocatively down. In man and beast and all green things, the sap came racing up to meet it. There didn't seem to be so much call to carry on about a young man being in a girl's room at night. My sakes, didn't he marry her? Were they the first in this Valley . . . ? The malignant feeble ones bringing up the rear began in the midst of their virtuous denunciations to feel that their listeners' eyes were ironic, were silently saying, "How about that ahead-of-time first baby of yours?" "What was it I used to hear old people say about your mother when she was a girl?" "You sound like Almira Boardman." Unwillingly they saw that they had come to the end of the happy period when mob feeling brought the finer spirits down to their level. The "Hurrah!" days of communal uncharitableness were past. They must fall back again on their own poor personal ability to be venomous, on mere private back-biting, discounted in advance because it came from them.

People remembered now and smiled over Miss Gussie's remark—amusing only because it came from such an ignorant, innocent old maiden-lady. She had said as if wondering at everybody's excitement, "But isn't that nater?" And so it was, of course. How could folks ever get married and have families if 'tweren't for nater!

The grass greened; the brooks ran brimful of noisy water; life centered about the care of capering lambs and baby chicks and tottering calves; a girl in every other house, seems though, was sewing on her wedding outfit; showers for prospective brides were reported every week in the Ashley *Record*: M'Sanna was called up at all hours for babies arriving; finally, incredible miracle of every May, clouds of pink and white bloomed in apple orchards

where yesterday the children had been tunneling in snowdrifts. And in hearts that had been dry and matter-of-fact, inner springs melted too and ran brimful; flowers burst into bloom in minds that had been heaped with snow, and—secretly—separately—many of the tall men in overalls, plowing or harrowing or spreading manure, or silently seeding down with old ritual gestures a stony buckwheat field, thought of Anson Craft with more liking than they had ever had for him, felt less on their guard against his superior education, felt him—let the women folks talk as they would —to be human, to be a brother, to be a whole man like themselves. A comment of Sherwin Dewey's began to go the rounds, "Well, be all that as it may, I think more of him than if he'd married a rich summer woman." There was lots *in* that, people said, and now you came to think of it, Doctor Anson might ha' been crabbed and he might ha' been cussed, but nobody could say he was on the make. He wa'n't trying to git more for himself, darned if he was. Nor to stand in with rich folks. No, sir, it was the high-and-mighty he was always knocking, them and the folks that say everything was all right because *they* are all right. It was the pizen-good he couldn't stand, folks who wanted to slam doors in poor folks' faces. And hadn't he proved he meant what he said, he, a Craft from The Street, marrying somebody from off Searles Shelf which a person would *hardly* want to risk, himself, would you, now? But at that, the girl might be all right—seems she was only half Burdick. She don't look—dark as she is—to be so much as a half to all them Burdick tow-heads. Her father might ha' *been* somebody, you couldn't tell. Why not wait and see how she turns out? Everybody says she's a good hand to learn. Even Miss Bessie says that.

As for the matter of who could have wanted to shoot the doctor, that remained a mystery so insoluble that it soon began to seem improbable. And then incredible. Simply not to be believed in a county where for a hundred and fifty years every man and boy had owned a gun and where since the American Revolution no one had ever aimed a gun at another human being. Conjecture exhausted itself, and gave up. It *must* ha' been a spent ball. Some drunk off a logging camp on The Wall, flourishin' around. What

else? They tell me those new rifles carry for miles. By and by, after it had been talked about long enough, some people even claimed to know which lumber-jack it was who, trying out a rifle won in a poker-game, had crazily fired it off into the air from the road in front of a house in Clifford Four Corners.

Down at the Academy spring fever was raging too, though the young people plowed not neither did they clean house. Unaware that they were thin-blooded descendants of morose life-hating Puritans, Cornelia and Olivia and their boy friends and all the rest of the eighteen- and nineteen-year-olds in the Senior Class danced, had picnic suppers, took Saturday hikes back up on The Wall, played tennis and baseball, sat on porch steps in the May moonlight, ardently fell in and out of love with each other, and light-heartedly eluded the attempts of the Principal and faculty to prepare them for final examinations. Isabel Foote resolutely played some tennis but sat on no porch steps, being indoors of an evening, working hard over her books. People said loyally to each other that she needed to stand high if she was to be welcome at the Boston hospital training school.

To her mother she said no word, nor to her father, nor above all to her old comrades. But once or twice when her heart's bitterness threatened to choke her she turned to M'Sanna again as she had so trustingly back there in the past, so far behind her now, a month ago, when she had been a happy and confident child. Now as then, it was almost as a sick person turning in piteous bewilderment to one learned in healing. "Will it ever get any better, M'Sanna, do you think? Sometimes I think it *is* better, the way you do a toothache when it lets up a little. And I think, 'Oh, perhaps I've got over it! Perhaps now it has gone!'—and then it comes again, oh, *frightful!* The ache so bad I can't think of anything else, boring into me like something burning hot. It *is* like a toothache, don't laugh, M'Sanna." But M'Sanna was not laughing. "Oh, *why* should I have to bear it? If I could only get over it. Will I ever get over it, do you think?"

"Other people have, Isabel."

Once standing with her outdoors beside a lilac bush in blossom, the lilac bush to which she had been bright flowering sister so short a time ago, the nurse was shocked by her pinched look. "Isabel, don't you ever cry? Perhaps you are wearing yourself out, keeping it all down."

The girl did not lift her heavy eyelids. She said, shredding a leaf between her fingers, "I can't cry long enough to do any good, M'Sanna. I always get worn out long before it would help any." She dropped the ragged leaf, took M'Sanna's hand and said, still looking down, "But I've been wanting to tell you—don't think I blame him. Or hate him. Or her. Or you. It's nothing anybody's to blame for. And you mustn't think that it's all the time. The worst are the dreams. I dream that he . . . If only I didn't. Mornings when I open my eyes and know that . . . M'Sanna, I can *feel* his head heavy and warm on my shoulder, long, long after I wake up. And . . ." She shuddered and was silent. Then, "But in the daytime mostly I don't feel much of anything . . . except empty. It's only when something makes me remember him—really remember—his voice, or the way his hair used to . . . or his hands as they . . ." She broke out into a moaning cry, *"His hands!"* and turned away to hide her face. Anna stood silent, all one ache of sympathy. Isabel, looking up into her face, misread the shadow on it and said, in a low, humble tone, "I don't mean I hate him then . . . or love him. It's only that all my strength drains out as if I were bleeding to death."

Commencement drew nearer. Waking late one night and finding his wife's place empty, Doctor Foote went downstairs in his nightgown to see where she was. Pale and worn, she bent over the sheer white material of Isabel's graduation dress, her needle flashing. "You're foolish to put so much work on a dress!" he protested.

She looked up at him, really looked at him and said, "Oh, Merrill, if I could only think of something else I could do to it!"

"Why, Hilda!" he cried. They clung to each other for a moment, nearer than they had been since their betrothal.

Isabel passed her final examinations well. Very well. Brilliantly in fact. And without flinching, every time her mother asked her, she tried on the white dress that looked so like a bride's.

Finding M'Sanna alone in her office one afternoon, she said, "Before I go away, I wanted to tell you . . . that I'm really better, I think. It doesn't come so often. Some days I feel almost the way I used to." But having said so much she could not stop. "But then, 'way off . . . it's like a storm coming around the mountain, you know how dark it gets . . . I try not to pay any attention to it . . . it seems as though I could keep it off if I could think of something else *hard,* every minute. But everything gets darker and darker— and then—*oh!*" She flung herself into M'Sanna's arms, her teeth chattering, her face gray.

But this was the last time she ever spoke of it. Commencement was there, a turning point in every Senior's life as in hers. All at once everybody was grown up, grown-up plans replacing the sky-larks of adolescence. Mrs. Browne not only formally announced Cornelia's engagement to Charlie Dean (which was no news to anybody) but said the young people were planning to be married that very August. Charlie, graduating that June from the College of Pharmacy, had secured a position, she said, with a decently concealed satisfaction, at the Peltier drugstore in Ashley. People smilingly surmised that it was not the lackadaisical, novel-reading, verse-scribbling Charlie who had landed that job, but his practical sensible fiancée. Charlie was lucky, they said, always to have had Cornelia to look out for him. The other member of that school-girl threefold friendship, Olivia, was already enrolled in the next Freshman class at the State University. Funny to think of the crazy, quicksilver Olivia as a "college woman." She'd show 'em in Burlington what a live wire was! There was special applause on Commencement Day as Isabel, composed and steady, Cornelia, tall, blonde and phlegmatic, and Olivia, small, dark and vivid, passed across the platform to get their diplomas. They were three fine girls, everybody thought, girls that would do honor to the old town.

When Isabel went to say good-by to M'Sanna her mother went

with her. The talk ran on training-school regulations as to the wearing of caps.

The students scattered, the Academy shutters were closed, patient grass began once more to grow on school playgrounds. The Community House was shut up. The Cannon Ball stopped at Clifford Depot almost every afternoon, depositing piles of trunks and suitcases and returning summer people. After the roar of the train's departure had died down, they felt their eardrums muffled in the same old Clifford cotton wool. In the silence they looked around them, saw Frank Barney still chewing on that same old straw and gazing into the same old vacancy, noted that Henry Gardner's Ford taxi hadn't been washed yet, told each other genially that it was a comfort to have one old hole-in-the-ground where nothing ever happened, and facetiously asked Henry what the news was.

Henry understood that this was their idea of joke and played up to it as always, "Nothin'!"

"What? No births? No deaths? No marriages?"

"Oh, sure, some of *them!*" He fished in his memory for enough items to satisfy them. "Well, we've got a new boy at our house." Pause. "And the young doctor's got married!" Pause. "And old Mis' Everts—her that they called Aunt P'liny—we buried her last week."

3

HENRIETTA was having trouble with one of her kittens that summer. Or no, not Henrietta who as long as she was nursing her kittens thought that everything they did was perfect. It was the housekeeper who had the trouble, and after her, Jo Danby. The kittens were always drowned of course, each summer, although Mr. Stewart didn't like to have them drowned too young, because Henrietta bothered him by prowling around the house crying and calling. But it wasn't that the housekeeper minded drowning them. No, she enjoyed it. She was that kind of person. But this year either she couldn't count them correctly or there was

one that didn't stay with the others. She thought she had seen five of the wriggling blind worms when she first discovered the dark corner in under the woodshed-chamber stairs where Henrietta's this year's nest was made. But after they were old enough to run around there seemed to be only four. When the time came to drown them, four being all she could find, four was the number she dropped into her pail of water, and four were the little draggled pink-toed wet corpses that Jo Danby buried.

Henrietta did not prowl or cry or call at all that year, not once. She still spent most of her time in the woodshed, and presently Mr. Stewart, prowling himself in the manner so disapproved of by his help, saw from a distance Henrietta lying in a motherly attitude, the nose of a sizable kitten buried in her flank. After a disagreeable passage of "Why did you leave one kitten this year?" "I didn't," "You did," "I did not," the housekeeper was dispatched to drown this one. But she could not find it. Henrietta sat in the sun, her paws tucked under her, and on being spoken crossly to, lifted inscrutable eyes to her questioner and slowly sauntered away.

A game of hide-and-seek followed, murderous in intent on the part of the housekeeper. Yes, there really was a kitten. If she looked from the extreme side of the kitchen window she could catch an occasional glimpse of it. But as soon as she opened the screen door and stepped out, there was no one but Henrietta crouched over her pan of milk. "It's awful shy," she told Mr. Stewart. "It runs under the floor of the woodshed as soon as anybody comes around." But she found that shyness was not the explanation of its behavior. Coming down early one morning she came on it lying asleep beside Henrietta, as innocent and deliciously woolly a brindled ball as ever kitten looked. "Ah, now I've got you!" she said triumphantly as she pounced.

Her screams were so loud that they brought Jo Danby running in from the barn in his overalls, and Mr. Stewart down from the sleeping porch in his pajamas. They found her, empty-handed, bleeding scratches on her face and arms, one thumb bitten through to the bone. Henrietta perfidiously purred at her feet and undulated against her ankles. Although Mr. Stewart was delighted to see her

face scratched and would have liked to have done it himself, he decreed, of course, that the matter had now gone beyond a woman's handling and told Jo Danby to attend to it.

"Attend to it!" thought Jo in the weeks that followed. Attend to it! That was Mr. Stewart all over! He'd like to see anybody attend to a critter nobody could lay eyes on. For if their encounter had taught the housekeeper a lesson about the nature of the kitten, it had apparently taught the kitten a lesson about life in general. Never again was he caught asleep in the enemy's camp. All that Jo could see of him was an occasional fleeting brindled shadow at dawn or dusk, scuttling under the woodshed. He also often saw Henrietta carrying a mouse or bird in under that floor, so, "It lives under the woodshed and I can't get at it," he reported briefly to his employer, pushing his dirty old felt hat to the back of his bald head and moving his chewing gum from the left to the right side of his mouth. Mr. Stewart paid dearly for his consistency in having no imported professional help, and many times felt that it might be worth giving up that part of his little summer rôle if he could secure thereby a few "Yes, sirs," and "No, Mr. Stewarts," and doffed hats. He looked hard at Jo's head, and at his moving jaws and said irritably, "Don't tell me you can't get at a kitten here on our own place. Stop up the holes so it can't get under the woodshed floor."

"If it happened to be in there when I did it would stink something fierce," said Jo, between chews.

"Well, *shoot* it, then!" cried Mr. Stewart, turning away, "as you would any other wild animal."

"I'd like to see you draw a bead on a moving target in the dark," thought Jo, looking venomously after the well-tailored pale-gray back.

The housekeeper suggested that Jo put out some poisoned meat, but of course that might kill Henrietta, and they both knew how indispensable to Mr. Stewart's talk and hence to their jobs was the unbroken continuity of Henrietta. "Maybe it'll run away after a while," she hoped, "if I always feed Henrietta inside the house."

"I see lots of bird feathers around. Guess he's quite a hunter,"

demurred Jo. "Them wild ones are always a lot smarter than the tame ones."

Then at the same moment they both had the same soothing idea, a perfect interlocking combination, "As long as he keeps out of sight so he can't be shot, Mr. Stewart will never know he's still there. If he gets so tame he comes out where Mr. Stewart could see him, why, it'll be easy to shoot him."

It was not often things came out so restfully for the help in the Stewart house.

All this had taken time. Most of the summer in fact. And of course it had not been the only happening in Clifford. The usual events had taken place, and one or two that didn't happen every year. While this had been going on at the back of the Stewart house, the usual limousines had rolled up to the front, discharging the usual marvelously coifed white heads and marvelously corseted overweight, seeing whom the housekeeper had crossly but cautiously reached into the china closet for that damned set of blue willow-ware, each time reminding the that-year's waitress that the old man would have a stroke and they'd all lose their jobs if a piece of it were broken or cracked. Beyond the Stewart place the usual things went on as usual; Miss Gussie gardened, her peas perfect though it was a damp summer and other people's mildewed. Miss Bessie in a grimly solitary kitchen canned and preserved. The Foote twins, old enough this year to be admitted to the Tennis Club, spent all their spare time on the courts, and showed promise in their forehand strokes. Miss Ingraham had as usual gone back to Newark to spend her vacation with her married sister. M'Sanna incessantly came and went to the hospital. On fair days old Sherwin Dewey cruised back and forth on Old Hemlock, Don at his heels, ostensibly planning his next year's cutting operations, but sometimes on his return so rapt after his day on the heights that he didn't see you or hear you when you said "Good evening" to him as he passed. On rainy days he pored over his collection of yellowed old papers. This summer he began to feel the need of help, he said, and insisted on Doctor Foote's taking hold of the work with him. At first Isabel's

father had resisted, saying plainly that he felt little interest in researches about where the first trails and paths had run and in establishing an accurate list of the Clifford men who had taken part in the Battle of Bennington. But old Mr. Dewey had given him no rest, and before long he began to find like other men before him that local history is not a bad opiate.

Of the unusual happenings of the summer, Cornelia Browne's wedding to Charlie Dean took up most time in preparation before and in talk afterward. Cornelia herself, who favored her father's family, the easy-going stodgy Brownes, didn't care whether she was married in church or at home, being chiefly concerned with the furnishing of her new kitchen. And Charlie, being sensitive and romantic, having all the Deans' self-conscious shyness and not being very decorative in person, longed to elope and be married at midnight by a justice of the peace far away from prying eyes. But Mrs. Browne had been a Merrill and took social events seriously, as the Merrills do. Poor widow though she was, she was bound that her only child should have a formal wedding with every possible High Church trimming. And so she did, even to a Bishop from a Western state, some connection of the Deans, who happened to be in New England on a visit. Clifford gardens were stripped to the stalks for the church and house decorations. Everybody said how foolish it was for Cornelia's mother, who was rather an invalid, to fuss so—and prophesied a breakdown for her after this. Everybody helped with the preparations for the wedding breakfast, everybody knew about the extravagant underwear Cornelia had, and what her mother-in-law-to-be thought about it, knew which house on Maple Avenue in Ashley the young people were to live in, knew how much rent they would pay, knew what pay Charlie was to get at the Peltier drugstore. Olivia made a brilliant maid of honor, rather eclipsing with her sparkle the somewhat static bride. Isabel, locked fast in the early stages of training school discipline, could not leave the Boston hospital. "Just as well, too," people said, under their breath. "A wedding's no place for her now."

What with the preparations for the event, and the success of it on a hot July day—and a bad automobile accident soon after, down

where the road from Lathrop's Gap crosses the railroad tracks—and a wind-blow that twisted the tops out of some of the best elms on The Street, and the annual visit of the circus, and a drop in the price of milk, it was not surprising that nobody noticed particularly about Doctor Anson's being finally discharged from the hospital in August and going to live in a house up in Ashley that had been got ready for him by his young wife aided by M'Sanna—or when you stopped to think what was more likely, the other way around probably.

4

FATHER KIRBY had said, "Now you've got a situation to rise to, Anna, if you ever had!"

She had answered, "No, no, it's too much for me. I never shall have wisdom to rise to it."

But no situation is too much for us if we are introduced into it gradually enough. The inability of human beings to continue long in the same state of mind always dissolves the drama out of any facts. Acceptable or not, the new and strange, simply by the passage of time becomes—what nobody's effort could ever have made it— the familiar and accepted.

As a nurse, Anna shared in the professional excitement of the fight for Anson's life, shared in the professional satisfaction over the response made by Lixlee's young body to the care given it. The clean way that jagged wound in the smooth white shoulder was mending—it was glorious! Everybody on the hospital staff was talking about it.

"You're doing grand, Mrs. Craft!" the head nurse would say, touching the cleanly healing shoulder with an expression that would almost have done for the contemplation of spiritual virtue. "Just keep it up now, and we'll all get our names in the Medical Journal." As she went out she shook her finger playfully at the invalid. "Now remember, Mrs. Craft, I've let your sister-in-law in to see you, although it's against doctor's orders, because she's a nurse. But *you're*

not to say a word. I don't want your temperature going up on me. Doctor Millet would skin me alive."

So Anna, day by day, heard Lixlee called Mrs. Craft; heard herself spoken of as the sister of the girl from Searles Shelf, exchanged silent smiles with a dark-haired, dark-eyed young woman whose rather long, oddly modeled face with its high cheek bones was now, through loss of blood, of a spiritual transparency, mentioned that the daffodils in Miss Gussie's garden were two inches high and that the blue birds were back; and lost little by little the sharpest of her sense of strangeness in what had happened.

"But the time must come, of course," she told Fred Kirby, "when we'll have to face it and really say something to each other."

Anson's case was not so simple. Long after Lixlee was up in a wheeled chair, he was still having dreadful relapses, hemorrhages from his perforated lungs that took him down time and again to the very doors of death. And when he finally turned the corner, he seemed morally exhausted, could not be roused to interest in his own recovery, in anything. Doctor Millet asked his patient's sister to make some plans with his young wife about their future and cautiously to bring back to Doctor Craft's mind the life to which he would return. His illness had lasted long, he had lost far too much blood, he had been down very low. There was danger that things outside his sickroom might be dimmed to invisibility. So, "How would you like to have a house and office of your own, here in Ashley?" asked Miss Craft, one day in a casual tone. "Doctor Cole is agreed, if we have a special telephone line put in between his bedroom and yours, so he can ring you direct for a hurry call without depending on Central. Charlie and Cornelia Dean have told me about a little house next door to them on Maple Avenue that's vacant. It would do very well. The wing has a couple of rooms that would make a nice office and waiting-room. Only twenty-five dollars a month. Aunt Jennie Moffatt, it seems, left you and me what she had in the savings bank. And she had more than anybody thought. Your share will be nearly six thousand dollars. You could afford, and not notice it, to put a bathroom into the house and have

running water in your office. And there are plenty of extra pieces in our big Clifford house to furnish it."

There was no response from the sick man, wrapped in the austere indifference to daily life of mortal illness.

"What would we Vermonters ever do," said Doctor Millet in a jocular tone, his eyes anxiously fixed on his patient, "without those bits of savings bank accounts from our aunts and grandmothers?"

The bloodless corpse-face on the pillow kept its unearthly remoteness. The doctor shook his head forebodingly.

Anna said, "Anson, Lixlee and I have talked it over and she thinks it would be a good idea."

Doctor Craft was too weak to turn his head or lift his hand, but at the words, "Lixlee and I," a smile came into his blue eyes, sunk in cavernous sockets. He made a motion with his eyelids that signified, "Yes. All right. I like that." Doctor Millet and Anson's devoted nurse exchanged a look of relief and satisfaction.

Anna said afterwards to Fred Kirby, who came into her office every day to get the news, "I don't know whether he smiled to hear that Lixlee and I are on friendly terms, or just to hear her name." She added, "And that's only *one* of the things I don't know! I certainly don't know a single thing more about Lixlee."

She repeated this again another day, when he looked in to ask how Anson was. This was after she and Lixlee had begun going and coming together to and from the house on Maple Avenue.

Mr. Kirby insisted incredulously that with all her daily contacts with Lixlee in the matter of furnishing the house she must know the girl much better by this time.

"No, I don't," said Anna. "All we talk about somehow is where to put the sideboard, and what kind of curtains to have. I still haven't any idea about what happened the night of . . . the accident. She never says a word about what's past. Acts as natural . . . ! Like any young wife arranging the new house."

"Perhaps her mind heals as promptly as her body," suggested Mr. Kirby.

The idea struck Miss Craft's imagination. "Why, yes! Perhaps!"

she exclaimed, Lixlee's silences at once taking on to her nurse's eye pleasant aspects of health and soundness.

She did not notice that the clergyman's expression was of patience, rather than interest, and went on, after a moment's pause, "It's wonderful how she has profited by Miss Gussie's English lessons. And by all that Miss Bessie taught her."

"Some women seem to be geniuses in that line," said Father Kirby, and told an anecdote about the uncouth youth of a Boston acquaintance of his, now not only presentable, but an accomplished woman of the world."

"Yes, with Lixlee too it's more than correct manners," insisted Anna. "There's something unusual about her that sets her off from girls that have ten times her social advantages. It's not just physical charm either, though I do think she has the most beautiful figure. It's something about her, herself. About her presence in a room. Perhaps she makes that impression on me at this time because I can't get over her taking everything so naturally. How can anybody who's been through what she has, be always so the same, quiet and smiling! It gives her a sort of mystery. And you know what prestige it gives anybody to seem mysterious. How *can* she be so composed, emerging from a cyclone of emotion as she must!"

Mr. Kirby doing his best to keep up his half of this talk considered the question gravely, "Well, I should say there were three possible explanations. She may be just dumb and insensitive. She may have acquired a special skill for concealing what she feels. That would be natural for anybody who has survived such a friendless childhood as hers seems to have been. Or she may be one of those people with a special gift for living in the present. Since she's a member of the human race, most likely it's a mixture of all three qualities."

Anna dissented, "No, I believe it's the last—I do believe she is one of those people you read about, who *can* live in the present. Maybe that was what Anson felt in her—he's always saying, you know, that New Englanders waste half their time worrying about the future and the other half worshiping the past." After a thoughtful pause she went on musingly, "It still seems awfully queer, of

course, and there's a great deal I don't understand about it and probably never shall, but I do begin to believe that Lixlee and I will get along very pleasantly together. I must try to think of some way to let Anson know that."

Father Kirby had been turning his hat around in his hands, looking absently into its inverted crown. He crushed it together now, looked at her unconscious face, took a decision and said sharply, "Don't do that, Anna! Don't say anything to Anson about it! Can't you leave him alone!"

"What do you mean?" she asked, startled. His tone had been like the crack of a whip for decisiveness. He did not retreat now, though she looked at him hard, hurt and resentful.

"Why, I mean—I've never dared to say it before but—see here, Anna, if it were anybody else you could see it plainly enough! You're not so very much older than Anson, much too young to be his mother, but you've had to take the part of mother to him, and you're hanging onto him now with all a mother's stranglehold."

"I am *not!*" she said, astounded and indignant. "Why, I've been on my guard against that all my life. I've never asked Anson to do one single thing for me in all his life. All I want is his happiness and you know it."

Their voices were loud as though they were quarreling.

"Oh, Anna! With every breath you draw you ask him to keep you in the center of his life . . . or next to it. And all you want of him is that he go on everlastingly providing a goal for your efforts. Honestly, Anna, a person doesn't know whether to laugh or to cry over you! The other day weren't you telling me you didn't know whether the first smile he'd had on his face for weeks was because you had showed him you and Lixlee were doing things together . . . or just the mention of her name. You didn't *know* which!" He gave a short laugh. "If he loves her, he can't think of anybody else on the same plane with her . . . and he shouldn't. He shouldn't, I tell you. That's what it is to love. Anything else is mere . . . *friendliness!*"

He stood up, clapped his clerical hat on his head as if it had been a derby or a Fedora, and said with authority, "You've just got

to get it through your head, Anna Craft, that you must let *go* of Anson."

She watched his upright back as he walked off, thinking bitterly that it was only when he tried to talk of God that Fred felt any humility or self-doubt. When he was disposing of *her* life, he felt no hesitation in wiping off with one sweep the devotion, the self-sacrifice of all her years.

He turned and came back threateningly to where she was sitting. Looking up at him Anna was so held by the fire of his gray eyes that she could not look away from them to see his birthmark. She had the experience of distinctly seeing his face as it would have been had it not been scarred. He said in a deep passionate voice, "I can feel you resisting me to the marrow of your bones. Very well then, I *will* tell you! I wasn't going to. Anson all but made me promise I wouldn't. I found it out by chance—happened to meet a Doctor Something or other, head of some laboratory and it came out that he's wanted Anson to stay on and do research work for him. And Anson was crazy to."

"Well? Why . . . ?" Anna began.

"Why, there wasn't enough salary attached for anybody to live on. Anson couldn't, of course, take any more from you, and anyhow he thought it his duty to you—and so did that other doctor —and so would anybody—to come back and go into general practice till he'd earned enough to pay his debt. 'At least my money debt,' he said. That's what Anson has done for *you!*"

Anna was beside herself. "Oh! Oh! He shouldn't! He mustn't! Why didn't he tell me!"

Mr. Kirby broke in roughly, "You're the last person in the world he could tell."

He spoke loudly, but she did not hear him. Wringing her hands, she said, "It's not too late! He could go back and go on. . . . I could manage. I could make it possible. . . ."

He shouted her down, *"That's* why he didn't tell you!"

Still intent on her own forward-rushing impulses, she said as if to herself, "Oh, I must go to him and tell . . ." She half sprang up.

The clergyman's patience gave out. He put both hands on her

shoulders, pushed her down in her chair and held her there as he told her roughly, "No, you mustn't! Don't you tell him anything! Anna, you can't live his life. Haven't you got any of your own? *Let Anson alone!*"

Consternation came into his face. He snatched his hands away, stared at them, and looking up met Anna's startled eyes. The room that had been so full of Anson contained nothing now but a strangeness that rose and breathed around the man and woman looking fixedly at each other. This fixity was broken by a flood of color dyeing all of Anna's pale face from chin to brow with red. She looked down at her desk. The man before her flung up his head and stood taut. Then letting out his breath in a long sigh, without another word he went away, his head hanging, humble enough now, in all conscience.

5

WHEN Anson's slowly recovering body was able to send enough blood up to his brain so that it could register something more than a blurred wonder over a crack in the ceiling at which he lay gazing, his days and nights began to be colored by two emotions—anxiety about his work—exaltation about his love. He was increasingly alarmed about the long interruption to his medical observations. The whole point of keeping those cardiac records was of course their unbroken continuity, and here it was—weeks, months wasted with nobody noting what went on in old Mrs. Everts' fascinating pulse, with nobody verifying the gradual change in the second sound of Tom Merrill's heart. As the blood made its life-giving way again to the cells of the cortex, one after another of the hearts on his list was a reproach to him—suppose old Miss Bessie—suppose that mechanic at the garage with atheroma had another attack with nobody to make an electrocardiogram—damnation! what a loss!

"Pain somewhere, Doctor Craft?" The flat face of his devoted attendant nurse hung over him solicitously.

He restrained himself from whispering (he had not strength

enough yet to speak aloud), "Damn you, no. Leave me alone," shot
out at her a curt, "Quite all right, thanks," and closed his eyes, con-
gratulating himself on his skill in hiding his impatience. All in all,
he hadn't done so badly, he thought, since his return to Windward
County, in controlling his Craft temper. And he deserved some
credit, for it hadn't been easy those first months when he had been
as sore as a boil over giving up his work with Colchester. He hoped
he never again would be as wretched as then, shut up in a Black
Hole of trivial personal life with nothing to look forward to but
attending to the measly health of unimportant yokels. Queer, how
listlessly he had taken up this business of making cardiac records,
crazy as he had been for a goal in life. It had looked like the merest
stop-gap. No, not queer. Old Doctor Neale himself when he suggested the work, hadn't had the faintest idea of its far-reaching implications, of how much more original and vital it was than Colchester's narrow laboratory research. The hard old Caledonian was
all right on detail, but he had no creative fire. Weak as Anson was
now, his imagination kindled anew at the thought of the immense
possibilities in it for usefulness, for fame, for ever renewed interest.

With a life's work like that, and with such a lover as Lixlee
waiting at home to renew his vitality, life in Windward County
didn't look so bad—even if the only juice in most of the local ex-
istences was the ooze of self-satisfaction. So long as they provided
him plenty of bad hearts to observe and let Lixlee alone he could
put up with their gregarious smugness. What would make everything completely right of course would be to have Anna get some
personal life of her own. If she only would! That would roll off
his back the intolerable responsibility for all those years she had
given to his needs. Good old Anna! How she had stood by! Not so
old at that! Not at all too old—though that was hard to remember—
to get her share of personal life in the usual way by marrying and
having children. If any man on earth could get at her through her
impersonality! A red-headed woman with her quick temper and
hair-trigger reactions wasn't cold, that was one sure thing. But her
habit of mind had become so rigidly extrovert—it would take dynamite to make her think of herself long enough to have a personal

emotion. And when had the Necronsett Valley produced a man with any dynamite in him!

He knew where there was a girl with plenty of dynamite in her, all right. At the thought of Lixlee, his white face relaxed and smiled so that the nurse told herself, "That snappishness of his is just nervous weakness. He really likes to know I'm watching him closely."

Lixlee! Long before he had blood enough in his body again to desire her, even to remember how desirable she was, the thought of her was life-giving. There was a real woman for you, none of these martyrized, well-brought-up, denatured girls who had been put through the wringer of convention with old women of both sexes turning the handle, till they were as flattened out and dried as table napkins. The only full-blooded, unspoiled, full-sexed, right woman in the whole valley, and because she was technically somebody's hired girl, he the only man with sense enough to see her, and courage enough to take her. Ha! He wondered proudly what they had thought when they heard he'd married her! He'd like to have seen their faces. His tiny stock of strength was used up now, his eyelids fell shut, he slept, with a smile on his lips. The nurse noiselessly noted on her case-record the time when that nap began.

As his strength came back and with it his ability to fret, he began to use his vivid sense-memories of Lixlee to push out of his mind the bitter impotent regret over his interrupted work; to recall one by one, from the first on, his dramatic contacts with her. The evening she had gone down to the front hall to let him out, when he had first noticed her beautiful shoulders and breast, and had—to prolong the moment—asked her if she weren't sometimes rather lonely, shut up with two old ladies. Instead of answering him she had raised her eyes to his and looked at him silently. He had drowned himself in her eyes many times since, but never could he forget that first time. How long had he stood there, plunging his gaze into those mysterious pansy-dark pools? He never knew. Coming to himself and going out of the door rather fast he had told himself dizzily that he had only been trying to see whether there really was

a slight deviation in one eye. Remembering that feeble attempt at self-deception his smile now was so broad as greatly to enliven the case-record kept by the flat-faced nurse at his bedside. And that irrevocable first time when with a falsely paternal gesture he had put his hands on her shoulders! How many times he lived over the electric shock that had taught him what contact with her body meant to his. Before that shock, how densely insulated by self-deception he had been! But from that time on there hadn't been any doubt in his mind as to what he wanted. What was the pompous nonsense he had begun to say to her—"You're a brave girl to nurse so uncomplainingly a fretful old lady. . . ." As a matter of fact he had never known what his words had been, so startled was he to feel the living warmth of her under his hand. His blood had leaped up hotly to meet hers. If that deaf old woman had not been moving around in the next room, he would have snatched her to him then and there—she on fire, too, her eyes fixed on him with her glorious absence of shame.

"Now, now, Doctor Craft, aren't you tossing around *rather* a good deal for a man with a hole through his lung?"

If those ugly women only wouldn't try to be playful! Or any woman for that matter. How he loathed playfulness! One of the things he adored in Lixlee was her grave absence of it. Yet he deplored the absence of playfulness in Anna. The answer was of course that he adored everything about Lixlee.

But one day Anna, not realizing that old Mrs. Everts' abnormal heart was one of his chief fields of research, brought the news that she had died. Anna was not to blame. She couldn't know that the death of that insignificant old woman up on The Other Side would be a blow. It was, all the same. His weakness made him almost weep over the loss. So far as he knew, that was the only case of acquired pulmonary stenosis in Vermont and it had several features that even Doctor Neale himself had never observed. He *had* counted so on noting exactly what happened to that astonishing heart in its last illness.

The busy cells of his body having by this time replaced with red

and white corpuscles the quarts of salt water that had been injected
after his last hemorrhage, he had more strength to rage over this
disappointment. To ward it off he turned his mind resolutely again
to Lixlee. But now his irritation suggested to him that what these
local oafs with beetle-minds would think was that he had married
Lixlee out of conscience, had been forced, by their being discovered
together, to "make an honest woman" out of a girl whose reputation
would be lost if he didn't. He was between wrath and laughter.
"Make an honest woman out of her." The damfool phrase. He'd
like to see anything or anybody make a dull, dumb, "honest woman"
out of that magnificently sensual wildcat. Just let anybody intimate
to him—just once!—that he had "done his duty" by her. Just let
anybody hint that he'd married her for any reason except that she
was one of the most desirable women the world had ever held.
Wasn't she the first woman in this valley in a century and a half
that had fired any man to do murder for her? How frantic he had
been that March day when Anna so casually had touched off the
bomb, when he had driven off like mad hell from where she stood
repeating that Searles Shelf gossip. By the time he was in the Kemp
house he was so beside himself that if he had seen an unknown man
merely standing in the kitchen beside Lixlee he would have murdered him before asking any questions. He had indeed almost
murdered Lixlee, clawing at her, yelling his questions like a crazy
man. A good thing old Miss Gussie was stone deaf. How gallant
Lixlee had been, her lovely eyes fixed on his, clear and wide so
that he saw down to the bottom of her brave heart as she made
that reticent self-respecting revelation of the lonely battle an unfriended girl must wage to protect herself from what other girls
never even hear spoken of. How his fury of suspicion had transformed itself into a fury of indignant sympathy and understanding
and then into a fury of love and passion. What a girl! She made
a bonfire of a man and touched him off with a look. Yes, he understood all right what had crooked the finger around the trigger.
Poor devil out there on the woodshed roof looking in to see Lixlee
in another man's arms! If it had been the other way around he
too would have shot to kill.

A clinical thermometer was inserted under his tongue. "I don't *think* you have a rise in temperature, Doctor Craft, but your face looks rather red to me—not but what that's a nice change!"

He was asleep before she took it out—it was astonishing how even thoughts tired him out.

But, of course, the time came when he was really better, strong enough to have a visit from Lixlee in her wheel chair, looking amusingly saintlike with her transparent face, and long dark braids over her shoulders. But that was one of the spicy things about Lixlee —the two different people she looked, according to whether she did or did not open her eyes on you. Most people had never seen her real face. It was almost as good as being an old-time Turk and knowing that your wife's face was veiled to anyone but you. Yes, he liked the deliciously secret way Lixlee had of pulling the shades down and putting the light out when somebody she wanted to exclude knocked at her door—as he liked everything else about her—her hair that had enough vitality of its own to fit out two or three Clifford women, her neck, the firm elastic tautness of her beautiful, beautiful bosom. To have her face opaque to everybody but him—it was one of the most seductive things about her.

She smiled at him now, from under lowered white eyelids, held his hand a moment, murmured in answer to his question that she felt "pretty well" now, and was wheeled away by her vigilant nurse who apparently thought that just looking at the woman you loved was what a man wanted. The difference between that pale little social call and what their first night together would be, made his eyes so scornful and gay that his nurse told Lixlee's nurse it had done him worlds of good to see his wife. After that, they often wheeled her in for a moment. Rather to his tantalized exasperation than otherwise. Whatever else she was, Lixlee wasn't one of those tame women a man wanted to *talk* to!

And then, a fortnight later, he was actually strong enough to sit up a few moments, and the day after that a little longer and then long enough to write with his own hand the letter to Doctor Neale which he had written mentally so many times. His writing

was still rather sprawling, but it could be read. Three days later, when old Sandy's answer came back, he snatched the letter jealously from the nurse's hand.

Doctor Neale (first name Alexander, middle name McPhail) began with a few formal expressions of sympathy for Anson's "accident" and illness, and good wishes about his marriage, a notice of which he had happened to see in the Alumni News Column of the college paper. "I hope she'll be a help to you. A doctor's wife can make or mar him more than most! 'A man must ask his wife's leave to thrive,' my grandfather used to say." He added to these guarded Caledonia County comments on Anson's marriage, a blunt Caledonia County statement that yes, the break in those cardiac records would greatly impair, almost destroy their value. Absolute continuity of observation was the crux of the matter as Doctor Craft very well knew. It was regrettable. However, doubtless when Doctor Craft resumed practice he would make a fresh start. Probably new cases as interesting as those he had started on would present themselves, which according to their program he could watch without interruption from the very beginning and indeed before what was usually considered the beginning, if his theory of the significance of those nervous symptoms were valid. Doctor Neale advised very particular attention to cases of true angina in women, if any came under his observations, even if quite advanced. Any evidence of coronary closure diagnosed from the electrocardiogram with conspicuously abnormal T wave and convexity of the S-T phase *without* a previous attack of angina pectoris in the history of the case would be especially interesting as filling in gaps in existing records. If that old woman—Everts was the name—with the rare case of acquired pulmonary stenosis was still living, he would take the time to go down to Clifford and make an observation on it himself. In closing he wished Doctor Craft a quick recovery.

The letter dropped from the white thin hand. "However—doubtless—probably— It's not a year lost out of *his* life!" Doctor Craft thought, bitterly.

But the hemoglobin and red and white blood cells count of his blood being by this time somewhere near normal, there rose in his

heart his share of the old instinct to shake a fist at Fate which keeps the race alive. What was the loss of a year? Nothing, compared to a man's will! He *would* start again. There *would* be cases which he could follow from the first beginning through to death. And follow them he would, sleeplessly, unrelentingly, like a wolf on a deer's track. Give him ten years, twelve years in which to keep full records himself and correlate them with the records of the hearts of the same families kept by his father and grandfather—he'd have a collection of absolutely top-notch material that would knock the spots off those truncated odds and ends of hospital records of cases never under observation till everything important had happened. They'd be discarded as worthless compared to records kept in actual practice. It was of course a blow that Mrs. Everts had died. But as to angina in a woman, he had a case right under his hand, old Miss Bessie Kemp. If nothing else—and there was plenty else—her sense of apprehension, her great fear of death, would show it to be true angina. He'd keep her alive for five or six years longer if it took all of him to do it!

The flat-faced nurse noted noiselessly: "hands clenched, jaw set, frown and tension of lips, general expression of much greater vitality."

6

WITH the old-Greek narrowness of local feeling characteristic of the settlements up and down Vermont valleys, Ashley people though only seventeen miles away had few personal contacts with Clifford. They had all read in the *Record* about the mysterious wounding by a stray bullet of the young doctor who was assistant to their own old Doctor Cole. And gossip about where he had been when shot and with whom trickled up The Valley by word of mouth. It seemed, of course, a little more real than the violent deeds you read about in your Boston paper. But only a little. Not at all, for instance, as though it had happened to an Ashley man.

So there was not much comment on Maple Avenue when Doctor and Mrs. Craft finally began to live there. Those Deans, the bashful young pharmacist and his nice sensible wife who had taken the next house, they were Clifford people, too, weren't they? Mrs. Doctor Craft seemed to be just a young housekeeper like Mrs. Charlie Dean. The two brides were busy around their houses in clean percale dresses of a morning, sat dressed in pretty summer fabrics on their front porches of late afternoons, waiting for their husbands; and did not forget to put out the milk bottles at night on their respective back porches. Mrs. Dean went to the Episcopal Church (all Clifford people were Episcopalians if anything), Mrs. Craft didn't go to church at all. But that seemed about the only difference between them. Even in Clifford, there was not much talk when five long months after Town Meeting Anson resumed his tri-weekly office hours there. His practice, like that of most young doctors, was largely among poorer folks. And he generally came alone. Clifford hardly ever saw his new wife.

Moreover, his marriage now had stopped being a thing of the present, new enough to be molded and shaped with talk. It had slid into the class of fixed past events, along with the Spanish War, and the Battle of Bennington. You had your opinions about those happenings but what good did it do to talk about them! What few comments were made about the Crafts were divided between, "I can't see that she's wild and fast at all—what I should call a very nice-appearing young woman. I told you, you can never believe what Miss Bessie says! M'Sanna seems to like her brother's wife all right. And anybody can see that Doctor Anson's more than satisfied!" and a more dubious, "Well, wait a while—when you've made the bed you're lying on, you don't let on about there being lumps in it."

If anybody had asked Anson Craft's opinion, he would have said that his life in those days suited him to perfection. Physically he was on the rocket-like upward rush towards health of a sound organism that has successfully repelled a deadly attack. After those endless weeks of mortal weakness and suffering it made him feel like shouting just to feel the strength pouring back into his vigorous

young body. Mentally, his condition was as inspiriting. His attitude towards his work was wholly transformed by the revelation,
full and complete in his mind now after the long hours of convalescent meditation, of the capital importance of the research he
could carry on side by side with his daily routine. He was no
longer wandering in circles in a dismal swamp of trivial routine;
his every step in his practice now was forward, was part of his
steady, purposeful push through unexplored country, towards a distant goal of understanding and certainty. The grind of general practice no longer exasperated and disheartened him with its meaningless accumulation of petty detail. Not a day but gave him some
addition to the carefully kept records of the disease to the attack
on which he had dedicated his professional life.

And this deep satisfying confidence in the value of his work was
matched by the boundless satisfaction his personal life gave him.
From having been starved, his every hunger seemed now richly
fed. The debt to Anna that had shadowed him so long was discharged by the stroke of his pen that had transferred to her his
share of that unexpected bequest. He had been afraid she would
refuse it, and had consulted Fred Kirby about what he should do
next if she did. But Fred's steady "She'll take it all right" had
proved true. And with the disappearance of that obligation had
gone the unavowed element of strain in his relation with Anna;
he could be natural with her, and since he was, she lost that old
anxious defensive expectation of being hurt which had so often
out of sheer nervous tension wrought him perversely to give her
the very blow she dreaded.

And of course this—all this—was nothing, literally nonexistent,
compared to the astounded, intoxicated revelation of the joy that
love could give. . . .

It was depressing late summer, hot and humid. The subtle modeling of the mountains was stupidly muffled under the woolly green
blanket of trees in full leaf. The Valley looked as summer people
thought it looked. Everyone drooped and perspired and sat around
laxly, loosened and unvibrant as damp violin strings. But Anson
when touched gave out a taut twanging as though his eyes were

thrilling to the reds and yellows of autumn—walked down the
street as though October frost were in the air. When he stepped
into the Craft house in Clifford where, during the vacation absence
of Cora Ingraham, Anna was living alone, every fiber in her vibrated in a reflected wave of pure feeling, happier and freer than
any she had shared with Anson since he had grown up. "I owe
this to Fred," she often thought, to Fred whom she rarely saw in
these days, who had little to say to her, who had not so much
as been in town on the day when Anson proposed to turn over to
her his share of their inheritance. But, distant though he was, he
had towered suddenly over her, filling the room with his peremptory, *"Let go of Anson!"* So, in a matter-of-fact voice, "Why, yes,
brother, if you'd feel better about it," she said, opening her hand
sadly to let fall what she most prized.

But it had not fallen. Never had Anson seemed so near to her
as now since she had let him go. Where now was the irritable
temper they had thought an inevitable part of their Craft inheritance? And where the self-conscious silences that had shut her out
of all he cared about? Almost at their every meeting he said the
something real, for which she had vainly longed, talked to her open-
heartedly of his work, as never before. She was carried away by
what he told her of the research he was beginning alongside his
general practice. During his convalescence he had been turning
over and over in his creative mind the suggestion given him by
old Doctor Neale and had divined in it possibilities for probing
into stubbornly hidden truths, far beyond anything the rather lit-
eral-minded old specialist had seen. To take an obscure disease that
was certainly not wholly physical and material, and study it day
by day, year by year, not in dead tissue but in living men and
women, all of whose lives were open to your eyes, the medical records of whose fathers and grandfathers lay under your hand—good
heavens, yes! who would not see that it was a bigger life-work for
a whole man than sitting in a laboratory, his eye glued to a microscope. To amass authentic information about the progress of a
malady that took years to kill—that was work for a scientist in
intimate, uninterrupted contact with it during all its phases, not

merely with those of the very end. Strange that it had occurred to no one before that the only possible method of research was to apply to the whole course of the disease the same sort of intensive, minute scrutiny now given only to those cases which—always too late—were brought into hospitals to die. But of course such research to be successful required a combination seldom found, an impassioned scientific temperament, soundly trained in the austere methods of modern laboratory inquiry, but actually engaged in general medical practice. The usual easy-going family doctor would have no more idea of how to gather and collate the necessary facts than his bridge-playing wife. Yes, she could see how it was an opportunity for Anson alone among medical research men.

Listening as creatively as he thought and spoke, her sympathy and understanding drew him on to formulate an idea that was as yet only a seed in his mind—his conviction that *true* medicine must more and more concern itself with the obscure self-inflicted causes of physical misery as well as with enemies from without.

"I haven't told anybody but you, yet, but I am keeping two sets of these records of cardiac cases. One to go up to Doctor Neale about the actual material changes in pulse and so on, and reports on any post-mortems I make—for his laboratory boys who can't take into account anything that can't be smeared on a slide and put under a microscope. But I'm keeping for my own purposes just as complete records of every single item in the general conditions of a patient's life. Take angina now—you'll think I'm cracked on angina! It's because of the way nobody has plotted a single one of its curves yet. Do you realize that nobody understands even the mechanism of death from angina pectoris? Did you ever happen to think that apparently there is nothing in common between the people who have it? You can give one look at a boy and know he'll have trouble with his digestion all his life, and at a girl and predict she'll die of T.B. But what are the physical traits that predispose to angina? *You* tell! Nobody knows. Maybe it's something not physical at all. You'll find a blacksmith with it, and a broker maybe—what have they in common? And a mechanic in a garage like Tom Weeks here in Clifford, and again a high-stepper like

Elliott that never did any work in his life. And why didn't women use to have it, or hardly ever? And why do they begin to, now? Is it because of differences in physiology, or because men have been the wage-earners and have had a heavier responsibility? I'm going to collect angina cases, Anna, like a summer dame collecting Bennington pottery. I'm going to keep a *complete* life-record of everybody in my practice that has it, and when I say complete I mean complete. Not just how his heart reacts to this or that drug or muscular effort, but how he likes his work, how he gets on with his wife, whether his mother-in-law bothers him, what he does on his vacations, what kind of books he reads, whether he goes to church—everything that could affect his liking to live or not. Ten years, twelve years from now, when I get enough of these so they can be tabulated, and I can make some graphs—I'm going to keep up on everything that's learned about graph-making—there may be some conclusions to be drawn that'll put medicine where it belongs!

"Of course," he went on, "there's nothing new about the idea that general life-conditions can cause organic changes in tissue. Christian Science has been groping around in that dark corner. And a lot of modern books are written about it—if you can call novels books. There's a regular fad of literary belly-aching. But who takes fiction seriously? Everybody knows that novelists are just ignorant excitable peasants of the intelligence, with only the peasants' intuition and guess-work to go on. Like the old women and herb doctors that preceded modern medicine. There's a reason why nobody pays any attention to novelists but uneducated women and half-baked kids. But once let doctors put their trained, informed minds to work on human nature, not just human bodies, and you'd *have* something!"

His sister, listening intently to him, felt her imagination, stirred by each of his hints, leaping up with them to run far. She had been right—everybody had been right who had divined a real superiority in the saturnine young man he had been. His was the rare ability to scatter living seeds in other minds. And it was love that had unlocked his door and let him out. And love that had blighted and

blackened a vigorously flowering organism like Isabel's. Strange to
have lived in the world so long as she, and not once to have felt
a single shock from that life-giving, death-dealing current. Not
once? The color came up in her pale face, and with it a self-conscious expression that made her brother stop talking about his young
wife and turn the conversation to something neutral. It was scarcely
fair to let a celibate have a hint of what she was missing.

He did not often remember that it was perhaps kinder not to
speak of satisfied love to an old maid, and did not by any means
confine his talk to his work. One day soon after his return to active
life her usual inquiry of "How's Lixlee?" brought from him an
involuntary boyish, "Oh, wonderful!" And before he knew it he
had let her look into his heart. "It's a revelation to know that anyone can feel so at peace as I do, so reconciled to life," he said in a
shaken voice. "I wish it could come to you, Anna." She made no
answer to this.

There were other times when the floodtide pouring through his
life overflowed into hers because he could not hold it back. One
September night they had both been working till very late on a
case of septicæmia in a poor house on a back road. It was long
past midnight when they drove off in her car back towards the
valley. They were both tired, the barriers of personality lowered
by excitement, and by effort together. Their wills, released from the
taut professional tension in which they had been held, relaxed to
a floating vagueness; their thoughts wandered undirected. Anson
sat silent for a time in the dark car, his arms folded. Beside him,
Anna, driving by second nature, leaned her head towards the window to watch the thick-sown stars, spangling with gold the black
roof that stretched from mountain top to mountain top across the
valley. From time to time as the road turned, the headlights of
the car lighted an autumnal maple tree which in the same instant
flared up to a pillar of red flame and died out to blackness. Once
Anna swerved sharply to avoid a scudding white-tailed rabbit. From
a hemlock thicket the eyes of a deer caught the lights, gleamed like
living jewels and went out. Presently as if he were thinking aloud
Anson said, "Why do we hide from young people what the love

of man and woman can be,—how magnificently more it is than magnificent physical gratification! We tell them, right enough, that sharing life with someone else takes the poison from your wounds and makes life a glory. But we never give them a hint that nothing but love, violent love that tramples your self-control to bits, can work the miracle of making you *able* to share life with another." He said no more. Perhaps had not known he had said this. For the rest of the drive they sat in silence, the echo of his words spangling the darkness with gold.

When she stopped to let him out, she waited while he raced up his front walk like a boy. When the house door closed behind him she still sat motionless in the car. Only after the light in the hall had gone out and the house lay dark like all the others on the street, did she drive on to her own dark empty house.

7

ANSON knew that he raced back to his love like a passionate boy, and that Anna saw him doing it. He was glad to have her see it. He would have gloried in showing all the world how he felt. He was proud of the violence of his delight in Lixlee, proud of being crazy about her. "I'm literally mad about you!" he often told her. "About every single thing you do and are!"

It was true. Every expression of her mouth ravished him. He adored the deep-veiled voice that gave her words a mysterious color. His rancor against complacent triviality was appeased by her indifference to the childish occupations of ordinary women—bridge playing, paying calls, dressing for each other's eyes. He was amused and enchanted by her epic ignorance of his profession (so much more dignified than the foolish half-knowledge that made most people nuisances to a doctor). The complete absence in her mind of any formal knowledge made her, he thought, seem timeless and universal Woman, free as in the dawn of time from the rote-learned odds and ends of information which impeded the breathing and moving and loving of lesser Eves. To his imagination there

was something grandly primitive in her ignoring of all that is usually called news. If he did not unfold the newspaper in the morning, he found it at evening still twisted together on the front porch as the newsboy had left it. It gave him a picture of her day, all centered about her absent lover, that made him tell her, fancifully, "It's Eternity you live in, not Time!"

But above all he was wrought to almost unbearable ecstasy by her bodily presence. The way she sometimes sat dreaming, one long white arm up over her head, brought tears to his eyes like the loveliest poetry. He could never decide which of her physical attributes gave him most joy. Sometimes he thought it was her hair, which had an electric life of its own; sometimes it was her firm smooth elastic skin, which he could not leave alone. "It would take dozens of lifetimes for a man to get enough of you!" he told her madly, himself astonished by the sharpness of his ever-renewed hunger. "I could spend forty years just kissing your flower-petal cheek and not be satisfied!" It was by no means only what was literally beautiful in her looks that stirred his blood to fever—it was everything! Her high cheek-bones; that fascinating slight deviation in the focus of her eyes which he could sometimes catch and sometimes could not see at all; the line of her jaw so long that it would have been a defect in another woman's face; her feet—because they were Lixlee's it seemed to him one more proof of her spacious, epic quality that they were not baby-small and conventionally arched, but strong and large, feet that drew from the earth on which they were planted, so Anson thought, the unabashed physical vitality which made her seem to him the only living woman in a collection of eviscerated wax figures.

He told her this. He told her everything. Not in the daytime. They never talked much then. Lixlee was never quick to speak. And there was not much time. Meals were hurried, like those of most young doctors. Anson came and went rapidly and irregularly, usually with no more than time enough to look Lixlee up for an instant and pounce on her for the embrace that was always his first impulse. "I never can remember what I had to tell you, because

the minute I see you all I can think about is hugging the breath
out of you."

It was during their long nights that their talk was intimate. At
least those were the hours when Anson's tongue was loosed as he
had never dreamed it could be. All that had been locked in his heart
and mind came to expression in the exquisite hours when, worn
out with loving but still awake, they lay clasped together. "I never
believed that anyone *could* be so at peace," he often murmured to
her, "so reconciled to life!"

Not only what he had consciously thought and kept to himself,
but thoughts and emotions he had always repressed with a savage
scorn for self-pity, flowed thus into words in this miraculous free-
ing of his locked heart. With his love's arm around his shoulders,
he could speak with compassion of the anxious, fatherless boy he
had been, he could yearn over his striving youth, shadowed, hard-
driven, over his furtive snatching at the poetry and great literature
he would have loved to add to his life. What exquisite relief from
a life-long tension to lie thus dreamy and tranced and feel the
hidden deep things of your heart pouring painlessly from you.
Locked in the impregnable stronghold of love, it was luxury to
him to remember the bitter ingrowing misery of the first months of
his home-coming, after he had renounced what seemed his only
chance at living. Holding his wife in his arms and thanking her
over and over for the joy she gave him, he tried—turning from one
impression to another as they fled through his mind—to share his
every thought with her, "You do see, don't you, Lixlee . . . oh, that
crazy name of yours, how I love it! Who ever had such an absurd,
adorable name! I *want* you to see, to know how much you mean to
me. It's more than just our personal happiness, though, by God!
that's all anything need to be! But it really does go deeper, down
to the depths, up to the heights. It gives me an intuition—honestly,
a mystic sort of intuition—about the hidden sources of life! I never
believed in anything mystic before. But really there is something
mysterious, that I can't understand, about the way our love widens
my intellectual conception of everything—of science, of knowledge,
of . . . I see as I never could before what the trouble with medical

research is . . . and of course now I see why a dry old stick like old Neale can't get anywhere, and why laboratory squinting can't locate the real root of anything human. For it can't! It hasn't! Do you know, Lixlee, that common as angina is, there is actually not one single decently probable guess about what causes it?"

Lixlee's voice came murmuring through the darkness, veiled and mysterious as the night, "Isn't there? What's angina?"

To hear her speak filled him with fresh amazement that she was really there, could really be there. He snatched at her exultantly. "Do you know who's the biggest fool in Windward County? It's a man in bed with the worst little demon that ever got inside a smooth skin—and wasting his time talking as if he'd married a trained nurse, God forbid! Never you mind what angina is! I'm going to talk about *you* now, Lixlee! Lixlee! Lixlee!—I'm going to start with your feet—yes, they're big! You can't get me to say they're not! But I love them for it. And I love . . ."

But of course other later nights found him again mixing talk of his work with all the rest of his self-revelation. How could he not? He could keep from her nothing that he was. In those moments of exhausted well-being it was not only his body that was relaxed and fulfilled, not only his heart that was at peace; his mind too. With no will of his own, what he had dimly dreamed, thought, guessed at, came flowing again and again over the lowered threshold. "This happiness of ours . . . it gives a greatness to life! It makes you stop being ashamed to be human. I'd known before—everybody knows—that ordinary human life is one long nightmare for anybody that's sensitive and intelligent. But what you can't believe till you feel it is what pure joy human life *can* be! It's the contrast that shows up what a strain on the heart unhappiness is. I tell you, Lixlee, if more men and women knew how to be just simply naturally happy, as you and I are this minute, there wouldn't be enough sick hearts left for an ambitious young doctor to get famous on. But of course you'd have to wring a lot of withered necks first—the prudes and the nay-sayers."

Lixlee was usually a passive listener to his monologues, cutting

them short when she had had enough, with an embrace or a beginning of tantalizing play. But she now said dreamily, "That's a
comical word. What does it mean?"

He laughed. "Exactly what you are not, Miss Wildcat. A nay-
sayer is somebody that won't let you have a good time without telling you it's your duty to stop and do something that's a bore."

Lixlee put her arms around him, and said she would never, never,
never make him stop having a good time, and that she had always
hated the folks who wanted to stop good times as much as he did.
"I didn't know you called'um no-sayers," she added. "A good name
for'um."

Anson thought, "If it were anybody else I'd wince at some of the
intonations Lixlee uses. Because they're hers I love them. It's all a
miracle." To her, he said aloud, "It doesn't make any difference
what you do, Lixlee, I like it better than anything else. You're not
just more important than anything else to me. I honestly don't care
about anything but you." He spoke with heartfelt sincerity. He
would have sworn he meant every word he said.

Another time, looking out from the circle of her arms at the rest
of humanity, he groaned aloud at the thought of their self-inflicted
misery, "Good gosh, when you think that people've spun out of
their own innards the very ideas they make Juggernauts of! They
don't have to lie down and be run over—they just think they have
to! Some days I feel like busting loose from medicine altogether
and spending my time blowing up the damnable conventions
that . . ."

"Why bother about'um now?" asked Lixlee in her rich dark
voice. As she spoke she rubbed her cheek softly up and down
against his. A very faint musky odor came to his nostrils as if from
this friction. He prostrated himself before the elemental wisdom of
her "now." "You see, I don't even know how not to spoil a perfect moment. You'll have to teach me, Lixlee. The way you live
in the present . . . it's the most wonderful thing about you, seeress!"

"I thought it was my feet," said Lixlee, holding one up in the
air and shaking it. He burst into laughter like a foolish little boy,
thanking the gods for the gift of non-ironic mirth, new to him.

Lixlee laughed too, wildly, happily, and said, "We *do* have good times, don't we?" A golden quality in her fun struck his ear, and for once turned his eyes away from himself and his own reactions. He said, surprised, "Why, Lixlee, I believe that is the first time I ever heard you laugh right out like that!"

Not with self-pity, only as a statement of fact, she answered, "What did I ever have to laugh at before now?"

A rare impulse of tenderness, not of passion, made him ask her, "Do I really make you happy? You *do* love me, Lixlee? How much do you love me?"

She made her first—her only—attempt to tell him in words how much. In other ways she had told him madly enough and often enough. "Well, listen—I never did anything but hate everybody before. Why wouldn't I? They all hated me. You needn't say they didn't. They did. The minute they laid eyes on me they hated the way I was and wanted to make me do different. All but Miss Gussie, maybe . . . she's kind o' queer. Well, I got so I kinda liked to hate'um back, and get even with'um. It was about all the fun I had. See? It *is* kinda fun. And easy! Folks fool'umselves so. You don't have to do much but keep still and watch'um do it." She lay still a moment, and then, taking his hand in both hers and holding it to her breast she said brokenly, "But now I love you in a minute as much as I hated everybody else all put together all my life. That's how much."

"It's literally a miracle," he told her, deeply moved.

She went on, her voice trembling, "I just couldn't take it in at first, that you liked me the way I am. Other folks had talked soft about wantin' to be good to me, but all they wanted was to get me where I couldn't help myself, and then make me stop doin' what I wanted to do, and do what *they* wanted me to. I thought at first maybe you would, too!"

"It's the strength of your wanting that makes you life-giving," he told her. "Do you know *now,* dear, how I will never, never try to . . . ?"

"Oh, I believe you *now,* all right," she said trustingly.

They fell asleep hand in hand.

Sometimes they both fell asleep at the same time. Sometimes they both lay awake in a haze, dissolved in silent senuous well-being. Sometimes she aroused herself first from this delicious languor to give him a teasing or an ardent caress. Sometimes it was he whose wandering sensations first turned into thoughts and then into words.

Late one October moonlit night that had been full of love, he came out of an exhausted sleep and looked over at her. She lay motionless, resting, long white arms folded under her head, her body relaxed in the physical composure that was one of her gifts. But she was awake. Her eyes were open. He drew one of her arms around his shoulder and began to murmur dreamy broken half words, first of love, of her, then little by little straying into his work, which more and more filled his waking thoughts, "You do understand, don't you, dear, why it is I have to get my notes down on paper the minute I come into the house? It's because I'd forget some detail if I waited. And every detail counts. Oh, Lixlee, the swell collection of heart-facts that I'm getting! Just you wait, my girl, you'll be the wife of a famous doctor yet!"

"Hey, there, mister," murmured Lixlee in his ear in a voice that showed she was recovering from her lassitude, "where do you think you are? In your office?" She drew closer the arm that was around his shoulder, and rising on her other elbow looked down at him smiling, provocative, her teeth white in the moonlight. Then still showing her teeth as though she were about to bite him, she stooped her face closer and closer to his till he caught fire from the flame in her eyes.

A quiver passed all through his flesh. "You little devil!" he cried, in adoring gratitude for her power to arouse him. He seized a handful of her long hair and with a random gesture began to pull her head from one side to the other. She lent herself to the rough play, her glistening laughing eyes gliding smoothly back and forth from side to side, always fixed on his. In the silence he could hear how her breath came faster as her eyes deepened from laughter to passion, as her face darkened into the grave contained fury that made

him feel a god, not a man. The pounding of his pulse spread from his breast to his temples, to his ears, to his finger-tips. Although he was awaiting her fall, when with a soft exhalation of her breath she dropped with all her warm weight, his heart stopped beating—and then sprang into a clamor of nervous pulsations.

But before he could raise his arms to put them around her, he was transfixed by a loud dissonant jangling in the room, close to him. With a quiver of his nerves, he recognized it as the telephone bell, the special one for emergencies. The first time it had been used.

He lay still, coming slowly to himself from an immense distance. Lixlee was softly winding herself around him, as if there had been no sound. Perhaps he had dreamed the bell.

"The telephone bell didn't ring just now, did it?" he asked, bewildered.

"Sure it did. But you don't have to answer it."

"Gosh, yes! I have to. *That* bell!" he reminded her, and waited for her to loosen her coils.

She tightened them. "No, no, no, no," she said fondly, in a coaxing, laughing, melting murmur. "No, you don't have to at all. You can say you were out. I'll swear you were away. I'll say you left right after dinner to drive over the mountain. It'll be fun. I'll tell'um you had to go over there for a case of an-an-gina. Who'd ever know?"

He thought, tender of her unreason, "What a kid she is!" And to her said in a gentle grown-up tone, "Oh, you know I couldn't do that, darling."

The bell rang again, longer. Every disciplined fiber in him vibrated to its peremptory summons. "I've *got* to get up, Lixlee," he told her as if he explained to her that as long as he lived he could not but breathe. "Let me go, dearest."

At the reasonableness of his voice, glinting like an icicle in the love-warmed room, she started away from him, and strained her eyes through the moonlight to see his face. Hers was very white. Her lips were shaking. And so was her frightened bewildered voice,

as she asked, "You don't *want* to go, do you, and leave me . . . now?"

"No, no! Good God, no!" he groaned. "I just have to. That's all. Don't make it any harder for me."

At this she showed her teeth again. But not in a smile. As if she were threatening him with death, she told him fiercely, "You don't have to at all! And you know it! It's nothing but an idea out of your own head! If you go it will be because you want to! And if you do . . ." she lowered her face steadily, menacingly towards his, "I'll never forgive you, never, never, never!"

She dropped her whole weight upon him, clinging to him madly, winding strong arms around him like ropes, pressing her face into his chest, oppressing his breathing. He was too astounded to stir.

The bell rang again, a long peal that sounded in his ear like a tocsin. With a spasmodic contraction and expansion of his will and of his muscles, he broke from the bonds that held him and sprang to the telephone. . . ."Yes? Anson Craft speaking. The third call? Sorry. I came as soon as I could. What? Mrs. who? *Oh* . . . ! Yes, yes, of course, not a minute to be lost. Right away. I'll be ready as soon as you can get here."

He hung up the receiver, flashed on the electric light and began to dress at top speed. Lixlee lay on her back on the bed completely covered with the sheet, even her head, as if when he had left her she had tried to shut out life. As Anson stooped and reached and buttoned and laced clothes and shoes, he explained to her, "You see, Lixlee, it *was* important. A patient at the hospital suddenly turned the wrong corner. We'll have to operate at once."

Lixlee tore the sheet down from her face to see what he was doing. When she saw him partly dressed she cried out in dismay, "Why, you're going! Right away!" The agonized sincerity of her astonishment was beyond question. This seemed actually to be her first notion that he might go.

"But, darling!" he protested, stooped over his shoes as he tied the laces. "How can I help it? Doctor Cole will be here for me in no time. Suppose I hadn't answered the phone. He would have found me here."

Now it was of willful bad faith that her indignant eyes accused him. "You're just sneaking out of it!" she cried. "I'd *told* you what we could do! When he got here I'd have gone to the door and told him you were out. You *knew* that!"

"Don't talk so foolishly, sweetheart," he exhorted her, tilting his chin as he buttoned his collar. "He'd know *you* must have heard the bell." His tone was a little absent. And so was his face. His mind had run away into the operation before him at the hospital. He had seen it performed only once in his medical training, and there were some details he could not remember. He would give anything for one glimpse of the drawing in his old text book that showed where the arteries ran. To be half responsible for getting them all tied, and tied solidly—he was frightened and elated at the prospect. His first really major operation! If he could only bring the course of these arteries clearly and completely before the eye of his memory!

Lixlee lay for a moment staring at the reflection cast by these thoughts on his face. Then with a groan of pain drew the sheet up over her head again, and lay like a corpse on a bier. The moan reached Anson's ear as her unreasonable words had not. He felt truly sorry for her. And for himself. Snatching open a bureau drawer he fumbled in it for a clean handkerchief, calling across to her sympathetically, "I feel as sore about this as you do, kid, but it's just one of the things we've got to put up with."

The body swathed in the sheet shrank together as if it had been struck. From it came in a heartbroken wail, "Oh, shut up! We have to put up with it because you want to, that's all! You're a liar! Just a plain ordinary liar!"

"Now, darling, have a heart!" Anson adjured her, some impatience in his tone. He had begun to have enough. A short tantrum was natural enough, part of her ability to let herself go. But she'd had time now to . . .

Lixlee pulled the sheet down from her face. Her cheeks were chalk-white, her eyes tragic. His astonishment brought him to a stand, "Why, Lixlee, what *is* the matter with you? You must know

I have to answer an emergency call for an operation. You knew you were marrying a doctor! It's a matter of life and death."

"Don't you pay *any* attention t-t-to what I say?" she implored him, desperately. "Didn't you hear me tell you how we could fix it so you wouldn't have to go? Don't you *see* what you're doing to me? When you t-t-tell me I'm all you l-l-live for . . . do you mean *any*thing? . . . or is it . . . are you just f-f-f-f . . . ?" Her teeth were chattering so that she could not go on.

He stared at her, trying to untangle what she was saying from the details of the anatomical plate in his text book which at that moment came distinct before his inner eye. For the time of a heart-beat the passion of her shocked resentment and despair almost battered its way to his heart through his absorption in himself. For an instant, just one out of all his lifetime, he was almost enough shaken from his rooted stand in the midst of his own values to guess at the existence of hers.

But she gave the swaying balance a violent push away from her. As if on a sudden suspicion, "Who is this patient?" she asked.

"Nobody you know. Oh, yes, you do. Mrs. Browne, Cornelia Dean's mother." He flung on his coat.

Lixlee sat up in bed, the sheet slipping down to her waist, "Do you mean to say," she asked in a loud rough voice that broke into a sob, "you're going to stop in the middle of loving *me* because of an old hag like that!"

Startled, confused and hurried as he was, he could not but laugh at the delicious unimaginable femininity of this. "You priceless little savage, you!" he cried from across the room, as with a mechanical gesture he felt in his vest pocket to make sure of his pipe. It was not there. His face went blank. Oh, there it was on the table. He snatched it up, slipped it into his pocket with one hand as he put the other arm around her bare shoulders. "Haven't we got all the rest of our lives to love each other? You're as primitive as Eve!" he told her, dotingly, gave her a one-armed hug, stepped rapidly into the hall and ran downstairs. Through the glass of the front door he could see the headlights of a car rushing along the street towards the house. He put his hand on the door knob. His name

was called menacingly from above. He looked up. Lixlee's face black and beautiful with fury hung over the stairs. Outside, the headlights slowed down and stopped before the house.

"I know you now, Anson Craft," called Lixlee, in a voice not loud but singularly penetrating, "and I'll never believe you again! Never! I know now you don't mean one damn word you say!"

How magnificent she looked when she was aroused! Outside the automobile horn gave a snarl of impatience. He flung a kiss to her, thinking how exciting it would be to love her out of this frenzy when he came back, and to go on where they had left off, only with even more of the agony of nervous pleasure. He opened the door. "You just wait, tiger, tiger, till I get back! I'll show you whether I mean what I say," he cried exultantly and stepped out.

"I warn you! You can't treat *me* like dirt and get away with it. I warn you! I warn you!" Lixlee's low, intense voice hurled itself over the railing. But he had closed the door.

8

IT was then half-past two, a late moon fainting on the ridge of Mount Weary. He had thought he would certainly be back at the house before dawn, before Lixlee was up. But the operation took much longer than he had expected. Not because of unexpected complications in what was to be done. Because of a frightful fumble of Doctor Cole's. It had given the younger doctor a shock to see his senior fail in so simple a routine detail. It might have been damn serious. It very nearly was. Together with the silently criticizing nurse, they had both worked their heads off to pull their patient out of the danger caused by the slipping ligature. Everything outside the operating room had faded into a distant blur, and so had everything personal within it. In their battle with the death which hovered over the middle-aged body for which they were responsible, they had needed—and given—all they were. If asked suddenly to give the name of the human being for whose life they were fighting, they would scarcely have remembered it.

Afterwards, as they washed their hands, Doctor Cole, ashy and aged, said, shamefaced, "Mrs. Cole has been worse lately. I am up and down with her a good deal, nights. It's—it's not very good for steadiness of hand."

Anson thought pitying, scorning, "An old man with an ailing wife. What surgery comes our way is evidently going to be up to me. I'll take that and leave the well-to-do women with the vapors to weep on *his* shoulder." And that would be all to the good. He hated that kind of patients.

The mention of the older doctor's sickly wife reminded him of a young doctor's wife who was anything but ailing. By that time he was very tired. His nerve had been shaken by his colleague's ghastly mistake. The thought of Lixlee's vitality was not an altogether reassuring one. In fact, as he stood there in his shirt sleeves, mechanically scrubbing his hands, it frightened him. For just long enough to conceive it, the idea occurred to him that what he had called "tantrum" might have been more serious than that; more lasting in effect than a mere nervous explosion; not what he had thought it,—a woman's equivalent for the raging "Damn! Damn! *Damn!*" with which a man frees his bosom of the perilous stuff of rebellion against the inevitable. "Could she really have *meant* that insanity about not answering the phone, and lying to Doctor Cole?" But Anson, son of one doctor and grandson of another, was incapable of more than one glimpse at that possibility. The brain cells he had inherited could not harbor such an idea.

Yet, though instantly dismissed, it left a darkness behind. To explain his low spirits he reminded himself that he had had no breakfast, although he had been up and squandering nerve-force at top speed for four hours. A doctor's was really a hell of a life to invite a woman to share, he thought gloomily, drying his hands. And of course it was only fair to remember that the same superb ignorance of cut-and-dried tradition that made Lixlee so brilliantly new to life, would make the inevitable sacrifices of a doctor's wife harder for her than for a conventionally brought-up girl. He would need to be extra patient with her till she was used to it. The pros-

pect was anything but to his taste, detesting the exercise of patience as he did—in everything except medical research.

He looked at his watch. Half-past seven. At ten he was due at the Clifford school for those confounded tonsil and adenoid examinations. Why in blazes didn't they send out seniors from the Medical College for routine stuff like that? He ran his finger-tips over his cheek, frowned over the thick-growing stubble they encountered, and started out from the hospital door. He had not gone twenty paces before a nurse came running after him. "Doctor Craft, please. The patient's heart . . ." Old Cole, trust him, had already gone. Grim and breakfastless, Anson worked for another hour over Mrs. Browne, not softened inwardly even by the distress of her daughter Cornelia who had wept all night in the hospital waiting-room. In fact, he was glad to see that it was possible to move the phlegmatic Cornelia out of what her friends called her "poise."

When he finally turned into Maple Avenue it was nearly nine. The air was crisp and sunny and cool—Vermont October. But his step was as heavy as if a July thunderstorm hung in the air. He was very hungry and very tired. But most of all he was uneasy to the point of alarm about how he would find his wife. On his front porch he halted, latch-key in hand. Looking fixedly at the closed door he heard a ghostly echo of Lixlee's wild, "I warn you! I warn you!" An ominous overtone of danger throbbed through it.

Astonished and ashamed, he thought, "Am I afraid to go into my own house?"

To self-respecting persons who feel fear there is left at least the resource of acting as though they did not. He straightened his tired back, opened the door and went in.

From the dining-room Lixlee greeted him at once with a quiet, cozy, "Hello, there, Anson!" Fresh in a clean print dress just as she looked every morning, she stood beside the table. It was set for breakfast. His vitals quivered at the heavenly smell of freshly made coffee.

"What'll you have first?" she asked him. "Peaches? Or your coffee?"

"Oh, coffee! Coffee!" he cried, trying by his tone to make a joke of his craving for it.

He was relieved almost to the breaking point to find food and rest and a good-natured wife, and staggered around the table to give her a grateful kiss. She put up a wifely cheek, said in a wifely voice, "*Boy!* You look all in!" and brought him in coffee, eggs, buttered toast, crisp savory bacon.

He ate and drank ravenously, one eye on the clock. The excellence of the food and the comfort it brought his empty stomach threw a blanket reassurance over all that had troubled him—Doctor Cole's failure to tie that artery properly, the prospect of taking on responsibility for all the surgery done, the possibility of Mrs. Browne's dying, Lixlee's flying off the handle. He poured himself another cup of coffee, and took another slice of toast. What a fool he had been to work himself up so about the scene Lixlee had made. Women proverbially made scenes. And forgot all about them the next minute. It was what you had to expect when you lived with one. She'd just boiled over and got it all out of her system. Not a bad way. Look how sunny and pleasant she was now. He was enchanted that he would not have to be patient with her.

She brought in the sliced peaches now, swimming in yellow cream, and sat down opposite him. "You're the second man I've served with breakfast this morning," she told him. And how might that be? Why, she had, it seemed, thought of poor Charlie Dean, left stranded by Cornelia's being at the hospital with her mother. Stepping across the back yard to the Deans' kitchen door she had, sure enough, found him burning his own toast and unable to find where Cornelia kept the bacon. "So I just had him over here and gave him a good feed," said Lixlee with a smile.

This was a kind neighborly side of Lixlee's nature Anson had not seen. "That was awfully thoughtful of you, dear," he said, surprise as well as approval in his voice.

Lixlee made no answer but she smiled a little more.

Cornelia Dean's mother was sick a long, long time that winter before she finally sank to her death in April. Both doctors (who had

their own remorseful reasons for extra attention to her case) attended her devotedly and so did Cornelia. Some days—even some nights, when the invalid was very low—Cornelia was at the hospital more than at her little new home on Maple Avenue. It was hard on a bride, people said, even a bride with such wonderful poise, to have a tragic anxiety the first year of her marriage, when she was expecting her first child. And hard on a bridegroom too to have, in addition to a baby coming right along, his young wife so taken up with sickness in her family.

"Why don't you ask Charlie over to dinner tonight?" Anson often said to Lixlee when he had left Cornelia staying on at the hospital. Lixlee always answered, smilingly, "All right, if *you* say so," and walked with her leisurely rhythmical step across the back yard to the other house to give the invitation. It was rather a bore to Anson to have an outsider there so much, but it seemed like a partial reparation for the mistake that threatened Cornelia's mother with death, and Charlie was a harmless, quiet fellow known to Anson and Anna all through his mild mooning boyhood and youth. He was no heavyweight intellectually, his taste in books being all for poetry, novels and other light reading; and, thin, sandy-haired and freckled as all the Deans were, he was not much to look at. But as a newly graduated pharmacist he had a professional background that gave him something in common with Anson to talk about. He and Lixlee had little to say to each other.

He was not the only guest who sat down informally at their table. Sometimes old Miss Gussie came up on the 'bus to spend a morning in the Ashley library, invited herself to lunch with Lixlee and Anson and drove back to Clifford with Anson. Sincere as was his scorn of gossip he was not sorry to have her do this, knowing (as did she) that nothing could contribute more to the stilling of Clifford talk. Also, steeped in the deaf person's life-long expectation of not having any attention paid to her, she was very little in his way. Her one-sided conversations with Lixlee even gave him considerable amusement. Lixlee could not sharpen and raise her rich deep voice to the sawmill screech which now alone could pierce

to the old woman's ears, and so wrote her half of the talk. From the bathroom where he shaved, or his office, Anson smiled to hear Miss Gussie's flat toneless voice holding forth *in vacuo*— "If you put a few cloves in, it won't." "No, don't bother to try to save 'em. I've got more in the garden than I know what to do with." "Well, I'm glad to hear it. It kinda worried me." "Now, Lixlee, you *know* better than that!"

She seldom said anything at all to him on their drives back to Clifford beyond an occasional comment on the weather or on life in general, which might have been a thought of her own spoken aloud as well as anything meant for him. Once indeed it turned out that she was definitely addressing him, although it did not sound like it. She roused herself from a long contemplative silence to say, "Yes, I remember that was what Grandfather always told us children . . . that we were to be extra respectful to folks that came of no-account families. Everybody's got to have *some*thing to be proud of as much as he's got to have vittles, Grandfather used to say, and folks like that hadn't got but just themselves to be proud of. 'Twas more like murder than just hurtin' somebody's feelings to slight one of *them,* he always told us."

Anson took for granted that she was thinking aloud and made no comment.

She turned her eyes on him, very clear though so sunken and old, and said mildly, "It's Lixlee I'm talking about, Anson."

Anson suppressed a smile and told the old maid loudly, "Oh, I'm always *very* respectful to Lixlee, Miss Gussie."

"See that you are!" she said firmly, and lapsed into her usual silence.

The next time he saw Anna he told her, laughing, "You know I've always told you one of the nicest things about Lixlee is that she brings me no sermonizing in-laws. Well, I'm not so sure. Miss Gussie—of all people—shows signs of taking on the rôle of mother-in-law."

But rough winter weather came on, the footing was icy and uncertain, old ladies stayed at home. Miss Gussie seldom appeared in the Crafts' house. Plenty of other people did. Sometimes Anna in

Ashley on an errand telephoned to ask if she might stay to dinner, bringing perhaps Father Kirby. The two of them were working together just then on the reports, repairs and preparation for next year's Windward County Boys' Camp. Once or twice another member of the Camp Committee came with them—a stout gray-haired farmer's wife from The Other Side, perhaps, or a civic-minded business man from Clifford Depot. There was an occasional official from the State Health Department or a classmate of Anson's driving through town. Sometimes the Anson Crafts had a dinner or lunch party of five or more. But, as like as not, the very next day Anson, delayed by an accident, would telephone Lixlee that he was grabbing a bite at the lunch counter at Clifford Depot and wouldn't be home for dinner, so that she sat down quite alone. No one at all to eat dinner with her, or many—Lixlee took what came with a quietness that reassured her doctor-husband. His colleagues had led him to believe that irregularity at meals was one never-failing source of friction in doctors' households. "It doesn't seem to bother *my* wife in the least," he sometimes told another doctor. Nothing seemed to bother Lixlee. Quiet and competent she moved about her work, rather silent—she never was a chatterbox—but often with a smile on her lips that did not, her husband thought, speak of any suppressed dissatisfaction with her lot, even though there was in it a good deal of slavery to the telephone and a marked uncertainty about her husband's coming home to meals.

Their marriage was going very well, he told himself. Not so much wildness in it now but that was normal. You couldn't keep any emotion always keyed to its highest pitch. You wouldn't want to. There was enough wildness left . . . plenty! He still thought there was no joke so good as the contrast between the sleek decorum Lixlee showed the world by day, and her tigerish response to his touch when they were alone.

November blew into The Valley a frosty air that made elderly plow horses prance, and sent middle-aged cats like Henrietta madly chasing dry leaves and their own tails. Miss Bessie Kemp had a magnificent attack of angina lasting long enough to get a clear electrocardiogram showing an abnormal T wave that Anson was

proud to send to Doctor Neale, together with a positive assurance
that there had been no stenocardia in her history.

His day-by-day observations on the various hearts in his practice
grew greatly in volume. Occasionally—though it was much too
soon for this—he caught an exciting glimpse at this or that possible base for generalizing from the facts he was gathering. On
entering the house the first thing he did was to go at once, often
without waiting to take off his overcoat, into his office, to set down
on paper the dated record of what he had heard that day in pulses.
It was wonderful, he often thought, how a big worth-while motive
carried you over the dustiest routine. A scientific mind like his,
to which accuracy and exhaustive information were essentials of
thought, would naturally have found general medical practice intolerable with its copious guessing and its necessity to base its reasoning on insufficient data. But because the continued observation
of living human beings in their normal round was the only source
of the data he sought, he endured general practice not only patiently but gladly, working his head off, for instance, in the thank-
less undertaking of keeping Cornelia Dean's mother alive, as she
begged him, at least till April so that she could see her first grand-
child before dying. "You know Cornelia's expecting then," she reminded him every day he stepped into her room at the hospital.
Once, very full of Cornelia's good news, "No interesting event expected in *your* family, Doctor?" she asked him. "Not yet," he answered, and had a passing thought that this was a little odd, he
and Lixlee both so vital, both so crazy about each other and quite
willing to begin their family now in their youth.

Basketball at the Ashley High School began. One of the first
matches played was with the Clifford Academy. The Crafts and
the Deans bought tickets and intended to go all four together to
cheer the home team. But Cornelia's mother had one of her low
spells, and at the last minute Anson was sent for to a premature
confinement case. Charlie Dean and Lixlee went together, Charlie
reporting afterwards that they had sat successively in all four seats
to get the good of their money.

December was there. Ashley saw much less of Anna now. She was struggling with the details of furnishing and organizing that Out-of-town Students' Home she had made so much fuss about last year. Applications were coming in. It was to be opened next September—if Anna didn't pass away first from overwork. Anson who saw her twice every week in Clifford reported that Cora Ingraham was being helpful about the new venture. "Those charmless women have to do something to justify their being let to go on living," he told Lixlee. Christmas came. The Crafts invited Anna, Father Kirby, Cora Ingraham and Charlie Dean to dinner. (Cornelia was at the hospital with her mother.)

"Ye gods!" whispered Anson in Lixlee's ear as they stood in the dining-room together, just before calling in their guests, "was there ever such a dim virtuous crowd? Not enough devil in all of them put together to steal a postage stamp!"

Lixlee smiled, looked down at the table, said, "There! I've forgotten the olives!" and turned away.

Anson caught at her, "Here, let me kiss that subtle smile of yours first."

Cornelia was not very well, which surprised nobody. A young wife who was "expecting" and whose mother was slowly dying, naturally wouldn't have much pep, her friends said. Anson who was her attending physician was fascinated by the paroxysmal tachycardia which troubled her at this time. Any other doctor would have thought it reflex, due to the emotional strain of her mother's illness and the physical strain of her own condition. But he had several relatives of her father's under observation, had noted that the older women of that family had an unusual amount of mitral stenosis. Consulting his father's and grandfather's medical diaries, he found that many of the earlier generation of Brownes had died of valvular diseases. Perhaps in Cornelia, though it looked like simple neurotic tachycardia, he had an incipient case of something serious he had been looking for, which he would watch from before the beginning. For the hundredth time, he thanked Providence that he had behind him two generations of doctors working

with the same families in the same place. It gave him eighty years of pertinent medical data.

He spoke of this to Doctor Neale when in January the specialist came to spend the day with him. And he showed the old doctor not only his own minutely exact and detailed records but his father's and his grandfather's notes, beginning in 1852. Doctor Neale, whose own father and grandfathers had been back-road farmers, was impressed. Although given to Caledonia County silences about other people's work, he gave Anson distinctly to understand that he was satisfied, more than satisfied, surprised by the possibilities in what Anson was doing.

It was at the dinner table, after the day's work was over, that he said this, gruffly, as ungraciously as possible. Anson had often told Lixlee how greatly he prized Doctor Neale's opinion, and shot across the table at her a proud, sharing glance. Doctor Neale caught this and followed it with his eyes to where Lixlee sat behind her wifely teapot, her dark hair burnished with brushing and vitality. She wore a yellow voile dress, with a net fichu open at her white throat, its converging folds drawing the eye to the lovely fullness of her bosom. The old doctor stared at her as though he had not noticed before that she was there. Anson was proud to have him look, proud of what he saw. Amused, too, by the perfect defense against those formidable cold eyes made by Lixlee's "lights out and shades pulled down" look. Meeting Doctor Neale's scrutiny with her half smile she held him at arm's length by a play of inquiring eyebrow that conveyed her expectation of a question from him about something on the table, and her hospitable readiness to pass him the salt or sugar.

What he grimly asked was, "How do *you* stand being a doctor's wife?"

She broadened her smile, and made a gesture with her shoulders to indicate that she found nothing very difficult in that undertaking.

Anson spoke proudly for her, "She's a perfect doctor's wife!"

Doctor Neale shifted his cold-steel eyes from Lixlee to her husband, and inspected Anson's face silently for an instant. Anson had

not Lixlee's ability to resist what was in a look, and bristling under this one, explained resentfully, "I don't mean she's one of those intolerable prying women who 'take an interest' in all the details of their husband's work. I mean she makes a perfect home. And isn't jealous of my women patients. And keeps my mind free from care so that I can concentrate . . ." He stopped himself now, nettled that his old teacher could still make him feel and act so young and touchy.

Doctor Neale looked down at the food on his plate and went on with his dinner.

Anson thought wrathfully, "The old brute has the worst manners in Vermont! And could you say more!"

But he was soothed to see that Lixlee did not care a hang, any more than she ever did. It was a strength in her he envied.

Still smiling, she said in her easy natural tone, "How about another cup of coffee, Doctor Neale?"

She could hold her own with anybody, thought her husband admiringly.

9

JANUARY had three days of what would have been called a blizzard elsewhere, what was called in The Valley a real good fall o' snow. Everybody except very old people and housebound invalids was delighted to see it. It meant jobs in the woods for choppers, easy hauling on runners over good slipping, and glorious coasting for young folks. And then on general principles Valley people liked snow. They told each other it made everything look "kinda pretty, like in 'Snow Bound.'" But the real reason was that cold and winter made them feel ten times more up and doing than humid Augusts. And to feel up and doing seemed to them enjoyable. "Let them that wants to, lay 'round in hammocks" was how they expressed this sentiment.

The winter weeks went by. Anson grew used to Lixlee's acceptance of the unpredictable irregularity of a doctor's life. As com-

pletely and naturally as he had forgotten what he had had for supper on that night or any other night he had forgotten his first emergency night call, his wife's objection to it, which patient of all the many on his mind had been involved. Most later calls had found them sound asleep. He took for granted in the same way Lixlee's not minding his uncertainty about meals. He was under the impression that he was being unusually thoughtful about domestic arrangements because when delayed he made a point of telephoning her as soon as possible so that she would know what to expect.

Detained at the hospital one late afternoon in January by a leg broken in a coasting accident, he telephoned her he would not be home for dinner. But just as he was getting the X-ray photograph taken, Doctor Cole appeared in one of his jealous fits, and claimed the patient as his.

"Just as you like," said Anson, a little scornful, a little amused, considerably annoyed, but relieved at the prospect of a decent dinner. He thought of telephoning Lixlee again but someone was using the hospital telephone booth and, "I'll be home by the time I could get her on the phone," he thought, and drove quickly to the house.

Fresh-fallen snow lay thickly on the front walk, and deadened the sound of his footsteps. He took out his key, opened the door, stepped into the front hall. The door to the dining-room was closed. Charlie Dean's hat and coat were hanging on the rack. Oh, yes, he remembered now he had seen Cornelia at the hospital just as he left. "Hello there, Charlie," he called, going through the living-room into his office to set down his notes on hearts while they were fresh in his mind.

He was half through this desk work when his nerves sent up to his brain a belated impression of incompleteness. Charlie hadn't answered that hail, had he? Yet that had been his hat and coat. Perhaps he didn't hear. Perhaps he'd stepped back to his house for something. The doctor's fingers continued busily to set down the symbols he had invented to indicate the slight changes in the pitch and quality of the aortic closure; but the silence that had filled the hall now displaced the air in his office. His thoughts keen and ordered were still on his notes, but inside his body fibers duller

than nerves and closer to the core of his being, set up a dark throbbing. In the midst of a sentence he stood up suddenly and stepped back through the living-room. The dining-room door was still closed. He turned the knob and opened it. Charlie Dean sat there, sure enough, in his usual place. His sandy hair was rather tousled as though he had not been home to wash and brush up. In the kitchen a replaced stove lid rattled audibly.

"Oh, hello, Charlie, you *are* here then," said Anson. "I didn't hear your answer just now when I called to you."

Charlie had not lifted his protuberant eyes. Nor did he now. He hesitated and looked towards the door to the kitchen. His face was rather pale. Perhaps a little set. In a flat voice he said, "Oh, didn't you? I said 'hello.'" He looked down at his tea and stirred it around and around.

"See here, see here, see here, see here!" said Anson to himself. A very disagreeable taste came into his mouth. His pulse leaped up. There was not a thought in his head. There seemed to be nothing of him at all but unrecognizable and savagely unpleasant sensations.

Lixlee appeared bringing a plate of hot soup which she set down at Anson's plate. In her usual voice she said, "Hello, Anson, glad to see you back. What did you do with the broken leg?"

The inimitable naturalness of her voice and manner filled her husband with a relief as sensory as his discomfort had been. He took a great gulp of air. His mind caught up and overtook his hurrying senses, perceived that Lixlee had asked him a question and after an instant's effort remembered what the question had been. "Oh, Doctor Cole took on the broken leg," he exclaimed, sitting down, a little dizzy. Good grief! What hell it must be to be jealous if just a faint momentary awkwardness canceled out everything in you but reflex spasms of striped tissue a thousand times more quickly than your will-power could summon up your common sense. "I bet my pulse is a hundred and twenty this minute," he thought.

"Did I get too much salt in that soup?" asked Lixlee. "It's one of Miss Bessie's recipes."

He tasted it. "No. It's all right."

It was in fact, very good, as Miss Bessie's recipes carried out by Lixlee always were. And so was the onion-smothered beefsteak which followed. By the time he had finished that, Anson's pulse was at normal, and he had figured out reasonably what that odd little passage meant. Poor Charlie had fallen under Lixlee's spell— who wouldn't? Especially a fellow whose only experience of women had been a cambric-tea specimen like Cornelia. Being decent, Charlie felt miserable about it. Being honest he was no good at hiding the fact that he was miserable. To his credit.

Anson looked over at Lixlee. She raised her beautiful eyebrows inquiringly. Evidently no suspicion of any of this had occurred to her. Yes, Anson remembered now that he had been amused to see how casually she took Charlie, as if he were a piece of furniture. But of course Charlie was a poor stick if there ever was one, born to be treated by women as if he were a chair or a table. Still he was a human being. Anson didn't want him to get hurt too much, didn't want to be in any way responsible for spoiling a marriage, even of a poor stick with a wet sponge like Cornelia. And it had been really his own idea, having the poor sap around the house so much.

By the time he had dispatched his dish of the excellent chocolate dessert he was feeling sorry for Charlie. A little scornful, too. And then professionally interested. . . . "Gosh! I'd like to know what *his* pulse is! I bet it's going like a trip-hammer!" For a wild instant he wondered if there weren't some pretext by which he could take it. Then seeing the element of real comedy in this, he broke into an involuntary laugh. Lixlee's eyebrows asked their butterfly question again, and he hastily invented something amusing that had happened to him that day. This reminded Lixlee of a ridiculous scene in a movie to which she had recently gone. And when she had finished, Charlie Dean, now quite his usual color, brought out a humorous aphorism of his grandfather's that was apropos.

"I remember your grandfather very well," commented Anson. "It was seeing my father set his broken collar-bone that decided me as a boy to go into medicine."

The reef was passed. They floated smoothly in deep water again. But Anson had no mind to repeat that sickening scrape of the keel. When the pharmacist went away he called out good-naturedly enough, "Well, good night, Charlie," but the moment the door closed behind him he said seriously, "Lixlee darling, come here."

She came at once and perched on his knee. "What's the matter with you tonight?" she asked, her eyebrows arched.

He put what he had to say in a question, "See here, you seductive little demon you, has it ever entered your head that Charlie Dean might—that maybe he is—falling for you harder than what's proper for a man with a new wife of his own?"

He expected her to be too astonished to answer him at once. But although she was silent, the expression of her attentive face did not look like surprise. Her eyebrows were level now. She looked at him so keenly that he felt a little ashamed of himself. After a pause she said gravely, "Well, perhaps."

How reasonable she was! It was going to be perfectly simple. "You see, once you think of it, it's plain," he said, at his ease, stepping forward confidently like a man wading in shallow waters. "Not really his fault either. Our fault. We've been foolish to let him hang around so much." He thought he saw a protest rising in Lixlee's serious eyes and added hastily, "Not our fault. Mine. I know, I know it was my idea, not yours. I had a . . . a sort of a professional reason for wanting to help the Deans out. But I ought to have known better. Well, now let's put our heads together to see how we can stop it without making real trouble. Of course poor old Charlie's the mildest guy that ever wore pants. It won't be hard. But we've got to think of some way of putting it." He waited for a suggestion from her.

Lixlee's breast rose in a deeply taken breath. "You might just speak to Cornelia about it and ask her to stay at home with him more," she suggested steadily.

"Great Scott, no! That'd be the same thing as telling her!" Anson protested. He was astonished that Lixlee hadn't seen this. "Cornelia's having a hard enough time as it is. Her mother is dying.

Her heart is going back on her. You wouldn't want to make it any harder for her!"

"Wouldn't I?" asked Lixlee, her eyes deeply on his.

Puzzled, half laughing at the idea, Anson said, "Why, you haven't got anything against Cornelia!"

"Or her mother?" asked Lixlee, never shifting her eyes.

"Her *mother!*" exclaimed Anson, stupid with wonder. "You never so much as spoke to her mother, did you?"

At her answer he stepped off from safe shallows and sank like a stone into fathomless cold depths.

"No," said Lixlee in a low ominous voice.

There followed a moment in which the two searched each other's faces, desperately looking for what they did not see. Then from his very heart Anson said honestly, "I haven't the faintest idea what you are talking about."

She sprang up from his knee with a cry of horror. . . . "You don't *know* . . . ?" She struck her hands together. "Oh, you *must* . . . !" But plunging a despairing gaze into his depths she saw that he spoke the truth.

Before he could stir, she put both her hands over her eyes and bowed herself together as if she would fall. "Why, you don't love me at all. You never have." She said this in a voice so low and broken he could scarcely make the words out.

But they brought him to his feet, immensely relieved, the whole mysterious scene taking on at once in his eyes the comforting aspect of something natural and to be expected. Her words, the traditional phrase of nervous young brides, told him what all this was. It was hysteria. Just regulation feminine hysteria. All women were subject to it. Novels were full of heroines crying out that their husbands did not love them any more. Perhaps Lixlee was pregnant and had not told him. To have a text-book label for what he did not understand made it seem simple and intelligible. Tying a technical word tightly over his eyes, he saw no mystery anywhere, and with confidence in his mastery of the situation, took his wife into strong loving arms that were very practiced in holding her. "Why, darling! Darling! *Darling!*" he cried. "How can you be so crazy!

You know there's nothing of me but loving you! Love you . . . why, no woman was ever loved as you are! (His professional experience taught him that arguing with a hysterical person is like arguing with a deranged mind, a mere loss of time. To bring logic to bear on a delusion only deepened it. The thing to do was to change the whole emotional color of the moment, to flood the sufferer with tenderness till the delusion was washed away by love.) "Why, I can't think of anything in the world but you, Lixlee. I'm a perfect idiot about you! Everybody knows that! You're my life! You're all that makes life worth living for me. Love you . . . why . . ."

But no matter what he said, she hung limp in his arms, both hands pressed over her face in a spasmodic rigidity he could not break. She spoke twice. Once, whispering sadly, "There's no use telling me those lies again. You'll never make a fool of me any more." And once, half strangled with sobbing, "Just you wait! I was only trying to get even with you . . . but now!" The words, the tone sounded angry and bodeful. But when he held her off, he could see the tears streaming down from under her fingers. He redoubled his caresses that began by being tender but soon were passionate. Let him once kindle her into the flame that was her natural element (he thought) and all this nonsense whatever it was would be burned to ashes and blow away.

But he was soon frightened and shocked by the austere hostility of the dear body that had always been so volcanic in its response to him. He lost his head. He forgot his scientific decision not to go into explanations with her. His own voice broke with emotion as he begged her, "Oh, darling, don't torture me. If I don't even know what it is, how can I be to blame? But if you'd tell me what the matter is, I'd . . . I'd . . . I'd . . . do anything to make it up to you!"

He meant what he said, yes, but it was as an indulgent grown person coaxing a frantic child that he persisted, "Lixlee, dearest, why can't you just tell me? . . ."

She snatched herself from his touch, turned her back on him,

said darkly from behind her hands, "It's *your not knowing* that's
the matter! I'd die before I'd *tell* you! Any woman would!"

His first stupid blankness came back like a black bag flung over
his head.

The office bell rang. A patient must have come into the waiting-
room. To his surprise Lixlee said in a smothered voice, "That's
your office bell. You'd better go."

In great relief that she had been the one to suggest it, he answered,
"Well, I will. But I'll be right back here with you the minute office
hours are over."

She said nothing more. But she had stopped crying. The worst
of the storm is over, he thought. He kissed a piece of her cheek
that was not covered by her hands, and stepped away not very
steadily across the hall into the living-room. A mirror on the opposite wall showed his hair rumpled, his necktie loosened, his face
pale and haggard. Good grief! how scenes did take it out of your
nerves! Partly to give himself time to quiet down before confront-
ing a patient, he cupped his hands over his head for a stroke at his
hair, straightened his vest, and raised his hands to pull his necktie
into place. As he thus made himself neat, uneasiness struck deep
into his back, like a hard-flung knife. Turning around with a start
he saw that Lixlee had taken her hands down from her face and
was looking at him. The dining-room light was behind her and
he could not see the expression of her face but her silhouette was
tautly attentive to what he was doing.

He opened his mouth to explain how he happened to be thinking
of his hair and necktie but there was something so daunting in her
silent scrutiny that no words came. Between resentment and shame
he took a step back towards her. His office bell rang again.

"There's another patient," she said quietly. "You'd better go."

Well, all right, he would! He went on into his office. His half-
finished card catalogue records lay scattered on his desk. Was it
only an hour ago that his mind, free and clear, had been pressing
forward towards that impersonal goal? He could scarcely focus
his eyes now to read what he had written, could not at all focus
his memory on what he had meant to add. He frowned at the cards,

opened a drawer and swept them into it in a disorderly pile. A day lost, that was what it was. He stepped to the waiting-room door to call in his patient.

The work that evening was the usual uninteresting routine—a felon to be lanced, a case of eczema, an indigestion, coryza—"Drugstore stuff," he called it scornfully to himself and with a start remembered Charlie Dean. How completely that poor chap had dropped from his mind in this explosion. Lixlee had gone off halfcocked so fast she had evidently scarcely heard what he said. Well, they could take that up another time. It was a matter of no consequence anyhow. If they couldn't do anything else without calling Cornelia's attention, they could always move back and live in Clifford. But apparently he and Lixlee had been quarreling—had that been a quarrel?—not about Charlie Dean but about his mother-in-law! Trying to follow women's whims certainly was enough to addle a man's brains. The conviction came to him . . . it would explain a good deal . . . that in spite of Lixlee's saying that she had never spoken to the old lady, that Mrs. Browne had sometime snubbed her. She had all of the Merrill snobbishness, and would like nothing better than to drive home her low birth to a young woman more attractive than her own daughter. And, just as old Miss Gussie had warned him, Lixlee would desperately resent what she considered a slight to her dignity. Perhaps she had said something to Miss Gussie about Cornelia's mother that very day that Miss Gussie had spoken to him. Yes, that must have been it. That was what Miss Gussie had meant. All the same, even though he now knew the cause, he wouldn't bring it all up again and talk it over with Lixlee unless she started it. Those hysterical phobias merely throve on attention. The best treatment—and, oh, in this case infinitely the less painful for him—was to ignore them. She might be over it by this time.

Sure enough, when at nine o'clock he shut up his office and went upstairs, he found Lixlee in their bedroom, quietly brushing her hair and getting ready for bed. She was in a loose flame-colored dressing-gown she had made herself, a favorite of his. He stood

looking at the rich mantle of her hair falling almost to the floor as she leaned forward. One white arm rose and fell with the flying brush. Apparently she had not heard him come in.

"How are you, dear?" he asked tentatively.

She sat up at once and flung the shining mane back of her. She looked just as usual. "Oh, I'm all right," she said in a reasonable tone.

And there was neither austerity nor passivity in the lovely body he took in his arms. "Oh, good! Fine!" thought Anson, relieved, only too glad to let it drop, whatever it had been.

As he lay awake, later that night, he told himself almost with pride, "Well, my hot-blooded girl doesn't make scenes often, but when she does . . ."

But she never made another.

Just before he dropped heavily to sleep he thought, "That's the first time I ever saw Lixlee shed tears."

It was also the last.

PART FOUR

1

LIFE and death entered the little world on Maple Avenue in Ashley that spring. Cornelia Dean's poor mother who had been ill in the hospital so long, died on April 10, two days after Cornelia's baby was born in the same hospital. The young mother, of course, could not take any responsibility for the funeral— in fact, her heart rather going back on her after the strain of her confinement she was not told at once of her mother's death. Young Mrs. Craft made all the arrangements, took all the care off the young husband's shoulders, showed herself as competent as she had been all winter, kind and neighborly. After Cornelia was at home again with her baby, fairly well except for her unsteady heart, she often told callers she didn't know what she and Charlie would have done that difficult sad winter if it hadn't been for the Crafts. When she said "the Crafts" she meant Lixlee, for she always had been a little afraid of Doctor Anson. You could never tell, she told Charlie, *how* he was going to take things. "I'll say you can't!" Charlie agreed.

Her naming the baby Alix, for instance. Anybody would think he'd like that. But, "Alix!" he'd said, pretending he didn't understand. "Why Alix?"

"For your lovely Alix Lee, doctor," she had said; and seeing him still looking queer, had felt awkward about his making her explain that Lixlee had made a confidante of her.

To Charlie that night she said, talking with some heat about this encounter with Doctor Anson, "He put on that thundercloud look of his as if Lixlee had done something wrong in telling me. Why in the world—? It's just *sad*—nothing to be ashamed of—that mother-

232

less little girl losing her splendid father and being sent back North
to those dreadful relatives of her poor mother's. Nobody but a born
snob would see anything to be ashamed of in it! He has the queer-
est ways, anyhow, the doctor has!"

"I'll say he has," agreed Charlie.

"Still, if he didn't like her telling me, I'm sorry I mentioned it.
I don't want to make trouble for Lixlee. I bet she doesn't always
have the easiest time with that grouch, as it is. You can just bet I'll
never tell him anything else. Nor you either, Charlie."

"Not on your life," agreed Charlie.

"He's simply hateful, that's all. He doesn't even like to have
Lixlee praised. Every time I say something about how nice she was
to you and me when poor Mamma was sick he looks as black! I
believe the safest thing is for us just not to mention her to him at
all."

"O.K. by me," agreed Charlie.

He agreed with everything she said in these days. Or that Anson
said. Or that anybody said. "O.K." or "all right, sure"; he never
said anything else to Cornelia's frequent proposals that they invite
Lixlee over to dinner on evenings when they knew Doctor Anson
had telephoned that he was detained on a case; or that they run
over to spend the evening in the Crafts' living-room instead of their
own, talking, to the accompaniment of the radio. They had tried
playing bridge on such evenings but Lixlee could not seem to "get"
the game at all, showing a rather complete inability to reason from
the cards that had been played to those that must be still held.
After two or three evenings of this, Cornelia asked her husband as
they got ready for bed, "Charlie, does Lixlee ever seem dumb to
you?"

"How do you mean, dumb?" asked Charlie cautiously.

"Why, just plain dumb!" She hastened to add, "I don't mean
it as anything *against* her—lots of nice folks are. Mamma was.
Brains aren't everything. Only—in Lixlee—she kind of puts it over
on you that she's somebody. You know—the way she carries sail
generally. Maybe it's because she doesn't talk much. Or maybe that
deep voice makes anything she does say sound sort of important.

But sometimes when Lixlee and I are visiting together, just ourselves, she gets off something that makes me think she doesn't know *any*thing."

"She hasn't had much chance for book learning, of course," said Charlie.

"Oh, I don't mean that! It's not what you study about—dates and literature and things. But she doesn't seem to—well, this, for instance—the other day she told me she'd cooked an egg too hard because the water had boiled up hotter than usual, and I started to explain to her why water can't get any hotter than boiling. Honestly, I thought I'd go crazy—she didn't seem to be able to follow anything I said. Yet she's a real good cook, you know. Well, for heaven's sake let's keep off bridge. Another evening like tonight would give me brain fever. I don't believe Lixlee could learn the rule of tit-tat-toe."

"O.K. by me," agreed Charlie.

So after that when they went over to the Crafts of an evening Cornelia took some sewing along, and Charlie a book, from which, when conversation gave out, and the radio was dull, he read aloud. Cornelia was one of those who are made nervous by reading aloud, but didn't mind if she had something to do with her hands. Lixlee listened without sewing. Even when it was poetry.

It was convenient having the two houses so close. Cornelia could run back every half hour if she wished to look at little Alix, who was rather delicate. And the doctor could step into his office when a patient called. These flittings rather broke up the group. But Lixlee and Charlie were always good-natured about waiting for the other two to come back. As an unusually warm spring came on, Lixlee sometimes slipped on a wrap and they moved out on the side porch to wait. Sometimes strolled off for a short walk.

Time after time that spring, when Anson came back into the house from his office, he found the radio volubly talking to itself in the empty living-room while over in the Dean house he could see the nursery lighted. Sometimes he found his wife and Cornelia's husband on the side porch in the dusk. Sometimes they were not to be seen anywhere.

He liked this less and less, grew more and more grim to Charlie, felt more and more at a loss.

One evening in May, he stopped short in the midst of filing some notes, because he could not fix his attention on what he was doing, and went back into the house. In the empty living-room, a disembodied voice was explaining unctuously the merits of a toothpaste. There was no one in the dining-room. The kitchen was dark. Anson looked out of the open window and in the Dean house saw Cornelia leaning over the baby's crib. He walked rapidly, his pounding step jarring the house, to the side porch, and flicked the light on. The porch was empty. "Lixlee!" he called, and was shocked by the quality of his voice. There was no answer. Behind him, with a loud false geniality, a voice announced, "And now, dear unseen friends of the air, we are going to turn you over to . . ." Anson plunged back, turned off the radio, and returned to the door. "Lixlee!" he shouted, menacingly, as he had never before pronounced her name. There was no answer. Inside the semi-circle of light cast by the bulb from the porch the grass glistened wetly with dew. Outside it, the spring blackness lay softly impenetrable. He waited, his muscles tense, darting his eyes to one side and the other. Then the black pool of silence around him was broken by a faint sound. He gave a start. But it was a homely and familiar sound, the click made by the opening of the refrigerator door. He looked back. The kitchen was lighted. He was at the door in two strides, saying furiously all in one word to Lixlee's beautiful amphora-shaped back, "Why-didn't-you-answer-me?"

She turned around carefully, her eyes fixed on a brimming basin of milk she had taken from the icebox. "I didn't hear you call," she told him, her quiet voice in harmony with the steadiness of her hands as she walked slowly towards the table. She set the pan down, the line of yellow cream unbroken, and asked Anson peaceably, "What did you want of me?"

"*Where's Charlie?*" asked Anson, his eyes fixed on her shoes glistening with dew.

"Oh, was he the one you wanted? He forgot his watch at the store and had to go back to get it," said Lixlee. "What did you want

of him?" She walked in her wet shoes with her light, rhythmical step back to the refrigerator, shut the door with a gentle click of the latch, and looked at Anson inquiringly as if she wondered why he did not answer.

He could not. His vitals stirred sickly in him in the primitive physical qualm that precedes nausea.

Lixlee looked past him, her face brightening into a smile, "Oh, *hello*, Cornelia! Wouldn't Alix go back to sleep? The bad little girl! Isn't she the cute thing! How sweet you look with her!" Cornelia, looking like a Flemish madonna, came into the kitchen. She moved slowly with the same controlled concentration of care Lixlee had shown for the brimming basin of milk. Her eyes were fixed in adoration on the tiny face, now grotesquely writhing. "I do believe she has gas, doctor!" said the young mother anxiously.

"Many do," said Anson, and walked off to his office, his heavy step jarring the house.

He made up his mind that evening not to let this sort of thing run on. He would speak to Lixlee about it and sternly put a stop to it. But he was in no condition of nerves to make a success of any interview that night. It would be wise to wait a few days till he had cooled off. By the time he had cooled off he could not believe that he, Anson Craft, had lowered himself to the thoughts of the man who, his muscles tense, his face congested, had stood at the front door, glaring out into the perfumed silence of the May night. He felt like a man who has had a fever and, his temperature at normal again, remembers with shame the strange delusions that had seemed reality to him.

He thought mornings, shaving a rather haggard face—the only time he glanced at a mirror—that he not only felt but looked like a man who has had a fever, and was afraid Anna would ask questions about his health. But she seemed to notice nothing unusual. She had seemed rather worn herself, and now was busy getting her work ready to leave with a substitute during what she called her vacation—six weeks spent in a settlement house in Boston, studying the organization of their home for needy out-of-town students, especially their system of buying supplies, and their account

keeping. This was not the first time she had made this temporary exchange with a city nurse. Anson could not see why her attention was now so absorbed by it that she hardly heard him when he spoke to her. But it was all to the good not to have her notice that he was looking seedy—even though it did make him feel slightly aggrieved. Long before she came back from her "vacation" he would have had his plain talk with Lixlee and together they would have devised some way for pushing that unpalatable Charlie off their map. It was absurd to let yourself be ruffled by a fellow old Miss Bessie had described as a "cipher with the rim off." He let several days go by, and several evenings too, forcing himself not to notice whether the Deans were at their house or his, and then one night he chose, as favorable to coolness and self-possession, the time when he was brushing his teeth in the bathroom, to call out over his shoulder, "Say, Lixlee, I thought we were going to hold Charlie Dean off a little. Seems to me he's around the house more than ever."

He had been afraid of what he called to himself "fireworks" from his wife, but her tone was as casual as his as she called back, "That was *your* idea."

Whatever he had expected it was not this, and, genuinely surprised, he stepped back into the bedroom to remind her, "Why, you agreed with me, Lixlee. You know you did. You said you did."

Lixlee sat before the mirror pulling at the ribbon in the neck of her nightgown. "No, I didn't," she answered absently, leaning forward and trying to get a better view of the knot in the mirror.

"You did too!" said Anson, emphatically, his temperature beginning to rise.

Her fingers still picking at the ribbon, her eyes fixed on the knot, she said in a matter-of-fact voice, "No, Anson. Honest! Just remember back. That time you spoke of it all I said was, 'perhaps so.' But goodness! The minute I really thought, I could see there wasn't anything to it! There! I've broken it! Damn ribbon anyhow! See if you can get hold of it before it slips all the way back." She went over to him, tipping back her head and turning her shoulders so that he could see the broken end. He put his hand up mechani-

cally, and began to fumble with it, his fingers brushing the warm, fine-textured skin of her breast. "Can you get hold of an end of it?" she asked him. "Just stick it back and forth through a few of the holes in the beading, will you, so I can make it do for tonight. Why, about Charlie, I didn't suppose you meant it seriously even. I'd forgotten all about it." She took the end of the ribbon from his fingers and, pulling the thin fabric together, asked, her face lifted to his, "Whatever put such a funny idea into your head, anyhow? Was it something Charlie said that you didn't like, maybe?" She turned away to the mirror, took up her hairbrush, remarking over her shoulder, "He does say dumb things sometimes."

She had asked him a direct question. But Anson, staring at the close-grained ivory of her nape, did not answer it. How could he, caught and held in that matter-of-fact atmosphere which she had so softly, so quickly spun about them? How could he say that the aspect of a shut door, four months ago, the feel of a night silence the other evening, had warned centers of his being deeper and surer than his intelligence? As far as that went, he did not believe in such centers himself, but placed his whole trust in his brains. He now brought up to mind the items recognizable by the brain. Her not answering when he called. But she had explained she had not heard him. Her shoes glistening wet with dew. It would make him sick to speak of the suspicions they had suggested to him, but even suppose he could, she would say, "Oh, I'd just stepped out to bring in something I'd hung on the line." And perhaps she had. Perhaps Charlie *had* forgotten his watch. Perhaps he *was* making a fool of himself. He knew with what contemptuous pity he would listen to any other husband talking about shut doors and thick silences, and wet shoes.

His legs were tired. As if he had walked far. He sat down heavily on the edge of the bed, his hands hanging between his knees, his eyes still on the back of Lixlee's neck, up from which she was brushing her hair in long, regular strokes. At the end of each sweep of the brush the shining silken mass hung for an instant in a soft cloud, the ends of the hairs quivering. He could almost hear them tingle. He himself had rarely had so little vitality. Too little to hold

up his head. Too little to push out of his mind a distasteful thought he had resolutely banished weeks ago. "That Alix business! The aristocratic Virginia father . . . !"

He had been thunderstruck at first, when that had come out in Cornelia's prattle. But turning it over and over in his mind it had occurred to him that this was what Miss Gussie had referred to. Perhaps Lixlee had brought out that story in her hearing, and the old woman had wished to put in his mind beforehand the idea that on the part of a proud girl with such a wretched family background as poor Lixlee, it was no more than a natural and harmless, indeed necessary, defense-mechanism to protect her self-respect. He had accepted that argument. He had considered that the matter was wholly disposed of by it. But here it was again, as immediate a bad taste in his mouth as aloes.

His troubled eyes met in the mirror the reflection of Lixlee's. Hers were clear and quiet. She laid down her brush, rose and went to him. The comforting arm she laid around his neck brought with it a thousand touch-memories of the sweet dark hours of intimacy that were his happiest time.

"Why, Anson, you're not really worried about that?" she asked. "If you are, if Charlie bothers you, just tell him to get out and stay out. *I* don't care. If you'd feel better."

He turned to her, his back straightening, relief in his eyes.

"Only," she added, "I remember your saying once you didn't want Cornelia worried, on account of her heart. You'll have to tell me what to say to her about it that won't worry her."

He sank together wearily.

Lixlee broke into a murmur of laughter. "Oh, you old nit-wit, quit fussing and come to bed," she said caressingly in his ear. Her loosened hair fell around him like a silken web.

So the next day and the next and the next all went on as before; Cornelia laying on weight, happily insane about her baby, and more than satisfied with the daily routine of the life on Maple Avenue, which kept Charlie contented without asking her to leave little Alix for the "running around" to movies and dances that most

young men wanted of an evening even after they were fathers. Charlie was perfectly satisfied, too. And so was Lixlee, going around her work, or brushing her hair of an evening with the smile on her lips that had looked to Anson, some months earlier, so pleasant a proof that she liked what she was getting out of life. Anson was the only one who could not settle down. He was stiffly unresponsive to Cornelia. When Anna dropped in to see them and said something about his happiness, he was depressed to gloom by the unconscious wistfulness of her face. He returned a glum taciturnity to Charlie's attempts to be sociable. Yet he was furious when Charlie desisted, and sat silent instead, looking at his cigarette tip with a faint smile. He made constant attempts to reason as Cornelia did, from the unsuspicious American premise that a nice young American husband is not also a man; and once in a while, for several days at a time, he succeeded.

But even when things were at their best he found it hard to keep his mind on his research work which by the worst of misfortunes was now tied by an association of ideas to this nagging uneasiness. The act of sitting down to transcribe his rough notes to the cards of his permanent record now brought back that snowy evening in January when with no volition of his own he had risen so hastily from his desk, and the evening in May when that hideous moment of insanity had overtaken him. Every time he began to work on his files he was obliged to make an especial effort to fix his attention on what he was doing, especially if, as often happened, he had just seen Lixlee sitting on the porch, her eyes fixed on Charlie as he read aloud out of one of his accursed poetry books—or perhaps had not seen either of them anywhere, and had scorned to look. At such times he fumbled with his cards, shifted them around causelessly, told himself he was an idiot, worked for a few moments and found that he was once more trying to imagine just how Lixlee had told Cornelia that fairy tale about her Virginia father and all the rest of it. "Could it have been in that 'natural' voice of hers?" Sometimes when he had torn his thoughts away from the sequence of ideas following that question, he discovered that he was staring at a card he had filled with a meaningless tangle

of lines. The first time this happened he was annoyed; the second time he was startled. The third time he got up and poured himself a drink of prescription whiskey. After that he tried the whiskey first.

Then Charlie began, apparently of his own account, to be much less in evidence. Days passed without his being in the Craft house at all as far as Anson knew. Between relief and uncertainty Anson told himself that perhaps it would just blow over of itself. But presently a change crept into Lixlee's way of talking. Although she still never read a line, an occasional literary word began incongruously to appear in the plain, decently grammatical speech which she had taken over from Miss Gussie's instructions and which Anson liked for its homeliness and straight-grained unpretentiousness. Once in a while she used a word like "exquisite" or "poignant" or "gracious." Every time she did this a perspective was opened into Charlie Dean's poetry and novel-reading habits that made Anson wince. But he said nothing till one evening as she stood at the window watching a gray day loweringly sulk itself into night, Lixlee said casually, "How austere it looks!"

Anson went off like a bomb, "Who taught you that word?"

Lixlee continued to look out of the window, "Oh, I don't know, really," she murmured with a dreaminess that sounded provocative to Anson, "where I did hear it. At a movie probably."

The day after that Anson went out of his way to be so disagreeable to Charlie that there could be no mistaking his meaning. The next morning Lixlee said at the breakfast table, "Cornelia is pestering the life out of me to know what's the matter with you, Anson. What do you want me to tell her?"

He sprang up from the table in a rage. "You don't have to tell her anything. I'll do the telling!" he said violently and strode across the grass to the Deans' door. But when Cornelia, mild blonde madonna, the baby in her arms, came to open the door to him, he was helplessly her physician, not a plain man. He knew her heart had been in bad shape since her confinement, knew how wildly her pulse would flutter and how her lips would turn blue if he . . . The truth was that he could strangle her as easily as tell her what

he had come to say. He coughed, stammered, looked away; ended by saying he had had a series of bad headaches that made him unsociable lately. Going back to his office, he poured himself another drink.

But after a week or so of determining not to pay any attention to Charlie, and of seeing, wherever he looked, nothing but the red spark kindling in Charlie's eyes when he brushed against Lixlee in the casual contacts of their shared daily life, Anson once more strung his will taut, and said firmly to Lixlee, "Just quit fooling now. You can't help seeing that that fellow's crazy about you!" He looked straight into her eyes as he spoke—or tried to. But this was one of the times when the almost imperceptible obliquity of one eye baffled his gaze.

Not the slightest answering tension came into body or voice. Her hand hung loose and casual in his. Good-humored, indulgent, she dropped down on the couch beside him in a relaxed pose, saying, "Why, he's not, either! How can you be so foolish! The trouble with you is, Anson, you don't want folks to have good times."

Grim, sitting up very straight, he told her, "There's no good time ahead for Cornelia." But in his heart he knew that this appeal, like the others, was unavailing. It was like bringing your hammer down, not on an anvil but on a pillow.

Lixlee moved over to lean against him. "Oh, who'd be so mean as to put the idea into Cornelia's head?" she asked. "You're the only person that's got it anyhow, and you say yourself she's the last person you'd want to have think of it."

(From the back of Anson's mind a thought curled out like the lash of a whip and flicked him on the raw. "She's counting on my not wanting Cornelia to know.")

Lixlee's face was close to his now. He could see the finished perfection of every familiar and lovely detail of eye and skin. But he was again mortally tired and felt no answering stir. She drew his head down on her breast, soft as nothing else in the world is soft. "Now, Anson, don't be like those nay-sayers you're always tellin' about. I thought you believed in enjoyin' life."

"I'm not enjoying it very much," he told her sadly.

"Well, the only thing that keeps you from it," she said reasonably, "is just an idea you've made up yourself."

So the next day and the next and the next everything went on as before. Then, "Isn't this sort of trash awfully expensive, Lixlee?" Anson pointed to a cluster of cut-glass jars of cold cream and colored bottles of cosmetics on Lixlee's dressing table.

"Oh, Charlie gets them for me for next to nothing."

Anson's face ran up the storm signal. "Does he get them for Cornelia, too?"

"Now, Anson! Of course he does. There you go! You just don't like people to have pretty things, that's the trouble with you. You'd like a woman to rub her hands with mutton tallow."

"If she paid the market price for it. Can't you understand it's a question of principle, Lixlee?"

"I don't know what principle you're talking about," she said with the most evident sincerity. But she was unruffled, ready to show herself, as always, indulgent to any of his notions. "But anything you say goes, of course. I'll make Charlie take these things back. Here, I'll take them right over there now. . . ." She began to gather them up. "I'll tell Cornelia . . ." She stopped short. "Well, what shall I tell Cornelia?"

Anson roared brutally, "Put those things down! Put them *down*, I say!" She set them down. There was a pause. He tried to fix her with his eye but could not find her through her steady natural expression. "Only don't let him give you any more of them. Or anything else."

"Just as *you* say," Lixlee told him, smiling.

He went away into his office and, snatching up a half-made report to Doctor Neale on recent heart observations, plunged into work on it. But though he fortified himself with several drinks and gave it half the night, at the end he tore it up and flung it in his waste-basket, horrified by its lack of sequence.

This could not go on. Anson tried to bring himself to speak directly to Charlie. But he could think of no words that would not humiliate him beyond endurance to pronounce. And he did not

trust his self-control. He knew very well that if, as he began to speak, Charlie should look at him with a certain satisfied smile, he should knock him down. And that would inflict on him the ludicrous indignity of seeming jealous of Charlie! That there should be grounds for believing *him*—Anson Craft—to be jealous of such a nothing-at-all as Charlie Dean . . . He felt his pulse hammeringly drive the blood up into his congested brain at the mere idea.

It was early in June that, after a good many other ideas, most of them materially impossible, it occurred to Anson that geographical separation was the simplest way out, as it often is. It had always been understood between Doctor Cole and himself that the two doctors would some time divide the practice of The Valley between them, he taking Clifford and the scattered difficult country practice, leaving the easy, well-paid practice of the larger Ashley for the older man. It was really too early in their partnership to do this, but by putting some pressure on Doctor Cole he arranged to make a try at it.

He chose to announce this decision the evening that Anna had come to say good-by before going off on her laborious six weeks' vacation. Before he was through with the first sentence he was ashamed of the impulse that had made him avoid telling Lixlee of this change of homes when he was alone with her. He realized that he put her, before a witness, in that most uncomfortable situation of a wife who has not her husband's full confidence. But she showed no resentment. "Oh, that'll be fine!" she said, falling in with the idea good-naturedly. "Sort of like going back home."

There was a silence in which their minds all ran forward into the future, imagining what life in Clifford would be for them. They all encountered the question—"Will people . . . women . . . be hateful to Lixlee as they would have been a year ago?" Anson's code and Anna's forbade their acknowledging this possibility in words. But not Lixlee's. With an easy laugh she brought it out into the light and flung it down before them, "Probably some of the old cats will hump their backs at me. But no matter. Cornelia's friends

will be nice to me, anyhow. And Miss Gussie is always benevolent."

Anson scowled at the literary adjective, but Anna's face was warm with her admiration of Lixlee's Olympian lack of resentment.

"To have me in the same town with her will give Miss Bessie a fit a day, I suppose," Lixlee went on, amused. "But there'll be one advantage of the plan, Anson likes her to have fits so he can make notes on her heart."

"I don't *like* to have her have those attacks, Lixlee! What an idea! If you knew a little more about how frightfully people suffer with angina you'd talk differently. I am just very much interested when she does have one."

"Same thing," pronounced Lixlee.

Anna broke in to suggest that they move into the old Craft house in Clifford. But she did not insist—she never insisted any more—when Anson said, "No, no, there's no use upsetting all your living arrangements for an experiment that may not work."

Anna answered confidently, "Experiment nothing! It's just what everybody's looked forward to ever since Father died." She turned to Lixlee. "If you'd just as soon?"

"Oh, I'd *rather,*" Lixlee assured her. "To tell the truth, the Deans are rather getting on my nerves. I don't mean I don't like them. Cornelia's my best friend. But one can have too much even of a good thing."

Anna thought, "Lixlee's picking up cultivated ways of speech as readily as she did table manners." Aloud she said to Anson, "Well then, if Lixlee is satisfied, of course it'll work, Anson. Why wouldn't it?"

2

BUT IT didn't work. Or Anson couldn't see that it did. Not that Clifford people were actively disagreeable to Lixlee as they would have been a year earlier. The passage of time had grown a protective tissue over that story which turned the edge of comment. The year had provided other items of scandal, recent enough so that sharp tongues could still draw blood from them. And people had been favorably affected by Cornelia's reports of Lixlee's sedate home-keeping and neighborliness; by the Deans having given their baby the name people now learned was Mrs. Doctor Craft's real one; and by a vague rumor about Lixlee's distinguished parentage which rolled its snowball way from one whispered version to another. Lixlee's father had been, it was said in strictest confidence, "a distinguished young Southern lawyer who, up North for his vacation and fishing in Hawley Lake, had . . ." "He had been a Congressman . . ." "No, not young at all, the Governor of a Southern state . . ." "Spanish blood, New Orleans," "Virginia," "South Carolina." ". . . couldn't marry Lixlee's mother because of rigid laws against divorce from an insane wife." "Ambassador to . . ."

". . . oh, nonsense! I don't believe a word of all that. Fairy tales!"

"Well, now, don't be too sure. No smoke without some fire. Everybody's saying it."

"People'll say anything!"

"But she *does* look kind of foreign. You know she does. Or Southern anyhow."

"Go off! She looks like a French Canuck, that's what she looks like."

"But if her name really is Alix Lee, you know—the Virginia Lees—"

"Miss Bessie says her name was . . ."

"Miss Bessie talks to herself. Cornelia's been living next door to them for a year, a'most, and *she* says . . ."

"What does Miss Gussie say?"

"Oh, it's too much trouble to make her hear to get anything out of her."

The upshot of all this was no more than uncertainty. But that is a good deal. The middle-aged matrons responsible for upholding the tone of the town did not know exactly what attitude to take. They decided to hold a middle course, to speak to Doctor Anson's wife when they met her, but to be stiff and hold her off at arm's length.

All except Miss Gussie Kemp, who ran in and out on the usual neighborly errands. But the deaf old maid could hardly count as a matron, and anyhow always did things nobody could understand. She was growing even more silent and for all her bulky body seemed scarcely, any more, to cast a shadow. Once, then once again some weeks later, she asked, "Lixlee, are ye all right?" To which the young wife, shades pulled down and all the lights out, answered steadily, "Oh, yes, I'm all right, Miss Gussie."

The younger people, at least Cornelia's friends—came often to the Craft house to see Cornelia and the baby. For from the first the Deans were frequently there. It was June, glorious weather, little Alix was now old enough to be presentable, and Cornelia felt lonely in Ashley with her only Clifford neighbors gone. She often persuaded Charlie to drive them to Clifford where, naturally enough, they made their headquarters at the house of their ex-neighbors. One day Miss Gussie stopped for a moment on her way out, on the front porch where Anson's self-possessed young wife was being unobstrusive hostess to a group of lively young people clustered around Cornelia Dean's baby. Lixlee was standing behind them, looking down as they did. Her long pale face was quiet and inexpressive. Miss Gussie looked intently at her, so intently that Lixlee involuntarily lifted her eyes. She looked down again at once, and in an instant turned away and went back into the house. Miss Gussie went away, too, shaking her head and murmuring to herself. The young people smiled mockingly over her queer ways.

It seemed to Anson that Charlie was underfoot on the porch or in the living-room of the Clifford house more even than in Ashley.

And more often without Cornelia. Anson himself was at home less, his office being in the wing of Anna's house, several blocks away. The situation seemed to be hardening into a formula even less to his taste than the former one. Cornelia's business in town was to show off her baby, of course. Friends of her own age, Olivia and the rest, ran into the Craft house to gloat and to burn the incense expected of them. But there were many older people, friends of Cornelia's mother, whom because of their age it was fitting for her to go to see in their own homes.

As she prepared little Alix for these expeditions, Charlie, sitting on the porch steps with a book of poems, or just looking off at the mountains, always asked dutifully, "Like me to go with you, 'Neely?"

"No, you'd be bored," she answered. She really did not want him along. The local folkways did not expect the father to be one of a baby-party. His presence, indeed, would be rather damping to the enthusiasm. "No, you stay here, Charlie, and read aloud to Lixlee. I won't be gone long."

After a week of this, Anson made it his business to return often to the house, to ask pointedly about Cornelia if she were not there, and to settle down grimly to stay until she came back.

Presently Lixlee mentioned to him at breakfast that Cornelia had suggested she learn to drive a car. "I'm pretty nearly the only person in town my age who can't," she reminded him. All right. Why not? Anson agreed without thinking about it. But that afternoon when the Deans were there it came out that Charlie was to teach her. He had taught several other girls. It was natural enough. Anson opened his mouth to say forcibly, "If anybody's going to teach my wife to drive, I will," but was ashamed of the position this would put him in. Afraid, too, if Cornelia should repeat it, of the guide-board for gossips it would make. He could hear Almira Boardman whispering, "Did you hear he wouldn't let Charlie Dean teach his wife to drive? Made a regular scene. Charlie, of all people! Anson must be . . . She must be . . ."

"It won't take long," said Cornelia placatingly to Anson's dark-

ening eyes. "Charlie's had quite a bit of experience teaching people to drive."

So Charlie and Lixlee soon began to motor off together "to some back road quiet enough for Alix to practice backing on," said Charlie.

"Alix!" Anson winced. He had never said anything to Lixlee about that story, did not dream that it had gone beyond Cornelia, still explained it as a piece of justifiable defense-mechanism. But every time the name was pronounced it literally set his teeth on edge.

The son of a patient complained, "When Mother's pulse began to get so weak I had them try and try all the afternoon to call you on the phone. But Central said nobody answered. Your wife must have been out driving."

One of the substantial farmers on The Other Side said to him in the tone of voice that went with the words, "I was up on the Sam Perkins lot yesterday and saw your wife and that Dean fellow driving down the Black Hole Hollow road. Never saw a car *there* before! Must ha' wanted to try out their brakes."

Fred Kirby, thinner than ever, came to see him about a poor patient, and Anson, nettled and offended, felt in the clergyman's manner towards him an anxious gentleness. Anson was thankful that Anna was away.

Going into the Merrill drugstore for some supplies, he passed Almira Boardman coming out and she looked at him with a certain relishing expression of eyes and lips.

That night he told Lixlee bluntly that people were talking about her and Charlie Dean. She answered comfortably, "Oh, they're bound to gossip about something." Seeing his face still clouded, she exclaimed, with the accent of a reasonable person whose long-suffering patience begins to wear thin, "For goodness' sakes, Anson, are you going to start worrying about gossip! You always told me never to pay any attention to it."

He waited a week longer and put his foot down. It might make him seem a fool. He didn't care. When Charlie and Lixlee drove up to the house, they found him waiting on the front walk. He told

them shortly, "These driving lessons have lasted long enough. This is to be the last one." Now what would they say?

They turned to each other in astonishment and exclaimed over a coincidence. "Why, we were just going to tell *you* this was the last one!"

"I backed a quarter of a mile today on a narrow wood road."

"She's ready for her driving examination now."

They had planned this together, thought Anson, had had it ready for the time he wouldn't stand it any longer. Shame at his own suspicions sent him into a shocked reaction. How could he think that? Good God! What a dirty mind he had!

He continued to have. One day when he came in for lunch, Lixlee showed him with pride a surprise she had for him, a used-car bargain she had picked up, a little blue runabout, as good as new, for eighty dollars.

He looked at it in astonishment. "Why, I never saw such a bargain!" He examined it. He got in and tried it around the block. "Miraculous!" he said.

"It's mine," she told him happily. "I've paid down the forty dollars I've saved from the housekeeping money" (he had not known of these savings) "and I'm to pay ten dollars a month for . . ."

She was smiling at him as she spoke, the smile that was one of her compelling charms. For the first time Anson saw something sinuous in it. "Who told you about this car?" he broke in.

"Cornelia," she said. "She heard about it from a friend of theirs." She flicked a speck of dust from the radiator-hood and looked back at him, a cheerful, clear look.

All the blood in Anson's body rushed to his brain. He said hoarsely, breathlessly, "That car was never sold for eighty dollars!"

She was astonished. "Why, it must have been. Cornelia said so."

"You must take me for a fool, Lixlee!" he told her bitterly. "You know as well as I do . . ." He stopped. Here in broad daylight, he could not put the ugly thing into words.

"No, I don't know, either!" From her look, from her accent, she could not imagine, though she now made a guess, "Do you mean you don't *want* me to have a car? Are you afraid if I do I'll be out

and miss your phone calls? Mrs. Cole doesn't answer her husband's phone. But if you think I ought never to . . ."

"Stop that!" he raged at her. "You know it's not that!"

"Well, *what* then?" Gravely waiting for him to explain himself she forced him to bring out words like mud in his mouth. And when he did, she said, not impatient, almost sympathetic, but taken by surprise as she always was, "Oh, *that* again!" She looked at him and shook her head. "You get so excited, Anson. You don't listen to what I say. Didn't you understand this was Cornelia who . . . ?"

His fist crashing down on the radiator cut her short. He had had a literally unbearable impression that she was gloating over his shame and pain. It was like a nightmare . . . brought on a cold sweat, loosened the tendons of his joints.

She made with her shoulders a patient gesture of resignation. "Oh, I didn't understand you wanted me not to be friendly to Cornelia, too. But all right. Just as you say, Anson. I'll tell Cornelia you don't want me to take it because you think Charlie . . . Oh, dear, what *can* I tell Cornelia?" She made a reasonable appeal to his good sense. "Anson, *why* can't you just let us all have a good time?"

So clear were her eyes, so natural every intonation of her voice, so penetrating the physical influence her nearness always had on him, and, above all, so fatiguing and distasteful to him what was in his own mind, that often by the end of one of these scenes he was persuaded that he really was making a fool of himself.

That car was sent back, and Anson bought her another one, paying the three hundred dollars for it that he had been saving for some therapeutic electrical devices.

There followed a week or so of uncertain weather. At times the odious uneasiness blew out of Anson's mind entirely, like clouds out of a sky, leaving the blue so clear that clouds were not only absent but incredible. At other moments, dark ones, he seemed helplessly to become somebody else than Anson Craft. He hung for dear life to his research work. There at least his will, so powerless against those black rages, was still valid.

Not all of his physician's lore and experience gave him, by anything he knew of himself, or by anything in the situation, an ex-

planation of the violence of those paroxysms. They would look from the outside, he knew, like the explosions of physical jealousy. But— he told himself this a hundred times—if there was one thing he absolutely knew it was that he was not and could not be jealous of Charlie. Nobody could be jealous of such a poor fellow. You had only to look at him to know that. More than that, anybody could tell from Lixlee's every easy tone and accent and casual expression that she did not take Charlie seriously. How could she? No woman could. Over and over Anson restated the case to himself, passed the situation in review, and saw it clearly as a mildly bothering one which he himself had inadvertently created. A poor stick of a man had fallen for Lixlee; she was so young, so inexperienced, cared so little about him that she had a childlike inability to understand that what was of no consequence to her might be serious for anyone. The only thing to be concerned about, therefore, was the possibility that the commonplace marriage of those commonplace people might be spoiled for the young wife. But the uninteresting Cornelia aroused in him the merest impersonal humanity. Where in that annoying but merely annoying situation lay concealed the unknown element which was such a vicious irritant to his nerves as to bring on those sudden thunder-claps of fury?

Yet they continued at the most unexpected moments to lay low his self-control. They were, he thought, as unconnected with conscious will on his part as epileptic seizures, except that such seizures give some warning, and these spasms of his came on him from one breath to the next. Often with no visible provocation. After the episode of the car, never with any provocation from Lixlee. He, the man, the mature responsible personality, was now the one who made all the hysterical scenes. And he made them over nothing.

One of these uncalled-for rages, though only momentary, left an inexplicable somberness after it. Sitting reading the newspaper one evening, opposite Lixlee darning a stocking, he observed that as she looked down at the work a faint smile curved her lips. Over his newspaper he spied moodily on her and amazed himself finally by flinging the newspaper to the floor and bursting out, "What the devil are you smiling at?" He had not known he was going to say

this till the words were out of his mouth. He had been suddenly overmastered by the insane idea that she sat there secretly smiling over some joke on him. The doctor in him recognized this suspicious referring of everything to himself as a true psychopathic symptom. Why, he was getting mentally unbalanced. He looked down on and pitied patients of his who showed such symptoms! This was insanity.

Lixlee laid down her stocking to answer. She said good-naturedly, "Well, all right, I won't smile." She got up and came over to perch on the arm of his chair. "Poor Anson, I know you didn't get much sleep last night."

The words were kind, the arm around his shoulder was soft. But—and again he recognized a familiar symptom of the remoteness from reality which is the misery of mental unbalance—he could not *feel* these proofs of kindness. He knew they were given, but with helpless unreason he could not take them to himself.

He reached up to pat the smooth young hand, said with the accent of contrition, "Sorry! I *am* rather tired." But he felt himself bound hand and foot and sinking down into a bottomless sea of unhappiness so primitive that it was like physical pain.

Strange how long this tiny incident—no incident! nothing at all!—affected him. Or if not that, what was it that cast over the next days a cloud of bleak suffering such as he had never known? His cherished work turned under his eyes to a jumble of meaningless details; there was no savor in his food; no life in the air; and his still surviving passion for his wife was bitterness.

Sometimes it was almost fear he felt for the lovely body burning its way through his wretchedness to his helpless senses. He did not know himself, could not recognize as the Anson Craft he had always been, this bewildered, strengthless man, undone with conflicting feelings raging back and forth in his heart like armies at war.

One night after he had yielded wholly to Lixlee's seductiveness and when all his barriers were down in the ensuing exhaustion, he felt his pride, his self-control, his self-respect crumble away till there was nothing left of him but the aching impulse to throw himself on

Lixlee's mercy. Brokenly, in whatever poor words came, he told her how much he was suffering, admitted that he must have been in the wrong, claimed nothing as his right, suggested no definite steps she might take—he knew now that he could never command her obedience—complained of no definite acts of hers, only abjectly begged for help in his pain, implored her to use her skill and finesse not against him but for him.

He felt her listening intently. When he finished, her whole body relaxed. "Why, Anson, have I really made you feel as bad as that?" she whispered through the darkness. He could not see the expression of her face, but her voice was low as gentleness itself and—he was sure, so bitterly did he need her—remorseful and sympathetic. "I have reached her!" he thought, and, exhausted with the effort, leaned to pillow his wet cheek on her breast. How soft it was—the heart of which it was the home could not but be compassionate. He drew long broken breaths and lay still. He had wanted comforting. The very touch of her gave it to him. How sweet it was! He lay in unguarded peace on the lovely breast that felt as soft as pity.

But it was only ten days after this that he had so terrifying and humiliating an attack of his black fury that it shocked him into making a vow—which he kept—never to let himself go again, no matter what happened.

Lixlee was once more quite blameless. Everything had been going unusually well. He was very busy. The city nurse who was supposed to be doing Anna's work was a woman of rather flimsy physical stamina who, confronted by the thousand difficulties of being an outsider, often gave out under them, so that sometimes he had virtually to do Anna's work as well as his own. But he liked work. Lixlee was absorbed by her new car—as everyone is by his first car and his first baby. She sought out all the neighbors who had no cars of their own and took them for rides. Anson often met her, smiling, animated, with a load of noisy children or happy old ladies, and shamefacedly altered the color of his mental associations with the car. The Deans stayed away for days, for a

week, for ten days. Anson thought gratefully that Lixlee had invented some way for keeping them off. His spirits rose again. Several interesting developments occurred in the sick hearts he was observing. Lixlee was delicious to him. Something of the ardent strength-giving confidence of the first weeks of his marriage flowed back around him. What could have made him act like such a fool?

The day before Anna was due to return was a sultry July scorcher. In the middle of his morning round of calls Anson, finding he needed some medical supplies, stepped into the local drugstore to buy them. Behind the counter there, talking to the elderly proprietor, was a man whose back was familiar. Anson looked at it hard, a wave of heat congesting the blood vessels in his head. Charlie Dean turned around, very spruce in a cool new suit of tan Panama cloth, and nodded pleasantly. Anson nodded back, without a smile, his teeth on edge, his mind filled with a senseless loathing of light brown. He made a stiff comment on Charlie's being rather far from his job in working hours.

Charlie explained, "Oh, I'm here on business. Mr. Peltier is thinking of making a combination with Mr. Merrill here, and having me run this store as a branch of the one in Ashley."

A sudden sweat flowed from Anson's pores, drenching his undergarments with cold.

Old Mr. Merrill said, "I been sort of looking for a chance to get out. You know, Doc, you told me to take it easy from now on."

Charlie added, "Ever since you folks left Ashley, Cornelia's been wanting to get back here to Clifford to live. Maple Avenue's lonesome for her without Alix." Then, leaning his new light brown elbows on the counter, he grinned, his pale eyes glistening. Or did Anson imagine this?

He turned away and made for the door.

"Wait a minute, Doc," called the old proprietor, pained. "I was just going to wait on you."

But the screen door had fallen shut with its cheap weightless rattle. Anson was in his car pressing his foot hard on the starter, saying to himself over and over, "If he thinks he can make a monkey out of me . . ." He was in no state to call on his next patient.

Nor to go home. He drove straight before him blindly, rather fast, wherever the road took him, and found himself out on The Other Side beyond the Foster farm.

A wood road led off to the left through its green tunnel of trees. He remembered from his fishing boyhood that it went to a solitary pond, buried in the forest, and he turned his car in on its grass-grown ruts. But still driving fast he took at random one of three trails at a fork, and soon came to the end of the road. It was in a clearing new to him, probably a cutting of last winter. He brought his car to a stop and looked around him.

The clearing lay at the edge of the steep pitch down to the valley. It was open to the sky and to the west. From it, the man sitting in the motionless car looked out across the lush emerald of the valley below him, to Hemlock Mountain, dreaming its endless blue dream in the distance.

There it lay, the great pile—every fold of it, every shadow, every golden light, every lovely down-dropping line as familiar to Anson as himself. Brooding, serene, resigned.

He had forgotten it was there. He felt that he had risked losing it by forgetting it. To find it still steadfast in his world was like a deliverance from a danger. He drew a long breath and took off his hat, his eyes held by the mountain. Open to the full stare of the midsummer sun though it was, the cool peacefulness of eternity flowed from its unchanging stillness, flowed over the humble green mortality of the valley, upward again to the man in the clearing; and laid an appeasing touch on the pulses hammering at his temples.

His hair, clammy with the sweat that still lay cold in the garments against his skin, stirred in the breeze. His pulse slowed down. His hands loosened their clutch on the steering wheel and dropped to his knees.

He sat there till he was warm and dry from sun and wind, till he was ashamed of his rage, wondered at it. "The only way to meet this is to rise above it, to live on another plane," he thought. Later, "It's literally true that everything in human relations is the result

of the way you take them. By reacting in a violent, resentful way
to this petty problem, I am just making it bigger." And finally he
answered the mountain, "Yes, yes, that's true—turn a straight and
generous face to life if you want straightness and generosity out
of it."

He turned his car and drove slowly back to The Street towards
his next call. The inner poison was gone. He had no definite plan
for action, no recipe for making over the situation, only the serene
determination—which made him feel invincible—not to allow his
human dignity to be brought low by actions and feelings unworthy
of him.

He entered town, passed several streets and was about to pass the
lane leading back of the row of houses at the far end of which his
own stood. Slackening his speed as he came opposite, he looked up
the alleyway, thinking he might get a glimpse of Lixlee in the garden or on the back porch.

Down at the end, a man in light brown clothes was just disap-
pearing into the back door of his house.

Between one beat of his pulse and the next, he stopped being
Anson Craft, the disciplined professional man, and became black,
breathless fury. He turned his car wildly and drove it wildly up
the lane, his will and purpose groveling in mud. He leaped from
the car and ran up the path to his back door. It was shut. He
turned the knob. The door would not open. He put out all his
strength to turn the knob. The door was locked. It was never
locked in the daytime.

On the key ring in his pocket hung a key to every door in the
house. But the wild man he now was remembered nothing of keys.
He flung himself against the door, once, twice. It held. There was
no sound from within. He stopped an instant to get breath, drew
back, lunged forward with all his strength. With a crash the door
burst open. As he plunged in at one side of the back hall Lixlee
came in from the kitchen at the other. Everything he suspected
was confirmed by her face. She made no pretence of surprise. For
once he saw her undone with naked emotion so that he scarcely

knew her. He tried to speak, found he had no air in his lungs, flung at her soundlessly, "Who . . . who . . . ?" She gave him no answer, looking at him dumbly. In two steps he passed her and was in the kitchen, murder in his fists.

The man who stood there, his profile to the door, leaning over the table, was not Charlie Dean at all. Only an itinerant berry-picker, a lean, tall, ordinary-looking countryman in rough clothes, weather-beaten and faded to tan by sun and rain. He held a tin pail of blue-berries in his hand and had evidently been about to pour them into a pan that stood on the table. At Anson's entrance he stopped, his pail suspended in midair, turning towards the door a leathery rustic face that might have been that of any back-roads mountaineer.

Anson came to himself with a crash of nerves that shook him from head to foot. *"Oh!"* he cried, in a shuddering indrawn breath, and leaned against the wall. And *"Oh!"* again in a great groan of shame. The berry-picker lowered his pail and stood irresolute.

Anson motioned him to go on. "That's all right. Go ahead. I thought . . . ! Never mind." The man's eyes flicked to something back of Anson. He turned and saw Lixlee, her face very white, swaying towards the floor. He sprang to catch her. She had not fainted, for she looked up at him now, her face all open to his eyes. In its deathlike pallor he saw as in a mirror how like a mur-derer he must have looked as he burst through the broken door. He abased himself to the dust. "Oh, darling, I'm so *ashamed*. How could I? I never was so ashamed of myself in my life. It's because I love you so. I *care* so! *Do* forgive me. I could die of shame. Never again, Lixlee, never, never, never again. I swear it, never!"

He carried her through to the couch in the living-room, and ran back to the kitchen to get some cold water. The berry-picker had taken his pail and gone away; he could be heard at that moment walking heavily down the back steps. Anson did not wonder. "He must have thought he'd got into an insane asylum," he told him-self, sinking deeper into humiliation. He drew a glass of water and went back quickly with it to Lixlee. Her condition startled him. How frightful he must have looked. Her pulse gave every indica-tion of her having had a nervous shock severe enough to shake to

the last fiber even her wonderfully vigorous. organism. He could scarcely feel it beat—a weak, soft, almost imperceptible flutter. Good God! What an idiot he had made of himself! He made her drink the water, cautioned her not to raise her head and, hurrying into his office, came back with a dose of whiskey. She took it silently, not opening her eyes. He sat down then, his finger on her wrist, and was soon relieved at what he felt. She would be all right in a moment. What a superb mechanism a normal heart was! Miraculous to feel that dreadful formless flutter steady down, strengthen, begin to knock firmly and rhythmically, if still too rapidly. But as he sat thus, his eyes on her white face with its shut eyes, his finger on her wrist, her pulse shot up hard and strong, racing like the reports of a machine-gun. She had opened her eyes. They were fixed on his. "You're taking notes on my heart. You—you . . . !" she told him, and tore her wrist away. "You're a perfect . . . You deserve to . . ." She could find no words. But her color had come back and her energy too. She sat up, turned her feet from the couch and walked steadily out to the kitchen.

He wanted to hurry after her to tell her he had only been re-joicing in the signs her heart gave him that he had not really killed her by his brutal violence, that he had never dreamed of thinking of his professional observations. But for a moment he had not strength to get up from his chair. He was beaten. His own heart, which he had not noticed before, was thundering in his ears. His hands were shaking. When he could stir, he went into his office and took a long drink of prescription whiskey. "I'm a mess!" he told himself. "Just a dead loss. How did I get this way?"

Then he looked up Lixlee, who had gone out for air on the back porch, and with many abject promises for the future made his peace with her. It was not so hard to do this as he feared. She too seemed worn out. Towards the last of their reconciliation she even clung to him in a way he found touching when she had such good reasons for punishing him. It seemed to him that this time the storm had washed the air clean once for all. He had had his lesson. It had been coming to him, and now he'd had it. One of that kind was enough.

Lixlee got an early lunch for him and he went out to make the calls he should have made in the morning. They filled the afternoon—the last round of his extra heavy work, since Anna was coming back the next day. Even at the end he could not go home to rest because of an emergency call from Doctor Cole for help in an amputation after an automobile accident. But when he reached the hospital operating room his hands were still quivering from his nervous explosion. If he had needed anything to confirm him in his humiliated vow never again to yield to his ugly obsession, this would have been enough. Shamefacedly he excused himself and stood back like a nurse or a raw student, handing instruments and ligatures to the other doctor, whose long face was so ashy with the heat and with age, yet who was able to stand valiantly to his guns. Never again, never, never again.

Reaching home late, with an apology for that on his lips, he found Lixlee still rather pale, but in an ardent mood. Their supper was a lovefeast. Afterwards, looking through the kitchen at the back door, he found she had had it repaired. But she had said nothing about it. "You just haven't a smallness in your whole body, sweetheart," he told her gratefully. "I never thought a woman could be so big-hearted." They went to bed worn out, appeased.

As the clock struck two that night, Anson woke up out of a sound sleep to a question as loud in his ear as if someone had shouted it through the window, "But why was the door locked?" He shrank back as a mortally beaten man shrinks from another blow. This could be nothing but a temptation of the Evil One to drag him once more into that self-created hell he thought he had left behind forever. Never *mind* why that door was locked! Perhaps a mere mechanical gesture of Lixlee's. It could be nothing but a meaningless accident. A serious one. For if it hadn't been locked, his fit of insanity would have been over before it rose to the pitch that had terrified Lixlee and had left his hands in that shaking palsy all the rest of the day.

He promised himself once more, "Never again," turned over and composed himself to sleep. But it was the ebbtide hour of early-

morning darkness, when the will, resting from its long struggle with human nature, is hardest to summon up to action. How could that door have been locked! It was never locked. If Charlie had been there! But it hadn't been Charlie. The facts, grotesque in their bald detachment from any conceivable meaning, drew themselves up out of his unloosed imagination like the djinn out of the un-stoppered bottle, and filled the room with formless shadows. His breathing grew difficult.

And then it occurred to him to ask Lixlee. There was probably some perfectly natural explanation. Hadn't he heard something about back-porch sneak thieves lately? Perhaps she had formed the habit of keeping that door locked now. He hadn't happened to enter the house that way for weeks. Yes, of course, there must be some perfectly natural reason.

Through the darkness he said gently, "Lixlee?"

"Yes," she answered. She had not been asleep either.

"I'm ashamed to speak of—all that again, but—how ever did you happen to lock the back door this morning? It's of no consequence, of course, but finding it locked was what—I just got to wondering why . . ."

With the intonation of surprise, "It wasn't locked," she answered.

"Yes, it was too!" he said. "I turned the knob. I know."

"It couldn't have been," she said, quiet and assured. "I never lock that door. You must have been too excited to really turn the knob. Sometimes it sticks." Nothing could have been more natural and matter-of-fact than her voice.

There was a silence. Then, "Well, yes, perhaps," Anson said. But only because he was afraid to say anything else. For that door had been locked. Not that it could—under the circumstances—have been anything but an accident. But it had been locked.

Lixlee turned towards him, put an arm around him and her head on his shoulder.

But the door had been locked. He admitted to himself perfectly that the fact had no possible meaning. But it was a fact.

She moved closer to him, and finding his lips in the dark, set hers on them—soft, soft and warm as life.

But it had been locked.

"Don't you love me any more at *all?*" she murmured.

He took her in his arms.

All right, it hadn't been locked.

3

A NEW gray roadster was coming along the river road back of Windward Mountain. It was being driven much faster than local cars were ever taken over those curves. People in the cars which it passed looked at its license plate, smiled and thought, "Just you wait, young man from Wisconsin, till you strike the road up to the Gap." They had seen other people in high-priced cars from out West trying to make time on Windward County roads.

The plump young man behind the wheel would have described his progress as "just driving along." He was there to look at the country, not to break records. Not that there was anything to look at. He had been thinking all the morning that it certainly was one hot little hike from Milwaukee to Vermont and—so far—nothing here to write home about. On the other hand! Im gegenteil! He pulled out an elegantly thin gold watch, looked at it admiringly, yawned, and glanced down at his speedometer.

His yawn ended with a snap. Lines appeared on his amiable face. He slid the watch back into his pocket, and sat up, his lips compressed. Damn that salesman! Hadn't he guaranteed no vibration under 65 and here, idling along at 35, she was shaking the insides right out of her! But hold on a minute! Let's be sure! Maybe that wasn't engine vibration. Maybe these crazy rocky roads had shaken something loose. He slowed down. Everything quiet. He brought the speed up gradually. Back to 45 again, up to 50, not a whisper out of her! Well, wouldn't that eat you! Just *like* a gas-engine! You never knew what was the trouble with them, when it was going on or after it was over. You heard people say women were like that.

Driving with one hand, he fumbled in his pocket and took out a cigarette and a cigarette lighter. It was of gold. He smiled down

at it. Boy, oh, boy! Did it seem good to buy yourself the right things! All those nickel-plated lighters, all those hand-me-down clothes, all those Ingersoll watches, all those verfluchte cheap cars— season after season nothing better than another Ford or Chevy! Mamma had certainly put it over on him. He pursed his good-natured mouth and thought, "If *I* ever have a boy, you can bet I won't keep him down till he's nearly twenty-five. I'll treat him square."

But, though now, of course, he could think anything he pleased, such thoughts made him uneasy. It was nicer to keep your mind on your car. "She sounds so good at 50 now, I wonder how fast she'd go without starting trouble?" If you could only find a straight-away. Their big idea up here in the mountains seemed to be to tie bowknots in their roads. Well, here goes. He increased the pressure on the accelerator till the speedometer was past 65. She was humming for fair. Started vibrating at 60, didn't she? But that was all right at the higher speeds. You liked it. Exhilarated by swiftness, he rose to an abstract thought—yes, there were lots of things that were fine at high speeds but made you sick when you were going slow— love-making, being drunk— He stopped philosophizing to snatch his car neatly around a sudden curve with a deep drop to one side. Another curve! Say, brother! Look out! That left wheel all but went over that last turn! And here was a corkscrew one! Ouch! Help! A downhill drop like a roller coaster! Steady now, hold her! *Hold* her!—whew!

He drew up beside the road and put his hand on his heart. Well, what an absolutely God-damn rotten country! Mamma was right!

He looked around him. This cowtrack can't be the main road. Must have taken a wrong turning somewhere back there. "They told me it was an *up*hill road." He pushed the blond hair away from his forehead. It was damp with sweat. "Is Vermont hot!" he thought, surprised. "I thought Mamma said the air was like a breath from the tomb all the year around." He took off his coat.

"Say, hey, you!"—a Ford was grinding steadily past—"How do I get to Clifford?"

A laconic thumb jerked forward. This *was* the road then. He

drove ahead, turned a right angle curve and saw what looked to him like a narrow ladder of gravel leading straight up. Well, Rug, old boy, enough foolishness for one day. You crawl up after the Ford!

He put his car in second. The road, climbing like a cat, wound back and forth in long zigzags through dense forest trees. Black water and white foam raced among bowlders at the bottom of the hollow. The mossy green walls of the ravine dripped moisture over feathery maiden-hair ferns. The road continued to ascend and came to Lathrop's Falls, the place where the river jumps off from the level of the higher Necronsett Valley and in one sliding plunge falls sixty feet, strikes a granite ledge and with a roar rebounds in a cloud of iridescent spray.

"If I don't get a chance to pass that Ford soon," thought the young man in the roadster, "I'll drop dead of the fidgets!"

From now on the river was too violent a guide even for that road which turned away from the Hollow and struck out in a long slant for the top of Lathrop's Gap, narrower than ever and darkly walled in by the forest. No chance to pass. The laboring Ford ahead threw out a cloud of blue smoke. A memory from the past put an acrid taste into the mouth of the young man. "That Ford I had in '24 used to smoke like that. God! I was ashamed to go out in it. And Mamma all the time with enough to run a fleet of Packards."

They had come now to the top of the pass. The road dipped, turned to the left and led out of the woods. For half a mile it ran north along a sun-flooded shelf of rocks, from which to the right there was a clear view down into a green, green valley. Its fields, marked off by stonewalls and hedgerows, were laced together by the winding silver cord of a river and the winding white thread of a road. North and south on the far side of this valley a long wooded mountain proudly reared its rocky crest like a great wave fixed at the top of its surge. On the other side lay a mountain of another temperament, rounded, suave of line, one that had done with the struggle against gravity, with all struggles, and now was sinking

down towards the common level, submitting with resignation to the dissolving action of rain and frost and sun and wind.

The young man's eyes wandered over all this and came back to the rear of the car rattling along before him. Its exhaust-pipe was still smoking. "I could buy me a new straight eight every six months as long as I live," he thought wistfully, "but it wouldn't make up for all those Fords. Nothing can ever make up for what happened to you when you were a kid. Mamma meant all right, but she ought to have thought of that."

The Ford, shamelessly smoking, led the way in a road that was soon as outrageously down as the road on the other side of the pass had been up. The car from Milwaukee lifted crazily up and plunged down over the water-bars. "If Mamma wanted to keep me away from here why didn't she tell me about the *roads!* Um Gottes willen, whatever made me bring a decent car into such a place?" Then, all at once, it was over—a level stretch through tamarack swamps and there he was, in a road wide enough for cars to pass.

His guide turned to the right. He was sick of the sight of that Ford with the memories of oppressed youth evoked by it, and turned to the left. The road was wider here, and almost level. He could make some speed. His spirits rose. But he saw ahead of him a group of wooden buildings and hastily took his foot off the accelerator. He didn't want to run slam into Clifford without thinking. It took him by surprise to see it. He perceived now that he had never believed there was such a place.

He drew up beside the road to consider. What had he wanted to come for anyhow? Probably only what makes every kid want to look inside a locked trunk. If Mamma had let him go to that boys' camp that summer, years ago, probably he never would have thought of it again. But Mamma hadn't let him. When had she ever? "As long as I live no child of mine shall ever set foot in Vermont." When Mamma looked like that you could as easy argue with her as pick up a red-hot poker. No wonder an easy-going Dutchman like Papa had been afraid of her. So of course it had been another German summer for him, dressed up in short pants and embroidered suspenders, hiking twenty miles a day with a pack

and shoes that weighed fifteen pounds apiece. It had been that summer, dragging along through some picture gallery or other, he had decided that before he died he'd go to look at Clifford.

Well, now here he was and Clifford was a little hole-in-the-ground, as he might have known. Well, where do we go from here? It looked to him like "home James." Nothing to see. Oh, since he was here, he'd just drive through, slow, try to locate the house from that photograph, take one good look at it and pass on back to God's country.

But before he drove on he reminded himself to continue here, even more guardedly than back in Milwaukee, Mamma's sound policy of not letting anybody know how much money Papa had left. He hadn't needed poor Mamma's deathbed warning about what designing women and sharp-practice lawyers would do to him if they ever found out what the rise in the value of Milwaukee real estate had done for the Milner holdings. And his own good sense told him that here of all places it wouldn't do to be known as rich. There might be a swarm of poor relations in Clifford who'd fasten on him like horse-flies if they had any idea who he was or how much he had inherited. Easy-going as he was, he never could stand them off. Mamma had always told him that any Yankee with one hand tied behind him could outcheat a gypsy horsetrader. He'd better keep it dark he had any connection with the place.

But was this Clifford? From a long weather-beaten wooden building across the road came a steady zooming of machinery and an occasional scream of a saw. A wood-working plant. To his right stretched a row of small, painted, wooden houses, gray, yellow, and chocolate brown, with small front porches, and small, very green, clipped lawns. None of them looked at all like that photograph. Of course he had had only one glimpse of that before Mamma coming up behind him had snatched and torn it up with a fury that had told him it must be her old home in Clifford. Maybe this wasn't Clifford. A small boy in faded blue overalls, carrying a pail of blueberries, trotted noiselessly by on bare feet. The young man called, "Say, kid!" The little boy stopped. "Is this Clifford?"

"No. It's the Depot," answered the child seriously.

"Oh, I see. Is Clifford up that hill?"

"No. That's The Street."

"Oh. Well, where *is* Clifford?"

The little boy hesitated and looked around him blankly.

"Well, see here! Where would I come to if I went along this road the way I'm pointing?"

"To North Clifford."

"Oh, *North* Clifford!" The young man from Milwaukee gave a great laugh and asked, "Maybe Clifford's off *that* way?"

"No. That's Clifford Four Corners."

"You don't say." Ironically, "Is there a South Clifford?"

The child stared, and hung his head shyly but he answered conscientiously, "Yes. You must ha' come through it."

"I did, did I?" He leaned over and dropped a half dollar into the pocket of the faded overalls. "Here, son, here's a nickel for you if you'll tell me where they've got Clifford hid?" he said, laughing.

The little boy held his head up, took out the coin, threw it back into the car, said dryly, "There's your fifty cents," and walked away.

"That was the first Vermonter to know he was one, I ever saw," thought the young man very much nettled, "and I should say Mamma was dead right."

The gray roadster took a long look at the signs at the crossroads that told the way to Boston, Portland, Pittsfield, Keene and other unwanted places and began slowly to climb the hill. On both sides of the steep road were white houses digging their toes into the hill, looking down from their front porches into the chimneys of the houses below them. Oh, boy! What a grade! Wasn't it swell to have a car that could take it in high! At the top a long street led both to the right and left. He hesitated, and began to say facetiously, "My mother *told* me *to* take *this* . . ." but stopped suddenly, rather shocked by the inappropriateness of the jingle. If there was one road poor Mamma had told him *not* to take—

He turned to the left on a chance, drove slowly along a double street, shaded by large elms, with a wide strip of closely cut grass

down the middle. On each side were old square or long, white, clapboarded houses buried in trees. It might not be Clifford but it looked a good deal like the photograph Mamma had torn up. Well, what was the matter with it? There were flowers around most of the houses and green lawns in front of every one. The church had ivy or something on its walls that made it look like a nice postcard view. The gold hands of the clock-face in the tower caught the sun and glittered. In a yard near him a bunch of little kids in bathing suits were playing with a hose, hollering and running around just as he and the kids on his street used to. Down farther somebody in a white dress with a wide-brimmed hat stood in a graceful pose on the sidewalk looking idly up and down. Up at the other end he saw tennis rackets flashing and a white net. On the front porch of the long low house across the street from the church sat an old woman rocking and reading, a cat in her lap. It looked as though they had good times, all right. Of course there was the cemetery, just as Mamma had told him, but this nice hot summer day it didn't look as she said, as though they wanted it right where they lived to remind them of dead bodies and worms. If it had been a German dorf, he bet Mamma would have thought it just looked peaceful.

In front of the house where the old woman sat reading he drew up and got out to make inquiries, but stopped to look down at the stones of the walk. They were white marble. Can you beat that, a marble sidewalk! The old woman shut her book and looked at him. Looked at him so hard that she made him feel funny. Maybe he should have put on his coat. Easterners were said to be damn particular about shirt-sleeves. But no, this was a very ordinary old woman in a calico Mother Hubbard wrapper. He said to her, "I beg your pardon. I'm a stranger here. I'm looking for the town of Clifford. Is this Clifford?"

Still keeping a penetrating gaze on his face the old woman murmured, "My goodness gracious!"

The Alice-in-Wonderland unexpectedness of this took his breath away. For an instant he stood helpless. Behind him there was a sound that might have been a laugh. He turned around. The person in a white dress was strolling by. The dress was thin and sleeveless.

"That old lady is deaf," she said in a low pleasant voice. "She's very nice, but she can't hear a thing you say." The brim of her white hat was lined with yellowish pink and cast a tea-rose-colored reflection down on her face. She stood still now, smiling to see him stare. What gorgeous arms she had! And shoulders! "Were you asking your way? Ask me—I can tell you. Where did you want to go?" He had never heard a voice like that, so deep and husky. She had dark hair, very thick.

Another fat old person in a calico dress now appeared at the house door. But she looked bad-tempered and he walked back towards the graceful woman in white. "All I want to know is where I am," he said. "I was looking for the town of Clifford."

"I'll tell you where you are if you'll tell me why in the world you want to get to Clifford," she said. Before he could speak, she added, "Some of your ancestors came from here."

He tore his eyes away from her arms and shoulders and looked at her, startled. She explained, smiling, "Why else would anybody ever come to Clifford?" And added, "Many people from out West come here for that."

A door slammed. Looking back he saw that the porch was empty, the front door shut. "That's because I came along," said the young woman pensively.

"You don't mean to say anybody would go in and slam the door just because somebody came by the house?" asked the young man, shocked.

"You don't know Clifford."

"What've they got against *you*?"

"The cross one didn't like my getting married."

"Why, that sounds just like what Mamma used to tell me," said the young man.

"Oh, it was your mother that came from here?" said the other. "Well, she evidently knew this town very well."

The young man felt a qualm. This was not so hot. Here inside the first five minutes he'd let out what he wasn't going to tell at all. Mamma never could have done that. Nobody ever got anything out of Mamma she didn't want to tell. A cold breath of self-doubt

blew across his mind. He was going to miss Mamma. But he set his jaw. Nobody was going to get that other piece of information out of him. He had an inspiration. Looking straight at the attractive person in white he said firmly, "Yes. My mother did come from here. But we never got around to come back in her lifetime. The trip costs a good deal, you know. I've just lost my job and while I was looking for another I thought I'd run up and see what the place looked like."

"There's nothing the matter with its looks," said the other.

They both looked at it, up and down the trim, grass-bordered, elm-shaded street. There was no reason for their continuing to stand together. But the young man now felt no need to beat a retreat. That losing his job had been a swell idea. Poor relations wouldn't bother a fellow looking for work. It would be safe to make some inquiries about them. But his companion said, "I'm sorry I can't offer to help you find out about your family. But I don't know local history. I'm not from Clifford. My father was a Southerner, one of the Lees."

"Well, I *thought* you didn't look like any Vermonter I ever saw," cried the young man from Wisconsin, "or act like one, either. My name is Rug Milner," he said, bowing from the waist as Mamma liked to have him.

She nodded, pronounced her own name, "Mrs. Anson Craft. My husband is the doctor here," and added with a slow turn of a lovely neck, "I'd better move on or the cross old maid inside that house will drop dead. She has fits when she loses her temper."

He was startled. "Is she looking at us *now?*" he asked, glancing askance at the house.

"She and everybody else in town," she answered, smiling. She had a wonderful smile.

"It sure does sound like what Mamma used to tell me," he exclaimed, laughing. No harm now in speaking of Mamma's connection with the town.

"She and I would have had a good deal in common," surmised Mrs. Craft, beginning to saunter along the sidewalk. He had never seen such a back as was outlined by her white dress. The undulating

line from her slim waist to her hips made him feel funny. It was the first time he had ever thought a back could be beautiful.

He had no mind to lose her. It was as if he had found a compatriot in a foreign country. "If you don't mind," he said politely, falling in beside her, "I'll just walk a way with you and find out who could tell me something about my mother's family." They were passing his car now. Remembering Mamma, he wondered if she would notice that it was a very expensive one. She did not give it a look. "She's a *lady!*" he thought. "You can tell every time." The sight of his coat on the back of the seat reminded him of his shirt-sleeves. Reaching an arm in he pulled it out, slipped it on and smoothed back his fair hair with both hands. He saw his companion glance at the crape band on his gray sleeve. "My mother only died last month," he said. He was surprised and moved to hear a quaver in his voice. When you said the word right out like that, it came over you that this wasn't just a vacation, sort of, but that Mamma was *dead*. That you'd never see her again. And Mamma might have been bossy and she might have been close, but you could count on her. As long as she was there nobody could get at you. It was going to be lonesome without anybody to stand by you.

His companion had heard the quaver in his voice too. She said seriously, "I lost my own mother when I was very young, when I needed a mother most. My life would have been utterly different if she had lived."

"That *was* hard luck!" he told her. So she was motherless too. What a refined way of speaking she had—a regular educated Easterner. And yet so pleasant and friendly.

They walked on. He had been lucky to come across her—not a glum tight-mouthed Vermonter—somebody he could really talk to. A nice married woman too, not a girl making up to you because you drove a good car. He knew well enough that had been one of the reasons why Mamma had always made him drive cheap ones. But here was somebody it would be safe to talk to. A wide road with plenty of room to pass.

He turned to the safe person. "I don't know whether any of my relatives are still alive. Mamma didn't keep track of things back

here. I never heard her speak about anybody but a younger brother, Lawrence. Lawrence Stewart. Did you ever hear of him?"

"Oh, yes. He lives here now. His house is not far. I'll show you which one it is, if you like."

"That'd be swell," said Lawrence Stewart's nephew.

They stepped off a little more briskly now that they had a goal.

"I never knew Mr. Stewart had had an older sister," Mrs. Craft mused. "He's rather old himself. But as I told you, I don't know Clifford family histories."

"I don't know much about this one myself," said the young man. "Mamma never told me any of it. I just sort of pieced it together. It seems that she and her father didn't get on together any too well. In fact, fought like merry hell, I should say—and she ran away when she was young."

"Ran away?" inquired Mrs. Craft with a special accent.

"Oh, I don't mean eloped or anything. Just beat it. No, as a matter of fact, she wasn't married till quite a while later."

"What does anybody do who just runs away?" murmured the woman beside him as if she were thinking aloud.

Mr. Milner found something wistful in the quality of her tone. It made him think, although she was far too much of a lady to say anything complaining, that she was envying Mamma's pep in getting out of here. Right from the first there'd been something about her that made him think of Mamma. Probably because she was in some such fix as Mamma ran away from. Maybe *her* father was— oh, no, she was married. Well, probably her husband was a regular Vermonter, as pleasant to live with as an icicle. Or maybe like what Mamma used to say her father was, "just a plain old devil."

"I suppose she taught school," surmised Mrs. Craft. "They say New England girls who went West usually—"

"She did not teach school!" her son repudiated the idea indignantly. "Mamma was a crackerjack of a business woman. The kind that'd make money if you let her down a well, as the saying goes. She got to Milwaukee somehow—I never heard about that part— and went into the real estate . . ." He bit off the next words and swallowed them down. Du lieber! what was he saying? In an-

other tone he went on, more slowly, picking his words, "She got a job in a real estate office. That's how she met my father. He was— he was working there too."

But she evidently had noticed nothing. He went on, "Papa was a German, that is, his folks had been. He never cared anything about it, couldn't even talk German, but Mamma was crazy about it. You'd think to hear her go on she was the one that had the German family. I did think that till I was quite a big boy. Papa told me once it was probably because her father had been so mean to her that she had no use for anything American. Well, for anything New England or Vermont, anyhow."

"Oh, yes indeed," murmured Mrs. Craft, with a melancholy accent. They walked on side by side silently.

"Well, here we are," she said. They came to a halt.

The young man from Wisconsin looked at a three-story white house. It had a huge central chimney, carved ornamentation under the overhanging eaves, an old doorway with leaded glass and white pillars with Corinthian capitals. Around it stood four immense elms. "Yes, sir," he exclaimed, "that's the one. I recognize it. My mother had a photograph of it once. Well, isn't it the old barn? The funny old before-the-flood model! So my uncle has always gone on living there? Wouldn't you think he'd have built himself a new one?"

"There hasn't been a new house built on The Street for—oh, since before the Civil War," Mrs. Craft told him.

"Everybody with pep went away then?" he surmised.

"Like your mother," she agreed. It almost seemed now that she had known his mother.

He looked back at the elm-shaded old house. "Not even a front porch!" he exclaimed pityingly, and inquired, "What family has he got?"

"Nobody but a cat."

"That's funny. What's his business? You'd think I'd know all this. But Mamma never would tell me much."

"He hasn't any business that I ever heard of. His father must

have made money—some, anyhow. Enough so Mr. Stewart has never had to work."

"You don't say! Wouldn't you think he'd rather have got out and hustled and have made enough to fix up the place, anyhow? Well, everybody has his own ideas. What *does* he do?"

Mrs. Craft smiled and lifting one end of the fine-spun invisible thread that now lay between them flung it out from the present to the future, where it caught and hung, a firm airy first cable. "You come and tell *me* what he does, after you've found out," she said. Then for the first time she lifted her eyes and looked directly at him as she added a few words.

He stood blinking, startled, under the impression that something intimate had passed between them. But when he really heard them, he perceived that her words had been only, "There's no bell. Just raise the knocker and let it fall." What had taken his breath away was that for the first time he had seen what wonderful eyes she had.

She nodded and walked slowly away with an easy flexible step. She was leaving him all alone to cope with Vermont! And he didn't even know where she lived! He took a few hasty steps after her. Apparently she did not hear him. He halted, not wanting to seem pushing, and thought hard. Then, his face lighter, he went up the marble walk to his uncle's front door. He had thought, "There's no hurry. I don't have to go right on. I can just wait over till tomorrow."

4

A S MR. STEWART and his nephew sat on the side porch that afternoon talking over family matters and getting cautiously acquainted, Mr. Stewart was very conscious, but his nephew was not, that Jo Danby made a good many errands to that part of the yard, walked past the porch with a sickle in his hand, or the oilcan for the lawn mower, or the rake. Every time he did this, Mr. Stewart lowered his voice, or stopped talking to cough, or to stroke Henrietta who was somnolently of the party. But of course his nephew's city eye scarcely registered the fact that a bald-headed

hired man in overalls was working about the place, and saw no reason to stop the flow of conversation. Mr. Stewart thought wrathfully, "If I had a Japanese now, or a Swede, I could tell him to go to work somewhere else." But to tell Jo to go away would be to arouse suspicion worse than anything he could overhear. And anyhow what could he make out of the few scraps of talk that he could pick up?

They were still sitting there, having had tea together, at five o'clock when the Cannon Ball came crawling up the grade to the Depot and let off, among other people, Anna Craft back from the hard-worked period of special research she called her vacation.

It being midsummer, Cora Ingraham was away spending her vacation with her New Jersey family. Not wanting to be a bother to Anson and Lixlee, Anna had not written them which train she would take. This was part of her program of heeding Father Kirby's savage warning about not hanging onto Anson. And as to Fred Kirby himself, who in past years had usually come to meet her train, she had not written a line to him since she had been away and she had had no word from him. She did not even know whether he was back from his annual "retreat."

So there was no one at the station to meet her. No human presence, that is. But after the clatter of the train's departure had died away, the mountain silence welled softly up around her and bade her welcome home. Hay was a-making in the Barney meadow. The honeyed breath of new-cut grass made her a little girl again, fishing the Barney brook with her father. The Wall's long flank, flooded by the late afternoon sun, was golden as the ramparts of Heaven. Across the valley, Old Hemlock lay in shadow, dreaming its endless blue dream.

She stood still, her suitcase in her hand, gazing. Frank Barney, slouching in his ragged overalls, chewing on his straw, gazed with her. Their eyes met. "Same old place, M'Sanna," he said with the intonation of one apologizing for it.

"Same old place," she agreed soberly.

After a pause he asked, "How's Boston? Did ye see Doctor Foote's folks?"

Oh, yes, she told him, Eph and his wife had asked her out there for supper several times. Eph's business was doing very well.

"How's Isabel gittin' along at the hospital?"

"Why, splendidly," she said. "What do you think! She's considered the most brilliant student in her class. We didn't realize that she has a first-rate head-piece. And a wonderful worker—they told me she was, at it every minute. Steady as a clock. She'll be a grand nurse."

"The Nye comin' out in her," surmised Frank, dreamily, his eyes on Old Hemlock.

"Yes," said Anna, understanding him, "yes, the Nye is coming out in her very strong."

"Well, they're good folks, the Nyes are."

"Yes, they're good folks."

She asked him now, "Any news here?"

"Mr. Stewart's got company. Not summer folks. His nephew."

"I didn't know he had a nephew."

Henry Gardner, who as usual had not picked up a fare for his Ford, and was as usual glad he hadn't to bother with one, heard this. "Didn't your old folks ever tell about an older sister he had, a holy terror, that fit bloody murder with the old man and run away years ago?"

"Oh, yes. To be sure. Named Emma."

"Well," said Frank Barney, "it seems she went out West and married a German and had this boy. I was at the store when Jo came down to git some lawn-mower oil and he was tellin' about how she brought the kid up to be as Dutch as ever she could. But he ain't Dutch. Not even Stewart like his mother. Not a bit. I saw him out in the garden with Mr. Stewart when I came by and he's a perfect Merrill like his grandmother. You can see it on him a mile away."

Henry Gardner broke in. "Miss Bessie always says, 'Merrills are born to be bossed.'" He turned to the other man, "Speakin' of Miss Bessie—you heard what a turn this fellow give Miss Gussie? It

seems he's the very spit and image of his grandmother, same kind of pie-face, same tow head, same kind of milk-and-water look, and she was one of Miss Gussie's girl friends. Well, it seems he stepped up to her porch to ask his way, and she give one look at him and begun to cry and carry on. 'Who are you that brings my dear Emma Merrill back from the grave,' says she."

Frank Barney said, skeptically, "Oh, go off!" And then, on a suspicion, "Who told you that?"

"Almira Boardman," admitted the other, rather shamefaced.

"I thought so. Almira can't even make anything up so it *sounds* as if it happened. Miss Gussie ain't one to carry on. She never does. I bet she just stared and didn't open her mouth."

"Well, maybe. Likely," admitted Henry.

"What's his name?" asked M'Sanna.

Frank laughed. "Milner's his last name. And they tell me there's something funny about his first name. It seems his mother was bound she'd name the kid something that couldn't be nicknamed into American and so she give him three of the tongue-twistin'-est Dutch names! Sounded like Rudolph Oolrick and something that begins with G— Godleeb—only that ain't right. *She* always called him Oolrick, but the kids at school called him Rug from his initials. Rug Milner, that's the name he gives. And that's all the good his mother's bein' bossy did her. When anybody tries to be too bossy he only pulls it all over onto him, don't he?"

Henry began, "My grandfather used to tell about the time his father wouldn't let him—" But Anna had heard that story ever since her childhood and walked away. The men did not notice her departure, one absorbed in the story he was telling, the other in the story he was waiting for a pause to bring out.

Anna was only mildly interested in Lawrence Stewart's nephew, but she encountered nothing else on her way home. As she passed, the women, crisp in clean afternoon ginghams, sewing on their front porches or cutting out dead stalks in their perennial borders, greeted her, asked about Isabel, and spoke about the newcomer in the same breath. Jo Danby must have stopped at every front porch, she thought, to talk over the newcomer; and any gaps in what he

had overheard had been filled in by Mr. Stewart's waitress, whose afternoon-off it had been, and who had evidently been strolling around from back door to back door. To the items Anna had learned from the two men at the station, there was soon added the information that "he is a nice-appearin' fellow, only kinda fat. That's the only Dutch thing about him, that and the comical way he makes a bow—like in a square dance, salute-your-partner, sort of." She was told that Jo said, " 'Twould have made a horse laugh to hear Mr. Stewart standin' him off at first to be dead sure he had money so he wouldn't be wantin' to borrow. You know the twitter Mr. Stewart's always in about somebody gettin' some money away from him." Moving up to the top of Depot Hill and turning into The Street she met Mrs. Peter Merrill, whose hired girl had just seen Mr. Stewart's waitress, and learned among other things that "this Western nephew of his had lost his job he *says,* but Jo Danby says it must ha' been a nawful good paying job, he drives the best car that ever come into this town. Anyhow, he calc'lates on staying for a while, and playing some tennis. It seems his mother had him take tennis lessons, like on the piano, in Germany. She always hated Clifford—you can't blame her—and never would let him so much as speak the name of the place—on account of her feeling towards her father as she did. But Jo heard him tell Mr. Stewart that he took a liking to the place the minute he laid eyes on it—the way you *do* like something your folks wouldn't let you have. I told my Mattie the other day, 'My mother hated stripes and dressed me in plaids, and I never could bear plaids and so when you came along I always made your dresses out of striped material. I s'pose as soon as you can have things the way *you* want 'em, you'll take a throw-back to plaids.' And Mattie laughed kind o'surprised and said yes, she did think plaids had lots of style."

Anna smiled absently and walked on towards St. Andrew's.

The door to the church stood open as she passed. Fred must be back from his "retreat." He never could stand a shut church door. She looked in and saw the chancel windows burning red and gold and blue in the westerly sun. Her suitcase was small and so light

she scarcely felt its weight, but she set it down now, stood a moment to rest, and took it up in the other hand. Yet no one came down the steps to greet her. Walking on steadily, she told herself there could be no doubt that Fred was avoiding her more and more. She knew well enough what the trouble was. By her usual process of transferring herself into another's personality, she had again and again lived through from his side that last time he had been in her office—he had never stepped inside it since. She filled her mind once more as his had been filled, with righteous, intelligent impatience over the secret sin of possessiveness hidden so slyly under her devotion to Anson. With him, she lost her temper heartily over the woman half springing up to do again the worst possible thing for the brother she professed to love. With his hands she pushed the silly creature down in her chair and, looking out from the clergyman's startled eyes, she saw that betraying flood of color in her face, the conscious expression which must have told him more plainly than in any words how the touch of his hands on her shoulders had thrilled all through her body. There was but one impression he could have had, beholding her, the mature woman, usually so impersonal, blushing like a girl. No man could be blamed for taking it as Fred evidently had.

And yet it had meant nothing. She herself, sensible, informed, modern woman as she was, knew that that overpowering thrill, that living warmth softening her heart till it ached, had been the mere mechanical response of her woman's body to the touch of masculine hands. It was no more to be ashamed of, she told herself, feeling very much ashamed of it, than one is ashamed of running a temperature. A modern woman, she thought, just by understanding the bodily mechanics of personality could control and direct them, was freed from their tyranny. Yes, she thought resolutely, that exquisite fainting happiness that for an instant had meant everything—so much that to think of it now made her close her eyes and stand still an instant to get her breath—now meant nothing to her. Nothing at all, she repeated, opening her eyes and walking steadily on. She could almost have pointed out on a chart the nerve-centers whose involuntary reflex had caused it. It would certainly

vanish from her memory if she could only invent some casual, matter-of-fact way to make Fred realize that she attached no importance to her purely reflex response to his touch, to let him know that she did not hold him personally in the least responsible!

But it was not only because she was not clever and deft and "feminine" in personal relations that she had never dared to try to clear up the little misunderstanding. She was not sure that Fred had noticed anything. Perhaps the whole thing had happened in her imagination only. It had come and gone so soon. Rather like a flash of lightning. Perhaps he hadn't seen her silly blush and her heart in her eyes. If so, how silly to speak of it! She blushed again and for the hundredth time told over the many reasons for believing that he had seen nothing. He had been so exasperated with her. All his thoughts were concentrated on making her see how stupidly she tyrannized over Anson. Nothing in his mind but his attempt to make her see reason. She had now arrived at the conclusion to which these meditations always brought her which was that, of course, Fred had never stopped thinking of Anson, and had not noticed at all her foolish conscious look. And this reminded her again how right he had been about Anson! Queer about Fred, anyhow, so moony and impractical and absent-minded as he was— not to mention his being religious—he yet had for deep puzzling human problems the oddest sort of insight.

When she came opposite the Stewart house, Mr. Stewart stood in his garden looking as usual with his tall well-made body, beautiful gray hair and regular features like the distinguished forceful man of affairs he was not. With him, holding Henrietta in his arms, was a blond young man in a gray suit, with the small round Merrill nose and good-natured eyes. "My nephew, Rug Milner," said Mr. Stewart. "I don't believe you're old enough to remember my sister Emma."

"I've often heard people speak of her," said Anna discreetly. She smiled inwardly at the innocence of village ways which made Mr. Stewart think that because his nephew had been but a few hours

in town and since his arrival had not stepped out of the yard, it was necessary to tell anyone who he was.

"Rug, Miss Craft is our district nurse."

"Oh, you must be the sister of *Mrs*. Craft!" The young man's face lighted up.

"Sister-in-law," said Anna, wondering a little at his tone.

He explained, "Mrs. Craft was the first person I met here. I happened to ask my way of her and she kindly showed me how to find Uncle Lawrence's house." He added, "She's lovely, isn't she? A real Southern beauty."

Anna took the adjective as a random one referring to Lixlee's dark hair and eyes, and the whole speech as part of the effusive vocabulary of summer people.

"She *has* grown good-looking since her marriage," admitted Mr. Stewart, affably. "Quite bloomed out. I'd noticed it myself before Rug spoke of it."

The young man turned eagerly to the older one, "Uncle Lawrence, why don't you ask her over to tea tomorrow?" He added on a less eager note, "You, too, Miss Craft." And on another not eager at all, "And Doctor Craft, of course, if he could come. But I suppose he's very busy."

"So am I, unfortunately," said Anna, picking up her little suitcase. "But thank you just the same."

"Oh, you mustn't carry that!" cried the young man, dropping Henrietta, and taking it from her hand. She protested, he insisted. It ended by his walking along with her, chatting as he went. Having heard other newcomers to Clifford she took for granted that he would exclaim about white marble sidewalks, laugh over the way people here said "bahn" instead of bar-r-rn, and "yahd" instead of yar-r-rd, and remark that the sound of all these brooks everywhere made *him* "feel like somebody had left a faucet turned on." But he had a line of his own. He said she couldn't think how nice it seemed to him to find he had a real honest-to-goodness uncle and some old family things back here in the East. His mother, he explained, had been too much of a business woman to be very long on family ties, and his father had been an only child. . . . "I've

heard more about my relatives since I struck Uncle Lawrence's this morning than all the rest of my life put together."

"Yes, Vermonters are terrible on family history," said Anna.

"Oh, I don't mind," said the young man tolerantly. "It don't bore me so much as some other things—as going to a picture gallery, for instance. Mamma never bothered me about my relatives, but she sure was death on museums. I bet I've wended my weary way around a thousand miles of oil paintings. You know, like the plowman in the poem."

"You won't be troubled by many oil paintings in Clifford," said Anna, smiling.

"So I see! That's one of the things I like about it. People talk so much about the 'cultured East,' I had a notion it was most as bad as Europe. But I can't see but what it's like any place. Maybe it was meeting Mrs. Craft first off, and having her so nice to me, that gave me a good start. I hadn't really decided till then whether I'd stop over. But the minute she spoke to me she made me feel right at home. She has a swell voice, hasn't she? I never heard a lady's voice that was so deep and low." He laughed at his own phrase, "Sounds like 'Sweet and Low,' doesn't it? You know, the song."

They were at the front walk now. She took her suitcase from him, remembering in thanking him to use the extravagant hyperbole city people like, "I'm so *very* much obliged to you, Mr. Milner. It was *so* good of you! I don't know what I *would* have done without you, etc., etc." She added a friendly welcome to his mother's old home, and said she hoped he would stay long enough to let them get acquainted with him. This was not hyperbole. She liked his pleasant honest face and unaffected talk.

"Oh, nothing is stepping on my heels," he told her cheerfully. "I'm out of a job. Maybe I'll stay quite a while if Uncle Lawrence doesn't throw me out."

He nodded and started on. Anna's arrival had been seen by Mrs. Randall, she who for twenty years had come in from next door to help out in the housework and to tell the news. Iron-gray and four-square, she stood at the open front door now and called a wel-

come to Anna. At the same moment the young man halted as if struck by a sudden thought. "Would you tell me," he asked, turning back, "where Mrs. Craft lives?"

Anna told him, Mrs. Randall listening from the portico.

"Thank you. Thank you very much," he said, turning away again. "I thought perhaps I'd stop in. . . ."

Mrs. Randall raised her eyebrows, looked after his retreating back expressively, and said, "Here, give me that suitcase, Anna." She drew one of the long breaths that seemed to last her half an hour's flow of talk and began as they climbed the stairs to Anna's room. . . . "Almira Boardman's telling around that this very day he landed in town he and Anson's wife were walking up and down The Street together for an hour before she'd let him go. Why, it was no such thing! She happened to be going by when he was shouting at Miss Gussie to ask his way, and she just walked along with him to the Stewart house and left him the minute they got there. I saw them all the time myself. I don't know what's got into Almira anyhow. She's on the rampage *all* around. Her age, I guess. I hear she's been trying to make out that Charlie Dean got kinda too interested in Anson's wife when they were next door neighbors in Ashley. And that that's why Anson moved down here. Can you beat that!"

"Charlie *Dean* . . . !" said Anna, stopping her unpacking to give an incredulous laugh.

Mrs. Randall laughed too. "Comical, ain't it, to pick on Charlie to make that up about? Everybody knows the nearest he ever got to any girl but Cornelia was that summer he worked in the garage and taught two three of'em to drive. It took *all* the girl-nerve Charlie had, to get himself married. I wouldn't have a mind like Almira Boardman's for a million dollars. She goes to too many movies, that's what's the matter with her. Old maids with Boardman blood hadn't ought to be let in to the movies. You remember her Aunt Laura. Of course there's one thing! Nobody believes a word she says. All the same, I kinda wish this Dutch nephew of Lawrence Stewart's . . . Say, don't he strike you as kind of a simpleton, the way he looks and talks? He does me. . . . Well, it

mighta been as well if he'd waited a while before he looked up Anson's wife." She considered this a moment and gave it up as impractical. "But goodness, if a person started to run your life so Almira Boardman wouldn't talk, how much time would you have for anything else?"

She passed now without a break to canning and preserving. Raspberries were gone, it seemed, and blackberries not quite ripe, but there were plenty of blueberries being brought in from The Wall by fern pickers and their children. From that she passed to items about babies in the neighborhood, and then as to what she had prepared for Anna's supper waiting on the table downstairs. And finally she went away to get her own.

The moment she went out of the house, Anna started downstairs to telephone Anson. The gossip Mrs. Randall had told her was absurd of course but it touched Anson's welfare. It could do no harm to find out if he had any notion of it; perhaps to give him a hint to be careful of appearances for a while . . . or no, it would be better not to speak to Anson directly about it. That would only set him off in one of his rages. The thing to do was to get him and Lixlee to go away for a vacation somewhere. He hadn't had one since he started practice.

The many material difficulties of this plan came thronging into her mind now, and, her will leaping zestfully forward to the attack as it always did when confronted with obstacles, she began to think how she could surmount them one by one. She herself got on well with old Doctor Cole. By giving him extra medical help he could spare Anson for a while. Perhaps she could pay for a month's services of a clever student the medical school would send them. With that bequest that Anson had turned over to her she could . . . She could . . . she would . . . it would be easy for her to . . . if she gave up . . .

She was now beside the telephone table in the lower hall, dropped into the chair, and, her mind full of busy planning, raised her hand to the receiver. But she did not lift it from the hook. Fred Kirby's remembered voice said peremptorily in her ear, "Anna, can't you let Anson *alone?*"

She sighed, sat still for a moment and then started back up the stairs heavy with the burden of her repressed impulse. On the landing she paused, arguing with herself, "But this isn't the same thing as . . . To speak to Anson about *this* wouldn't be . . . Anson ought to know—or at least . . . Why, Fred himself couldn't object to my . . ."

It then occurred to her that the simplest thing to do was just to call up Father Kirby on the phone and ask him to come over so that she could put the matter to him. She was relieved at having thought of this, and ran downstairs again to the telephone. But in front of it she paused. She had forgotten for an instant Fred's changed attitude towards her, and her guess at the reason for it. She remembered it now and was shocked to find it shamed her as much as ever. "I shall certainly wait till he comes of his own accord," she thought with spirit and went back up the stairs.

At the top she told herself severely, "This is acting like a girl over a boy!" (For her this was the superlative of scorn.) "Allowing a mere personal consideration to interfere with . . ."

She walked firmly down the stairs again to the telephone, took the receiver off the hook and put it to her ear. But when the bodiless voice at the other end of the wire reached her ear with its singsong "What *num*ber, please?" she answered hastily, "Never mind. Never mind. It's no matter," and hung up. She had perceived that her real purpose in all this was to find a pretext to make Fred Kirby come to see her.

5

SHE STOOD there in the hallway beside the telephone in a state of divided personality as unusual as shocking to her. "I didn't get enough sleep in Boston," she told herself, dismayed, and began to go through some of the mechanical tricks for the control of the emotions she recommended to other people who let themselves get out of hand—drawing deep breaths, relaxing her muscles, letting her arms hang limp.

Through the open door she saw someone turning in to her front

walk; a tall thin man. The light flashed from a gold cross hanging on his breast.

Her confusion was gone as if it had never been. "Why, it's only Fred," she thought, in a phrase very familiar to her. She walked towards the door.

"How are you, Anna?" he asked quietly. They shook hands, and stood a moment looking at each other.

The well-remembered gray eyes were steady over the disfiguring blotch on cheek and temple.

Anna's self-confidence revived. "I didn't know whether your 'retreat' was due to be over." She kept her voice neutral, as she made a point of doing when any of his religious ways were mentioned. But as always such a mention put a distance between them. How could she have imagined she felt near to anyone with that obsession, so alien to her?

He told her, "The retreat isn't over. I came away."

They sat down on the broad eastward-facing marble doorstep, as in their childhood they had often sat after play, looking up at The Wall and the eastern sky above it. Now as then there was at this hour faint flushings and palings of rose and gold reflected from the sunset in Lathrop's Gap behind them. As children they had called it the shadow of the sunset.

"I didn't know you for a moment with a straw hat," she told him, smiling.

He tossed the unclerical hat down on the grass. "Still getting our sunsets in the east, aren't we? Colors by reflection," he remarked in a noncommittal tone, his eyes on the tea-rose flush in the sky above The Wall.

She leaned her head against the portico pillar. "The reflections are lovelier than the real colors in the west, don't you think?" she asked.

"I can't say I do." He was uncompromising.

She glanced at him inquiringly.

"I'm rather tired of it, Anna!" he said crossly.

She looked back at the faintly tinted sky and said, "Well, the reflected colors are clearer, more transparent, anyhow."

"Paler, you mean," he observed.

"Oh, have it your own way!" She gave in with a smile to his contrary streak, and enjoying her own renewed composure began to tell him about her Boston experiences. She had met a classmate of his there who had said the usual things about Fred's brilliant brains and baseball, and strange lack of ambition. He interrupted her to ask about Isabel. Anna repeated what she had said at the station and added, "She's driving herself, working at top speed every waking moment. Yet she looks strong. And steady. It's curious how she's changed physically. She looks not only years more mature, but . . . like another person. I hardly recognized her at first."

She went on from this to her study of coöperative homes, but presently, as if he had not been listening, the other broke in, "Anna, I know your first interest always is Anson; and I think I ought to tell you that I feel a little anxious about his wife."

Anna's mind darted back to Almira Boardman's absurd story. Could it be that? But no, all that Fred said was that both he and Miss Gussie had thought Anson's young wife did not look altogether happy.

"Why, what *do* you mean!" cried Anna, not as a question, as an astounded exclamation of justifiable indignation.

Mr. Kirby explained, "I don't say she isn't. I just wonder if she is." He went on patiently to remind her how this might concern her. "Of course if she is not happy with Anson he can't be happy with her."

There was a silence, in which Anna perceived that her exclamation had sounded like the vulgar outcry of a middle-class person over a low-caste girl's presuming to feel about her marriage to a professional man anything but humble lifelong gratitude. The flush in the east faded slowly, leaving in the sky only enough of the sun's yellow to turn its blue for a moment into a pale translucent green. Mr. Kirby said nothing. His gray eyes were but shadows in their deep sockets, yet presently something about their expression suggested to Anna that her exclamation had sounded vulgar because that was what it had been. With a shamed impulse at self-excuse, she tried to make it sound like something else, "Now, Fred, be

reasonable! What more could any woman have? What more does she *think* she could have?"

"Oh . . . 'have' . . ." he said slowly, his tone protesting against the word. "She might have found out that she loves Anson more than he loves her."

Anson's sister found this guess the wildest that could be made. "Why, Anson's *crazy* about her!"

"She's a primitive, you know. A Searles Shelf girl. You've told me yourself they ignore the laws and obligations that bind us."

"Oh, Fred, you don't get the point. It was her being a primitive that Anson liked her for."

"But Anson himself remains a civilized intellectual."

"Well . . . ?" Anna was lost.

"Can a man eat the cake of civilization and have it too?" inquired the clergyman, darkly.

The last tinge of sunset color drained slowly out of the sky as Anna sat trying to follow this. No . . . she gave it up. "I honestly don't know what you're talking about, Fred," she said. "Anson simply *couldn't* love his wife more than he does!"

There was a long pause. The first transparent veil of twilight dropped between them. "No . . . probably . . . he . . . couldn't." Mr. Kirby said the four words slowly.

Blue was now the world's wear. The mountain wall was luminous pale blue, like the essence of distance. Blue and dreamy-dark the shadows fell around them, dreamlike and brooding the mood evoked in Anna by her old comrade's silences and few slowly spoken words. She sat passive, all her muscles relaxed as half an hour before she had tried with conscious effort to make them. The firm opaque surfaces of her usual inner world wavered, thinned like mist slowly drifting before a current of air—beyond and through them she caught a glimpse of immeasurable spaces. A familiar formula floated through her mind. "I never understand a word Fred says when he's in a mystic mood. And yet . . ."

A faint rhythmical sound began to pulse softly in the silence, the pat, pat, pat of small bare feet on marble flagstones. Through

the twilight a child's form appeared down the street trotting towards them, a little boy in faded blue overalls, swinging a small tin pail. Anna's eye took him in absently. A little berry-picker off the mountain. But when he saw her, he slowed down abruptly. This made her look at him with more attention. She sprang to her feet in one startled movement. "Why, Eli Twombley," she exclaimed. The little boy turned as if to run away. "Stand still!" she commanded sharply and walked out towards him.

"How did you get here?"

He looked down into his pail and said nothing.

After a moment's thought Anna changed her tone and suggested in a conversational tone, "Perhaps your folks have moved back here to live?"

After a long wait, "I don't know," said the child in a low unwilling voice.

"You mean maybe it's not to live but just to stay for a while?"

The little boy hung his head and said nothing.

"Look up at me, Eli, and answer me," she begged and now her voice was trembling. The little boy silently lowered his head still further.

Anna turned her head towards Mr. Kirby. Her look was a call for help. He was instantly at her side, where, astonished, puzzled, "What is it?" he formed with his lips over the child's drooping head.

"Do you know who this is?" she asked as if now she were not sure herself.

"I gave him his name in baptism," said Mr. Kirby, putting a thin hand on the child's shoulder. "Haven't you a new little brother or sister now, Eli?"

"She died," breathed the little boy.

Mr. Kirby said something sympathetic and asked gently, "Have you gone back to Searles Shelf?"

The little boy shook his head, murmuring, "Fern picking."

Mr. Kirby understood the implications of this and said, "Oh, camping out on The Wall. That must be fun for you children."

There was a pause. At a loss, Mr. Kirby looked questioningly at

Anna. Her lips parted. She hesitated. Finally in a colorless voice she asked, "Is your father with you now, Eli?"

The child drew a long breath. "Sometimes," he said in a whisper. She let him go. "Well, run along, Eli."

He took noiselessly to his heels.

"What is the matter, Anna?"

She could only wring her hands and ask in a frightened whisper, "What *shall* I do? Oh, Fred! Oh, Fred!"

"Now I'm the one who doesn't know what you are talking about."

"I didn't dream he would ever come back!"

"Come, Anna, come," he said sharply, "unless you tell me what the trouble is . . ."

"Not *here!*" she whispered, looking over her shoulder at the darkening deserted street.

"Well, indoors then." He put out his hand impulsively as if to lead her back to the house. But drew it back. With a broken indrawn breath she turned and hurried him up the front walk and through her front door which she closed and locked behind them.

It did not take long to tell it but at that hour the darkness was falling rapidly. Before she had finished, the light had dimmed so that she could not see her listener's face. Without stopping her anxious confused explanation she groped for the pull-chain of the lamp on the table beside her, "I realized as soon as Mr. Dewey told me that Henry Twombley was hanging around Miss Bessie'n'Gussie's house and that he was a dangerous man—I realized then that he must have been the man who was hurrying up the hill to meet Lixlee that first time I ever saw her. And the man I saw tramping through the snow that zero night. He had probably come down from Searles Shelf then to find out whether Lixlee . . . whether Anson . . . Perhaps if he had had his rifle with him that night . . ." Her fingers found the chain and pulled it. The flood of light broke the thread of her story. She blinked, put her hand over her eyes, said from under it, "And the moment I heard Anson was shot and Lixlee with him, I knew it must have been the same man. But when the Twombleys all vanished from Searles Shelf,

I never dreamed he'd dare come back." She took down her hand, looked across the table and at the expression on the clergyman's face, asked in a panic, "Oh, Fred, does it seem as bad as that to you? Do you think Anson may be in real danger?"

"And Anson's wife."

The rebuke did not reach her through her agitation. "But what can I *do?*" she asked him.

"You must tell Anson that Henry Twombley has come back. It is his affair. Not ours."

"But I don't know that Anson so much as knows his name or anything about him," protested Anna, despairingly. "I've never had the least idea whether Lixlee ever told him. Yet she must have told him *some*thing."

"Oh, I didn't realize that Anson might not know . . ." said Mr. Kirby, and sat thinking.

Anna brought out another possible plan only to reject it with horror. "Suppose I just appealed to the sheriff. . . . No! No! That would mean another police inquiry. Publicity. Anson's name and Lixlee's dragged in the dirt."

"We would do that if we were good citizens."

"If you do I'd never forgive you in this life," said Anna, passionately.

They were at a standstill. This was their first encounter with violence.

Presently Anna said imploringly, "Fred, couldn't *you* do something? Go up on The Wall—pretend you were going fishing— any fern-picker on The Wall would tell you where the Twombleys' camp is, and talk to Henry? See if you couldn't. . . ."

"I daresay I could find out where he is," admitted the clergyman, thoughtfully. He tried this plan out in his mind for a moment and put it aside. "No, Anna, no. This is Anson's business. What man would want two other men talking behind his back about what his wife had or hadn't . . . You must just tell Anson and let him decide what he wants done."

Anna was almost in tears. "Fred, how can I tell Anson? Suppose I tell him, 'Henry Twombley has come back and is hiding on the

mountain somewhere,' and he says, 'Who is Henry Twombley?' Shall I tell him, 'He is the married man the Searles Shelf people thought was your wife's lover, the man who tried to kill you and Lixlee?' Why, if Anson found out I knew about that, if he ever guessed that you and I have been talking about him and Lixlee, that you know . . . that I have been . . . Oh, Fred, he would never speak to me again!"

"*I'll* tell him," said Mr. Kirby, getting up. "Where did I leave my hat? I'll go and tell him now."

But he could not find his hat. After a moment's search they both remembered that it had been dropped on the grass outside. Anna unlocked and opened the front door.

A small car was drawing up before the house. It stopped, the door clicked open, Anson stepped out, and started up the front walk, calling out, "Hello, Anna, you here already? I was planning to meet the evening train. How're you, Fred?" His footsteps, firm and rhythmical, rang on the marble flagstones. Hard, lean and vital, he appeared in the rectangle of brightness from the open door. Looking up at the two silhouetted against the light, he said as he drew nearer, "Say, Anna, what do you think, you know that mechanic in Danby's garage that lost his voice? Well, it's an aneurysm! Cole and I are going to try the gold wire and electrolysis. . . ." He took the two doorsteps in one vigorous stride. Fred and Anna moved back to let him in.

Even before he saw their faces he asked quickly, "What's the matter?" More sharply as he stepped into the hall between them, "Why, what's happened?" But his manner was that of the seasoned self-contained physician, used to things happening, professionally prepared to cope with them.

Anna was too frightened to speak.

Father Kirby's quiet voice said, "We have just heard that Henry Twombley has come back."

"Who is Henry Twombley?" asked Anson, blankly.

With an involuntary movement Anna put her hands over her eyes.

Father Kirby's left hand went to his cross. His gray eyes fixed themselves on Anson's face.

Anson's blue eyes stared back with a keenness that was almost fierce. And in a moment the change in their expression showed that he knew. He did not allow it to trouble him. When he answered, he gave himself the pleasure, dear to realistic people, of deflating a sensation proposed to them by someone else. "Oh, I know who you mean," he said, in an offhand tone, tossing his hat lightly on the hall table. "That Searles Shelf fellow who knew Lixlee as a girl and lost his head over her, and tried to put me out of the way."

Anna took her hands down from her face.

Anson began to fill his pipe. "Well, I can't say I'm overjoyed to know he's around again. But why throw fits? He'd never dare try any *more* fireworks." He was tamping the tobacco down with a steady finger. "Where're your matches, Anna?" he asked, glancing up at her over it.

Anna moved mechanically to find a matchbox, marveling once again at Anson's ability to turn mountains into mole hills; marveling too at his rocklike courage and coolness. When she came back from the kitchen with the matches, Anson was sitting on the sofa in the living-room, Father Kirby in a chair by the table. Anna sat down by Anson and watched him light his pipe with slow even puffs. When he finished, he said reassuringly, "Now, Anna, don't go up in the air so! Take it easy. A lot of water has gone under the bridge since then. And, anyhow, a man with a shooting on his mind who disappeared right after it wouldn't venture down into The Valley again whatever else he did. He'd know he would be recognized and that people might put two and two together."

He leaned his broad shoulders back on the sofa, and asked, "See here, how did you happen to know about his being here? Had you heard it, Fred? Did *you* tell Anna?" As he spoke, his voice sharpened in annoyance. His accent accused them of intrusion.

"No, no," said Anna, hastily. "One of the Twombley children went by the house just now."

"Where'd you say they were?" asked Anson, turning to his sister and laying an arm along the back of the sofa.

"Up on The Wall, somewhere."

"Not on Searles Shelf? What are they doing up there in the woods?"

"What people like that always do in summer. Picking ferns, selling berries, making . . ."

"Selling berries!" Anson said this so quickly that it was like the loud clap of an echo.

He sat motionless and silent, looking at her, all the expression gone from his face, his eyes stony. To her astonishment the sweat broke out on his forehead visibly, and ran down on his temples in little streams. He moved his right hand across to his left shoulder and gripped it hard. The pipe fell out of his left hand to the floor. His lips moved. She did not know whether she heard or saw him ask, "How does he look?"

Petrified by his strange stare, she scarcely knew what she said, "Why, a tall, thin, rough-looking man, like any back-road farmer . . . *Anson,*" she screamed, "what *is* it? What is the matter? Are you . . . ?"

But he was beyond speech now, sitting in stony immobility, his eyes glaring straight before him, his face gray and glistening with sweat, the hand holding the left shoulder set convulsively in a vise-like grip. Father Kirby gave a horrified exclamation.

But the attitude and aspect of the stricken man gave Anna's professional experience a clew. She sprang up wildly, darted into Anson's office, and ran back instantly. Not a muscle of the tortured man on the sofa had moved. But something had changed. His eyes, no longer stony but filled with abject terror, no longer stared at vacancy. They looked at Death now.

Father Kirby leaned over him from one side, his face white with pity, his hands clasped around his cross.

Anna held something up close before her brother's face. A small glass capsule, shaped like a falling teardrop. "Anson?" she asked urgently, as though he were far away. He could not turn away his eyes from the invisible horror threatening him, but as if he had answered, she laid the crystal in her handkerchief, crushed it. Then leaning over Anson where he sat, gray-faced with anguish, she

held it where he could not but breathe in the fumes which almost visibly streamed up from the saturated linen. He inhaled them with deep gasps. The tension of his body and hand relaxed. The sweat on his face dried. He drew in another lungful of the acrid gas and tried to speak. But it was too soon. His tongue was still thick, his lips stiff. Anna could make nothing of the few syllables he muttered, and, on a guess asked anxiously, "Chloroform?"

He shook his head, buried his face in the handkerchief again and breathed deeply. His right arm dropped heavily from his left shoulder. His right hand limp and trembling lay open on his knee.

When he looked up, nameless human anguish no longer lay sweating and cowering before Death. It was Anson Craft who leaned faintly against the back of the sofa, shaken and sunken together, his cheeks white and furrowed, but recognizably himself. In a tone meant to be peremptory but which came out as an anxious whisper, he asked, "Did you hear what I said just now?"

"No, the only word I could make out sounded like chloroform. I thought perhaps you were reminding me Father used to use a few whiffs of that when the amyl nitrite didn't give immediate relief."

He closed his eyes and was still. To see the look of life come back to his face was like seeing a resurrection. Father Kirby sat down heavily. Anna laid her fingers on Anson's wrist. After a time she told him, "That may have been only . . ."

Without opening his eyes he repudiated her half-offered reassurance, "Oh, that was angina, all right. *Me!*"

"You may never have another attack," she said.

He took his hand away and said, drawing in a long breath between each sentence, "I'm going to the bathroom. No, I can—no help—alone. Leave word in the office—can't see anyone tonight. All right—tomorrow." He stood up with an effort, stumbled across the room and into the hall.

Anna followed him and stood, one hand on the banister, watching his back as he slowly mounted the stairs. Father Kirby turned to her desk, found a large sheet of paper, wrote, "Doctor Craft will not be here this evening," and went into the south wing. No

one was in the waiting-room. He laid the notice on the table and went back to the hall. Anna was still standing there, looking fixedly up at the empty landing. He said in her ear, "Is it safe for him to be alone?"

She turned her head to whisper, her face close to his, "One of these seizures never follows another one at once. But people are always frightfully exhausted. Even after a short attack like this. I never saw anyone who could stand on his feet afterwards. He must be putting out his will power beyond anything we can imagine."

They started apart like conspirators. Anson appeared at the head of the stairs and began, slowly, slowly, to come down. His white face was impassive. His right hand gripped the stair rail hard.

"Let me drive you home, Anson," suggested Anna, timidly.

"No, I'd better," said Father Kirby.

Anson looked at them. But it took him a perceptible time to see them. And a moment more before he heard what they had said. By that time he was at the foot of the stairs. He turned his head slightly to the right and back again in a gesture of negation, and looked around for his hat. When he saw it on the table, he moved cautiously towards it and lifting his hand by inches put it on. Mr. Kirby had opened the door. Half way out Anson stopped and looking out into the night's blackness said in a muffled voice, "That matter—leave it to me, if you please." He took a step forward. "If anything needs to be done"—he lowered himself from the doorstep to the path—"I'll do it."

He stopped, stood an instant and turned around. Although he moved with anxious caution, the effort of turning almost threw him off his balance. Seeing him waver to and fro, Anna made as if to spring to his side. But Father Kirby's hand, firmly on her arm, held her back. Anson, standing in the rectangle of light, bowed together for weakness, lifted his head, tried in vain to throw his shoulders back, and breathed once or twice deeply. "I particularly do not wish you to mention that matter to my wife," he told them. "If anything needs to be said, I will . . ." His stern eyes read Anna's thought. "No, do not telephone her now that I have been . . .

slightly upset. . . . *Do you understand, Anna?* Do not telephone her at all or tell her anything."

He turned around and walked on slowly, setting his feet down with care. They saw his dim figure creep into the car. The headlights flared up, the starter burred, gears were shifted, the car disappeared. Father Kirby closed the door.

"Oh, Fred! Oh, Fred!" said Anna piteously. She had lost all sense of time or direction or purpose. She was fainting—not bodily but spiritually. For the first time she felt herself helpless and resourceless, as if she had been a dry leaf caught up by a wind suddenly pouring itself through the darkness and carrying her out to black nowhere. And now the wind fell dead. She was falling through space, whirling and falling, falling and whirling, helplessly. "Oh, Fred!" she cried out piteously as she fell.

He put his hands firmly on the abandoned controls. "Anna, it is long past eight, and you haven't had any supper. Nor I, either. Come out into the kitchen and show me where to find something to eat."

She felt the sickening downward pull slacken. A strong thin hand held hers. The eddying fall into nothingness steadied itself. Something that was not nothingness bore her up as outspread wings are upborne. She was not falling alone through space. Fred Kirby's hand guided a wide-winged circling flight with mastery, and from formless darkness she emerged into her own house. Her own kitchen floor was solid under her feet. He had brought her home. He was drawing her forward to where the teakettle drowsed somnolently on a turned-down burner of the oil stove. The teapot and the tea canister stood on the table beside them.

"Oh, tea!" said Fred Kirby. "That's what we need. Tea!"

The door was open into the dining-room. The table was set for one there, cold meat on a platter, salad in a bowl, slices of brown bread on a plate. Fred looked at Anna, smiled, and let go her hand. "You set another place at the table and I'll make the tea." He carried the teapot to the stove and lifted the teakettle.

She stood still, looking at his back, listening to the echoes in her ear of the tenderness of his voice.

"Go along, Anna," he said over his shoulder. "I'll be ready before you are." He spoke as though they had always prepared their meals together.

While they were eating he would not let her say a word. "No, no, let all that wait till later. Pass me the bread, please. And drink your tea." He spoke with authority. Anna passed him the bread and drank her tea as though they were in his house and not hers. It did not seem to be her house, she thought, looking around the familiar room. She seemed to have come out into a new place, where she had never been before.

"Isn't that a lemon pie I see on the sideboard?" asked Fred Kirby. He seemed familiarly at home in the place where they had come out. He got up now, brought the pie to the table, cut it, passed her a piece, and asked her to pour him another cup of tea. "I like eating with you," he told her. It sounded like something that had just come into his head. So he said it. When he had finished that cup, he sat back in his chair, and smiled at Anna again. "You look better," he said. "More like yourself."

She felt better but as unlike herself as if she were in a dream.

"Well, now let's see if we can get anywhere by talking it all out," he said, getting up from the table. "Come on into the living-room and let's start at the beginning."

It was nine o'clock when they sat down, Anna on the sofa, Fred in a chair across the table from her. He put his arms out on the table, his long thin hands loosely clasped, his quiet eyes on hers as she talked, as she asked questions, answered them. No, he told her, in those first words Anson had spoken so thickly he had not heard anything that sounded like "chloroform." It had sounded more like "they locked the door." Together they considered this with all their minds. "They locked the door." What could it mean? Together they decided that it did not mean anything and that neither of them had heard what Anson had really said.

Then from her professional experience she answered a question of his. No, she did not think that the news they had told Anson

could have had anything to do with that heart attack. In the first place, though emotion sometimes brought it on, angina was caused by something physical, usually sclerosis of the coronary arteries coming from overwork, too much coffee, too much smoking, too much . . . Anna hesitated, said, "Alcohol," and added, "I thought from his breath he had just had a drink. No, I never knew he drank." And secondly, Anson hadn't shown the slightest sign of being disturbed by that news. The hand filling his pipe had been as steady as a rock. He had been leaning back against the sofa as relaxed as they were now, and they were talking of nothing special —berry-picking and fern-gathering—when it had riven him like a stroke of lightning. But that's what angina does. The suffering's terrible. But the worst, they all say, is the frightful apprehension. That's what makes old Miss Bessie suffer so terribly from the fear of death. This reminded Fred that it had been Miss Gussie who had, with her clairvoyant eyes, seen a shadow on Lixlee's quiet face. Anna spoke then of Mrs. Randall's item of gossip about Charlie Dean. Fred had heard that too. People were talking about that— not only Almira Boardman. They considered this together and discarded it as of no consequence. No woman could take that bloodless tongue-tied book-worm seriously, even his wife did not. Anna asked then, might not the shadow on Lixlee's face, if there was one, have been because she had caught sight of Henry Twombley from a distance, or had heard he was back . . . Why, she knew the children, perhaps she too had seen little Eli. Yes, that must be the trouble, Anna decided, Lixlee knew that the evil genius of her youth was back, feared him, but dared not tell Anson. But now Anson had been told and by this time had probably found a way to reassure Lixlee. "You know how our own fear shrank to nothing just to hear his cool off-hand way of taking that news." (She thought, "Why, just so all my tenseness and excitement has melted away to nothing in the comfort of Fred's being with me. If only . . . oh, *why* must he keep up that barrier of religiousness!")

Fred was saying, "Yes, Anson is a man. A strong man. How indomitable he was, standing there on the walk, just escaped from

death, holding his shaking body up by sheer will-power and putting us both in our places with his eye and voice. No man of merely physical violence could stand against him."

Anna wondered dreamily, "Where *are* those inner fibers that vibrate so to Fred's voice? In the body? Or brain? Or . . . ?"

He said, now, "Yes, the woman he loves is safe in his arms." They both thought, "And that is where she is, now, this moment." They sat silent, seeing Anson's strong arms close about his love; his head bent over hers, his lips set like a seal on her mouth.

The man stirred, drew a breath, and said in a low tone that barely reached her ears, "All this is nothing you know, Anna, *nothing,* compared to their loving each other."

"No, nothing," repeated Anna after him, looking down at her hands. A lump came in to her throat at the thought of the marvel of that love. She seemed never to have looked at it before.

Yet when she spoke, it was of something else, "Fred, I've been wanting to ask you—do you think I've done better about Anson since you spoke to me that day? I've tried to. I've been so glad you warned me." The barriers were down. She had been able to devise no way to make it possible for her to speak of that. But now it came from her as naturally as breathing.

"You're all right, Anna," he said gently.

She got up restlessly then and asked aloud how could she sleep without knowing how Anson was. She asked herself what time it could be, walked aimlessly across the room, looked at her watch without seeing it, said, "I could telephone—?"

Fred sat still, following her with his eyes.

"But, oh, no, suppose he should be asleep. . . . It would be dreadful to wake him up just to quiet my own anxiety." She looked back at the silent man, asking wordlessly for advice.

He stood up and suggested patiently that they might walk around to Anson's house and see if it were still lighted.

It was a still night, very black. Although there were no clouds to veil the stars they were blurred and faint, visible but casting no light. Light was not needed by the two who walked side by

side along the deserted street. They knew their way without seeing it. Every rise and fall and turn of the path was familiar to their feet from a lifetime's coming and going. They could not see each other, knew that the other was there only through an occasional brushing contact of hand or arm or garment, and by the sound of near-by footsteps, quiet and light, echoing in the stillness, intermingled so that neither of them could tell his own step from the other's.

They passed a darkly silent house. Another. Another. It was past midnight. The town had gone to sleep. The mountains loomed huge, masses of unstarred darkness against the dimly lighted sky. Side by side the man and the woman walked steadily forward on their unseen path and presently came in sight of the house they sought. It was unlighted and silent. There it lay, dark and still, and hid what was within it. They halted.

"He must be safe asleep," murmured Anna, pacified.

"Look!" said the man beside her.

Above the mountains to the north an ineffable brightness slowly dawned. As they gazed a long finger of white light flared noiselessly up to the zenith.

Anna murmured, "Oh, the Northern Lights!" and threw back her head to follow the course of the ray which in one pulsing bound had bridged the darkness overhead. Something deep within her sprang up, too, from darkness and followed. Another shining beam sped up across the sky. And another. And another. Bodiless light was raying up and out from a hidden source of glory beyond the mountains' blackness, beyond the dark swinging speck of the globe, —beyond imagination.

She was awe-struck by the silence in which those rays flashed, leaped up and spanned infinity. She looked up steadfastly. Did time pass or did it stand still? Presently a fire and a heavenly whiteness filled all the northern sky. It paled and brightened, paled and brightened, as if the hidden source of light were a mighty pulsing heart. And now with each brightening pulsation, there, high in the blackness above them, shone out a floating immaterial white radiance. It did not travel out from the central splendor, not even on

one of those fleet rays, fleet as if space were not. Like a noble thought, it lay one instant at the mysterious heart of glory, and at the next was far beyond the outermost stars.

The man of God looked down and away from the symbol filling the universe with wonder, and turned his eyes with compassion upon the sullenly darkened houses around them. "And all the town asleep!" he said pityingly.

And now for the first time Anna understood the pity that was so often in his voice and in his eyes. She too was thrust through and through with that pity, now when at last she saw what he saw, what no words could ever tell.

"We are awake," she answered him, her face uplifted towards the radiating beams, luminous beyond light, yet filling the heavens with their tale of a brightness of which they were but pale reflections.

"Yes. Yes. Oh, *yes!*" said Anna in her heart to all she had said "no" to—to what, all her life and his, the silent man beside her had been trying to tell her. How often he had turned his face away from glory to knock on the door of her darkened house, and bid her "look."

"But I didn't know—I didn't dream—I hadn't a glimpse of what it is he sees."

His eyes were now on the unlighted black cube of Anson's house. He said sadly, "It is as opaque and shut as a human being." And on a still lower note, "So are we all to each other."

"Not you to me. Not now. Not ever!" The thought came as clearly into Anna's mind as though she had spoken it in words. And then she heard their echo in the stillness. She had spoken it in words. "Not you to me. Not now. Not ever!" she had said it aloud, all her passionate new certainty in her voice.

He said her name then— "Anna!" By saying her name, he set her apart from all other women who lived, who had ever lived.

"*Anna!*" he said.

PART FIVE

1

Aᴜɢᴜsᴛ and September that year had presumably the same number of hours and days as in other years. And for some of those living on The Street and in The Valley they were ordinary months, with nothing in them to drown out the dearly loved tinkle-tinkle of the daily round. But for others—they were not ordinary months.

The annual and seasonal functions of course took place as usual —the Bazaar of the Ladies' Guild of St. Andrew's, held in the open air on the common between the church and Miss Bessie'n'Gussie Kemp's house; the Saturday and Sunday afternoon baseball games on the Glebe field, passionately played and devotedly watched by quite another group of citizens of Clifford; the Boys' Camp up on the shore of Hawley Lake; the Girls' Camp in the Purdy woods and the combination Four H young people's camp filled with noisy, saddle-brown, vital boys and girls and emptied again with the usual miraculous record of nobody's neck broken; and the annual Tennis Tournament between the North and South Shires of Windward County ended as usual with a victory for the Ashley Club. This was expected, the Ashley organization being three times as numerous as that of Clifford.

But this time the Ashley victory was more dearly bought than ever before. Thanks to Rug Milner, the Clifford players made an unusually good showing. An impassioned tennis player and soon very popular with the young people of town, he brought up the level of the local Club's playing amazingly. His sound back-hand,

303

his steady errorless driving and impeccable second-service ball were object lessons in good form to the youngest members of the Club who till then had taken for granted that much spectacular slamming of the ball into the net was the last word in tennis.

He thought Olivia Merrill, who was back after her Freshman year at the University, very promising material, and had coached her as his partner in doubles with a care and attention such as nobody in Clifford had dreamed of applying to tennis. When the September tournament came, they downed Mr. and Mrs. Moore of Ashley who had won the doubles since the beginning of time.

The day after the tournament at their annual picnic supper Rug Milner gave the Tennis Club a wonderful pep talk. "If we step on the starter *now*," he told them earnestly, "that cup will be right in the middle of this party next year. If we all hang together, practice seriously, bring out our young players," his inspiring glance in their direction was their first public recognition as anything but nuisances, "by this time next year Ashley'll be swallowing our dust. The signal ahead is never a red stoplight unless you think it is, If you see it green, it is green. What we've got to do is—to—see— *green!*" His young Vermont audience not at all used to pep talks applauded. He was, as a matter of fact, quite the town hero at that time. Early in July Clifford had been shaken by an event that could easily have turned into a catastrophe for the town. This was the death of old Mr. Warren, the last of the family; and the consequent closing down of the woolen mills that had been run for more than a century by the Warrens. Would they be permanently closed? The question was an alarming one to the Clifford workmen who had always earned their wages in the Warren Mills, to their families, to the people to whom they owed money, to the whole town. The Warren Mills paid a considerable share of the taxes. For a fortnight nobody talked of anything else.

Rug Milner had come to the rescue, and had succeeded in selling the Mills to some company out West in Milwaukee where he came from. These big firms move fast, faster than Vermonters could believe. Only two weeks after old Mr. Warren's death, the Mills reopened and began to run again with the same manager, the same

foremen and workmen as before. For another fortnight people talked of nothing but this fortunate salvation of the town's prosperity, and began to call the round-faced young man who was so like his grandmother Merrill's pleasant family, Rug Merrill half the time instead of Milner. On the whole, in spite of being under an obligation to him, Clifford people liked Rug. He did not seem an outlander any more, in spite of his German expletives and other funny ways. He seemed a Merrill, a harmless good-natured Merrill, come home to live. Folks laughed a little over his dating everying in his life by which automobile he had owned at the time. The way he bowed like a poker breaking in two was funny of course. But Olivia maintained that he was cute. "No, I haven't either got a crush on him! I just think he's cute. And he is."

In addition to these communal goings-on, the usual crop of individual events occurred. It was that summer that Almira Boardman's disagreeable oddities went over the dividing line and became mental unbalance. And that summer that Mr. Dewey's cantankerous wife finally died, leaving the old man to a peace and quiet which, after his long martyrdom at her hands, seemed to echo hollowly in his ears. People who had sympathized with him were exasperated. It was perverse in him not to enjoy his new freedom. "It gives a person a nawful gone feeling . . . not to have anybody to do for," he told Doctor Foote sadly one Sunday afternoon when the two men were in the woods high on The Wall, trying with a much creased yellow map to trace out the course of the eighteenth-century "old road," the first road, that followed the still older Indian trail.

Don at their heels they were slowly working their way through a dismal swampy piece of brushland full of scraggy dead and dying alders. "I don't honestly know what to do with myself, seems though," Mr. Dewey was saying. "There don't really seem to be much use in my cumbering up the ground any more. It's pretty late to . . . What's Don barking over there about? What do you suppose he's run on to? Well, for the Lord's sake, look at that?" They had come up to Don, who was excitedly pointing out heavy

fresh shoe tracks in the soft muck. "Why in tunket was anybody in *here?*" Don's master asked himself, Doctor Foote and Don. They all three stood staring down at the sprawled muddy spoor.

"Fern-pickers?" suggested Doctor Foote.

"There don't a fern grow this side the 'Burnin''" Mr. Dewey reminded him. He gazed down intently. Water was beginning to ooze into the footprints. "Looks as though somebody had just this minute stepped out o' them, don't it? Hark!" Don ran forward, barking frantically. "Keep still! *Down!*" commanded Mr. Dewey sharply. Stricken with remorse for his sin, Don halted and was silent. But if that had been a twig snapping it was not repeated. The two local historians forgot the map and the Indian trail, set Don to follow the tracks, and themselves to follow him. But they came almost at once to a brook. The tracks vanished. Don ran up and down the bank, sniffing but not barking, and hoping he was being virtuous. Mr. Dewey looked at the running water with a mystified expression. "What could anybody ha' been up to at the back end of nowhere like this?"

"Well, we're here!"

"You don't suppose there's another such a fool in The Valley as we be, do ye?"

The usual and ordinary accidents, a fire, automobile collisions, a freight car off the track, happened that summer. But there was one most unusual. Mr. Lawrence Stewart was attacked by a cat and injured so badly that he stayed for weeks in a darkened room, his head and hands wound around with bandages, and couldn't receive his usual succession of summer colony ladies for afternoon tea. One of a litter of kittens his tame old house cat had had that spring, had gone "wild," as sometimes happened to one in the litter of even the most staid and domestic of house cats in a region so close to the forest as The Valley. It had grown up under the woodshed and in the barn, looking exactly like his mother, only handsomer, but as wild as any lynx. One evening, seeing it in a corner of the woodshed, poor Mr. Stewart had mistaken it for Henrietta and stooped to pet it. The wild thing had misinterpreted the friendly

gesture for a hostile one, had felt itself cornered and cut off from retreat, and had sprung desperately at the stooping man's face with teeth and talons trained to savagery by its long practice in killing for its food. The wounds had been serious—some danger even to his eyesight for a time—and he had lost a good deal of blood; but for a person of his age, the nervous shock was the worst. The few who saw him reported that he seemed shaken and feeble, all his spruce, well-preserved trimness gone. Sometimes now people spoke of him as old Mr. Stewart. It was providential that that good-natured nephew had turned up just then, so that he had someone of his own family with him in his illness, although Doctor Craft, who feared blood poisoning, made many professional calls and often sent his wife in to cheer the old gentleman up. At least she was often there.

Almira Boardman said up and down that Doctor Anson's wife went to sit with the good-looking young nephew, not with the sick old uncle. It was in fact her talk about Mrs. Craft that summer that made people realize what Almira's mental condition was. Everyone was so used to her and she had grown worse so gradually that it took the shock of her wild talk to startle Clifford into seeing that she was "going like her poor Aunt Laura." All the Boardmans were gossips, but a Boardman old maid was likely to be a very special kind of gossip. People as old as Miss Bessie'n'Gussie could remember scraps of forbidden talk heard in their childhood about a spinster great-aunt of Almira's, who—"what *was* that story, Gussie? Was she the one that told such crazy things about people's love-making that had never thought of such a thing, and began to take off her clothes at her younger sister's wedding, and . . ." "Sh! Bessie, what's the use of hauling all that misery up from its grave." And everybody, even quite young people, had heard about poor Almira's own aunt Laura. Like Almira she had been a girl who looked like other girls, but little by little had grown into a haggard old maid who could never talk of anything but you know what. She had seen and reported so much imaginary illicit love that finally she had gone quite beside herself, and had to be taken off,

tied hand and foot, to the Brattleboro Retreat, where she died a year later, just plain crazy.

Almira's actions that summer made people aware that she was far gone on the way to just such a mental breakdown. Her obsessions which had been wandering, scattered and relatively mild, were now sharply focused on young Mrs. Craft, and it was not long after the Crafts' return to live in Clifford, that what had been just "queerness" developed into what looked like true mania. She couldn't pass you in the street now without stopping to whisper greedily in your ear, "Anson Craft's wife has got Charlie Dean a-sittin' on thorns and now she's a-turnin' of that Western fellow's head. Somebody ought to *do* something. She's there in the Stewart house pretendin' to do something for his poor old uncle, or he's at her house, or they're off in the woods together, up to nobody knows what, every minute of the day and night, I tell ye. Why don't Anson put his foot down I'd like to know. He used to have plenty of spunk, if nothin' else."

The relishing glitter in Almira's faded eyes, boring into yours as she whispered volubly, stopped to catch a wheezing breath and whispered on again, was rather sickening. What would she be saying next? People began to tell their children that if Miss Almira stopped them in the street, they were to say their mothers had sent them on an errand in a hurry, and scoot along home as fast as they could leg it. When she managed to corner you somewhere and began to pour out that incoherent nasty talk, you usually tried to edge off, saying vaguely, "You don't say," or, "Well, well, think of that." A few people did try to argue with her, to say, "Why, Miss Almira, I guess you've got something twisted somewhere. *I* don't see Mrs. Anson going or coming to the Stewart house more than once in a while. Olivia's the one I see Rug Milner with mostly. He's always got Olivia in his car, driving, seem's though." But, of course, you never get anywhere trying to reason with a person who's off in the upper story. As the doctors tell you, it only makes them worse to remind them of facts. Almira always came back at you, talking so fast you could hardly make out what she said, with a rambling feverish fairy-story about your not seeing Mrs.

Craft go and come because there was a roundabout invisible back way between the Craft and the Stewart houses. . . . "There's a back door in the Craft barn" (she was one of the generation that went on calling garages "barns"), probably in the lower part where the horse-stall used to be—there *must* be—and the Deans' garden, the corn in that's high enough to hide a man, and across Miss Bessie'n'Gussie's back pasture—you know, that's lower than the graveyard—and has that high stonewall this side of it, so you can't see over into it from The Street, and along Cold Brook in the sumac bushes and under the bridge—" But you couldn't keep your mind on the poor daft thing's distracted talk for your fascinated watching of the saliva gathering in the corners of her pale lips. Sometimes it drooled down in two unpleasant streams before she could check her excited talk to wipe it off. Really, you thought, walking away from her in a hurry, she oughtn't to be let to wander hither and yon, making decent folks sick to their stomachs. She ought to be shut up.

How like a crazy person it was, everybody said, never to mention the one damaging thing a gossip could truthfully tell about the Crafts, which was that Doctor Anson was drinking heavily in these days, and once or twice had been seen when he scarcely knew what he was about. A mean person in his right mind, that wanted to hurt the Crafts by talking behind their backs, you argued, would have played up the doctor's whiskey. But no, Almira was a Boardman—nothing interested her but . . .

Her poor wits soon grew so cracked that she could not even keep her own inventions straight. She wandered and wavered in her versions, telling you the identical same story of secret meetings between young Mrs. Craft and a man—only one minute the man would be Charlie Dean, and with the next breath young Milner. She got *every*thing twisted! Sometimes it would be Charlie Dean who made his way through her imaginary hidden way from the Stewart to the Craft house, and if sometimes you couldn't help reminding her that, after all, Charlie Dean wasn't the one who lived in the Stewart house, her eyes glittered till your flesh crept on your bones, she put her fingers on her lips and went off into

even wilder fictions, talking about a mysterious third man—another one!—who on nights when the doctor had driven off on a night call emerged from the Craft barn and slunk into the back door of the house. Public opinion began nervously to demand that if Almira got one particle worse, something should be done about it. "Something" meant, of course, the Brattleboro Retreat where her aunt died.

Whenever this was mentioned in Miss Bessie Kemp's hearing, she said if you started taking folks to the insane asylum for telling tales about their neighbors, there soon wouldn't be anybody left in town to pay the taxes. And anyhow she maintained that there might very likely be something in what Almira was saying about that Searles Shelf hussy. But such malicious flings from her were discounted. Everybody knew her bossy ways, knew that as the old saying goes, she wanted to tell everybody when to breathe and when to hold his breath, and that she had never forgiven that girl for having a mind of her own and doing something Miss Bessie hadn't known about beforehand. Miss Gussie now bore the girl no grudge, always had a kind word for her when other people spoke of her, and another for her when she chanced to meet her on the street. And wouldn't Miss Gussie know as much about her as Miss Bessie?

To sum up the local news items during those two late summer months, there needs only to be said in addition to the important change in the ownership of the Warren Mills, the usual community events of Church Bazaars, Boy and Girl Scout Camps and baseball series, the usual accidents and fires, and the beginning of Almira Boardman's nervous breakdown, that two or three engagements were announced (that of the district nurse and the minister the most out of the common run), and that the customary number of babies were born. One of these, a baby girl arrived in the Jim Gardner family almost at the very moment when cranky old Mrs. Dewey finally died. "It certainly makes a person hope," Miss Gussie was heard to remark, talking to herself, "that there is nothing to this transmigration of souls business."

2

For the majority of the responsible tax-paying citizens of Clifford, the flurry of alarm over the closing of the Warren Mills and the relief when they were opened again with Rug Milner's help, may have been a more important event than the news that M'Sanna Craft was to marry Father Kirby. But in their own immediate world, these newly betrothed were talked about ten times as much as the danger of losing the biggest business concern in town. For a time, in fact, there was little talk of anything else.

People talked as they did everything else, according to their natures. Mr. Dewey exclaimed, looking after Fred and Anna as they walked down the street together, "Well, who'd have thought ever to see those two, lookin' like all engaged folks—as if they were the ones that had invented fallin' in love and gettin' married!"

Miss Gussie said nothing, except "Very nice, I'm sure." What she thought was "Anna's wick is turned up at last where it'll burn bright, instead of smoking."

When Mrs. Foote, Isabel's mother, was told the news, she said briefly from where, percale-crisp and gingham-aproned, she stood canning plums in the back-kitchen, "Oh, they've got around to it, have they?" After that she steadfastly talked and acted as though they had always been engaged. One of her caustic sayings, aimed at Miss Bessie Kemp, was "Nyes are no hands to talk the life out of their ideas."

For her part Miss Bessie told all comers that she'd as lief talk to Hemlock Mountain as to Hilda Nye. "Children shouldn't be allowed to let things happen without talkin' 'em over, any more'n they should be allowed to swill down their food without chewin' it." The young people who stopped to pass the time of day with Miss Bessie certainly had, in the matter of Anna's Craft's engagement, an object lesson in the art of talking things over. For days at a time Miss Bessie forgot to scold about "that Searles Shelf girl" she had cried shame on so long that people were tired of hearing her. As she sat on the front porch those hot August and crisp

September mornings, her gingham Mother Hubbard billowing over the arms of her grandmother's short-rockered hickory chair, her thoughts were full of speculation about the affianced two, and when anybody turned in from the front walk to lean over the porch railing for a chat, her tongue began with practiced rapidity to discharge what had been accumulating in her mind. After the ritual comments on the weather she would say, "What I'd like to know about Anna and Fred Kirby is . . . *what set'em off?* You know how such folks are . . . it takes a landslide or something like it to make either of them step out of their front doors where the other person can get at'em. Did I ever tell you about my grandmother and grandfather's courtin'? They'd never looked at anybody else from the time they played tag and hide-and-seek, just like Anna and Fred—but after they got to the marryin' and givin' in marriage age they could *not* seem to get *at* each other. Grandmother used to tell us young ones that as long as they talked about the weather and the crops they could gab along as good as anybody. But the minute they'd try to switch the talk to what they were both thinkin' about, why, *she'd* get shamefaced and *he'd* get bashful. The longer that lasted the worse it got of course, because you know if there's one habit that grows on you it's the weather-and-crop habit o'talk. In no time a person gets so he can't bring another word out. Well, they had been goin' together for four years and grandmother said she'd just about given up. 'Twa'n't just that *he* couldn't get over his bashfulness, you know. She couldn't either. If it'd only been one of them—the way it usually is—why, the other one could have managed. But 'twas a pair of'em for sheepishness. Every Sunday afternoon he'd come to see her. In fair weather they went for a walk. If 'twas stormy she made up a fire in the best room and they set there. Just like stotin' bottles, she used to tell us, boilin' hot inside, and stone on the outside. I suppose they'd never have busted through whatever 'twas kept'em apart, if it hadn't been that one Sunday in April they went up Dowling Hollow way lookin' for mayflowers. 'Twas so warm some snakes were out sunnin'emselves at the foot of the Crow Rocks, and before she knew it Grandmother stepped square on a big one." She paused to laugh

loudly at your blank face before she explained, "Why, don't you see, she was terribly scared of snakes, and when she felt this big fellow squirm so snaky under her foot, she let out a screech you'd ha' heard in Canada, 'Nat! Nat!' (Grandfather's name was Nathaniel) and flung her arms around him. But he had got his arms around her first, you bet, and had picked her up off the snake and carried her fifty feet before he could stop, huggin' the breath out of her. And by that time they were both kissin' each other for dear life and bawlin' like calves, they were so relieved. They were married before the next week was out. And had twelve children. And every year let mayflower time come around, those two—old folks they were when I knew'em—they'd hobble all the way to the Crow Rocks to pick mayflowers."

She rambled a good deal nowadays, old Miss Bessie did, and her listeners were apt to forget what it was she had been talking about. But she did not. She would always, give her time enough, bring her talk back to her theme. "But what I wish somebody would tell me is where Fred Kirby found a snake for Anna Craft to step on. I don't mean a real snake—for them, it'd have to be a kind of what you might call a soul-snake. Yes, for Anna too—she may not take Communion fasting—or any other way—but she's just as religious as Fred, every bit, and I don't know but more so. And where in Clifford, Vermont, this month of August that nothin's happened except a cat scratching Lawrence Stewart's face, did those two come across anything to jar their minds loose from makin' the world a better place to live in for folks that don't deserve to have it better, long enough to get their arms around each other is what I'd like to be told."

Extraordinary how much breath Miss Bessie had for talking! It made her puff and pant now, even to go up the three back-porch steps, her heart was so bad, but she could—and never notice it— wind her way through a sentence that would break a snake's back to follow. Her listeners might be breathless by the time she got to the end, but she wasn't.

Once old Mr. Dewey, stopping with Don to say good day over the porch rail, broke in on her to suggest tartly, "Maybe it didn't

happen that way, Bessie. Maybe you don't know all about every-thing in everybody's life, the way you think you do. Maybe she and Fred had understood each other long before this, but Anna had thought she oughtn't to marry, till she got Anson eddicated. Some folks do give up considerable when they think they ought to." He raised his voice and looked at Miss Gussie as he spoke.

"Gussie don't know what we're talkin' about," Miss Bessie told him. "She gets deefer all the time. We have to write most every-thing we want her to know now." She went on, "Well, there's one thing, Fred never could ha' found another woman with eyes in her head that would ha' had him. How *do* you suppose Anna can stand the prospect of bein' married to that birthmark? I've sat here by the hour tryin' to think how they manage. Do you imagine she ever kisses him? She certainly looks as if she did. You've noticed, I suppose, how all-over different she is. I never thought I'd live to see Anna Craft one of the kissin' kind. But can they really make love? Maybe in the dark she—"

Mr. Dewey's weather-beaten old face glowed hotly in a furious blush. "Shut your damn dirty mouth, Bessie Kemp!" he shouted, stamping away down the path as though he would like to break the flagstones with his feet, Don sadly slinking at his heels, stricken with remorse for the sin he must have committed to make God so angry.

Miss Bessie looked after them laughing, as she did at most things. Miss Gussie asked her, "What made Sherwin so mad?"

"Nothin' in particklar. Sherwin always did get mad over nothin'. He stays just the way he was as a boy anyhow."

"What?" asked Miss Gussie.

Miss Bessie repeated in a shout, "I said he stays just the way he was as a boy. Hadn't you noticed that?"

The tears rose to Miss Gussie's eyes.

Miss Bessie stared, reached for the other's pad of paper and wrote, "I guess you didn't understand what I said. I said Sherwin stays just—"

"I heard what you said," said Miss Gussie, getting up and going into the house.

Miss Bessie shook her head. "Poor Gussie gets queerer all the time," she told the next person who came to lean on the porch railing.

Miss Bessie was not the only person in Clifford to wonder about the disfiguring birthmark, nor the only one to mention it. Along with the joy in the faces of the newly betrothed couple, it was in the thoughts of many people. And Anson brought it out into words almost at once when Anna told him she loved and was going to marry Fred Kirby. She told him this the very day after the Northern Lights, although the evening before she would have thought that now was the last time to ask Anson's attention for anything but his own affairs.

But the next day had brought her, from one source and another, an almost complete reassurance about Anson and the menace of Henry Twombley.

She had wakened the morning after the Northern Lights to astonishment at everything in the world and in herself. She was astonished by the still lambent gold of the summer sunshine flooding her bedroom. She had never before seen how thickly it gilded to its own resplendence all it fell upon. She was astonished by the profound dreamless sleep which lay behind her, sleep into which she had fallen as soon as—exalted and quivering from her lover's good night at the door—she had lain down in her bed. She had wakened refreshened by that sleep as by no other in her life. "It's like waking up in the World-to-Come!" she thought. "It's the first time in my life that I ever felt *rested*." She was astonished above everything to find that it was not the revelation of last night that now seemed dreamlike and unreal, but all the pale and shadowy years before that. Had she ever been anywhere else than in Fred's arms? She felt them about her now as, still half asleep, she sat on the edge of her bed, dreaming in the sun. "They will always be around me, now and forever, amen," she said aloud, her certainty far outrunning the metes and bounds of mere mortality.

She accepted this immeasurable happiness and security as effort-

lessly as her eye had followed the light-beam's joyous play across infinity last night. She had not been surprised then, only exalted. She was not surprised now. She could scarcely remember back to the old unhappy days before last night. She thought, "How laughable to try to write poems about love. Its smallest part cannot be told." But even as she told herself, "No, it can never find expression, never," tears sprang into her eyes and rained down on her cheeks, expressing for her exquisitely what words could never say.

Her alarm clock set off its rattle. It was time to dress and go to work. She unbraided the red-gold of her hair and began to brush it. She had always known she had fine hair and she thought now, "I'm glad I have *some*thing nice for Fred," but when, the gleaming fleece of it hanging loose, she went to the mirror to pin it up, she was startled by the luminous clear face and red-brown eyes of the woman she saw there. "Can that be Anna Craft?" thought Anna, and saw the firm red mouth in the mirror quiver and soften to beauty.

The door from the kitchen to the back hall slammed. Mrs. Randall's voice called up the stairs, "Say, Anna, your coffee's made. I've got to run over home now. I put the things in the oven and on the back of the stove. And Mr. Kirby left a letter for you he said to give you as soon as you were up. I'm putting it here on the newel-post—something about his going to look up one of your poor families today, he said it was."

The front door shut. The benediction of solitude thick around her, Anna ran down and at thirty-seven years of age read her first love letter. When she turned and went slowly back to her room, she put out her hand to feel her way up the stairs and along the hall, her eyes dazzled, like those of a person who has looked into the sun.

As she laid the envelope down on her bureau she saw a postscript scrawled on it. He was off for the day to Searles Shelf and The Wall to see what he could find out indirectly about "the family in question." Oh, she would not see him then till that night! He had written, "Not back till after dark." She wondered a little at

the turn of his phrase. How could he be so sure? Why only after dark?

She dressed, slipped the letter into the bosom of her dress, and went down to her breakfast in the same room where she had sat at supper with Fred last night. Long after she had finished she sat dreaming at the table, bringing up to her inner ear over and over the tenderness of his voice, feeling again and again his dear thin fingers clasped about her hand.

The clock struck. She should have been at her office by now. She came to herself and thought, "So poor Isabel sat and dreamed of Anson and the touch of his hand." And then, "If I had any idea then what she was feeling, I could never have lived through her pain at the last!"

At that hour the familiar streets were deserted. She saw no one till from a distance she noticed that a woman and two children were sitting on the steps before the battered front door of the Town Hall waiting for her. The first human being she saw after her first parting from her lover was Henry Twombley's wife. She had been one of those who had never liked M'Sanna and as the nurse drew near, she stood up with a forlorn attempt to look casual and matter-of-fact. She was very thin, very shabby, far advanced in pregnancy. Two ragged unwashed little girls stood up with her, fixing frightened furtive eyes on the approaching nurse.

"Well, here I am again, you see, M'Sanna," she said in the flat dry voice of a person too self-respecting to try to force sympathy by lamentations. "I've come down to see if you've got any shoes that'll fit the children. And some medicine for me. Henery has run away and left me. And you see how I am."

Anna thought overjoyed, "Oh, he has gone! Anson is safe!" And, because she was ashamed of this first primitive reflex, she drew the woman and the two miserable children into the office with unwonted warmth of word and manner, so sympathetic that the other's thin set face began to work pitifully. "Oh, M'Sanna, I've had a hard time of it. I've had a hard, hard time, M'Sanna," she sobbed, and put up her hands to hide her tears.

Seeing their mother weeping, the little girls set up a frightened wail, clutching at her skirts with dirty claws. Anna sat down at her desk, lifted the smaller child to her lap and put her arm around the other. The child in her arms cried less loudly, nestling her frowzy unkempt head into the nurse's shoulder. "Just shut the door, Mrs. Twombley, will you please," she said, "and then take a chair." After the other woman was seated, she asked, "Now let's hear. When did Henry go? What makes you think he won't come back? I remember he used to leave you before and be gone for a while."

"Yes, that's the way he done here, after we came back in June. He'd be away for a week at a time, maybe. Then he'd come back and knock us all around for a day or two and go off again. He told the kids he'd kill'em if they told anybody he was ever with us, and they used to have to sneak off to go sellin' berries—he wouldn't let'em come down off The Wall into The Valley if he knew it, not if we was starvin' to death. He used to tell us that was the best thing that could happen to us, starve to death, all of us. And him along with us. And then he went away and didn't come back. And yesterday I had this letter from him down Boston way, you see the postmark."

M'Sanna opened the torn dingy envelope, read the few words scrawled on the cheap blue-lined paper, looked at the postmark and the date of the stamp cancellation and handed it back with a nod. "He's probably in South America by now. But you and the children will be better off without him. Where have you been all this time?"

At this, all the story came out in a rush. A familiar story. M'Sanna had heard many a one like it. Drink, savage fits of temper, brutality to the children, bestiality to the wife. "What'd he have to go and get me this way for? He hadn't no use for me any more. He did it just to be mean! He's *been* mean, M'Sanna! He's been a perfect devil, Henery has! He didn't use to act so! He was do-less, but he wasn't mean. Maybe he's gone crazy. He acts crazy." Her loud voice was rancid with bitterness. But it broke and failed her as she tried to tell of the indignities she had undergone during their hungry wanderings from town to town, from one foul hovel to another,

met everywhere by ungentle, often by ignoble efforts on the part of the town authorities to frighten or force the miserable family to move on before they became public charges. "I've been shamed to the dirt, M'Sanna—the way nobody ought to be shamed, no matter what they done. And I haven't done nothin'. I hadn't *never* done nothin' to deserve to have folks shame me like that. I don't know what made Henery act so! I wasn't to blame for it. I've worked hard all my life and put up with . . ."

Like a mounting tide, Anna's pity had risen word by word to meet and match the misery being laid before her. Pure pity such as she had never known. To feel such pity she had not been forced to think herself into the other woman's narrow, clouded, bitter mind, and so was now rent by none of her bewildered hate and resentment. She remained herself, Anna Craft, whose heart, widened by love, was now great enough to hold not only sympathy but understanding. Her compassion was not only for the undeserved shame and sorrow of the woman before her, but for the misery of the man who had made her suffer so. Even as she leaned forward to take the other's knotted fingers in a sisterly clasp, she sent a thought of mercy to wherever the wretched man had taken himself and his pain.

Mrs. Twombley said brokenly, "I know you don't want to see us any more'n anybody else, M'Sanna, but if me and the children belong anywhere it's here in The Valley, ain't it? I've *got* to have some help. I'm eight months gone. Henery won't never bother anybody around here any more. You needn't to think of him ever again. Me and the children couldn't help bein' born. And we was born here."

"Yes, you belong here," M'Sanna told her. "You did just the right thing to come back home with the children. We'll all help you bring them up. I think I can get work for you in that new Students' Home as soon as the Academy opens. Your confinement will be over by that time. You can keep the new baby and the children with you there."

Mrs. Twombley strained her faded eyes towards Anna as if a mist had risen in the room. When Anna's voice finally made its

way through her doubt and fear, she burst again into sobs, wilder and more uncontrolled than those which had frightened her children before. But they recognized this weeping for what it was, and were not troubled. The older girl looked unconcernedly around at the colored charts and pictures on the wall. The little one lifted her head from Anna's shoulder, and, her eye caught by the burnished red-gold of Anna's hair, dreamily put up a small grimy hand to touch it. Seeing that this involuntary action was observed, she cowered back. Anna smiled at her, and pulled off her hat so that the whole gleaming casque was within the reach of the little fingers. The other child leaned closer against her knee.

"Well, now let's do some planning," said Anna.

Mrs. Twombley stopped crying, wiped her eyes and set her battered hat straight.

Going out later, very much relieved as to Anson's safety by this interview, Anna went downtown to get her mail. A woman was standing on the Post Office steps reading a letter. "Who in the world can be writing to Lixlee?" Anna asked herself, looking up at the beautiful vase-shaped back, and aloud, "How are you, Lixlee?" With Anson's command still in her ears she did not dare to ask, "How is Anson?" Lixlee turned around, folding the letter together between her fingers, with a slow rhythmic gesture that was like the turn of her body. Whatever she did was to an unhurried inner cadence of its own. "Well, Anna! You're back! Have a good time in Boston?" The Boston of yesterday morning was already so far behind Anna that she stared and said, "Boston?" before answering hastily, "Oh, yes! I had a good time in Boston. Learned a lot I'll need to know."

"See Isabel Foote?"

"She's very well, doing finely." She asked now looking more closely at her sister-in-law, "Are *you*, Lixlee? Seems to me you're thinner than you were." She thought, "How fascinating it makes her irregular face to have those subtle hollows in cheek and temple."

"Well, maybe I have lost a few pounds," admitted Lixlee.

"It's very becoming," said Anna, gazing into the other woman's

dark eyes, admiring the masterly modeling of the delicate bones in which they were set.

"Oh, I feel all right," said Lixlee, closing the handbag into which she had put her letter.

Anna ventured now to ask in a casual tone, "How's Anson today?"

"Fine and dandy. Collecting symptoms till he forgets to shave or change his collar. But that's what he likes, so it's perfectly O.K. by me. He *has* taken a day off today—for a wonder! Gone up on The Wall, fishing."

"Is that so?" remarked Anna, in a colorless tone.

Lixlee nodded and passed on. Anna thought, "Well, he must be all right or nearly so after his night's sleep. If he'd looked badly, Lixlee would have noticed it. Heavens! If it hadn't been for Mrs. Twombley's visit how anxious I'd have been to know he is on The Wall!" She luxuriated for a moment in the delicious freedom from that sharp anxiety. Anson was safe anywhere in The Valley now. The only thing for her to worry about was his health.

But his appearance in her office later that afternoon made concern about his health seem rather foolish, too. He was in old clothes and hip boots, just back from his expedition on The Wall. He had learned, he told her, from some fern-pickers that Henry Twombley had gone for a sailor and had shipped on a long cruise from Boston.

"Yes, I know," said Anna apologetically. "I saw his wife this morning. I am very sorry I bothered you about that at all, Anson. If I'd only waited. I'm always making dumb mistakes when I try to be helpful."

Her brother did not answer at once. Then looking away from her, "Anna, I'd like to have you know that I don't . . . just take for granted . . . the way I used to, your caring so much about my being all right. I may not speak about it very often. But I think about it a good deal . . . lately."

At this Anna's full heart brimmed over and she told him her news.

He was not exactly surprised. But troubled. Physician and married man as he was, informed and experienced in human reflexes, he felt that he ought to warn his sister—as new to personal life, he felt, as any ignorant girl—that she might be running a greater risk than she realized. "She probably thinks of love-making as holding hands—*her* love-making that is," he thought. But it was one thing to recognize his duty, and quite another to think of how without wounding her he could remind her of the imperious rule over human personality of the senses so heightened in love, of the strange complex anguish caused in marriage by a disharmony between body and heart. He thought of the tragic cases known to all physicians, when a mere skin disease on the face, leaving the personality wholly unchanged, turns the heart of the valid partner in marriage into a battlefield on which love fights a long losing duel with disgust. But if he was a doctor, she was a nurse. She must know all that, have observed cases of it in her professional work. He would not need to inform her, only to recall known facts to her. "See here, Anna, have you ever considered that you and Fred might not be able to really come together because of . . ." He was embarrassed by the anxiety and alarm that came at once into Anna's face, halted, and felt his way. "Of course, I don't doubt you are very fond of him—I've always known you were—but marriage is . . . well, considerably more intimate than any relation you've ever known. Isn't it possible that with the best will in the world you may not be able to overcome . . . that between you, keeping you apart, there may always be . . ." No, he could not say it. Who could?

Anna said nervously, "You mean because I'm not a religious person? Yes, oh, yes, Anson, I have always felt that barrier between us. I had thought that would always keep us apart. And I'm afraid now that Fred doesn't realize . . . can't realize what I really think about that. Yes, that does trouble me. I mean to have a frank talk with him about that at once." She hesitated, and said shyly, "But, Anson, I don't feel as I used to, about religion. I have had one glimpse of what it might . . ." She was silent, the white remembered radiance flooding her heart with its symbolic promise that the

years to come would not be dark. But she could no more take it out from her memory to show Anson than from its secret recess in her body she could have taken out her physical heart to show Anson that its every faithful beat promised her many years in which to love and be loved.

Anson was at first too much astonished by what his sister said to take it in. When he finally did, his reaction carried him out of his embarrassed hesitation into plain words. "No, no, Anna, not that! I never dreamed that such a thing as *religion* might separate you. I can't see, any more than you do, how any half-intelligent person can take religion seriously. No, I was talking about that disfiguring birthmark of poor Fred's. It's not a thing one likes to talk about, but you must know as well as I do . . . From your professional experience you must know, Anna, how a thing of that kind can get on the nerves of—a husband or wife—who has to look at it for a lifetime."

Having flung his bolt Anson kept his eyes intently on his sister's face to see how she took it.

She passed from a blankness as dumb as his to astonishment. And with a vivid flash as from pole to pole, from astonishment to extreme relief. She drew a long breath and expended it all on the exclamation, "Oh, *that!*" Her anxiety was gone. "Anson! What an idea! As if that could make any difference. To me! Why, mostly I don't even *see* Fred's birthmark any more. Haven't for a long time." She was almost amused.

He persisted. "You say that 'mostly' you don't see it," he said earnestly. "But when you do . . . ? It's no laughing matter. Think honestly about it, Anna. It might be serious business for both you and Fred."

She obediently set herself to think honestly about it, sitting with folded hands and searching inturned look. Anson's gaze did not leave her face. At what she found in her heart and memory her eyes began to glow and brighten, her lips curved in a tremulous smile of such loveliness that her brother thought, incredulously, "Why, Anna's a beautiful woman!" She turned her gaze from what she saw within, and looked at her brother now, the transfiguring

smile still on her lips. "Well, Anson, when I do see it, it just means
. . . *Fred* . . . to me," she said in a tremulous voice that was like
her smile.

He started up from his chair as if he had been stabbed.

"Why, what is it, Anson?"

"I envy you, Anna!" he said, and went quickly away.

3

A FLICKER of heat lightning darted spitefully through the blackness above The Wall as Anna Craft sat down on her doorstep to wait for Fred's return. "It looks like the flash of an
angry eye," she thought. The tense waiting stillness of the air was
ominous. She herself was strung taut. Hour by hour since she had
seen Anson, she had been bending her will like a bow to the effort
of telling Fred what she had always concealed from him.

When the human will, with its full, fatal power, pulls all it can
of the deep life of tranquil instinct up into the harsh atmosphere
of self-conscious reason, it is always burdened and oppressed. It was
so now with Anna. Her mental preparation for the ordeal before
her had drained her memory of that white remembered radiance,
and her body of strength.

"I must have been crazy last night," she told herself, folding
her hands tightly together, "to imagine that Fred and I are any
less fatally far apart than ever. How sentimental to have imagined
that the Northern Lights could make any difference!"

She did not lean back against the pillar of her portico as she sat
thus thinking and resolving. She held herself straight, and pressed
her hands together hard. "I forgot Fred's side of it, that was what
I did. That's what being in love does to your sense of fairness! I
selfishly longed for him so much I forgot that even if I don't care
what he believes, he's bound—being what he is—to care everything
about what I don't believe. But, of course," she reminded herself
sadly, "he has no idea what I don't believe. Probably he couldn't
even imagine what is in the mind of a really irreligious person like

me. But I must tell him. Just because I am in love with him is no reason for betraying him in what's more important to him than anything else in life. And I will tell him. If it kills me—if at the first words I say, he starts up and leaves me forever. It's the center of all his inner life." She gave the screw of her will another turn, grinding it down into her heart as she thought fiercely, "I must have been out of my mind last night. Knowing that Fred has no idea how I feel—it was dastardly. Why did it take Anson's reminder to make me realize it?" (By this time she had convinced herself that it had been of this that Anson had warned her.) "I must get it straight with the first breath I draw after Fred is here."

Through the blackness came the distant beat of a step on the flagstones. She leaned her ear to listen. It was his step—so dear, so his, so no one's else that at the thought of what it was approaching, Isabel's remembered voice said despairingly in her ear, ". . . it's only that all my strength drains out as though I were bleeding to death."

"But I am not Isabel," she told herself sternly, and walked down her path. Through the darkness she heard his step quicken like a startled pulse, and turn in from the street. But she called at once in a low urgent voice, "No, Fred, no. There's something—something that stands between us. I shouldn't have—I ought to have told you last night."

He stopped short. Not far from her, she knew. But though she strained her eyes towards where he stood, the night rose impenetrably between them. She stood alone in darkness. The only sound in her ears was the dying throb-throb of her heart as her life ebbed out of it. Then the heat lightning flickered sardonically again and she had one sight of him, standing still, his bared head bent, his left hand clasped about his cross. At that, to her perfect astonishment, with no warning she began to cry. She could no more have stopped her tears than her breathing.

In an instant he was beside her—a dim tall figure that kept its distance, a trembling voice that told her gently, "No, no, Anna— I understand. You're right, of course. I've always quite understood that was something no woman could ignore. You're right. And

honest, not to . . . I've felt all day I had done you a wrong . . . taking advantage of a moment of emotion when you were already worn out with anxiety and excitement . . . taking advantage of our being in the dark where I . . . where you . . ."

As unexpectedly and involuntarily as she had burst into tears, Anna now burst into fury, "How dare you say such a thing to me, Fred Kirby! How dare you think such a thing of me! I'll never forgive you . . . never, do you hear me . . . if you ever intimate again that I'm the kind of woman who'd care about such a thing as a birthmark. You make me so angry! You make me so ashamed! Don't you know me, at *all!* What must you think of me to imagine that . . . you must think I'm . . . How could you, Fred? Oh, how could you?" She was crying now, raging and weeping and winding her arms around her lover. And then she spoke no more, but only wept as she felt his arms around her and his lips against her tear-wet cheek.

"Haven't you the red-headed temper, Anna!" his shaken voice was murmuring in her ear. "You scare a man to death!"

"Well, I hope so," she flung back hotly on a sob, the embers of her wrath still smoldering. "You deserve worse than that." She drew a long breath. "Why, Fred, all day today when I thought of your birthmark I've thought, 'It wouldn't be his face without that!' It tells me what you've suffered. It's like a seal showing what you've become. It means *you.* . . ."

In all those words he heard but one thing. "Why, Anna, you love me!" He cried it out in an astonished passion of certainty that shook them both.

She clung hard to his hand lest she be literally swept away by what she felt. They turned back, and by a common impulse swerved away from the path, its white flagstones faintly gleaming, and felt their way over the black grass to the great rock at the foot of which they had talked away so many hours of their childhood. They sank down at its base. Fred took out a handkerchief and dried Anna's eyes and cheeks. She waited till she could control her voice and breath before she said shamefacedly, "How I do act! I don't know myself!"

"You seem to me to act very much like yourself," Fred told her dryly, and made her laugh. He added, "Maybe you don't know yourself. But I do."

"Have you had any supper?" she asked him now on a sudden thought.

"Plenty. In Ashley. I came down from The Wall that way. I found out about Henry Twombley. It's all right. He's shipped as a . . ."

"Yes, yes, I know. The first person I saw this morning was his poor wife."

She told him briefly the various items of reassurance the day had brought her, ending with, "Anson looked so just as usual—such a natural color and all—that I feel sure his attack last night wasn't as serious as I thought."

"You know more about that than I. It certainly looked infernal!"

"I don't mean that he didn't suffer frightfully. Only that it may mean nothing dangerous for the future. As I told him last night he may never have another. If he doesn't work too hard. Or have much nervous strain." She ran on quickly, involuntarily, "Perhaps Anson'd better not try to do any operating. Now with good roads a surgeon could be brought so quickly. Perhaps it would be better for Anson to . . ."

"Look out, Anna," came through the darkness.

After an instant's silent resentful wonder Anna said with spirit, "Good gracious! You surely don't call *that* 'trying to live his life for him.' "

He took her hand. "You just put in your time from now on living *my* life for *me*," he told her. She knew from his voice that he was smiling. "The more you live my life the better! I've been starved to have you bossing me, Anna. Why waste it on anybody else when I want it all?"

An intuition flashed a sudden way across Anna's mind. In its light she saw—come and gone like the precise images caught in a flicker of lightning—that the relative strength of the personalities in her world were not at all as she had thought them. She told herself, astonished, "He says that because he knows it's safe for him

to! He knows I'll never be able to do it at all—not really. He knows that people who rely only on their own strength like Anson, like me . . ." The flash was gone, quenched in the blackness of what she had meant to say, ought to have said at once before she had once more been guilty of a tacit betrayal of his love and trust.

She had done no more than fall silent, had not taken her hand from his, nor stirred to put a distance between them. But he asked at once gravely, "What is it, Anna?" laid her hand down and waited.

She thought, "If I don't get it all out at once with my first breath I can never tell him," and said tragically, desperately, "Fred, I've never let you know what I . . . that I'm a completely irreligious person. I haven't any religion at all. I don't believe in any."

Helpless involuntary laughter came through the darkness, its quality telling as though in words, that it was as unexpected to himself as to her.

Anna thought wistfully, "He can't, of course, even take in what I mean." And said, miserably firm, "No, I don't mean just theological dogmas, Fred. I mean everything. I suppose you can hardly imagine what is in the mind of a total unbeliever like me. It's . . ."

He broke in, "Anna, I deserve to be shot for laughing. It took me unawares, the turn of your phrase. Your saying you had never let me know what you felt about religion, but that you would reveal it to me now. It *was* funny! I've hardly thought about anything else since I can remember."

Her exclamation was of pure astonishment.

"Why, Anna, what do you think I've been doing all these years but trying to grow up to a conception of religion that would be good enough to take in the one you live by. What's in your mind about religion has been my touchstone. It's saved me over and over from accepting something that wouldn't have been big enough to last me. The idea of your starting to tell *me* what *you* feel about *religion!* I know more about that than you do, by a long shot!"

As he talked, she turned cold with distress. "No, Fred, no, no. You don't know how serious this is. There's some dreadful misunderstanding. You . . ."

"No, there isn't either. Oh, stop—I think I know what you mean. You're feeling guilty over having deceived me—once in a while using a phrase when you were talking to me that you thought sounded like what I say. Anna, *darling,* you don't suppose I was taken in by that!" But he was not resentful. He was laughing tenderly again. "If I've looked pleased when you did that—or almost every time—it was because I didn't pay any attention to the words. What your dear voice—Anna, do you know you have a beautiful voice—what your voice said was 'Perhaps this will give Fred a moment's pleasure.' It's *sweet* the way you go around doing that to people! But it hasn't anything to do with what I'm talking about now. The point is simply that if there is one subject I know all about, Anna Craft, it's this one. What makes you think you're the only person who divines what other people are thinking? Not a day has passed since I've grown up that I haven't made a trip into your mind to look at your religion!"

"But, Fred, I haven't any!" she told him shortly, bewildered and impatient. Along with the other confused impressions lying criss-cross in her mind, she perceived that she was on the point of losing her temper again. She was astonished, remembering the mournful solemnity with which she had begun this conversation.

"Oh, Anna, you can't imagine what a relief it is to me," he told her, "not to go all to pieces with panic when your voice gets hot that way, and your red hair begins to throw off sparks. You've scared me out of my senses—literally for years. But now I've had you in my arms, you never will again. I used to feel as if I were trying to show you something infinitely frail, and I was terrified for fear you'd make me drop and break it. As easy to drop the North Star and break that, I see now. Now *wait . . . !*" Feeling her stir, he laid his arm across her shoulder, holding her quiet. "I know what you're opening your mouth to say. I'll say it for you. You're going to say, 'But, Fred, it's not just candles on the altar and fasting before Communion that I shockingly don't believe in. I don't believe in God, do you understand me, Fred? And I not only don't call that Jewish prophet "Our Lord and Master" as you do, but I don't like his ideas very well, and I think Charles Darwin

discovered a thing or two that shows that upside-down Christian morality to be unwise and dangerous . . . unless maybe you call it "slave morality." ' I know what's in your mind, all right, but I don't know just the labels you've put on it. Why don't you consider all that said?"

Disconcerted, Anna tried to collect her thoughts, did not succeed and said guardedly, "Go on."

"You mean," he told her with humor, "go on as religious fanatics always do from premises that are acceptable to reasonable people and somehow arrive at conclusions that nobody but a theologian could swallow."

"Why, Fred!" she faltered, shocked by the accuracy of his divination.

He laughed at her. "Will you believe now that I have had some idea of what's in your mind, Anna?" He groped for her hands and said from his heart, "I'll tell you something else about what's in your mind, Anna, that's just as true—it is all filled to the outermost corners with your love for God. Oh, blessed woman who can so love God."

She began a hasty movement that was to be a denial, but he held her hands closely. "It's just wasting your breath to tell me, Anna, who have watched you all your life, that you don't believe in God or love God. All you mean is, that you don't believe in the white-bearded policeman in the sky, and don't see how anybody can love him. *You* not love that 'Jewish prophet'! There's nothing to you, Anna Craft, but your trying to make human life more as Jesus Christ would have it."

She thought in breathless self-defense, "If only those inner fibers did not vibrate so to his mere voice!"

"See here, Anna. I thought today of a way to say it so you can't help but understand. You want to do what's right, don't you? You do admit that. *Where do you think you got that wanting? And don't you suppose there must be more there than just what you took away?"*

This reached her through her determined resistance. For the first

time she was surprised into considering what he was saying, instead of automatically resisting it.

"Anna, everybody loves and worships and serves *some*thing—success, or power, or safety, or malice, or money. . . . That's the law of human life. As long as we live, we bow ourselves down before a secret god. And what by the laws of your nature you love and worship and serve is that wanting to do what's right. Why, whenever you see a spark of it in somebody's heart there's no holding you, you fly so to protect it, to keep it from being blown out. . . ."

She appealed to his sense of fairness. "Fred, you're taking an advantage of me—how can I think of anything but your hands on mine!"

He kissed her hands and gave them back. "But I'm not conducting an argument with you, Anna, that you have to meet. I'm just telling you some plain facts about yourself. Or trying to. . . ."

His deep voice dropped to so low a pitch now that as he went on, Anna heard through it the small crystal murmur of the brook behind them talking to itself in the darkness. She leaned her head back against the unshakeable steadfastness of the old rock, listening to the two voices as in a dream. "If there's one thing I know all about, Anna, it's you. You don't, of course, because you take yourself for granted. How can I make you understand? I can't—not in talk anyhow. Anything that's worth telling about you—about anything—can't be held in words. It's like trying to hold a beam of light in a net. Sometimes a symbol . . ." He paused, went on, "You know that symbolic sunken cathedral legend—the cathedral that lies far below the surface in everybody's heart, and how on our best days we hear its bells ringing faintly from the depths? Well, Anna dear—you can't help it—that cathedral is your home. You keep house in it, and never dream that it's not like everybody's housekeeping. But I've found the way in. . . . You're not going to live there alone from now on."

He drew breath, went on musingly, his voice no more than a vibration in the air, "I wonder if you understand a single thing I'm trying to say? Not that understanding matters. . . . It's all far, far beyond understanding."

The brook's singing treble rose clear in silence. The heat lightning flickered lightly, harmlessly, and showed them to each other, dreaming, relaxed, at peace.

Anna stirred, "No, Fred, I never do understand what you say about that sort of thing. I never have. But it always makes me feel differently about everything. And it has now. Yet, after all, it says no more to me than that you love me." She had said the words quietly enough, almost unwittingly; but their echo in her ears was like the reverberation of an explosion. She cried out his name on a fierce, low, passionate note, and flung herself towards him with a fierce gesture of passion.

Afterwards, steadied by his arms around her, she said in his ear, startled, shaken, "But I didn't mean to do that, Fred. Why, I didn't even know I was going to, till I had. It scares me to death to lose my self-control like that. It scares me to death to feel the way I do about you, anyhow. It . . . scares . . . me . . . to . . . death!" Life blazed up hotly from her every word.

"It doesn't scare me," he told her. "What'd scare me to death would be if you didn't. Nobody can advance a long step into deeper life, Anna—any kind of deeper life—without passion that shakes you clear out of yourself. That abandonment of the will is what opens the door for the entrance of something greater than the will."

Was there an overtone of sadness in his deep voice? Silent, resting in his arms, Anna was listening to something deep within her which, tuned to something deep within him, answered that overtone with a shaken throb. Had he meant to open the door only to the love of God?

Presently, her lips against his cheek, she asked, "Fred, are you ever sorry that you love me—humanly? Won't it exile you from . . ."

He broke in, "I've spent years and years trying not to, Anna, if that's what you mean. I suppose it is stupid of me not to be able to help it. I've done my level best. Sometimes I almost thought I had. But the moment I saw you again, it was all up with me." He used the accent of apology.

She felt herself drowning in the smiling gentleness of his voice.

But he had not answered her question. "Fred, be honest with me. *Do* you, in the back of your mind, feel that you are falling short of what you were meant for—to love a woman instead of . . ."

He corrected her sharply, with authority, "It's not 'instead of . . .'!" For the first time he showed an impatience at her slowness of understanding. And then, "No. Wait. Wait a moment. I see I haven't given you any idea yet. I'll try again. But, Anna, do your share! *Try* to understand. I can't say it of course—but if you'll do your half . . ."

She drew herself out of his arms to listen, bringing her will at last to the determination to hear and to understand. He said, opening to her the last and most secret chamber of his heart, "Yes, Anna, there is a security in the selfless life that's lost when you step out of it into a life where you yourself are important because of another's love for you. You too, Anna, you're giving up that security. Both of us are stepping out of a convent into whole human life. Yes, we're spiritually less safe. We must face that." She felt him straighten his back and draw in a deep breath. "But by God! spiritually greater!"

She had listened, she had heard, she had understood; she said with humility, "Fred, I believe you know more about what really matters than I do."

"You don't have to know. You are," he told her, taking her hand. They sat silent, in peace.

She was astonished to hear the St. Andrew's clock striking endlessly. "Why, I haven't heard it strike before! Have you, Fred? Can it have struck hour after hour without our hearing it? What time do you suppose it can be? Come in and let's see."

She felt her way across the grass to the side door, stepped in, turned on a light, looked up at the face of the old clock and exclaimed, turning around, "Eleven o'clock! It must have struck three times without our hearing a sound." But there was no one in the lighted room with her.

"Fred!" she called, going to the open door. He did not answer.

She stood in the door for an instant, astonished, looking from one side to the other, and then walked out into the darkness. She

saw him then, a dim figure, standing in the shadow of the rock. With her physical eyes she could not so much as make out whether he was facing her or turned from her. But she felt, and with a shock that took her breath, every line of his shrinking averted body. She ran to him, took his arm in her two hands, "Fred, you're *not* worrying about . . ."

"Don't scold me, Anna!" He drew a long breath of pain. She felt with her hands how he winced at her touch. He who had been so bold when she had been fearful, so strong where she had been weak, stood now, a strengthless, tortured boy, defeated by an old pain.

"Stay here with me, Anna. Don't make me go into the light. Suppose it should be pity that you . . . Not tonight. Just this once more!"

She told him bitterly, "You'll break my heart, Fred. You'll simply break my heart till I die of it, if you don't believe me!"

"I can't help it," he told her helplessly. "It's lasted too long. I *can't* believe you. It's too strong for me."

Her love, her passion, rose towering like a wave against his doubt, beat it to pieces and swept it away out of their future in a swirling flood. "It's not too strong for *me!*" she cried. "I said you knew more than I do! But you don't know *any*thing! I'm not going to let you break my heart! Do you hear? That's what you want to do—that's what you're trying to do. But you can't!"

She did not know what she was saying as she dragged him along towards the open door. Nor did he. Words were nothing.

The door was there before them. They had passed it. With a cry of triumph she slammed it behind them, shutting him in to love and to light.

PART SIX

1

THE TURBID vitality of summer which since June had filled The Valley with sultry life, began to lose some of its reeking force, and for days at a time stood still in its curved green cup like roily water in a quiet glass. The sediment began to drop, the air to cool and clear. September came.

Clifford people looking dreamily from their ripening orchards and gardens and fields, up into the cloudless sky, looked into light itself, unveiled. The thin purified air affirmed the beauty of emptiness. People said peaceably to each other, "Summer's gone, ain't it? Well, let it go. We've had enough."

Only to the eye of the imagination was the empty air above those scattered human homes filled with the intertangled graphs of their human lives, rising, falling, united, separating, ending and beginning.

Cora Ingraham would have said hers ended. Anna had written her—only that she would have a piece of news to tell her when she got back to Clifford. So Cora came back at once. But no one can get from New Jersey to Vermont literally "at once." Between the arrival of Anna's letter in Newark and Cora's descent from the Cannon Ball at Clifford Depot, there stretched a day and two nights—many, many hours. And much can be lived through in an hour! Yet when Cora looked out of the window of the train as it slowed down for the Depot, and saw the September sunshine gleaming on Anna's hair and luminous, clear face, she felt for one dreadful moment that all that she had lived through in those many hours had been useless suffering; that her attempt to rise above the limita-

tions of her own nature had availed her nothing; that she would fail Anna, after all.

But that was the last paroxysm of her old self before it died. She had laid it in its grave with the snow falling over it, by the time she had shuffled her way down the aisle knocking her suitcase clumsily against the seat ends, had climbed clumsily with her too-short legs down from the too-high step, and, her hat knocked to one side, stood on the station platform looking around for Anna.

Anna saw her, ran to her, took her hand and kissed her. The quality of the kiss told Cora. They stood together at one end of the platform, hand in hand, looking into each other's eyes.

Cora asked at once, "Anna, is it something that makes you happy?"

Tears veiled Anna's brown eyes. She nodded.

"Then I'm glad of it."

"Cora! You are the best woman I ever knew!"

"Oh, nothing extra."

Anna had told her she was to be married, and Cora had answered that she would not be a bother. They went together to find Anna's Ford, carrying her suitcase between them.

But that evening, just before they separated for the night, Cora said something more. All that she ever said.

Till bedtime they had been talking about the local news. At least Anna, shy of saying much about her engagement, kept bringing the conversation around to such items, after each of her rather nervous answers to the questions which from time to time Cora conscientiously asked about her plans. No, they had not decided on the day yet. They wanted the simplest of weddings, of course. Such old friends, and not young people—marrying wasn't for them the social event it was for girls like Cornelia Dean. Oh, yes, indeed, she expected to go on with her district nursing service after her marriage. Why not? Ye-e-s, they were going to live in the Rectory— it was the natural thing to do. And ye-e-es, Anson probably would move in to live here in this house, which was, after all, his own old home. (It had been Cora's home for eight years.)

Cora kept her plain, broad face quiet, and her voice matter-of-fact, but Anna felt unspoken pain about her like an atmospheric pressure. She continually sheered off into neutral items of general news—had Cora heard that Mr. Merrill who ran the drugstore was going to retire and Charlie Dean was to run it. Wasn't it strange that so serious and dangerous an accident had happened to Mr. Lawrence Stewart, who had never in all his life taken a risk of any kind, even the smallest? Had anybody told her that just at the time when Mr. Stewart needed some family, a good-natured nephew from the West had turned up and was staying with him till he recovered. "Have I written you about Almira Boardman—another tragedy of inheritance? The poor thing's condition is so bad that her married nieces are starting the legal machinery to have her sent to the Retreat, and high time I gather from what people tell me. I don't know anything about it at first hand, for her obsessions seem, strangely enough, to center around Anson's wife, and of course she wouldn't talk to me about that. Curious, she hardly knows Lixlee. I doubt if she ever said a word to her. Insanity goes like that. No logic to it."

But local news gave out before the evening was over. Anna was reduced to talking about Anson, although she knew that he was no favorite of Cora's. She described in lengthy detail his research work, and quoted Doctor Neale's high opinion of its value. She spoke anxiously about his inexplicable attack of angina, ". . . he was sitting quietly on this very sofa, where I am now, smoking his pipe and chatting to Fred and me, one evening." Cora winced at the "Fred and me," and Anna, wishing confusedly to make amends by telling Cora something she wouldn't have mentioned to anyone else, confessed that she was anxious about Anson's drinking. "But I can't believe that he will let that go too far. Why in the world should he? He has everything in the world to keep a man satisfied. Fred and I can't see . . ." Strange how she could not keep Fred's name from her lips— "At least when a man who's never had any tendency that way begins to drink, it usually is to take his mind off of some worry. Could Anson have, do you suppose, any reason to fear some

illness—could he have known that he is subject to angina? Perhaps that *wasn't* his first attack."

For an instant Cora's control of herself failed. "Mightn't it be," she asked harshly, "just that it's an intolerable blow to him to have you gone from his life? With no warning, by no fault of his?" Anna hung her head remorsefully, protesting in confusion, "No, Cora, no . . ."

Cora flushed, swallowed, and went on, choosing her words to make it plain that she had been referring to no one but Anson, "Till now, he has always had you, Anna, you know, all there was of you!"

Anna said, tactlessly, "Yes, I'm afraid I've been rather in his way with my . . ." and horrified lest Cora take this to herself, asked abruptly, "But see here, I haven't told you a thing about the developments in my Coöperative Students' Home."

"You wrote me that after Mrs. Dewey died, Mr. Dewey moved into the south wing of his house, and told me you could have all the rest of it for your young people."

"Did I tell you that with what furniture he left, and what I've been able to collect from people's attics, that I have sleeping quarters for sixteen? The girls in the second and third floors of the main part, and the boys in the north wing?"

"I didn't remember how many. When you last wrote it was mostly about trying to see how you could get the housework done with almost no money to pay wages."

"Oh, that's all settled now. In the first place, the girls and boys can do a good deal of it without interfering with their studies at all. And I've got just the person to work in the kitchen. One of my poor families has been deserted by the father, so that the mother must make her living and the children's. They can live in the three rooms over the long woodshed—there's a chimney and a stovehole there. The windows face south, and have the winter sun. The rooms can be made quite cozy. The children can get their food as pay for Mrs. Twombley's work in the kitchen—food is something there'll be plenty of, of course, with all those farms and gardens to supply apples and potatoes and milk and eggs. And it will be good for the

big boys and girls to have some little children around to look out for. There'll be a new baby by the time school opens, too, and the girls will learn a lot they ought to know, just by helping take care of a baby. The hitch now—and I can*not* see how to get around it— is where to find a housemother. Mrs. Twombley's fit for nothing but housework. She's a perfect barbarian, of course, as far as manners go. And of course any woman that would be of use along those lines is decidedly not looking for an unpaid job with lots of responsibility."

These details were of no interest to other people. Anna knew that. But the subject was an impersonal one. She was safe as long as she could think of something to say about it.

Miss Ingraham had been listening apathetically. She had as usual chosen her seat with no thought for her appearance, and was sitting as she often did, the abdomen of her square, uncorseted figure protruding as she leaned too far back in a chair too deep for her. But now she straightened her back, sat forward, interrupted Anna abruptly. "Let *me* do that, Anna!" Her sallow face was white. "Let *me* be the housemother." She was almost breathless. "No, it wouldn't interfere with my teaching. I'd have plenty of time."

As if she were a comely woman and not a plain one, she pressed a hand hard over her heart in the old instinctive gesture of deep feeling, "Oh, Anna, *let—me—do—it!*"

For the first time the tears were in her eyes, "To think there is something I can do—that you want done—without being in your way!"

She sprang up from her badly chosen chair, and impulsively, forgetting that she was a stout graceless woman no longer young, she went to kneel like a girl beside Anna's sofa, "You couldn't be so unkind as not to let me, Anna. Think what it would mean to me to return a little of what I owe you."

A crimson flood of remorse rushed to Anna's cheeks. "What *you* owe *me!*" she said, faintly.

"Why, Anna, yes! I've loved you! Where could such a woman as I ever hope to find a chance to love?"

Her lips and chin began to tremble. "Anna, now that you know what it is to love . . ."

With her trembling lips she smiled at Anna. Blinded by the selfless sweetness of that smile, Anna put her hands over her eyes. Cora's trembling voice went on, "Think, Anna, what it would be to have missed it! To have just kept going on, day after day, over all that sandy desert, and never to have felt the living waters of your heart unsealed. . . ." She laid her cheek against Anna's hands.

"Good night."

From the door she said, and now in a clear and steady voice, "Oh, Anna, I'm so glad you're happy! I am, too."

2

AMONG the sayings of her forebears devoutly quoted by Miss Bessie was, "The only thing about a person that's worth taking notice of, is whether he's goin' uphill or down." Miss Bessie's gloss on this was, "Don't make any difference where you are *now,* I always tell young folks. If you're going uphill from there, you're all right, I tell 'em. If you're started down, you're a goner."

In the light of this aphorism she insisted that what had looked to sentimental people like the breaking to pieces of Isabel Foote's life was in reality her great good fortune. "You can't wish a body any worse luck than to get what he wants. Look at Anson Craft. All that that disapp'intment did for Isabel was to start her right up the grade. Seems from what I hear that she's got brains! How'd she ever have found that out, tell me, if she'd got what she wanted?" She pooh-poohed the soft-hearted ones who went on pitying Isabel, "Oh, girls at the fallin'-in-love age! They're all made of lime. Don't take more'n cold water to make 'em boil up hot. But lime has got to be slaked, ain't it, if your mortar's goin' to hold? That was the best of experience for Isabel. She's got it out of her system now and can tend to business and get somethin' done."

Once Sherwin Dewey demurred, "You call that experience, Bessie? I call it just a mistake all around."

"Well, well, Sherwin, what else *is* experience?" Miss Bessie had reminded him impatiently.

All this talk about the going up and down of people's lives was brought out by the fact, more and more obvious all the time, that Doctor Anson was not on the upgrade. All the other subjects of talk, from the change in ownership of the Warren Mills to M'Sanna Craft's engagement to the minister, sank into second place for a day or so when it was told around that a patient had found the doctor in his office one evening so dazed with drink that he could not understand the simplest statement. It is true that the next day, when every eye was focused on him as he made his rounds, he seemed like himself, except that his manner had a raw March bleakness about it. That might come from a hang-over. But just as likely from an ordinary bilious headache.

It was not long before the chill of this news struck Anna, even through the warm peace to which she opened her eyes in the morning, in which she sank to sleep at night. Mrs. Randall told it to her one day, beginning baldly, "I don't hold with repeatin' gossip, as you know, Anna, but since you've got engaged you don't hardly seem to be able to see your hand before your face, and *some*body ought to . . ." and ending, "There's something a-goin' wrong over there, Anna. I don't believe in relatives buttin' in, but *some*body ought to . . ."

"Yes. I think so too."

She had begun by asking Lixlee cautiously if Anson seemed well. Lixlee took an instant to reflect—she had gone back to this earlier habit of hers—decided apparently on plain speech, and said soberly, "He's drinking worse than any lumberjack, Anna."

"Good heavens!" cried Anna, aghast. Her eyes searched the other's serious young face for an indication of something more than her words. "Haven't you the least idea what's the matter, Lixlee?"

Lixlee shook her head slowly, looked down at her hands and was silent. Anna saw now that the ivory of her face was paler than usual. After a pause, "He'll be all right for a while and then all of a sudden he acts as if he'd gone crazy. There're days when I'm afraid of him, Anna."

"Oh, Lixlee, why didn't you tell me about it before?"

"I hated to. A person would."

Yes, Anna could understand that. "It's terrible for you," she said humbly as if she were partly responsible.

Lixlee said nothing. The two sat silent, Anna feeling her way in thought around the blank walls that shut them in. Then with a start, "Well, I'll see," she said, getting up to go.

It had come to her with another of those staggering shocks of joy that she was no longer alone in life. The very thought of sharing this blow with Fred flung open a door in the wall. Lixlee stood up, too, with the slow, flexible grace that made poetry out of her most ordinary movements. Her eyes were intently on Anna's face. They expressed the sincerest anxiety and fear.

Anna was touched. Putting her arm around her brother's wife, she told her comfortingly, "I'm sure something can be done, Lixlee. We'll think of something."

"Oh, if somebody only could!" cried Anson's wife, with a sob that came from her heart.

Anna had never given Lixlee a caress before. Half-way down the street as she hurried towards the Rectory, the arm that had encircled that warm, yielding firmness still felt quite different from the other.

But Fred was not at the Rectory. Nor was the slightest indication as to where he was to be extracted from cross, incompetent old Hiram Rudd, who detested Anna as heartily as she disliked him. "No idee!" he said, slamming the door in her face.

On a chance she went down Depot Hill. She was thinking so deeply about Anson that she felt startled and self-conscious when he unexpectedly emerged from the telegraph office as she went by it. He did not look as she had been imagining him, wild and lost and disintegrated. He looked like what he was, a powerfully built, rather distinguished, young professional man, with a doctor's keen eye in his head.

"Hello there, Anna," he called in his usual voice. "Wait a minute

and I'll walk along with you. I've just been sending a wire to Philadelphia, to poke up the Atwater and Jenkins people. It's more than two weeks ago that I sent them that order." He fell into step beside his sister. "Mrs. Cole is worse. I had to put off going to Boston till Thursday," he told her.

The shirt-sleeved telegraph operator appeared at the door behind them. "Oh, say, Doc, hold on a minute!" he called. "Was that address on Mrs. Craft's wire Waterbury or Watertown?"

"What are you talking about?" asked Anson, blankly.

"Oh!" said the operator; and retreating too late, "No. Never mind." Anson thrust out a long arm and snatched the yellow paper. As he looked at it his face turned to stone.

After a moment he said, "No, I'm not sure of the address myself. Better telephone Mrs. Craft. Unless perhaps my sister knows." He turned the telegram. Anna read, "Joe Howe, Waterbury, Conn. Not till Thursday." It was not signed. Astounded, Anna looked from it into Anson's granite face. "No, no. How should I know?" she said flatly.

Anson consulted his watch. "Mrs. Craft is out now. But she will be in at eleven," he told the operator. "Telephone then."

Anna began to say that she knew Lixlee was at the house now; but Anson silenced her with a look like a hand pressed over her mouth. The operator turned back into his office and shut the door. Anna made as if to walk on.

"No, you don't. You're coming back to the house with me," said Anson, and pushed his sister into his waiting car. "I want somebody else there."

"What in the world . . ." she began, and stopped, her protest struck from her lips by the sight of Anson's face as he stooped forward and leaned back to push his lever through the gears into high. It was darkly swollen. The big vein in his neck throbbed as though it would burst.

His first words carried her into the heart of the waking nightmare which the next ten minutes were to her, in which she heard what it was impossible for Anson to have said. "I know no more

about what in the world it is than you do," he told her in a tone of cold fury. "Henry Twombley, Charlie Dean, Rug Milner, Lawrence Stewart—I thought I knew them all, but this is one even *I* never heard of."

His long fingers gripping the steering wheel tightened as he wrenched the car around a corner. One rear wheel struck the curbing and rode up over it. The lurch of the car flung Anna against her brother. It was like being thrown against a pillar of stone.

She recovered herself, raised her arm to straighten her hat, and thought distractedly, "The instant he stops the car before the house I shall get out and walk away. That's the only decent thing to do."

They turned another corner, again on three wheels, Anson having chosen that time to drive with one hand as he pulled out his watch. It showed three minutes of eleven. He pressed his foot down on the accelerator. The houses flew by on each side of them. His own appeared at the end of the next block. Anna, the self-respecting woman, thought, "Anything in the world except being the third person present at a quarrel between man and wife!" Anna, the nurse, giving one look at his terrifying face, thought, "Leave a man who's had one attack of angina and looks on the point of having another because of some genteel nonsense about your own dignity!"

Anson stopped the car, got out of it and lunged heavily up his front walk, stumbling as though he were not sure of how far down under his feet the stones were. Anna followed him, sick with dread. "In a few moments from now something irrevocable will have happened; things never to be taken back will have been said—something decisive will have been lived through that we can never live again and live differently."

Anson went in through the front door. An irresistible impulse to run away took hold of Anna's feet. "I couldn't stand it." But after that, "If Fred were here," she thought, "he would close his fingers around his cross and pray that Christ's spirit might be with him." Her heart righted itself. Her feet carried her forward into the house to whatever opportunity to help awaited her there.

None at all, as it turned out. It was all the other way around. When she stepped in, Lixlee, a white cloth in her hand, glanced down over the upper banister to see who had come, nodded to them, and walked on along the upper hall.

The telephone bell was ringing. Anna saw her brother take off the receiver and listen. "I'll get Mrs. Craft," he said, and stepping to the foot of the stairs, called loudly and very distinctly, "Lixlee, the telegraph operator wants to ask you about the telegram you sent this morning."

The air curdled in the long moment of silence that followed. Then Lixlee appeared at the head of the stairs and came down with her unhurried rhythmical step. Without looking at Anson she took up the receiver. "This is Mrs. Craft," she said into it, in her usual tone, and stood listening, presenting her lovely back to the others.

Anna was terrified to see the ominous dark red in Anson's face turn almost to black as he waited, his hands thrust into his pockets, the tension of the hidden fists apparent in every taut line of his body.

"No . . ." said Lixlee, into the telephone. "No . . ." And then, "Yes, that's right." She hung up the receiver and turned around, looking just as usual.

"Well . . . ?" said Anson threateningly.

Lixlee looked at him inquiringly.

His self-control broke into frenzy. Like a clap of thunder, "Don't you dare lift your eyebrows at *me!*" he shouted at her.

Lixlee straightened her brows, her jewel-like eyes steady under them, and waited.

"What's all this?" asked Anson, his fists clenched, his face congested.

"All what?"

"None of that, now! Who are you telegraphing to?"

The beautiful eyes set in the delicately modeled bones fixed themselves on Anson's face. After a moment's pause, "To a dry-cleaner's," she explained, patient and dignified—a little dry. "The one in Ashley couldn't get out that coffee spot on my yellow dress that you—

that you used to like. But he gave me the address of one in Connecticut that he thought perhaps could."

Anna felt an immense, almost unendurable relief. Shame for Anson. And a sudden panic about him that drove everything else out of her head. For as he stood looking at his wife, all the dark blood drained itself out from his face. His lips shriveled and grew pale, deep lines appeared in his cheeks, gray-white now. The nurse was aghast. "Oh, no heart can stand that sort of strain!" she thought.

But he did not faint. Nor even waver on his feet. He stood a moment, looking intently at a spot on the wall before him. Then he looked back at his wife and laughed a little, disagreeably. He put his hands over his face, pressing them hard, so that he shook as if in a spasm of repressed nausea. He took them down. His eyes, dulled and vacant, wandered around the room. "Oh, well, what do I care?" he said listlessly.

"You've been drinking again, Anson Craft," Lixlee accused him gravely. Anna had had the same thought.

"That's an idea!" he said, and lurched off towards his office.

Lixlee looked at Anna, shook her head, made a small weary gesture with her shoulders and went back upstairs.

Overcome with shame and pity and alarm, Anna followed her brother into his office. He was stooping over the lowest drawer in his desk. "Can he be meaning to turn to his research cards, *now?*" his sister asked herself. To his back she said, distractedly, "Anson, how *can* you?"

Over his shoulder he said, fumbling in the drawer, "You believed all that?" He straightened himself and turned towards her, an uncorked bottle in his hand, "Well, you would."

"Why should anybody doubt it?"

"Because my plausible wife said it." He held the bottle out towards his sister. "Have a drink, Anna," he urged her. *"Have* a drink. You're soon to be married. You might as well start now."

He took a long drink himself. It brought the color to his white lips. "That's better," he said, and took another.

He laughed. "I forgot to tell Lixlee something," he said. "I'm always forgetting to tell her the most important thing. She gets me

rattled. I'll tell her now." Without moving, still leaning against his desk, he called hoarsely, "Lixlee! Lixlee . . . *ee* . . . !"

There was no answer. He took another drink, set the bottle down, said in a conversational tone, "You'd better go on your way, Anna. I don't see how you can make the world any better right here," and, steadying himself by the furniture, walked heavily to the foot of the stairs. "Lixlee!" he shouted, towards the upper floor. "I forgot to tell you something you'll be interested to know. I've put off that trip to Boston. I'm not going on Thursday. I'm going to be right here on Thursday. And the day after that. And so on. Lixlee, do you hear me? My trip to Boston is in-def-i-nitely postponed."

There was no answer.

3

H ENRIETTA's summer had not been satisfactory. Her house, usually so quiet except for an hour or so in the afternoon at tea-time, had been invaded by strangers who came and went at all hours—nurses, the doctor, the doctor's wife. And the spare-room, which had always been kept for show, was cluttered up with a new young man who seemed to have taken root. But the worst was the disturbing behavior of Mr. Stewart himself, especially at night.

Nobody understood the value of traditions better than Henrietta. Although as far as her natural tastes went, she would have preferred to sleep on her woodshed cushion near her refrigerator where the smells were more interesting, she had always been willing enough to sleep on the foot of Mr. Stewart's bed as her ancestors had. Till now this had cost her no trouble, Mr. Stewart's habits being so regular—always in bed by eleven and up by eight, with no more bother to the sleeper on the foot of his bed than occasional turnings over with an inconsiderate lack of care as to where he put his feet.

But for weeks now she had been out of all patience with him. She had almost forgotten what it was to have a decent night's sleep. First there had been all that hullabaloo about a few scratches on his

face;—nights and nights of wakefulness for Henrietta as nurses rustled in and out with medicine. Remembering the glorious fights conducted by the big tom from off The Wall last year, Henrietta asked herself with amused scorn what Mr. Stewart would do if he were *really* scratched by somebody who meant business. Lie down and die, probably, she thought, yawning widely.

But that was not the end of it. Even now when his scratches were quite healed he tossed to and fro; he was forever turning on the light (Henrietta did detest a light shining in her eyes when she was trying to sleep) to look at the clock; he walked the bedroom floor; he went to the bathroom to draw himself a drink of water, and came out again, the door squeaking and slamming; he got back into bed groaning and pulling her blankets out of place. He was worn out, mornings. And so was she.

It was getting worse instead of better. As time went on, he not only tramped up and down the bedroom, he put on his dressing-gown, took a flashlight and prowled all over the house, his every heavy step painfully jarring the delicate hammer-and-anvil bones in Henrietta's ears. Did he think a cat was as deaf as a human—as the intruding young man in the spare-room, who—let Mr. Stewart bang around the house all night—never opened his door till breakfast time. "It's enough," thought Henrietta, outraged, another muffled collision with a chair downstairs startling her awake once more, "to make one go wild."

But she did not mean this. She had no intention of ever going more than a very little wild. She admitted that it was hard to put up with senseless human prejudices against half-eaten mice on rugs and bird-feathers on chairs. Henrietta knew human beings too well to be taken in by their myth of their own superiority. She had not the slightest idea that their code was any better than hers. Yet she never really considered running away from them to live in the woods and hunt for her living. There was no denying that raw meat, hot, bloody and still half alive, was exquisite eating. But much could be said for an unfailing supply of sweet milk in a clean dish. And more could be said for the untroubled safety of days and nights under human roofs. And for hearth-fires. And cush-

ions. Safety, warmth, shelter and food went along with human rules and regulations; Henrietta knew that. She was not an exceptionally intelligent cat; but almost any cat has brains enough to grasp the fact that cake may not be both had and eaten too.

So although she put her ears back and looked as cross as she could, she lay still on the foot of the bed when, night after night, after wandering around the house, Mr. Stewart stumbled back to her room, turned on the light, looked at the clock once more, and sank down on the edge of the bed, his red-rimmed eyes fixed on space, his pajama-legs flapping limply around his withered hairy shanks. Nights in the Stewart house brought little rest to Henrietta.

Nor to the owner of the house. He was often so tired when he went to bed that as his head touched the pillow he fell asleep, his jaw sagging open. But the disordered scurry in his mind apparently could not sleep. Its clatter woke him up again as soon as his body had recovered ever so little from the extremity of its need for rest.

He was like a man meaning to take a little pleasure trip who finds himself shut into a through express train. When he had stepped aboard, nobody had given him the faintest warning that it would make no stops till it reached its destination. Stops? It never even slackened speed. He was half wild with the—he did not know whether it was exhilaration or terror—in which he ran from one window to another trying to locate a familiar landmark in the new and strange landscape reeling backwards from his forward rush. At times he simply gave out, but it was not real sleep into which he fell then, it was more like that momentary unconsciousness which comes to the exhausted railway traveler dozing in his seat, his hanging head flung from one side to the other by the swaying of the train. But even these half-respites from consciousness were brief. And after one of them when the roar and rattle of the warring impulses in his mind once more roused him, and he looked out to see where he was, it was to find himself still hurtling through unfamiliar country towards a goal remote beyond his imagination.

Each time he felt himself beginning to wake up, he made a

pitiful effort at least to lie still in his bed and rest—his dear, comfortable bed, arranged exactly to his taste, where he had known such peaceful years of sleep, and such happy, happy wakings-up. For years his sleep had been troubled by a recurrent nightmare that his father was still alive and in the house somewhere. But although this dream had caused Lawrence the most intolerable horror, it was almost worth having because of his bliss when he came clear awake and remembered that his father was really dead and buried! In later years, when he was middle-aged, when that had worn off, the joy of waking had been, though not so piercing, almost as great. It was bliss to be aware from the first blurred opening of his eyes that he was safe; and then to lie awake, drowned in that sweetness. Like spring flowers, like poetry, like music, like the most exquisite food—all that such joys are to other people, Lawrence Stewart's safety had been to him, lying awake in his own bed, in his own room, in his own house, with his father safe in his grave, and he himself walled around from danger by all that money—ten times what he had expected, ten times what anybody in Clifford thought.

But now the very first sleepy awareness of being in his own dear bed was linked to a confused perspective of changing it for God knew what others with God knew what lumpy foreign mattresses and skimpy pillows and grimy, threadbare, suspicious blankets. The misery of this idea always startled him awake, and as soon as he was awake he remembered once more that those were not the beds before him but behind him, the foreign beds of his oppressed boyhood, the cheap beds in poor lodgings where his father, damn him, had made him live. Now it would be entirely different—yes, as Alix was obliged continually to remind him, now he would be going to the very best hotels in any city in the world.

Before him, in his darkened Clifford bedroom, rose the glittering image of those best hotels as they had looked to the shabby boy, envious and intimidated, slinking by their double doorways on his way to his dingy lodgings. Yes, now that boy could swagger in through any of those imposing entrances. He who had looked sidewise with rancorous shyness at the arrogant uniformed concierge

would be revenged and appeased to see that gold-braided cap snatched humbly from the bullet head, the broad lackey's back bent low. Mr. Stewart's chest expanded with a deeply taken breath that vitalized his every drop of blood as he walked past that servile imaginary doorman. He did not give him so much as the glance that would acknowledge his existence, but he saw into that thick, obsequiously bent head, saw that he was thinking the newcomer a distinguished member of the diplomatic corps, no longer exactly young perhaps, but not too middle-aged to be adored by young princesses like the dashing exotic beauty hanging on his arm. Sometimes the concierge in Mr. Stewart's imagination thought slyly to himself, "Oh, là! là! that old roué! He's had experience. He knows how to pick them out!" Mr. Stewart would not at all mind being thought an old roué by the concierges of the best hotels in Nice and Cannes and Biarritz. Lying in his own dear home bed in Vermont, he sometimes smiled happily over what he saw in the concierge's mind, and knew a moment of cloudless satisfaction, colored with the quality most surprising and exciting to him at his age—novelty.

But they could not always be passing in front of concierges. They moved on, he knew now how Alix would always move him on, on into the lobby and into the plate-glass elevator and so up to their expensive suite. And whenever the door in Mr. Stewart's imagination closed behind them, shutting him into that suite, so wild an agitation took possession of his sixty-year-old body, so cold a sweat, so hot a rush of blood into the brain, so mad a beating of the heart, that there was nothing for it but to fling himself out of bed, turn on the light, and wide, stark, staring awake, look at the clock imploringly to see if it wasn't almost time to get up.

But it never was time. Only half-past one, or two at the most. He was so tired! He longed to crawl back into his open bed but did not dare. Looking fearfully over his shoulder at the tumbled thrown-back sheet, Mr. Stewart felt that its folds were still saturated with those choking fumes. If he lay down there again they would strangle him again. Better give them time to evaporate.

"Perhaps if I stirred around a little, it might make me feel

sleepy." He put on his dressing-gown. Where was the flashlight? It would not do to turn on the lights downstairs. If his windows were lighted at two in the morning, by breakfast time everybody in town would be commenting on them. As Alix had told him, it was "just fierce" to live where everybody knew everything you did as soon as you did it. Yes, she had been right when she had told him it would be "just grand" for him to be free of this imbecile village life. Why had he taken so long to realize that? Well, it was the kind of thing you didn't think of for yourself, unless you were absolutely self-centered. You needed someone's else affectionate thought for you to point the way. And he had never had that—till now—never.

He turned out his bedroom light and began to feel his way downstairs in the dark, thinking hard about her—"the first time in my life—the very first time a living soul has wanted anything out of me but money." A lump came into his throat at the thought of no longer living in cold solitude among paid attendants and tea-drinking acquaintances. An affection in his life at last, a real affection, warm and tender—and young.

Reaching the lower hall, he turned on his electric lamp for an instant to see where the library door was. And stood transfixed by the vision of perfection painted on the darkness by its flash. *His* perfection! He owned it. The grandfather clock—how many times had he stood by it proudly listening to the envying admiration of connoisseurs. Nobody else knew as he did how to keep that discreet not-too-glossy gleam on the brown surface of the Sheraton side-table. And the set, perfectly preserved, not one missing, of the six curly-maple chairs, mellowed richly by time! How often he had blessed his grandmother (otherwise in no way estimable) for her taste in chairs! And the two prints hanging on each side of the clock—that specialist from the Metropolitan who had come to call with Mrs. Levering Peabody had said they were unique. What was the cheap and dangerous admiration of Grand Hotel concierges compared to such moments! Like jewels they clustered in his past. They beckoned him ahead into more and yet more safe years filled with the felicity of being envied. He was shocked at the recollec-

tion of the perilous madness that had been in his mind upstairs just now. Quite another kind of emotional cold sweat stood out on him. He must have been still half asleep to let such notions into his head for an instant. Yes, it must have been something left over from a dream. What possessed him to begin to have dreams again—at his age?

He moved forward into the library, knocked his knee—his lame one, too—against a chair, and stood bent over, drawing in his breath sharply, nursing his hurt. He *felt* hurts more than other people, he thought, repressing a groan as he let his breath out. Alix was right when she had quaintly and anxiously said that he really was "awful sensitive."

Strange how the child's personality pervaded all she did. At the beginning, before he had begun to teach her, she could scarcely open her mouth without bringing out some rustic or slangy inelegancy that would have jarred on him frightfully if it had come from someone else. All mixed up with absurd incongruous bookwords—picked up from her reading, probably. Yet because they were hers, he had found something touching in her rusticities of speech and her misdirected efforts to improve them. Her eagerness to be corrected and to learn was so childlike and sincere! She had to the full that sure proof of innate superiority, the instinct to form herself on the best model in her reach—she wanted, she often told him, to be as much like him as she possibly could. And what a pupil she was! Mr. Stewart had never dreamed that teaching could be so absorbing and fascinating.

He sank into a chair, smiling to himself. She never made the same mistake twice. One hint was enough. "Oh, Alix child, the fork! The fork!" Or, "Lovely ladies don't use words like 'roseate' and 'nebulous.' They leave those to the dictionaries and to spectacled professors of literature. Well-bred people use plain neutral words like 'pink' and 'cloudy.'" Or, "Slim young ankles should always be close to each other." Not even once after that would she begin to use a spoon for the wrong food, or bring out that pretentious or that slang word, or sit down with her feet apart and then with a telltale start correct her mistake. No, as though she had

done it from her childhood, she reached for the right utensil at table, and sat down with quiet elegance added to her slow, provocative, native grace. Blood would tell in all the things that really matter, he often thought. Even without knowing the secret of her fine ancestry, one look at Alix was enough to show anyone who knew good breeding that she came of distinguished stock.

And even more than good form in speech and manner how she assimilated culture! She was now letter-perfect in the styles of old American furniture, could hold her own with anyone in the summer colony in talk about Bennington pottery, and had listened so attentively to his explanations of fanlights that when, yesterday, he had heard her talking to Mrs. Schuyler about New England doors, he had recognized many of his very phrases. No one had ever before treated Mr. Stewart as an apostle. Strange, new, enchanting satisfaction to hear his words earnestly repeated by a devout young disciple. Yes, thought Mr. Stewart, leaning back in his chair in the dark, yes, it is the plainest of duties to feed such hungriness for the finer things of life.

Yet all that was nothing compared to the primitive, literal responsibility that anyone with a heart could not but feel to protect defenselessness against violence. Good heavens! Think of any so-called civilized man acting like Anson Craft! "He's just a brute," thought Mr. Stewart, sitting up, his muscles tightening, "that's all Anson Craft is, all he ever was—in spite of his brains." Who but a brute, the worst variety, the intellectual brute, could have struck down ruthlessly as he had the poor child's first timid claims to the respect and consideration due a wife. Who else, when she protested, would have broken her heart by giving her cynically to understand that he had never wanted a wife of his own class who could enforce such claims, and had picked Alix out exactly because, poor and friendless as she was, he could take her up and fling her down as it suited his convenience.

On the day when her pitiful longing for help and protection had broken down her self-respecting reserve and for the first time she had confided in Mr. Stewart, she had not been able to keep back her tears. Nor had he—not yet fully recovered from his injury. He

had wiped his eyes a good many times as she sobbed on, "Anson thinks I'm dirt under his feet because I was brought up on Searles Shelf. But, compared to him, they are *gentlemen* up there! There isn't a man there who'd shame a woman that was ready to love him, the way Anson shamed me. And no Searles Shelf woman would have stood it, the way I did. They'd have had more pride. I would have too, only I just couldn't take it in at first. But I know him now. He's just a plain liar. 'I love you,' he'll tell you. I thought he meant it. And I loved him back. How'd I know that what he did mean was that when he got all through everything else . . . He wouldn't expect a meal of vittles to stay the way he likes to eat it till he gets around to sitting down to the table, would he? But a woman . . ." At the end she had let herself wildly go into a frenzy that shook her listener as the untamed wind shakes a human habitation. It made him tremble now even to remember her writhing body, sick with shame. "And he can't even keep his mind on it enough to remember that he *has* spit in his own wife's face! It's so little to him he can't even remember doing it!"

Mr. Stewart, terribly harrowed, but of course very ignorant of married as of all other life, never did understand exactly in literal detail—and certainly hoped he never would—the indignities which Craft's helpless young wife had undergone; but there was no mis-understanding the dreadful reality of her suffering. It was the first time in forty years that anyone had made him witness of feeling deeper than a cook's bad temper. He was shocked and horrified and indignant. And vitalized to the tips of his fingers.

And not surprised. A detestable man would naturally make a de-testable husband. Anson Craft had always been a sneering egotist, even before he went through the dehumanizing experience of medical training. Mr. Stewart winced at memories of the cold mockery in the boy Anson's eye, fixed on him as he escorted a summer-colony tea-time lady out to her car, or as he stood around being genial at some idiotic church supper or school picnic. De-testable as Anson had been to begin with, utterly spoiled by his sister, brutalized by the materialism of a medical school—that a

timid, inexperienced, friendless orphan girl child had fallen into his hands—it was frightful beyond imagining.

Mr. Stewart's hands doubled up into fists at the thought of what unthinkable treatment the poor girl must have had to reduce her to the terror she felt at the idea of appealing to her husband for protection. The danger that threatened her, alarming as that would be to any woman, even the bravest, was nothing apparently compared to her fear of her husband. Her agitation, already overpowering, rose to panic at the mention of Anson's name. And how wildly lovely she was in agitation! Mr. Stewart had never dreamed that anything in life could so take his breath away with beauty as she had that day when, pale, panting, looking fearfully over her shoulder, electric with life, she had whispered in his ear that she was suddenly in danger of death. A man crazed with love for her (Mr. Stewart, his hands shaking on the arm of his chair, his heart beating chokingly in his throat, could understand that) who had threatened her as a girl in Searles Shelf, was back in The Valley. A man who stopped at nothing—who had already— "Listen, Mr. Stewart! He'd kill me, I know he would . . . He's tried to already. When Anson and I . . . He was the man who . . . Look!" Shuddering, she tore at the fastenings of her waist, pulled it open and laid a trembling forefinger on a jagged white scar in the warm ivory of her shoulder.

When Alix had recovered from her wound, he had disappeared— she had thought forever. "And then yesterday—oh, Mr. Stewart, I thought I'd die—I was in the kitchen—I heard somebody come in the back door and lock it behind him and then stand a minute in the back hall. Before he opened the door and walked in—I knew. If I could have run away I would—but I couldn't move . . ." She had been again before his eyes physically paralyzed with fear, so that before she could go on he had had to take her in his arms to soothe her. It was the same ruffian who had terrorized her youth— as mad about her as ever and as strong and savage and wily and quick-witted as ever—there was nothing that he would not dare to do, or not be cool and bold enough to do. He was afraid of nobody. And he cared for nothing in all the world but her. He wanted her,

and he'd kill her and himself if he couldn't have her. Of course he was a nobody, a dirty, ignorant, backwoods hick without a cent to his name. But he put the woman he loved first, first, *first*—and not last.

For an instant as she poured this out, her pale face and wild, dark eyes close to his, the hot sweating surface of what Mr. Stewart thought was his sympathy for her contracted sharply, chilled by the piercing guess that mixed with Alix's fear of Henry Twombley there was unbounded fascinated admiration. This passing rigor of cold had been quite the most intolerable sensation of Lawrence Stewart's life (—*so* far). But it had lasted hardly long enough to notice. Whatever obscure door in the depths had opened a crack to let in that icy draught had been instantly slammed shut. In his incessantly recurring memory of the scene there was nothing but Alix's beautiful eyes swimming in tears, the pathetic clutch of her poor little hands on his, her husky, heartbroken voice. It echoed now in Mr. Stewart's ear. His heart melted, absolutely melted. With an unconscious gesture he opened his arms to her in the darkness, murmuring tenderly, "There! There! Poor *child!* Don't be frightened. Count on me! You'll find Henry Twombley is not the only real man in the world. You are not alone any more. I'm here."

But at the agonizingly vivid touch-memories which sprang into his arms that had held her, his shoulder on which her head had lain, his body against which hers had pressed, he leaped wildly from his chair astounded and shocked to hear himself make a moaning, animal-like outcry. But he couldn't help it! It was like having the dentist touch a live nerve. You couldn't help . . . Well, no—not exactly like the dentist. But quite as impossible to resist by self-control. At least for an instant.

He got his breath back, remembered where he was, and lifting his flashlight turned it for an instant on the mantel clock. Oh, God! Only half-past two! He must get some sleep or he would break down. His heart was racing. He must simply stop this helpless hypnotized living over of moments too exciting for his nerves. Perhaps if he ate something . . . ? Yes, he would go into the kitchen and get a bite of food. That might draw the blood from his head.

The kitchen was at the back of the house. Its windows were not visible from the street. He turned on the light. Blinking in its glare, he caught sight of himself in the cook's mirror and bit savagely on the sore tooth offered him by the reflected image with its stringy neck above the pajama collar, its flaccid puckered flesh under the eyes and its lusterless hair, ruffled now from the precise orderliness which in the daytime masked the thinning places. A pretty specimen to be having emotional explosions like the one that had just now brought him to his feet, half crazy! He got himself a glass of milk and a cracker, and relentlessly watched the old fellow in the mirror chewing and swallowing. *You,* to think you could be anything but personally repulsive to a girl! You ought to be ashamed of having such thoughts about a poor child who turns to you because she has no one else to trust. Now come.—He set the empty glass down loudly on the table, his eyes on the battered elderly face in the mirror—a little rational thinking, if you please. Look at the situation as it really is. A young woman is in peril of her life from a gun-carrying thug, who has already nearly killed her. Something has frightened him away for the moment, but he threatens to come back at any moment, has now even set the day. Mr. Stewart had seen some of those scrawls and shuddered over their badly spelled ferocity and passion. She cannot appeal to her husband because he has a thousand times proved himself a brute. And insanely jealous of her. Has for months made her life a nightmare on account of his absurd jealousy of a neighbor—a poor harmless oaf to whom Alix had been kind because she liked his sick wife. Yes, that Dean fellow was—it is true—in love with Alix, but what male near her would not be! She was tinder that would touch off any man to flame. But unconscious of her power over men as she was, she had never dreamed that would happen, had been horrified when she knew it, and had turned to her husband for help and advice as to what to do. And he had responded by breaking into one of his terrifying jealous rages. Ever since, she had lived in fear of his losing all control of himself and spoiling the Deans' marriage forever. "I'd do anything, *anything,* Mr. Stewart, to prevent Anson's telling Cornelia. She'd never get over it.

And he'd do it in a minute just to spite me. He knows I think the world of Cornelia and he hates me! He simply hates me!" Could she appeal to such a man for help in this new and actual danger? A thousand times no. After learning what her life with Anson was Lawrence Stewart agreed with her there. Nor was there anything to be expected from the usual recourse to the protection of the law. That would but rake up and air old scandals, and be useless because so slow—the Searles Shelf rattlesnake would strike long before the clumsy law could be brought to bear. There was nothing for it. Alix was right. Her only safety lay in vanishing now at once. Before Thursday. Three days from now. And he was absolutely the only human being on the globe who could help her do it.

Mr. Stewart had long ago forgotten to look at the man in the mirror. All that he could see was a frightened girl, her dark eyes brimming with tears; all that he could feel was the warm, yielding firmness of her young body in his arms; all that he could hear was her husky broken voice, pleading, "You're the only friend I've got in the world! They all hate me here! They're all so mean to me. I've *got* to get away. Oh, Mr. Stewart, can't you . . . ?"

The trembling voice almost said—the next time he remembered it, it would say—"No, you're *not* old. I hate young men. I've had enough of them."

Mr. Stewart pressed a button. Darkness flooded the kitchen, annihilated the disheveled, elderly gentleman with his thinning hair and his stringy neck, and brought to life a champion of the friendless who went striding off through the dark house. (Striding as much, that is, as is consistent with occasional cautious flashings-on of his electric lamp to avoid collisions with the many objects harder than human knees all around him.)

He saw the situation clearly now; it was not in the least complicated. Of the barest simplicity. Here was a sensitive, ardent human being, set down by Fate in the midst of churlish, mean-minded villagers, as incapable of appreciating her as of any other generous emotion. Of course they hated her, as they hated anything fine and free and better than themselves. He knew them. He

had always hated them. To realize that he had, gave him now an exquisite sense of liberation from a pretense. Yes, he had always hated, loathed and despised their revengeful grudge against superior beings, their instinctive dislike of any existence like his own, lived on a higher level than their grubbing grind . . . Good God! Why had he put up with them his life long, with all the world to live in! To hell with them! Oh, new and ineffable joy of rage! How it fortified a human heart! Why had he denied it to himself? How it healed the wounds that had been dealt him, year after year, by the cold realism of the eyes around him. No matter how affable he was, how much money he gave to their damn sanctimonious "organizations," how carefully sociable he was, no matter how much sought after by wealthy connoisseurs of old furniture, Clifford eyes continued to tell him wordlessly, "You're nobody but yourself and you never will be. We know you. You're a whipped dog. Your old reprobate of a father broke your spirit once for all. No matter how much money he left you, you'll have your tail between your legs to the day of your death. Put on all the airs you want to—we won't hinder you! We won't give you away. But don't think you'll ever be anything but old Doc Stewart's do-less boy that's afraid of his hired man."

But now at last what they said, those cold eyes, was drowned out by a husky voice trembling with gratitude,—"Oh, Lawrence— It's a revelation to me that anyone can feel so safe, so at peace! To think that it has come to me!"

"Oh, Alix, darling Alix, a lifetime's devotion can never repay you for the salvation you bring! God's blessing on you for opening the door of life! Someone who needs me! Actually someone who needs *me!* Someone I and nobody else can help! Someone in danger I, even I, can protect and save. Something real to do with my life after all this lonely marching over the sands. Someone to love—yes, love, *love!*"

Mr. Stewart was hurrying up and down his darkened hall, his arms flung out, his hands clenched, tears in his eyes, his heart young with the youth he had been cheated of, forty years ago.

Dimly something from the external world of reality reached his

ear. A familiar sound close beside him. A faint unhuman stirring
of life began in the tall grandfather clock. The senseless parts,
little and big, of its cunningly devised mechanism engaged their
cogs in the manner decreed for them by their maker long ago, spun,
whirred and caught according to a plan that was none of theirs,
set in motion certain levers which released a catch, which by the
law of its being caused a metal hammer to leap up and strike
sonorously upon a wound-up metal spring. Musically, relentlessly,
another hour was told off, another morsel of eternity was droppd
down into the bottomless pit of the past—Mr. Stewart was another
hour nearer old age.

Could it be four o'clock? He lifted his eyes to the fanlight over
his front door. Sure enough, its beautiful leaf-vein tracery was black
against faint gray. Had he been walking about for more than two
hours? Yes, for more than two mortal hours excitement and emotion had strung him taut. No wonder his legs were trembling. He
was as lame as though he had just come off the mountain from
a climb too long and too hard for a person of his age. This night-
restlessness would be the death of him. Only four hours left to
rest—for if he slept on into the morning everybody would know
and speculate and say, "Poor Lawrence Stewart is beginning to
fail."

He turned his flashlight on for an instant to locate the newel
post, snapped it back to blindness and began to climb the stairs.
How heavy and strengthless his legs were. How his back ached!
Stooped and bowed and broken, he hauled himself up by the stair-
rail, thankful that he was alone and in the dark and could abandon
himself to his fatigue.

He did not flash his electric lamp on again. With sixty years'
familiarity he knew every step, and just where the turn on the
landing was. But half way up, as he slowly lifted a foot from one
stair to the next, a harsh inner light flicked itself on for an instant
in the darkness of his mind. What he saw in its crude glare was
that Alix was the common adventuress he had always been afraid
would get him and his money; that he himself was just the old fool

of vulgar tradition. Everything she had told him was probably a lie. Probably there was no Henry Twombley, nor was Anson jealous; nor was she from a distinguished family. She was just a low-down Searles Shelf woman such as he had never let into his kitchen. She would get him away from the only place on earth where he had any contact with life, and make but one mouthful of him. In a year's time she would be a brilliant, assured woman of the three-quarters world, and he half dead, a barely tolerated old hanger-on. A year? Six months!

The foot that had been raised fell jarringly on the stairs above. The inner flashlight snapped itself off. All conscious thought winked out to blackness too. But far below conscious thought, a blind, proud, vital force stirred in his heart for the first time, announced that it was there, and that it was right for it to be there. No matter what—no *matter* what—to stand up at your own peril for what lives against the threat of what might kill or maim it—for what else is a man born into the world? Never mind which kind of life— what is Man to pick and choose between this or that kind? Is not all life sacred? In all its degrees death is our only enemy.

Mr. Stewart was all but fainting with weariness and confusion of mind, but he was not beaten. Strange grotesque fate to suffer first from growing pains at sixty. He was far too tired now to remember how ever he came to be on those endless stairs, but there he was, and he would not give in to them. Stubbornly, doggedly, half proud, half ashamed, he crawled on from one step to the next.

But when he finally stood in the door of his bedroom there was nothing left of him but fatigue. Dawn had come. The windows glimmered gray. His disordered bed was only his bed. The danger had evaporated from the tossed-back sheet. He laid himself down and putting his hand on the covers began feebly to pull them towards him.

There was a stirring at the foot of the bed. Not the deadly mechanical rhythm of cogged wheels fitting helplessly into each other to produce a foreordained result. This was the unregulated, unpredictable stir of life—the sleepy cat crawled from under the disturbed blanket and turned a blinking, reproachful face upon the

man. The years fell away. Even so had the cat who slept on the little boy Lawrence's bed looked with amusing crossness at him when, restless with forebodings about one or another of the ordeals with his father which always threatened him, he tossed and turned and pulled the covers. Even so had that cat dragged herself up, yawning and stretching, and walked along the bed towards a hand reached out to stroke her. Even so had the anxious and exhausted boy taken her into his arms and loved her furry warmness and felt comforted to feel another heart beating against his own. Even so had he stretched himself out in his bed, the breathing, living thing clasped to him. Dear, unexacting, undemanding, uncomplex animal love! Dear safe animal beauty that can be loved and laid down at will!

Mr. Stewart drew a long breath and closed his eyes. Henrietta wriggled slightly in his arms till she was in a position that suited her; and closed her eyes. Lawrence Stewart and his cat were asleep, their heads on the same pillow.

4

EVERY morning during that last week in September, dawn broke over The Wall as grandly as though Waterloo were to be fought that day. Every evening the sun, dying in glory beyond The Gap, seemed to Clifford people to leave The Valley as it had found it. Not to Miss Gussie. Louder and louder into the silence around her sounded the ominous twanging of strings pulled closer to the breaking point. Night after night as she put on her long cotton nightgown and rubbed mutton tallow on her rough, earth-coarsened gardener's hands, she could hardly breathe, so thick was the suspense in the air of her room. And when she tied on her night-cap and opening her window wide leaned out, the solemn moonlit valley lay waiting as helplessly as she for those strings to break.

Sometimes her tense nervous expectancy simulated the very sound of straining fibers snapping apart, so that she clapped her hands

over her deaf ears to shut out Almira's mad laughter as she ran down The Street offering herself to any man she met—would it come like that? And to keep away Sister Bessie's frightened groaning in that last endless phase of her malady, when she would be forced into her bed to lie, month after month, watching death draw nearer, slow step by slow step.

From the irrevocable sentence that hung over those doomed ones, Miss Gussie sometimes turned away towards Lixlee with a wild impulse towards liberation at any cost while there was yet time.

Like all deaf people, it seemed to her that she would have been perfectly fluent, perfectly articulate, had she not dragged behind her the ball-and-chain of her infirmity. She held long imaginary conversations with the girl, saying to her what she thought she would have said if she could have been sure of hearing the answers; conversations in which Lixlee confirmed what Miss Gussie guessed from the expression on her impenetrably closed young face—that it was all wrong, a dreadful mistake, that Anson did not love her, had never loved her, did not value her, had never for an instant since their marriage stopped thinking of himself long enough to see her side of anything, had only married her in the first place to spite Clifford ideas, had been for years a secret drunkard, took drugs, had an illegitimate family somewhere else—the more Miss Gussie indulged her guesses, the wilder they grew. And to these imaginary revelations from the girl her unprincipled old friend returned incendiary imaginary incitements: "Why don't you just pick up and go away, Lixlee? If there's a chance of your fixing things so's to take some comfort in life, still—make a grab for it! There's so little comfort to be had! Any that anybody can get is that much to the good for everybody. I wish *I* had grabbed when I could! That boy's all right. You'd be safe with him. I knew his grandmother. He's just like her—good-hearted—simple. No more brains than you—and not a quarter your drive. You can wind him around your finger without half trying. He's not much but you could have *good* times with him. And you wouldn't be hurting anybody—not like me. Olivia would soon get her another beau. And Anson—deserves whatever he gets. He'd ought to have known better than to marry

you if he was going to act like this. He had brains! Plenty enough
to know what he was doing—if he hadn't kept'em all for his
doctoring. *You* couldn't know—he should ha' thought of that. He
just never for one *minute* thought of you, that's the why of it. Why
should you spend the rest of your life making up for a fool thing
Anson Craft did? Emma's boy couldn't be anything but good to
you—to any woman. And he's got money enough, it's plain to see,
for all he says he hasn't. Everybody knows that now. You could
just drive down The Valley with him and never come back—and
never once think again of Clifford or any of us here that didn't
ever give you a fair chance."

When she heard people gossiping as they increasingly did about
the scandal of a married woman making up to a young man—
what else was she doing in those long hours she spent in the Stewart house—Miss Gussie continued stoutly to flare up, to deny, to
challenge.

"How do *you* know? Maybe there's a perfectly good reason we
don't know anything about."

"You wouldn't believe anything else Almira says!"

"Why can't it be to take in something nice to a sick old man,
the way any neighbor might—whether there was a young man in
the house or not?"

"It is *not* the reason why—Anson had started drinking long before
Rug Milner ever thought of coming to town."

"Oh, don't bring up that silly Charlie Dean story. You *know*
there can't be anything in that!"

Because there was no one else, she kept saying what Lixlee's
family and friends would have said if she had had any. And on
the rare occasion when she saw Lixlee, who always asked at once
about her garden, she said matter-of-factly that the string beans
were about gone and that the Brussels sprouts looked promising.

But in her heart, too old now to bother about the little notions
that had bound her youth, the fire of rebellious sympathy burned its
way steadily through tradition and convention.

Sometimes she forgot, and when she was by herself, in the garden, in her room, she said aloud an occasional corner of a phrase

from these vehement imaginary conversations. Squatting to weed her carrot row, on the last Friday of September, she was saying fiercely to Lixlee, "*I* wouldn't blame you—not a mite. You acted as sensible as *you* knew how—and Anson didn't. He was just one of those men that think they can go fishing and not get their feet wet, that's all. And if they drown, it's no more than they deserve."

The intensity of her conviction had brought the last words out into blurred audibility. From the other end of the garden where she picked the beans for dinner, Miss Bessie screamed irritably, "Gussie! Stop mumbling to yourself that way! You drive me wild! Sounds as though you were crazy!"

Miss Gussie looked down at the ground to hide the pity that came into her face and went on silently weeding, her anxiety turning itself along another familiar channel. She knew why Bessie's voice was so cross. She was still scared sick over last week's heart attack. Miss Gussie quailed at what lay before them both. More than anything else in all her life she dreaded the last installment of her sister Bessie's story! Sometimes she shrank so from those last years, she felt it not wrong to pray she might die first. " 'Tisn't though there was anything I could do to make it easier for her," she thought for the hundredth time. "She's just got to go through with it. *I* can't keep it off. And it'll last for years. The Kemps die so slow. She'll have more and more attacks, worse and worse. And every time she thinks one is starting she'll have one of those terrible screaming fits—scared as if 'twas going to be the last one. And then be dragged out of it by the doctor to start all over again. Oh, I *never* could stand it. Let me die first, O Lord!"

She had reached the end of her row and struggled up to her feet, her old joints stiff. By the time she had walked to where her hoe leaned against a fence post, and with it in her hand had begun to hoe around the broccoli plants, she was ashamed of this prayer and had hastily withdrawn it. Desert Bessie at the very time of their long lives when she most needed help? Leave her to be roughly cared for by people who with the crassness of those who had ears, would let her fretful words blind them to the agony in her eyes! Anson Craft would probably say casually to them, as he had to

her, "Oh, that panic she always gets into, it's just one of the symptoms of the malady." And they would feel as he seemed to, that he had said something instead of nothing. Taking their cue from him they would feel justified in turning away from the dreadful sight of Bessie cringing and cowering, all her self-respect shattered by fear. They would think it was all right to leave her alone and unfriended except for material care. No, no, in the ordeal darkly drawing nearer, Bessie would need, as never before, somebody who cared enough about her to understand. "She'll soon have to take to her bed," Anson had said, his hand running with unfeeling lightness over the paper as he wrote out a prescription. "I don't say she mayn't last for years yet. But she'll be safer flat on her back."

Thinking of other times when her sister had lain flat on her back glaring at the menace closing in on her, Miss Gussie hoed harder and harder around her broccoli plants. Remembering and resenting the relaxed ease of that callously steady hand flying over the paper, she drew her own muscles into resolute knots, striking down the weeds as though they were the arrogant fears crowding around her sister's sick bed. She flung her hoe high and brought it down with a will—so and so and so would she—she resolved now—strike down those terrors. Somehow, when the time came, when gripping frantically at anything that might put off even for an instant the inevitable fall, Bessie felt herself slipping over the edge, somehow her own sister would know how to help her loosen peaceably the tentacles of life. The weeds, the arrogant weeds, fell prostrate before Miss Gussie's hoe. For an instant she felt unbeatable.

From the back porch where Bessie sat stringing the beans, she called now, "For the Lord's sake, Gussie, what do you think you're doing? Chopping down trees? You'll give yourself a stroke."

Miss Gussie had forgotten where she was. She stopped, pushed her sunbonnet back from her sweating face, and leaned on her hoe. Sure enough her old legs and arms were trembling with her exertion. But how her heart went plodding steadily along, slow and quiet. If she could only take that sound old muscle out of her breast and put it into Bessie's! As easy to do that, she knew, coming disheartened back to reality, as to share anything you had with the

one who needed it—as to give Bessie the least bit of her own feeling about death—her gardener's acceptance of it as part of the good cycle. If she could only say, "See here, Bessie, why need it scare you so to feel yourself slowin' down? Don't it make you feel sort of rested? It does me. Makes me feel the way things in the garden look these first cool days in th' fall o' th' year— 'Well, enough's enough,' is what they look like to me. And so 'tis."

Or, some time when the sleepy September garden stood dreaming in the sun, why couldn't she tell Bessie, "I don't know but what I like the garden this time of year—all through with what it set out to do—full as well as in July. There's times when these last still warm days before frost comes, feel to me the best of any.

"But, no, you can't say it," thought Miss Gussie, stirring the earth slowly now with light strokes, "when you get it out, it's never anything but words."

Across the garden, across the back yard, she saw Bessie turn her head as if she heard someone in the house. Yes, a woman appeared in the kitchen door. Jim Gardner's fat wife Ella, their next door neighbor. Probably stopped in to bring the mail. No, nothing white in her hand. Maybe to buy an extra cup of cream. Ella's married sister was visiting her. Miss Gussie went on hoeing. When she looked again, the newcomer stood on the other side of the table on which Bessie's beans were strewn. Something tense about her attitude made Miss Gussie stop working to watch her. Used to gathering her news from other sources than words the deaf woman knew whether a story that was being told was trivial or momentous, from a clenched fist or a relaxed open hand, from the placid balancing of a head on its neck, or its rigid thrust forward. By Ella's strung-up tautness, she who usually sagged as if made of dough, it was plain she was telling something that had startled her. She spread her hands out on the table and leaned far over it, her eyes grave with the satisfaction of the bringer of dramatic bad news, her lips writhing rapidly in the strange contortions of speech. People looked like that when telling about a fatal automobile accident. Couldn't people ever learn not to talk about death and dying to poor Bes-

sie? It was too late now to head Ella off. It was always too late. She looked anxiously to see how her sister took it.

All of Bessie's mountainous flesh had tautened, too. Her mouth had dropped open. Stupefaction was flung over her face like a heavy cloth. When Ella's chest heaved as she stopped to draw breath, Bessie's mouth shut and opened and shut in an exclamation. She pushed her hands against the table as if to stand up. The expression on her face, the gestures were those which go with the words, "You can't mean it! Can it be true!" The other woman nodded her head many times, rapidly. Her lips resumed their hurried writhing. Bessie got to her feet, tipping over the light table as she did so, but neither she nor Ella so much as glanced at it as it went down. She asked a question, waited for an answer, asked another. The stupid glare of blankness on her face thinned out now before another expression rising to take its place. It was amusement. Wild, enchanted hilarity. *Well* . . . ! It couldn't be an automobile or railroad accident then. What in the world could have happened as funny as that? For Bessie was laughing her greatest laugh. Gussie had never seen her sister so helpless before her sense of the ridiculous. She bowed her great bulk together, both hands pressing hard against her sides, she straightened up and flung herself backward, her mouth gaping wide. A ghostly echo of the yell of her laughter reached even Miss Gussie's ears. Yet Ella Gardner was not laughing at all, stood staring—disconcerted, half offended.

Her deaf sister was uneasy at the recollection of some of the things in the past which had seemed comic to Bessie. The hoe still in her hand, she started towards the back porch.

Then she flung her hoe away wildly and ran. Ran as she had not since her fleet girlhood.

But no one could have been fleet enough to outdistance the runner who had at last mercifully caught up with old Elizabeth Kemp.

Later, much later that night when everybody in the world, or so it seemed to Miss Gussie, had come and gone, when Anson Craft had made his disgraceful appearance so drunk that he could not write out the certificate of death and had been led away by old Doctor Cole, when Anna Craft and the neighbors, flinging them-

selves with brooms and mops and dustcloths into the only service there was to render, had driven the life out of the house and had set in its place a portentous dead orderliness, even then, at ten o'clock that night, Miss Gussie, pale, shrunken, her shoulders bowed, her hands shaking, but quiet and self-contained, still did not know what the joke was that Ella Gardner had told Bessie. There had been no moment when she could ask her, no instant when someone was not trying to make her hear a question about where the sheets were kept, or who among the relatives should be telegraphed to, or what was Bessie's favorite hymn. At this last she had not been able to suppress one of her unexpected laughs. "She despised them all, Fred, and you know it," she told the clergyman. She was too old to be mealy-mouthed. "Must she have a funeral? Can't we just bury her? She'd hate to be prayed and sung over."

They were standing at the head of the stairs, outside the closed door to Bessie's bedroom. Fred Kirby thought a moment. Then tearing a sheet from his pocket notebook, he wrote, "I'll see that whatever you want is done. You think it over now and tell me."

He drew her down to sit on the top step beside him—the first time she had been off her feet for hours—leaned his head against the wall and closed his eyes to wait. The house was silent now. Only Jim Gardner and his wife were in the living-room below, come over for the night so that Miss Gussie would not be alone. The undertaker had come and gone. Behind her closed door Bessie slept dreamlessly.

After a long silence, Miss Gussie said, "You're right, Fred. We better have a funeral. Bessie'll hate it, but she'd want to have it. She'd know Father and Mother wouldn't like it if we didn't."

The clergyman took her wrinkled roughened old hands in both his and held them an instant in a close loving clasp. He did not try to say a word, only looked at her, all that he was in his eyes. Miss Gussie began to cry. For the first time she knew what had happened. Till now the flurry and confusion and strain had not let her realize it. Why, Bessie was safe! Safe! She drew her hands away to find a handkerchief. While she was wiping her eyes and blowing her nose, Fred Kirby was writing something. He showed

it to her. "You don't think she'd mind, do you, my thanking God
that it came so quickly, without her knowing it? I can hardly help
doing that."

At this the sweet saltless tears streamed again from her eyes.
"No, Fred, no, she wouldn't mind that."

He smiled at her and stood up.

She told herself, "He's thought of a funeral service Bessie will
like."

He nodded and went away.

Looking after him, wiping her eyes and composing her face,
Miss Gussie thought, "Fred's *some*body! If I hadn't a-known him I
wouldn't ha' believed there ever *was* that kind." And then, "Kind of
a come-down for him, seems though, just to get married. Now he
ain't any different from anybody else."

She could not sleep, she knew, till she had asked Ella Gardner
that question. She stood up stiffly, and hobbled down the stairs to
find her. Ella's husband, the *Courier* in his hands, sat in the front
parlor shamefacedly reading the baseball news. In the back parlor
Ella tiptoed around picking at non-existent fluff on the furniture,
straightening the already straight pictures on the wall, twitching at
the curtains.

"Stop fussing, Ella," said Miss Gussie, in her flat deaf voice. "I
want you should tell me what it was so funny you told Sister
Bessie."

Ella took the question as the accusation she had been nervously
awaiting and, with the expression on her face that goes with self-
defense, hastily gabbled a long story. Miss Gussie was too tired for
the straining effort of lip reading. "I can't hear a word you say,"
she said, less patiently than usual. "Write it."

But all the familiar tools of daily life had been swept out of
sight with too dismal a thoroughness. Not one of Miss Gussie's
pads or pencils was to be found. Ella took the newspaper from her
husband's hand and a pencil from his pocket. Laying it down on
the table she wrote around the margin all in one long line, "It
wasn't a joke at all nothing funny about it I don't know what

possessed her to laugh I told her I had just heard that Doctor Anson's wife had run away with old Mr. Stewart."

Miss Gussie read this once, looked up at Ella, appalled, and as if she could not believe her eyes read it again.

"Not *Lawrence Stewart!*" she cried, horrified, incredulous, shocked. "Not *Lawrence*. . . ." Her legs gave way under her. She sank into a chair, looking for once in her life thoroughly scandalized.

Ella Gardner pursed her lips and nodded, gratified by Miss Gussie's appreciation of the event's enormity.

"Oh, that was too bad of Lixlee!" cried her old champion indignantly. "That was too bad! I never dreamed she'd do such a bad wicked thing! Why couldn't she pick on somebody else than that poor boy? What had he ever done to *her?*"

She could not be reconciled, "Oh, poor Lawrence, poor Lawrence," she mourned, "he never had any luck!"

She struck her hand violently on the table, outraged. "Why couldn't she leave him where he belonged?"

Then she who never sat in judgment, put on the black cap of condemnation. "Lixlee hadn't ought to have done that," she said with cold unforgiving severity. " 'Twan't *right.*"

5

DOCTOR NEALE of Caledonia County and Burlington, looking what he was, old and ugly, intelligent, bad-tempered and vital, driving with his usual intensity of concentration on something else, was outraged to feel his car not pulling well. "What's the matter with the damn thing?" he asked himself, stepping harder on the accelerator. The laboring engine did its best but he was obliged to shift gears, an operation he detested. Looking out, he was startled to see that he was climbing the steep hill from Clifford Depot to The Street. "Why, *I* never meant to take that right-hand turn at Mount Weary Four Corners," he thought. "Good Lord! I'll drive the bus into the lake yet."

The road was too steep and too narrow to turn around, so he drove on up towards the top, thinking in his absent-minded way, "Clifford? Clifford? Who is it lives in Clifford?—oh, yes, of course, Craft—heart data—angina facts—father and grandfather doctors here and he damn conceited about it." Well, since he was here, he would just stop and see how that research was getting on.

Not that there was any news to be expected from it so soon. You had to have a mountain of such material before it was safe to start generalizing. It was a life work, all right. Still it might be as well to keep some track of how Craft was getting on—"What was it the last time I saw him that made me wonder if for all his talk he was the kind to stick? It'd be a damn shame if he didn't. He's got hold of one end of something that might be worth a man's while." He was at the top of the hill. "Do I turn right here? Seems though I did before. Yes, I remember, I passed the Town Hall." He turned right, still fumbling in his memory for something that eluded him. "Perhaps it wasn't anything I saw when I was here. Perhaps it was something somebody told me about him. Haven't I heard about something's happening to him? Didn't his mother lose her mind, or his wife die, or something? No, that was old Cole in Ashley."

At a corner he turned left, and at the next one right again, thinking he remembered how to reach Craft's house. So he did. There it was.

But no one answered the bell. He rang again. No answer. His temperature rose. "This should never happen. Never, not once, in a practitioner's house!" he thought severely. But now he saw that dust and last year's dry leaves lay on the front porch and that the window nearest him gazed out forlornly from its curtainless hollow socket. "Maybe he's moved. Yes, that was probably all I heard about him. Say, you! Little girl! Doesn't Doctor Craft live here any more? No? Where *does* he live? What? What? *What?* Oh, well, never mind. Never *mind,* I say."

He got back into his car and drove along slowly, looking for some grown person to ask. But the marble sidewalks under the budding elms lay white and empty. "Nobody ever sets one foot be-

fore the other any more," grumbled the old doctor. "They'll be having the dogs and cats on wheels next thing!"

He turned a corner at random, and found himself on the same street with the church. In the front yard of the house next to it stood two women, and one of them was Craft's sister, the local district nurse. He remembered her distinctly, a tall, red-haired, competent woman with a quick temper. He drove up beside the curb and got out. "How'd do, Miss Craft. I'm looking for your brother. I hear he's moved." He raised his voice to be heard above the shrill singing of some children in the yard next door, playing a round game.

"It's Mrs. Kirby now," she corrected him. "Yes, my brother has moved. He's living in our old home now." She hesitated. "But I'm . . . I think he's not there now. Could you leave the message with me?"

"Oh, I haven't got anything to tell him. I want to hear what he's got to tell me. I'm interested in some medical research he's doing. I hadn't happened to hear anything from him for some time and thought I'd drop in. I'll stop at the house anyhow on the chance of finding him. Which one is it?"

A dismayed expression came into Mrs. Kirby's face. "Oh, *dear!*" she said faintly, and stood still, obviously trying to think what to say. "King *Will*yum was King *James*es son," sang the children next door.

Along Doctor Neale's nerves ran the hot prickle of wrath he always felt at the contact with human reactions that were not precise, definite and prompt. "Can't she answer a straight question?" he thought, and turned to the other woman. Adjusting the lenses of his mental microscope he focused them for an instant on her. She was a good-looking girl. The kind he called good-looking, anyhow, square shoulders, straight spine, wide hips, no soft fat anywhere. He liked too the impassivity of her face. Anything but one of those responsive personal women!

"Miss Foote, Doctor Neale," said Doctor Craft's sister. "Miss Foote is in training at the Boston City Hospital. Home on vacation for the first time in two years."

"How'd do, Miss Foote," said Doctor Neale, disappointed in her, thinking, "No, she wouldn't know." He turned back to Mrs. Kirby. "Well, I'll just dust along and find your brother. Where did you say his house is?"

"I didn't say," replied his sister, the flash in her eyes adding, "And you know very well I didn't." She looked hard into the craggy old face, and said firmly, "Doctor Neale, you don't want to see my brother about that work. Come up here on the porch and I'll tell you why. No, don't go, Isabel. It's nothing you don't know already."

But she was mistaken in this, or rather had forgotten that Isabel was now a professional woman—or almost—with something more than the personal in her life. As she finished what she had to say about Anson, and as old Doctor Neale broke into emotional profanity, the nurse in training asked with interest, "What records are you talking about?"

Oh, yes, Anna remembered now, all that business of Anson's research work had come up since Isabel had gone away and grown up. She opened her mouth to explain, but Doctor Neale rushed in with bitter words. "He's throwing away a first-rate opportunity, Miss Foote, as good as any man ever had, anywhere, right here in this hole-in-the-ground, to do some first-rate research, original first-rate research"—as he pronounced the words his harsh voice softened into reverence—"on a disease that needs facts known about it as much as any other in the list of human miseries, and maybe more. Good God!" The insanity of it took his breath away, "To give up an opportunity such as comes to not one man in a thousand—to let such a piece of work as that drop out of your hand . . . *because your wife runs away from you . . .* !"

"May I ask if you are married, Doctor Neale?" inquired Mrs. Kirby hotly.

"No, I'm not, thank God, and never was. Perhaps you think I regret it, hey?"

"You might know more what you're talking about, if you had been!" Mrs. Kirby's temper rose to match his. "And even without

knowing, you might be a little less callous and unfeeling if you knew some of the circumstances—that made it a blow not only to my brother's pride, but to his self-respect—to his confidence in himself—in anybody else. His wife must have been lying to him—must have been betraying him—and not with one man only—for months and months, when he had thought she was still his wife, when he was still— But of course *you* can't have any idea of what that means!"

Doctor Neale broke in on her with an exclamation. His subconsciousness had suddenly presented him with that elusive memory. "O-o-oh, yes, *I* remember his wife! I remember her very well. One of these damn high-powered dynamite females! Well, he's well rid of *her*. No man can get a lick of honest work done with one of them in the house. How'd you ever happen to have such a one around, anyhow? A fool in the head, too, if I remember, wasn't she? They mostly are." He flung her back into oblivion and implored Anna to contradict herself. "No, Miss Craft—Mrs. Kirby I mean—don't tell me he's just dropped the whole thing, it *can't* be true. What *is* he doing? He's still condescending to practice medicine, I suppose. Lancing boils and swabbing sore throats?"

Mrs. Kirby explained sadly, "He's lost, naturally, most of his practice here."

"Lost it? 'Naturally'? Do the people in this town stop going to a doctor because his wife runs away from him?"

Doctor Craft's sister hung her head. Then, reluctantly, "Well, he—drinks a good deal now. He lives alone with a shiftless old hired man. He's . . . you don't seem to understand . . . he's really . . . gone to pieces."

The pitch of Doctor Neale's scolding rose, "Of course, he's gone to pieces if he's drinking. What did you let him get to drinking for? He's not a drinking man. Don't you realize"—he shook his knotted forefinger in Anna's face—"that with your father's and your grandfather's records to go back to—observations made on two and three earlier generations of the same families now under your brother's care—that he has a perfectly unique and unparalleled

opportunity to collect some actual *evidence* that'd get us somewhere? Your brother could have added something real—and big!—
to medical knowledge. Don't you know enough to know that, and
you a nurse!" He crooked an angry forefinger inside his collar
and pulled it savagely away from his scraggy neck.

"I wish you'd tell me what disease? What records?" asked the
younger nurse again, in her cool, dry, professional voice.

As he told her, her young face relaxed from its gravity into
interest. "You don't say so! Why, I'm interested in hypertension
too. I've been working with Doctor Prellwitz—keeping records of
the frequency of individual symptoms in a group of out-patients
in his clinic with hypertension from pathological causes, compared
to those in a control group with a psychoneurosis."

"You are?" said Doctor Neale. "I thought Prellwitz was interested in the hereditary form of primary hypertension."

"So he is, I think," said the younger nurse, "but of course in a
city clinic you don't know much about parents and grandparents
and you don't have much chance to study it from that angle. Yes,
I've heard him say in a lecture that if we knew more in detail
about hereditary cases—only you'd have to be sure they *were* hereditary—a way might be found to detect it early, before the dilatability
of the arterial portion of—"

"Of course it might! I've always said so. And wasn't here the
place to do it!" cried Doctor Neale. "Medical records of the same
families for a century—well, eighty years—town records of inter-
marriage complete—every in and out of inheritance down in black
and white—and a town full of patients having their grandfathers'
diseases under the care of their grandfathers' physician's grandson.
Why, Craft had a case here he wrote me about of true angina in a
woman with an inheritance of—" He turned to Anna with a start,
"He didn't stop taking cardiograms of *that*—"

"She died eight months ago," said Anna, "late last September."

"Well, was your brother with her? Did he—?"

"No, she died instantly, dropped dead on her own back porch."
In the house a telephone bell rang. She held up her hand for

silence, listening. "Go *choose* the one that *you* love best," sang the children. The telephone rang again. "Excuse me," said Anna.

Ten minutes later when, hat and coat on, small professional bag in her hand, she came to the door, the two she had left were still sitting on the edge of the porch, their legs hanging over the side. She came out and closed the door rather loudly behind her. They did not turn their heads. Doctor Neale was in the middle of a long sentence. She stood a moment, waiting for a pause. Through the chanting of the children,

> "If she's not here to take her part
> Go *choose* another with *all* your heart,"

she heard the doctor saying rapidly, energetically, "I admit nothing of the kind! All that stuff is merely personal! How could a man with a brain allow it to paralyze what's of real importance? He *has* a fine brain, you know. Nobody here knows enough to appreciate that, but he has. A fool of course. But all young men are fools. I had the greatest hope of—"

There was no use in waiting. Anna came out and stood on the grass near them. Doctor Neale, dimly aware of this, turned his eyes for a moment on her, as he continued his quick incisive talk. Without having perceived her, he looked back at the intent young face on his other side "—ought to be somebody who could make him snap out of this self-indulgent idiocy. I could do it myself, if I had time. Anybody could who had sense enough to understand that—" he struck his fist on the porch pillar—*"that an actual contribution to medicine is at stake."* The battered granite of his face had now a stern beauty.

Anna broke in apologetically, "Sorry to leave you, Doctor Neale— an emergency case—"

They turned their eyes blindly on her. She said, "Why don't you go up on the porch and sit down in chairs? You'd be much more comfortable."

They looked back at each other and continued to sit where they were. Anna thought, "How Isabel grows to look like her mother."

Doctor Neale said urgently, "You understand, I hope, Miss Foote,

that certain features of Craft's situation here are unique—simply could not be duplicated in another setting."

Anna moved on down the path.

When she came in two hours later, the children were still indefatigably playing their immortal games. But her porch was empty.

6

WHEN Anna had married, in October, Anson refused any of the combination living arrangements she and Fred offered him. They would, they suggested, live on in the Craft house and he with them. No, he said. Well, if he would rather, the Rectory was plenty large enough to arrange quarters there for . . . No, he said again. Would he perhaps like them to take another house, in another part of town, where . . . It was in these discussions that a chance suggestion of Anna's brought from Anson the only reference they ever heard him make to Lixlee.

He had said, "No, Anna, not anywhere in town. There's no place for me in your life now, and I know it. I'm too late. You take Fred and I'll take his old Hiram—that'll be about the suitable division. You and Fred don't want to keep him on?"

"I should say not! I wouldn't let that lazy old malingerer set foot in our woodshed!" Anna had said with her usual moderation. "He's sponged off Fred just as long as he's going to."

"Well, I want him. Yes, I *want* him. He can cook enough to keep me alive. And answer the door bell and the telephone."

"But, Anson, if you're going to be in our old house, Mrs. Randall will be just next door, and she'd like nothing better than to go on doing for you, the way she always has for us. She's such a good cook. And she knows what you like, and where everything . . ."

Then it came out almost as if involuntarily, "She's a woman, Anna! I couldn't breathe with a woman in the house!"

His corrosive voice frightened her. He misinterpreted her quivering shadowed face and said darkly, "I know what you're thinking—

that it's never all on one side. But you don't know, Anna, you don't *know*. Anna, she was a demon! Possessed of a devil . . . ! There *was* no reason for it! I had absolutely given up my whole life to her—and she . . . she . . ." Trembling and ashy, he gave it up. "There's no use talking about it. No words could . . . ! A mind like yours simply couldn't imagine. . . ." But now he had begun he could not stop. With a groan of shamed misery, "She *enjoyed* torturing me, Anna. She'd rather slide a knife into my back than eat, any day. For no reason in the world—just plain devilish delight in giving pain. That's the woman of it. She had me where she could do anything she wanted with me, so, being a woman, she trod me down in the mud. And lie—she'd *rather* lie than tell the truth even when it would be to her advantage! From now on to the end of my life I never can believe a word anybody says to me. I *can't!* I've got her falsehood in every vein and artery."

Fred Kirby had been stirring protestingly in his chair. Anson turned to him now, fiercely, "You don't know anything about it, you others. She's so plausible that nobody who . . ."

Fred said, his deep voice laying the words down slowly one by one, "Anson! She wasn't . . . twenty-one . . . years old!"

"Oh, shut up, Fred! What do you know about women?"

To Anna, returning brusquely to his usual manner, and frowning resentfully over their having heard what he had been saying, "You send Hiram Rudd to me, Anna. I'll give him a job. It's enough for me that he wears pants."

Yet twelve months later, when, after an agitated talk with Isabel's father and mother, Anna went to see Anson, he insisted that he was not going back on this principle. "Isabel's not a woman," he told his sister, "she's a human being. Good God! Think what it means to me to have a human being to live with! Why, the first time she looked at me, said something to me, I knew that not from the first day had I had one single honest straight look or word from—oh, well—!" He did not attempt to defend his position. He understood perfectly why Doctor and Mrs. Foote were struck to the earth. "I am too. Don't blame *me!* I can't head her

off. I've tried to. Give me credit for that. *I* know she's throwing herself away! I'm not worth it. I've told her a thousand times there's no use trying to pick up the pieces. She'll never be able," he said in a dull, practical objective tone that cut his sister's heart out, "to put them together so they'll hold water. But there's no use talking to her."

Anna went away and telegraphed Isabel, "Implore you not give up training till I talk with you taking night train Boston Anna."

But she might as well have stayed in Clifford. The grave young nurse let her visitor say out without interruption all she had come to say. She told Isabel (what she herself could never believe) that Anson seemed a hopeless wreck. "He acts like a man who's been poisoned, almost to death but not quite. Every fiber of him acts sick. I can't understand it. I can't think what . . ." She hesitated, asked in a very low tone, "Anson hasn't ever let you know, has he, what . . . ?"

"No," said Isabel, steadily, "I don't want to know."

Anna went on sadly. "Well, she seems to have done for him however she did it. The connection between his will and life just seems to be cut. He never pays the slightest attention to that medical research he began. I subscribe to the medical journals for him. But he never even takes the covers off."

White in her starched uniform against the white walls, Isabel sat quietly waiting for her to say her say. But Anna was too heart-sick to go on. She began, "His practice has dwindled to nothing, or almost. People don't like to go even to the office any more. He and Hiram—Hiram is drinking, too. . . ."

It was a final imploring look rather than all these words that stirred Isabel to answer. "Anson has told me all this, already," she said. "He's tried his best to 'save' me, as he says. He's done everything anybody can—everything, that is, except to make me feel that he doesn't awfully, terribly need me."

"Oh, there's no doubt that he needs you," said Anna.

There was a brooding silence between them that lasted a long time. Then Anna pulled her heart up to go on. She emptied her mind of everything but Isabel. "But, dear girl, to step out of train-

ing six months before you'd get your diploma—to give up your profession—when you've made such a brilliant beginning—Doctor Prellwitz told me he expected to see you one of . . ."

Coldly patient with her incomprehension Isabel murmured, "What I care about my career . . . !"

And then, reasonably pointing out a fallacy in what Anna was saying, she went on, "As far as that goes, nothing I could do by myself would be a patch on what Anson and I could do together in Clifford if he'd brace up and start over. There are wonderful possibilities, Anna, in what he's begun. Thirty—forty years from now, we ought to have accumulated some facts and figures that would *count*. It'd be worth . . ."

Leaning forward and taking one of the girl's hands in hers, Anna broke in, "Isabel, do you still love Anson?"

From a long distance and from far away something cast a faint flicker of youth into the grave Nye eyes looking back at her. Isabel did not answer at once. Till that light had gone out. Her voice then was as serious as her eyes. "You must know without my telling you, Anna, that I'm marked with Anson to the marrow of my bones. There never could be any other man for me. I could never not love him. That is, I could never not want to live for him. For the best in him." She closed her eyes. "But I don't *feel* it as I used to." She opened them and added, "Thank God!"

After all if, as Fred had reminded them, Lixlee had not been twenty-one, Anson himself was not yet thirty. That showed in the resiliency of his physical rebound. Isabel had been right. She could do it. And Anna's dumb reserves of faith, behind and beyond her reasoning, had been right. It was not too late.

"A boy, he's been a mere boy till now," said Doctor Neale, once in the second year of their marriage, conferring with Isabel over the cardiogram files, helping her contrive a better system of cross-indexing.

"When you're looking forward to half a century's accumulation," he exhorted her, "it's exactly as important to know how to find your way around as to get the stuff together in the first place." Going

back to Anson, "Your husband never looked better. He's just had the nonsense burned out of him, that's all."

Isabel turned the conversation with a question about how to group cases where a thyrotoxic state coincided with a normal, or subnormal, basal metabolism. She would rather, she had found, hear old Doctor Neale talk about hypertension than about life in general. As far as that went she herself would rather think about hypertension than about life. And she wanted to get Doctor Neale out of the house before Anson came in, breathless, his rough clothes smeared with mud from the football field, full of talk about the afternoon's coaching. Doctor Neale did not approve of doctors who gave much time and thought to local affairs. "Let the storekeepers and the farmers be the 'j'iners,' " he often said. She had prepared an answer for any strictures from him on her husband's absorption in the Academy athletics, on his acting in amateur theatricals, on his having joined the Masons, on his taking up Bridge. "Isn't all that better than whiskey?" she meant to ask Doctor Neale. "Why wouldn't a man who's gone through what he has, be hungry for normal contacts with normal people!" But she would rather not discuss it with anybody. It was enough to cope with Anna's unspoken thought, when, day after day, she passed Anson, ruddy and active, bellowing at the team on the practice field, and found Isabel in the office, opening and shutting the big steel drawers of the filing cabinets, translating and copying off Anson's bedside notes. Isabel had known how without a word to keep Anna's protest unspoken. She was no longer a little girl, awestruck before M'Sanna's adult personality. As one grown woman to another she had closed Anna's mouth with a look. Doctor Neale was another matter. He was very much her superior officer, and said whatever he felt like saying, no matter how you looked. "There, I understand, I think," she said, one eye on the clock, "yes, I'm sure I do. I don't want to hurry you off, Doctor, but it begins to get dark early these October afternoons and the roads from here to Burlington aren't any too good."

Doctor Neale was never in any hurry to leave. He liked to be there with those big steel filing cabinets that, forty years from now when he had long been dead, would contain such heaped-up treas-

ures of classified facts. And he liked Craft's second wife. Once, pulling on his overcoat, the old man even told her so. "If I'd found a girl like you when I was young I might have married myself. And I'd have got somewhere. But there weren't any in my young days."

She had contradicted him, "Oh, yes there were. I know there were. My mother would have loved to have medical training. Any kind of training. She would have been very different if she'd had something to think about besides preserving and dusting and darning stockings." She added, handing him his gloves, "But you wouldn't have liked her if she had been in your class at medical college. You'd have turned your back on her for somebody who was fascinating."

He considered this, buttoning his coat over his woolen scarf. With the last button, "Yes, I suppose I would," he admitted.

This was, except for one other, the only personal talk they ever had, although they spent many hours together during the few years that remained of the old doctor's life. The other time was when her first pregnancy was far enough advanced to be visible. He said, drawing his stiff white eyebrows together, "Are you going to let— *that* interfere with *this?*"

"No, I'll manage," she reassured him. "I'm very strong. I'm built like my mother's family. Nye women are all very normal physically. I won't have any trouble." She added, the one time when irony ever edged her matter-of-fact voice, "My husband is anxious to have a family. He tells me he feels that children of his own will give him something really to live for."

The old doctor gazed into her quiet face with its faint smile, half indulgent, half bitter. He drew a long breath. "Well, you're quite a person," he told her. "I could do with more like you in the world. Hand me that pile of auricular fibrillation notes, will you— no, the thyroid ones."

"Don't they go here, under thyroid myocarditis?"

"How many times must I tell you," he stormed, "that there's no such thing?"

The second Mrs. Craft liked his being impersonal. So was she.

Even with herself. It was not the Nye way to talk the life out of things even in thought. When she thought, it was to tell herself sensibly that everything was all right. People liked to have their doctor take an interest in local affairs. They enjoyed having him at the same Bridge table with them. Hadn't his mother been a Merrill? Of course he played a good game. They liked having him one of them at Lodge meetings, too. It made them feel better acquainted with him. The wisdom of it showed in the way he had got his practice back, his practice that had been almost non-existent —and what little there was, mostly charity patients from below the Depot and up Clifford Four Corners way. Doctor Cole was scarcely ever called to Clifford any more, even for the well-to-do imaginary invalids who were the best pay. Anson was especially successful with them. They all said it did them good to have him step into the house, he was so cheerful. The thing to remember about Anson, she often told herself, was just that some people didn't enjoy being alone and quiet. It was their way of taking life. Why wasn't it as good as any other? Better. If you noticed, sociable people never had any trouble with their digestions. And neither did Anson since he had been rescued from old Hiram's fried horrors. He had not had a second attack of angina. He might never have another, if he had no personal emotional tensions, and that certainly seemed the most unlikely thing in the world, now. He hardly ever drank. He went to church once in a while, now that the Rector was his brother-in-law. He had joined the Fish and Game Club. What more did anybody want?

She was there, wasn't she, to see that he read his medical journals (and to read them herself so that she could discuss them with him) and to keep him from forgetting—yes, even when he groaned and showed he thought her insistence tiresome—to bring home the daily grist of notes on his sick hearts for her to work over, classify, index, copy, interpret and record. Tirelessly, patiently, competently, as her mother sorted table napkins and labeled fruit jars, she pored over the notes, trying to think how to cross-index the observations on the effects of epinephrin on hypertonic persons so that instances of its paradoxic inversion could be readily collated with notes on

lessened lactic acid in the vasomotor center, in case there proved to be a connection there. She pushed in one big steel drawer and pulled out another. It grew darker in the room. She turned on a light automatically, and sat down by the table to yesterday's records, not yet tabulated.

Her husband, coming in tired and rather depressed by a coaching session that had not gone well, found the living-room dark and silent, empty. The only sign of life in the house was an appetizing smell of cooking dinner and a humming of song from the kitchen. It would be comforting, he thought, to take his evening newspaper in there and read it by the stove, warmed by the burning wood and by good-natured old Maria's living presence. But of course a doctor could not sit in his kitchen. There was a light in the office. He had known there would be. He stepped quietly to the open door and saw his wife, her face still and intent, sitting at the big table, leaning over a litter of disordered cards. She took them up, she laid them down, she put this one with that, she read one twice and held it in her hand, thinking. He watched for a moment, turned away and stood irresolute. In the dark hall he looked around vaguely, absently, and drew a long breath that was like a sigh.

How long before dinner? He looked at his watch. Oh, only half-past five. He'd just step over to the basement of the Town Hall where the boys had a pool table. There'd be time for a game. Without making any noise he let himself out of the front door and closed it behind him, carefully.

7

ALTHOUGH Miss Bessie Kemp had died as quick as you'd blow a candle out, literally from one breath to the next, she went right on living in people's memories—at first as a real person, soon as a legend. A legend of a wonderful old woman such as you don't see nowadays, as smart as they make 'em, all her faculties as good at seventy-nine as at twenty—and full of juice, the kind of old woman that men—even young men—like to talk to and to hear

talk. There was no end to the old-time stories she could tell; 'twas a shame nobody had thought to write them down while she was alive. And what a hand for funny stories! For long after her death every amusing episode was greeted with, "Pity Miss Bessie ain't here to laugh over that one! I can hear that horse-laugh of hers now. The greatest hand to laugh this town ever saw. And brave! Brave as a lion. She died laughing, you know. Laughed in the very face of death, as you *might* say."

Comic happenings were not the only ones referred to her shade. Even if it occurred after her death, any event that cast a light on what makes folks act the way they do soon drifted to a place among the salty stories she had told. As a pendant to the story everybody had heard her tell about her grandmother's breaking the ice between her and her bashful beau by stepping on a snake and screaming, people soon hung the later story about how young Rug Milner and Olivia Merrill out taking a walk on the mountain back of The Other Side, found that man who'd committed suicide— his corpse that is—and Olivia fainted dead away—and they came back engaged. Rug hadn't been married a year before that story was being told as one of Miss Bessie's. At first every time Rug heard it, he set it straight. "No, no. You've got that twisted. Miss Bessie'd been dead a fortnight before that." But by and by he let it go. What difference did it make? It sounded like Miss Bessie, so people's talk just shoved it around to where it naturally belonged.

It's something to think about, anyhow, the way talk can—right before your eyes—change things that really happened into something else that sounds more natural. Take what happened at that same time, when somebody went into her office and told M'Sanna that the body of a man who'd shot himself on The Wall had been found. Remember, it was warm weather and the corpse was two weeks old then, and was—well, the only way it could be identified was by the clothes and rifle. Nobody then had the faintest notion who it could ha' been. But M'Sanna had turned as white as a candle, and said right off, "Henry Twombley. . . ."

That was the way it happened *when* it happened. But let folks talk about anything long enough and they'll fix it up to suit'em.

After that story had simmered in the pot long enough, whenever it was dished up, there was some more to it. It turned out that it was perfectly natural and just what you'd expect—her knowing about it before anybody else. She always knew lots of things before other folks because of her poor families. It seems this Twombley's wife had just had a baby and M'Sanna had taken care of her, and had heard about her husband's disappearin' two weeks before. Only *they* thought—it seems he was a poor miserable cuss and no provider—he'd run away to get out of being there when the baby was born and having to help out, maybe. You see—nothing queer about it. As soon as she heard about a body's being found on The Wall, why, of course, she'd think right away about—

It only took about six months for it to have happened that way, and to be told that way. It didn't make any difference anyhow. Who cared? The important thing for Clifford was that Rug and Olivia got engaged about that time, and were married in St. Andrew's that next winter—more greenhouse flowers in the church than ever had been in town before all put together—and went to live in the old Stewart house.

When his Uncle Lawrence had gone away with that Searles Shelf gold digger—and, by the way, would anybody ever have thought that old sissy had so much of his father in him! You know, old Doc Stewart was just a plain devil of an old rip. Funny how those things break out in folks! Well, when he lit out for France or wherever, he took all his money, you bet, but of course he couldn't take the old house. So he said his nephew could have it —or else Rug bought it of him, afterwards—folks tell it both ways. Anyhow that's where he and Olivia came back to after their honeymoon, and had it all done over new, the way that's in style now:—silver and gold radiator paint on the walls, the woodwork black or else bright red, zigzag chairs and tables and bookcases, beds with no head or foot, only about so high from the floor and broad enough to stack cordwood on, a bathroom for every single bedroom and one for the help, with devil-fishes and seaweed and you can't imagine what-all painted on the tiles. People laughed over this foolishness and talked the skin off their tongues about it, but

everybody liked Rug, for all he hadn't an idee in his head except about automobiles. That was one more than his Uncle Lawrence ever had, anyhow. And no doubt about it, he was going to be a great help to the town. He'd already given enough to get a paid librarian and have the library open every day; and said he'd double anything the P.T.A. could raise for hot lunches for the school children; and had had every brook and pond in Windward County stocked with trout, he footing the bill; and bought a new pool table for the Boys' Club in the basement of the Town Hall. But that wasn't why people liked him. Mr. Lawrence Stewart used to give money to things. Rug gave it different. You couldn't really explain out in words what the difference between them was. Rug had funny foreign ways just as bad as his uncle—funnier, when you came right down to it. Why was it that Mr. Stewart's had made you mad, and Rug's just made you laugh? He wasn't really any brighter than his uncle, nor so bright maybe. Well, all a person can say is that Rug is a *real good fellow*—the same all the way through that he is on top.

Maybe the point was just that you could see he liked Clifford. Why wouldn't Clifford like him? It did.

And it specially liked his letting one of Clifford's nice girls catch him on the rebound and not caring who knew that he thought more of her every day they lived. Clifford liked young married folks that were crazy about each other. That's nater, as Miss Gussie said.

Olivia certainly didn't care who knew that she was crazy about Rug. She even let him know it recklessly, whenever anything reminded her of it. He never could tell what was going to make her fall on him with a hug, and exclaim again that he was the sweetest thing in the whole world and that she simply adored him. "I don't know what you're talking about, 'Livie," he often told her. "You sound to me as though you weren't all there in the upper story. But I hope you keep it up."

Sometimes she was taken with a fit of this kind when he had been saying something rather important, sometimes it was over

nothing at all. The first time she had burst out that way was just when he wouldn't have expected her to, when, a week or so before they were married he told her all about how his head had been turned when he first came to town. 'Livie was such a good sport, straight and true and clear as a pane of window glass, that it wouldn't have been fair not being straight with her. "I want you to know all there is to know about me, 'Livie, and one of the things, I guess, is that I'm kind of soft in the head. You know what I mean, easy. Anybody can put it over on me. And that dame certainly did. I thought she had fallen for me, honest. She had me up in the air. She's the kind that *can* get men up in the air, you know. I might have known—just from that. Mamma always used to tell me that women that can get men going, never do it for nothing—not after the first time, anyhow. I'd seen lots of that kind around in Europe. I know just what she'll be like a year from now. She'll have the clothes and the lingo down so pat anybody'd take her for an Italian countess or a Bavarian Gräfin. Anybody but Mamma, that is. She could spot one of that kind a mile away, no matter how high their finish was. She used to step on the starter and roll us out of a hotel—out of a town—if one so much as came in sight down the road. But you see this was the first time I'd ever seen one of them before she really got going. And who'd ever think you'd find one in a dinky little old town like Clifford!

"Of course when you stop to think about it, they all have to start somewhere, and learn off anybody that's handy. Well, she darn near learned off me, I'm telling you. I didn't know for a while there whether I was coming or going. She certainly did have me up in the air! It turns me kind of sick now to think about it—the way you feel when you've skidded around an icy turn and *just* straightened out in time to skin through a narrow bridge. You know it's all over, and that you didn't crash. But you can't get your breath nor hold your hands steady for a while. No, no, 'Livie, don't be nice to me yet—not till I've told you all about it. I don't want you to think that it was any steering of mine that got me out of that tight place. No, it was just my dumbness. I never saw that what she wanted was to get out of here. She'd been *too*

smart, she'd made me think what she wanted was me. What put the brakes on and got the gas turned off was her hearing people tell—and when she asked me I told her so, too—well, it was true in a sort of way—about my getting a job at the Warren Mills. You know that bluff I ran for a while about looking for a job. Well, I take it that did make her believe I really hadn't any money and she thought that even if she *could* wind me around her finger I wasn't the travel-ticket she was looking for. I didn't know that, then.

"She never let on when I told her, 'Livie, she *never* let on about anything! She certainly is one smooth article. *I* didn't even know when she put the skids under me. But boy! looking back on it, even a dumb-head like me can see that right there was when Rug began to be the one that was going and Uncle Lawrence the one that was coming." He hung his head, and ended humbly, "I guess your poor old Rug isn't so much of a Don Juan as some other men."

And now it was all said. He stopped and smiled ruefully at Olivia. She took his breath away then. She sprang up from where she sat, listening seriously and intently to his story, she ran to him, flung her arms around his neck and told him a great many times that he was simply the sweetest thing that had ever lived on this globe.

"Nu, *liebste!*" he protested, bewildered. "Because I was a fool who couldn't keep his head?"

"Because you tell me about it! You didn't have to. Because you tell it the way it happened. You lamb! You perfect *lamb!* Don't you know any other man in the world would have told me *he* was the one who'd backed off and got out of it. Oh, Rug! I'm so glad I'm going to marry you! See here, Rug, if you told me I was standing on my head, right now this minute,—I'd believe you. You couldn't not tell the truth!"

Rug gathered her in his arms, and held her tight, drawing a long breath, laying his head down thankfully on her soft breast. "I wish Mamma could have known you, 'Livie liebchen," he said with all his heart.

But sometimes Olivia was seized with one of those fits over nothing at all. For instance, the spring after they were married, that old cat of Uncle Lawrence's had her kittens in the attic on one of the old sofas they had put up there with all the other discarded junk from the room downstairs. Rug had seen her streaking it up the attic stairs and followed her. And Olivia had followed him.

There was Henrietta with a mess of blind wriggling little worms. She did not roll over to show them off as most mother cats do. She froze just as she stooped over them, her body tense, her eyes, fixed on Rug and Olivia, wide with fear.

"They're kind of cute," said Olivia. "I suppose we'd better have them drowned though. Your Uncle Lawrence always did."

One of the blind worms was nosing vainly around his mother's neck. With a quick reflex movement Henrietta bent her head to give him a nervous rasping lick.

"Here, old man, you're in the wrong place," said Rug, pushing Henrietta over on her side and transferring the little warm helpless body to the right spot on her flank. As he withdrew his hand, he patted Henrietta's head.

Every muscle in her body relaxed. The glare of anxiety went out. She rolled over, stretched herself out to give her babies a better chance, and looked fondly from them up to Rug, her eyes soft and foolish with love.

Rug stood quite a time looking smilingly down at the little family. Olivia stood looking at him. The attic was filled with the soft unresonant music of the mother cat's purring.

Finally, the master of the house said, his eyes still on the greedy nuzzling little atoms, "What do you say we let the old girl bring them up this time—all of them?"

Olivia fell on him wildly, hugging him with all her strength— "Oh, Rug, you're the sweetest man I ever dreamed could live. Oh, how'd I ever have the luck to be married to you. Oh, Rug, I simply . . . I . . ." But she could not go on. She was *crying!* Could you beat that!

8

SHE HAD, of course, changed everything for everybody as she passed. Nobody could help knowing that. Charlie often thought about it. Without her there never would have been any support voted for Dewey House; Anna Craft and Mr. Kirby never would have married; Isabel Foote never would have had the education that made her now know more about some medical things than Anson; Olivia Merrill never would have caught a rich husband—they all owed everything to her. Yet everyone of them tried to forget her, to act as though she had never brought them to life for a time. Well, that was all right. It left her all the more alive in the memory of the only man of them all who had loved her.

Yes, the only one. That wild Indian who had shot himself had had sense enough to be crazy about her, and perhaps if people knew about who he really was, they might think that killing himself when he couldn't get her showed he loved her. But that wasn't what had been revealed to Charlie as love. To go on without her, a thousand times more of a man than if you hadn't loved her, never to forget her, always to bless her—that was the way for a man to prove himself worthy of the Fate that had swept him up out of the dust of everyday grubbing and from the top of the sacred hill had shown him what the meaning of everything is, had let him see why a man is born into human life.

To think that Fate should have picked him, poor old Charlie Dean who wasn't even good-looking, for the transfiguration of loving.

He wondered if that revelation of the meaning of everything, the goal of everything, had come to anyone else in town—now or ever? Certainly not to Anson—poor Anson who had had his chance and fumbled it. To Anna Kirby and her husband? No, no. They had something, of course—but something else, something with the cold light of eternity in it—all right for them maybe, but not what he meant. Olivia and her good-natured sap were just a couple of kids. Isabel never had got over the crush on Anson she'd had as

a child, and was living on what was left of that. Cornelia—well, Cornelia had loved him and married him the easy way water runs down hill.

But love does not run down hill, no! It flings itself up, up, up out of the heart, like a tall fountain. From a deep, unguessed-at reservoir of immortal life far below the surface, it shoots up in a noble column, held there high above the world by the very same heaviness of earth that weighs down all else.

And he had found that out, he only among the ordinary no-bodies in this ordinary town! He could not get over the miracle of it. He had been an ordinary nobody too—what had he ever done to deserve to be the cup into which was poured that draught so satisfying that even the memory of it was far beyond anything else life could offer.

What memories he had! Sometimes, alone in the back of the store, putting up a prescription, one of Lixlee's looks, just one, would flash across his inward eye, or one remembered intonation of that husky voice would echo in the empty room. Struck again by that blinding exalting revelation he would stand stock-still like a man struck by lightning.

How could people *endure* life, he wondered, who had never had the key to it in their hands, who had never seen for themselves what divine meaning may be in the turn of a head, in the slow widening of a smile, who had never soared clean and free from reality up into heaven—on a kiss. He was filled with pity for them, with gentleness for his wife who had so little to live for, for his children who had not one chance in a million to see the door of life's prison open before them as it had before their father.

A man could just never, never do enough to pay his debt to the woman who had aroused him to love! He was proud that when his great opportunity came, he had at least given everything he had— truth, honor, dignity, self-respect—all that he held precious he had given with his whole heart. Nor did he now regret one of those lost treasures. But what were they compared to the wonder and miracle of what she had done for him? Nothing that any man could give would have weighed down that balance—not the most instant "yes"

to anything she asked you to do or not to do, not the quickest completest sacrifice of yourself before the mysterious needs and urgencies of her own fate, not the most unquestioning certainty that all she did could not be otherwise.

He knew there were men who could not love like that, who wanted something for themselves in return for what they gave, and so missed this overwhelming benediction of wholeness. He pitied them. Destiny's arm was not long enough to reach a human being who loved as Lixlee had inspired him to love. Nothing could hurt you, nothing could happen to you, as long as that inner spring ran full with the waters of life. He never reached down a poetry book from his shelves any more. As well look at a picture of water when you are thirsty. He knew what the real thing was now.

9

ANDREW and Mattie Rollins were, though few people would have known it to look at them, having a good time at the party. Anna Kirby knew it, and said in thought to their mother, "Well, you willed Dewey House into existence for your children. Are you satisfied? I am." The two young people from Churchman's Road had not danced yet, but this was only because they did not want to risk this till they had inspected every detail of the way the young people from The Street danced. What they saw was reassuring. Round dances they disregarded, of course. As to quadrilles, any back-roads child in District No. 3 could do better than these big boys and girls stumbling through the simple figures. "After we come back from meeting the team," thought Andrew, from the doorway where with other shy boys new to Dewey House he gloweringly took stock of village people and ways, "I'll ask Mattie to dance the Tempest with me! We'll show'em! And after that I'll ask Phebe Foote. I bet she *never* danced a square dance with anybody that knew how."

Phebe Foote was his sister Mattie's special guest and her twin sister, Eliza Foote, was his. Every year that Miss Ingraham ran

Dewey House she laid down fewer regulations, but she never let up on the rule that each House student must invite a guest from outside to every party. The very idea of inviting one of these strange girls or boys had brought out the cold perspiration on Andrew; so Mattie had asked both the Foote twins, one for her and one for her brother. M'Singraham had let this pass. "She better!" thought Andrew.

It is all right for boys at parties to hang back and glower from doorways if they like. Nobody thinks the worse of them. Everybody knows they do it because they'd rather. But girls, Andrew's sister Mattie had thought despairingly, anybody knows when a girl sits around like a gawk, it's because she can't help it. She had dreaded the evening so much that by supper time she had felt sick. "No, *honest,* M'Singraham, I've got a terrible headache. And I'm kind o' dizzy, too. I think I'm goin' to have a bilious spell. I guess I better go right to bed." She had hated M'Singraham for the coolness with which she had looked at her tongue, and felt her forehead, and for the bossy way she said, "I'm sorry, Mattie, but I can't spare you. I haven't anybody else I can count on to pass the refreshments. You'll have to come down." She had added, "And I want you to wear that red crêpe your mother and I picked out for you."

"Oh, *no,* M'Singraham, not that! I'd feel a fool. People would laugh at me."

"No, they wouldn't either, Mattie. They'd laugh if you didn't. It's one of the rules of the House that everybody dresses up when we have parties. I can't let you break it."

So Mattie, shuddering, had washed herself, had brushed her soft brown hair till it crackled with electricity, had put on the red dress and blushed all over with astonishment to see that she looked just the way Phebe and the girls from The Street did when they dressed up, and had gone shyly down the back stairs to the kitchen to get her tray of refreshments before she appeared in the door of the parlor where the party was going on.

A tray held out in front of you was sort of like a shield, she soon found, you could hide enough of yourself behind it so that it wasn't too terrible having people look at you. And they didn't anyhow,

when you offered them a tray. They looked to see which glass they'd take and which doughnut. And it gave you something to say. "Take another glass, Phebe. You too, Eliza. It's made of our apples. I know it's good." With your arms outstretched to hold the tray, and your eyes fixed on the glasses to keep from spilling the cider, you didn't even mind walking straight from one end to the other of the big double parlors to do your duty by the elders sitting withdrawn into the bay-windows not to interfere with the dancing.

"Have some cider, Mr. Kirby, won't you? No, M'Sanna—Mrs. Kirby, I mean—Mother didn't make the doughnuts. Mrs. Twombley and us girls made them here."

"We girls," murmured Miss Ingraham, as if absent-mindedly, choosing a doughnut with care.

"Did you find your drawers I mended for you, Mattie?" asked Miss Gussie. "I left them on your bed." Not hearing anybody around her she often forgot they could hear her, and was always "saying something before folks."

"Yes, I found them. Thanks, Miss Gussie," said Mattie, nodding, blushing and trying not to laugh. Miss Gussie was certainly the most comic old woman that ever lived. She was nice though. It was a good idea having her at Dewey House to do the mending. "Have some cider, Mr. Milner. Won't you have some, Mrs. Milner?"

"See here, Mattie," said old Mr. Dewey scoldingly, in that quick twanging way he had of talking through his nose, "what'd I ever do to you? Don't you think I like cider? Or are you afraid I'll get drunk?"

"Oh, I *beg* your pardon, Mr. Dewey," said Mattie elegantly, passing the tray in a hurry. To herself she thought with exultation, "I said it! It sounded all right, too! Just as pretty as when Phebe says it! Now I'm going to try saying 'swell'!"

"That's a nice dress you've got on, Mattie," said Mr. Dewey. As he spoke he pushed Don's asking head away. "No, sir, no doughnuts for dogs."

"Ain't it too bright colored?" asked Mattie, looking down at it.

"Isn't it," breathed Miss Ingraham, straightening the ruffle around the girl's white neck.

"Oh, let up on our young people, Cora Ingraham!" said Mr. Dewey, only half laughing. "We don't want'em all slicked up till you can't tell'em from York State young ones!"

Miss Ingraham smiled. Mattie had noticed she liked it when some of the older people called her by her first name. Miss Gussie beckoned Don over to her and gave him half of her doughnut. Mr. Dewey said, "You spoil him, Gussie!" but you could tell he liked it.

The fiddler came across the floor to ask Miss Ingraham if she thought there would be time to have one more dance. No, she decided, looking at her watch, there would not be. Stepping to the middle of the floor she clapped her hands to get everybody's attention, and said loudly, "All those going to meet the team step upstairs and get their things on. Andrew Rollins is in charge of the torches. He'll hand them around. And at the station don't light them till he tells you. Not before the train whistles anyhow. We aren't sure they'll last all the way up here."

She caught Mattie sliding past her, and said pointedly, "No, no, Mattie, you're not going. It's a cold night, and you aren't feeling any too well, you know!"

"The mean thing!" thought Mattie. But she had too much self-respect to tease, and stood by silently while the others clattered up stairs and came down buttoning coats, chattering, laughing, calling back and forth, tucking in woolen scarves, pulling caps down tightly. Andrew was already standing outside the front door. As they came out he said boldly and importantly to each one, "Here you are!" handing out the birch-bark torches on long poles.

"Thanks!" they said. "Thanks!" Sometimes a girl said, "Thank you, Andrew."

Then the last one was gone, and Andrew too, running long-legged over the snow till he had caught up with the crowd. They were off, tramping down the middle of the street as if they owned the town. Somebody started a song—one of those often sung at Dewey House of a Sunday evening. Andrew knew every word of it. From the front door Mattie could see him, tall, straight, swinging along between Phebe and Eliza Foote, his voice rising above

the others. "Bring back! Bring back! Oh, bring back my bonnie to me," sang Andrew. Mattie, listening to the young voices growing fainter as the procession turned the corner and started down Depot Hill, thought, "It does sound pretty—singing out of doors. I must tell Mother about it." She stood a moment longer breathing deeply. "It must be zero this minute," she thought. Leaping up to meet the challenge of the pure cold air in her lungs, her young blood sped nimbly round and round in her veins and arteries. "How good cold weather makes a person feel!" she thought, and closed the door reluctantly.

There was nobody left in the house now but the elders, and not all of them, Mr. and Mrs. Milner and the fiddler having gone to the station with the young folks. When Mattie turned around from the front door, Mrs. Kirby was just starting up the stairs with her heavy slow step. Hearing Mattie behind her she stopped, turned around and asked, "Would you mind running up and seeing if little Cora's all right? She's asleep on the bed in the corner room."

"Sure I will, M'Sanna." Mattie sped up light-footed as a fawn, smiling to herself over the fussy ways of mothers. M'Sanna probably thought by this time her little girl had climbed out the window or evaporated or something. Mattie had told her mother how crazy M'Sanna was about little Cora, and her mother had said, "You wait. She'll take that one easier when the next one gets here." Mattie hadn't noticed till then that Mrs. Kirby was expecting another. It was plain enough now. She oughtn't to be climbing many stairs.

The door to the corner room squeaked so that Mattie was afraid little Cora would wake up. But no, not the faintest change came over the rosy sleeping face. The child had not stirred since her mother laid her down. The covers were still tucked tightly around her. But looking down at the defenseless bland little face, the young girl could not keep her hands from giving the blanket one gentle pull and patting it smoother. Then she touched the round cheek softly with the tip of one finger.

She did not notice the squeak of the door when she left the room. She walked down the hall, her finger-tip still remembering

the warm smooth child-flesh, came to the head of the stairs, looked down and stood still, holding her breath.

Tall in her flowing blue dress, one hand on the newel post, M'Sanna waited below. But she was not gazing up impatient for Mattie's return. She looked as if she had forgotten where she was. She stood there under the hall light, her head bent a little, her bright hair shining, her eyes dreamily fixed on nothing, a faint smile on her lips.

"She's thinking about the new baby that isn't here yet," thought Mattie. She did not take the first step that would startle the dreamer awake. She stood looking down, wondering, "What makes her look so . . . so sort of . . . *rich?* That dress is only mill ends from the Ashley Woolen Mills; Aunt Jenny had one made out of the same material. What makes it look—on M'Sanna—like something you'd read about in a book? Maybe it's because she is standing so still . . . as still as if she had roots. Yes, she looks like something growing in a garden, the way they stand sometimes on a warm sunshiny day with no wind, holding all their leaves up to the sun."

Consciousness of the outer world flowed back in transparent waves over the brooding luminous face below. Mrs. Kirby stirred, breathed, turned her head and looked up the stairs.

Mattie was just coming down.

"Was she all right?"

"Yes, she was all right, Mrs. Kirby."

"Thank you, Mattie."

The two went back together into the big double parlors. Miss Gussie and old Mr. Dewey were going around picking up the empty glasses and carrying them to the kitchen, Don trotting back and forth at their heels.

"Here! Hold on! That's my job," Mattie told them, running forward.

Miss Gussie did not hear, of course. So Mr. Dewey took hold of her hand and pulled her down into a chair and then sat down by her. Don stretched out at her feet. "Mattie says we're to sit down," he told her in his quick way, cutting off the last part of his words and running them together. "Haven't you found out yet, Gussie,

that old folks have got to mind young ones nowadays?" She smiled at his joke, and he smiled at her. He could always make her hear, seems though. Yet he didn't holler at her. Maybe it was because his voice was so high-pitched. Over her tray with its sticky heaped-up glasses Mattie looked at the two sitting side by side, smiling. They looked kinda nice, she thought,—for old folks.

M'Singraham was rushing around and bossing everybody as usual. She had sent Mr. Kirby to the telephone to ask the station-master to call up as soon as the train got in, so Mrs. Twombley could pull the boiler of coffee from the back of the stove to the front, and bring in the big pitchers of cream from where they waited in the back pantry. As soon as Mattie came in, she exclaimed blamingly, "Where *have* you been? Now hurry up with those glasses. When they telephone from the station I want you ready to run around and turn on the lights in every room. The attic too." She trotted into the kitchen—M'Singraham was too fat and too short legged to run—Mattie heard her telling the Twombley children not to dare to lay a finger on that sugar, and adding, "Here, help yourselves to the doughnuts, why don't you? There're plenty of them." A delicious whiff of coffee-smell eddied invisibly into the parlors. M'Singraham had pushed the boiler still farther back, and joggled the waiting coffee.

Mr. Kirby came back from the telephone, reporting that the train had left Ashley fifteen minutes late and would be at least twenty minutes late at Clifford.

"And fifteen after that before they can get going and get here," calculated Mr. Dewey. He turned his head towards the kitchen and shouted, "Cora! They wunt be here for a full half hour or more. For the Lord's sake, stop fussin' and come and set down."

"Well, I will," M'Singraham called back, "just as soon as I run up and give Nate his ten o'clock gargle."

They heard the back stairs creaking under her.

"Well, Mattie, you set down and keep quiet a spell, anyhow," said Mr. Dewey. "I will have *some*body mind me, *once* in a while."

Mattie laughed and dropped into the nearest chair. It stood near a west window so that by leaning her head against the frame she

could see Hemlock Mountain black against the stars. Although now it was all one dark blur, she knew the exact spot on the lower slope where Churchman's Road turned off and wound up through the burned-over pines, now the berry patch, and just where home was. "Father and mother must be asleep long ago," she thought. She saw her home, quiet now and sleeping, a tiny shrine of life on the dark bulk of the mountain. She was there in the yard before it. The snow on the roof and on the ground, and on the branches and twigs of the maple tree, glistened in the cold starlight. She stood on the front porch looking all around her. She pushed open the door that hung and scraped a little as it always did, and stepped inside, into the warm kitchen. The darkness there smelled of white-birch firewood and cookies and geraniums. She felt Rover's cold nose in her hand. She went to the foot of the stairs and listened, and heard all about her the good, safe, loving night-silence of home.

When she came back to the front parlor of Dewey House she perceived dimly, without moving her cheek from the cool wood of the window frame, that M'Singraham had come in and sat down quietly as Mr. Dewey had told her to. Mrs. Kirby was in an arm-chair, her feet up on a stool. Mr. Kirby was standing at the north window, looking out, as he often did, his head tilted back as if his eyes were on the stars. Mr. Dewey had brought out the checker board and was playing his usual evening game with Miss Gussie. M'Singraham had moved a chair up close beside Mrs. Kirby's. The two were having what Mattie's mother called "a good visit." Their voices came to Mattie's ear like something heard in a dream, or from far across still water. Sometimes she listened, sometimes she followed her eyes out into the starlit darkness on the other side of the window. "I guess I'm half asleep," she thought. "I was never up so late as this before."

M'Singraham and Mrs. Kirby were talking about little Nate's sore throat. It was better, they said. He would be all right tomor-row. He would not be behind with his school work. M'Singraham had helped him with his lessons. They were so sorry they told each other, for Nate's father and mother, that is, M'Singraham was sorry. M'Sanna was mad. "Hanging's too good for any man who'd fore-

close a mortgage on a farm home," she said, her words crackling as they did when she was mad.

M'Singraham said something Mattie didn't hear, and Mrs. Kirby flashed back, "I suppose you'd set up the legal rights of money against the human rights of Nate's little flesh and blood brothers and sisters?"

"Communism?" said M'Singraham, smiling.

"Call it anything you like," M'Sanna said in her spunky way. "Money nor nothing else oughtn't to give one human being, I don't care who it is, any such power over another man's family. Fred, what do *you* think?"

The man at the window answered without turning around, "Oh, Christian anarchy's my ideal."

Mr. Dewey looked up from his checkers and put in, "Now, Anna, you can't reduce it down to simply addition and subtraction like that. There's lots more to it than what you . . ."

But Mattie was trying to remember just the words M'Sanna had used—surely there had been something wrong with the grammar of that sentence. "Yet M'Singraham doesn't correct *her!*" thought the girl. Her eyelids were too heavy to let her keep her mind on grammar. How good it felt when they sank shut. She'd rest them that way—just a minute.

When she opened them again and slowly, swimmingly became aware once more of the two women's voices, they were speaking in a tender murmur of Mrs. Kirby's little Cora. "When I'm married if I have a little girl I'm going to dress her in bright-colored knitted things, like M'Sanna," thought Mattie. "They look cute that way."

She floated softly out now and weightless as a wandering thought drifted here and there over The Valley—over the Depot where the young folks scuffled and sang and laughed as they waited—over Downing Hollow, its spruces heaped with snow, smelling clean of the good cold of midwinter—over the lighted train thundering along the tracks from Ashley, proud of its burden of triumph.

Mrs. Twombley in the kitchen set down a lid on the stove. The faint click called Mattie back to the front parlor of Dewey House,

to lighted lamps blurred with sleepiness, to murmuring voices. She caught a word or two, "Isabel . . . records . . . writing up . . ." and knew they were talking as they often did about Doctor Craft's wife and how much she helped him with his work. Although they did not say that probably she was in his office this minute working away on his records while he was off in Ashley rooting for the team, she felt it as a reproach in their voices, knew that M'Sanna's face was sad as it always was when she thought of her brother. Mattie wanted to remind them, "See here, you've forgotten something, haven't you? Our boys haven't hardly lost a game—baseball, football, or basketball—since the doctor started coaching them, have they? I guess you're overlooking *that!*" But drowsiness billowed softly up around her and blotted out everything save a delicious loosening of every fiber.

"Hey, Mattie! Look out! You'll-fall-right-off-that-chair!" called Mr. Dewey, all in one word. "Why don't you lie down on the sofa and take forty winks?"

"Why, I'm not sleepy at all, Mr. Dewey!" She leaned farther forward and pressed her forehead against the icy glass of the windowpane, so that the cold could send its forkèd "wake up!" summons all along her nerves.

The talk behind her was more general now. Mr. Dewey was saying, "Who said that, I'd like to know? It ain't so. I've seen'em of a summer night, plenty of times. More often in winter, of course. There was a pretty good show of'em last night, along about midnight. Did you see'em?"

"Mercy, *no!*" said M'Singraham. "I've got too much to do daytimes to spend my nights hanging out of the window looking for the Northern Lights."

"Did you see'em, Fred?" asked Mr. Dewey of the man still standing by the other window.

There was a silence. Nobody spoke. Mattie, half awake, half asleep, her cheeks flushed, her forehead cold, wondered why Mr. Kirby didn't answer, leaned her ear to hear what he would say.

She heard him turn away from the window, walk across the room to where his wife sat and sit down beside her. Then he said—

how deep and round his way of talking was after Mr. Dewey's quick twang—his voice almost sounded like singing sometimes—this time—as he said, laying the words down slowly, one by one, "Yes. We saw them, Anna and I."

Far into the dreaming girl's heart, unguarded now by conscious thought, the deep voice sank, echoing. She felt it plumbing depths she had not dreamed were there. As it sank, it left its words behind it, and when it found and entered the unguessed secret center of her being, it was as music.

"Why, whatever in this world makes me cry?" thought Mattie, astonished to feel two tears slipping down over her round cheeks. She was glad her back was to the room so that they could not be seen. But she did not wipe them away.

The telephone rang. She heard M'Singraham's heavy trot across the room. "Oh, all right. Thanks," she said, and then, "Mattie! Wake up! It's time to get the house lighted. Mrs. Twombley, pull that boiler forward. Mr. Dewey, would you mind getting us a few dry sticks for the fireplace? Miss Gussie, they're coming! They're *coming,* I say."

It was as good as going to the Depot with the others—almost better—thought Mattie, scurrying from room to room turning on all the lights, and making sure that every shade was up to the top of its window—to stay here and have something important like this to do. She looked in on little Nate, his cheeks as red with excitement as the flannel bandage around his throat.

"They're coming," she told him.

"I hear them," he said, holding up a finger.

Sure enough, way off, you could hear singing. She went to the window. "Oh, I can see the lights!" she cried.

Nate sprang out of bed like a cricket and ran to the window.

"No, no, you mustn't," she told the younger child with anxious motherliness. "You'll take more cold."

"I've *got* to!" he told her fiercely, and pushed her to one side. M'Singraham passed by the open door. Mattie appealed to her, "Won't Nate take cold if he gets out of bed and stands by the window?"

M'Singraham came in, M'Sanna behind her, little Cora blinking in her arms. They had waked her up to see the procession. Nate's eyes were blazing. "Oh, M'Singraham, *let* me! I won't take cold! Honest, I won't!" He was almost crying. A boy!

M'Singraham and M'Sanna looked at each other. Mrs. Kirby shook her head. M'Singraham thought an instant. "I tell you," she said, "let's push his bed around till he can see out of the window from it. Get back into bed, Nate!"

Pushing and pulling together they shoved the bed into the right place. The procession was turning the corner of Church Street by that time, so they sat down where they were, on the edge of the bed.

It was beautiful! Mattie had never thought anything could be so lovely as the long double line of flaring yellow torches, zigzagging back and forth across the dark snowy street. "Oh, I wish Mother could see it!" she thought.

"They're doing the snake dance," Nate explained to her.

And they were singing! What a swell tune! Mattie couldn't make out the words but there was no misunderstanding what the music meant, "Goody! Goody! Goody! We won!" was what it loudly cried.

Nate began to sing with them, his voice husky with his sore throat,

> "Hail! Hail! the gang's all here!
> What the hell do we care
> What the hell do we care!"

Mattie was astonished by the meaningless words, and shocked by the profanity, but M'Singraham only said, "Now, Nate, you're still sick. You keep your mouth shut tight!" He was silent then, beating time with his small clenched fists on the counterpane.

The zigzagging line drew nearer, the shouting singing voices louder, and now at the end, around the corner strutted the Academy Band, its three cornets and two saxophones blaring out the tune loud above the roll of its drum. In front of it marched two tall boys carrying a banner made out of a white sheet, on which was scrawled in black paint, "CLIFFORD SEMINARY 21 ASHLEY HIGH 8." "Hail! Hail! the gang's all here! What the hell do we

care!" blared the band, wildly sang the dancing boys and girls. You could see them plain now, leaping high, changing step from one foot to the other, the smoking flares of their torches leaping with them. Behind the band, some grown-ups trudged soberly along in an irregular group, basketball fans who had been up to see the game.

M'Sanna chuckled and said to M'Singraham in a smiling voice, "Anybody'd think War had been outlawed, or poverty done away with."

"Oh, well . . . at their age!" said M'Singraham.

The head of the procession had now advanced within sight of Dewey House. When they saw every window in its three story bulk shining bright in welcome, they stopped singing, gave a hoarse cheer and waved their torches confusedly towards it in acknowledgment. For an instant Mattie could see the tall square old house as it looked to them—solid and steady as though it would stand forever. Compared to their smoking, flickering torches, how clear and still its lights—as though nothing could ever blow them out. Mattie's heart swelled high. She had lighted those lights!

It was all so bright and noisy that, she thought excitedly, it almost seemed as though—if Father and Mother happened to wake up and look out of the window—they could see from up on the mountain the yellow torch flames, hear the bragging music. She glanced up at Old Hemlock. There it stood, vast, dark, silent. Her glance turned into a long look. The singing and shouting died to a far-away insect hum: the flickering torch-flames were no more than fire-fly sparks.

When she looked down at the torch-light procession again, it was with a dreamy, indulgent half-smile.

She felt M'Sanna start and lean forward. "Cora! That's not *Anson!*"

"Where?"

"Right there at the front. Between those two boys. There! The one who just gave that great kick and jump!"

"Why, so it is!" said M'Singraham, in rather an embarrassed voice.

They both craned their necks to look down. "Goodness gracious!" breathed Mrs. Kirby.

Mattie looked too. Sure enough there was Doctor Craft, not back with the sober grown-ups but carrying on with the boys, kicking up his feet and hollering as they did. The torches turned in and began to flicker along the front walk. The Doctor was quite near now. Mattie looked gravely down at him as he gamboled a little stiffly between two boys as limber as birch saplings. In the flare of the torches she could see every detail of his contorted face, its singing mouth gaping wide. She thought to herself, "You wouldn't catch my father making such a fool of himself before folks."

M'Sanna lifted her sleepy little girl higher on her shoulder, got up from the bed and turned away from the window. Mattie didn't know whether she was talking to herself or to M'Singraham when she murmured, "Well, well, life certainly does teach you a great deal."

"Does it?" M'Singraham asked. "What does it teach a person, Anna?"

"Oh, Cora, I can't make up my mind just what," said Anna.